AND THE
TOMB
OF THE
KHAN

Also by Jonathan Stokes

Addison Cooke and the Treasure of the Incas

AND THE
TOMB
OF THE
KHAN

JONATHAN W. STOKES

Philomel Books

PHILOMEL BOOKS
an imprint of Penguin Random House LLC
375 Hudson Street
New York, NY 10014

Copyright © 2017 by Jonathan W. Stokes.
Map and chapter opener illustrations copyright © 2017 by David Elliot.

Library of Congress Cataloging-in-Publication Data
is available upon request.

Printed in the United States of America.
ISBN 9780399173783
1 3 5 7 9 10 8 6 4 2
Edited by Michael Green.
Text set in 11-point Garth.

For my family.

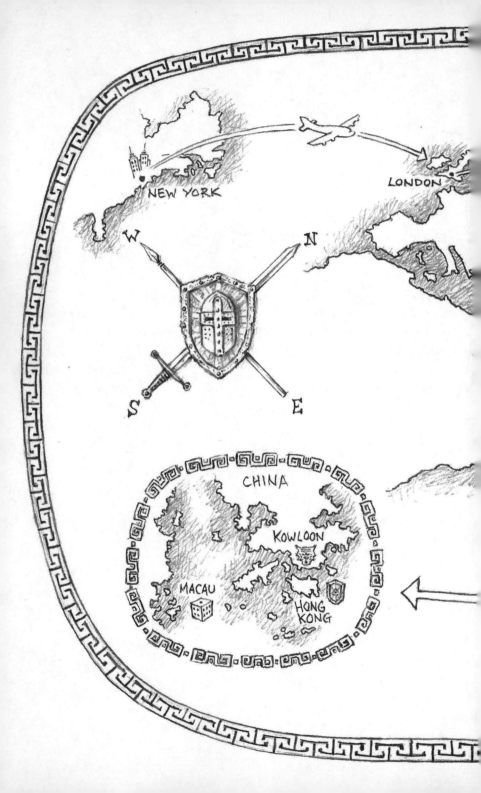

I

THE
SECRET
OF THE
KHAN

Chapter One

The Gentle Art of Persuasion

ALL THINGS CONSIDERED, TODAY was an otherwise excellent day in the life of one Addison H. Cooke. Summer was displaying its usual symptoms: immaculate blue sky, trace of freshly mown grass in the breeze, general feeling that all was well with the world, etc. There was a growing restlessness among the students of Public School 141, like inmates finally up for parole. Not only was June's thermostat set to perfection, but it was the last day of school and a Friday, to boot. Any way you cut it, Addison knew this was not a day to be spent in detention.

And yet here he was. He—Addison Cooke! The same

Addison Cooke who had crossed the Amazon, outwitted cartel criminals, and rescued an Incan treasure was now standing at humble attention in the school principal's office, Kangol cap in hand. "Touching on this business of skipping class," he began, "this is all just a simple misunderstanding."

"How?" asked the principal.

"I misunderstood that you would find out."

The principal leaned his elbows on the giant oak desk. He was scarcely tall enough to see over his own name plaque: Principal Ronald W. Stern. But what he lacked in stature he made up for in eyebrows. "You mind telling me why you were skipping gym class?"

"Not at all, I'd be happy to."

"Well?"

"I was reading a book, that's the true story. I mean, the book was fiction. But the fact that I was reading the book is true." Addison bit his lip; it was not his best opening salvo. He clarified, "The fact that I was reading fiction is not fiction."

"Reading a book is no excuse for missing out on your education."

Addison sighed. He had only himself to blame. After escaping Incan deathtraps in the jungles of Peru, he had a hard time convincing himself that seventh-grade gym class was of any real consequence. He had figured the administration wouldn't mind him skipping one measly gym class on a Friday afternoon on the last day of school. He had figured wrong.

Addison tried a different tack. The key to any hostage negotiation was simply to keep the kidnappers talking. "When Gertrude Stein studied at Harvard, she turned in a final exam paper to her philosophy professor. She wrote one sentence: 'I don't feel like taking an exam today; it's too nice out.'"

"Did she get a detention?"

"No. Her professor wrote back, 'Miss Stein, you truly understand the nature of philosophy,' and he gave her an A."

"Is that true?"

"In philosophy, anything can be true."

The principal frowned.

"The point isn't whether it's true," Addison continued quickly. "The point is to believe in the bigger picture."

"I'm not giving you an A for skipping class."

"I will settle for a B."

"I would give you more detentions," said Principal Stern, "but the school year is only so long."

Addison recognized it was time to improve his tactics. His aunt Delia and uncle Nigel had promised to take him on their summer archaeological dig in China if he could soldier through the last dregs of the school year with perfect behavior. Now here he was, staring down the barrel of a detention. It was like running a twenty-six-mile marathon, limping up to the finish line, and slipping on a banana peel.

"I'm writing out your detention slip now. You know the drill. The pink copy is for your aunt or uncle's signature."

Addison realized things were getting way out of hand. He made a T with his hands, signaling a time-out. He realized, as he did it, that this proved he actually had learned something in gym class.

"Time-out?" asked Principal Stern, confused. No student had ever called a time-out on him before.

"Yes. I'll take off my 'student' hat and you take off your 'principal' hat, and we'll just talk to each other like two human beings. Okay?"

Principal Stern slowly nodded, not sure where any of this was going.

Addison sat down in the button-tufted leather chair opposite the principal's oak desk. He crossed his legs urbanely, picking a speck of lint off the smooth crease of his trouser leg. He favored Principal Stern with his most frank and disarming smile. "A few million years ago, some monkeys climbed down out of trees, and now we have schools and principals and I have a detention."

"Are you blaming your detention on evolution?"

"I'm saying there are larger forces at work here. Here's the thing, Ron. May I call you Ron?"

"You may not call me Ron."

"Ronald, then."

"You may not address me by my first name."

"Yes, I can—we are in a time-out." Addison spoke quickly before the principal could retort. "Ronald, what did you want to do before you became a principal?"

Principal Stern decided to play along. It was, after all, a beautiful afternoon, and he had nowhere pressing to be. Besides, the detention slip was already written. "I was a teacher. Principal seemed like a smart career move. Although in this present moment, I am regretting that choice."

"How long were you a teacher?"

"Longer than you've been alive."

"And what do teachers do, Ronald?"

Principal Stern puckered his eyebrows, searching for a trap in the question. "Teach?"

"Precisely. They teach." Addison finally felt he was getting somewhere. He just needed to build the "yes ladder." "Do you value education, Ronald?"

"Yes."

"Do you value the pursuit of knowledge?"

"Of course."

"Do you value the Renaissance, the Enlightenment, and human reason?"

"I do."

"Look me in my eyes, Ron. Really look at me."

Principal Ronald Stern hoisted his eyebrows and really looked.

"If reading a book is wrong, I don't want to be right. Did you become an educator so you could punish students for reading books?"

"Well, not exactly. I—"

"Yes or no, Ron! Tell me to my face: are you going to stop punishing students for trying to learn?"

"No, I won't. I mean, yes, I will. Wait, what?"

Addison stood and crossed to the American flag that stood in the corner of the principal's office. The Stars and Stripes rippled proudly in the breeze of the open window. "Ronald, if you give me a detention for learning, you will be turning your back on education, on your life's work, and on America. You will be spitting in the face of progress, of science, and of your own dreams!"

Addison tilted his chin resolutely in the air as the flag fluttered behind him. "You shouldn't punish me for skipping gym class, you should pin a medal on me." He returned to his chair and crossed his legs. "Time in."

Ronald Stern sat back in his chair, unsure what to do. "Mr. Cooke, truancy is a crime in the state of New York. I can't have you skip class without consequences."

"Mr. Stern, if you punish me for this, the consequences will be only to the integrity of America's education system."

Principal Stern had heard enough. He suddenly felt

exhausted, like a boxer in the twelfth round, praying for the bell.

Addison knew he had the man against the ropes. He threw his widow-maker. "If you give me a detention, you will have to see me for three more hours. If you let me go, you won't have to see me again for three whole months." Addison watched the blow land.

The principal's eyebrows shot up to his hairline before settling back down to roost on his forehead. He crumpled the detention slip in his hand and sighed. "Addison, you are free to go."

Chapter Two

Eddie and Raj

IT WAS A CONTEMPLATIVE Addison Cooke who reclined on the top bunk in the bedroom he shared with his sister, Molly, in their fifth-floor walk-up on 86th Street. He thumbed through a monstrous library book on the stock market, but he found his interest in falling interest rates falling at a monstrous rate. He couldn't concentrate. He had, in a word, a problem.

At a museum fund-raiser two months earlier, giddy with good food and wine, Aunt Delia and Uncle Nigel had agreed to let Addison bring his friends Eddie Chang and Raj Bhandari along on their upcoming archaeological dig to China. A Song dynasty fortress had been unearthed in the Gobi Desert. Eddie and Raj were Addison's best friends, neighbors, and accomplices, and he could not conceive of going on an adventure without them.

Unfortunately for Addison, two months had given his aunt and uncle plenty of time to come to their senses. Addison, Molly, Eddie, and Raj had nearly been killed in myriad ways on their recent jaunt through South America, creating catastrophic damage in nearly every town that stood in their path. Aunt Delia and Uncle Nigel felt that it was one thing to unleash Addison and Molly on the unsuspecting Asian continent, but four kids was simply too much. Far better to leave Eddie and Raj at home in New York, a city they had caused considerable damage to in the past but not yet managed to destroy.

Across the room, Molly practiced palm strikes and side kicks against a punching bag she had hung from the slanted ceiling. She seemed to guess Addison's thoughts. "There's no way you're going to convince them."

"Molly, you disappoint me. Where is your can-do Cooke spirit?"

"It's been overwhelmed by Aunt Delia's can't-do Cooke spirit."

"Aunt Delia said she'll still *consider* it. I avoided detentions, I got decent grades, I did everything they asked. I lay six-to-one odds I'll convince them."

"All right. What's your plan?" Molly unleashed a fresh flurry of kicks on the punching bag. She had taken up kung fu lessons the instant she had returned from Peru. To Addison's amazement, Molly had proved to be a natural and the darling of her dojo. Sending Molly into a sparring match was like handing Shakespeare a parchment and quill. Addison had lived with Molly his whole life and never suspected he was in the presence of genius.

"Have you heard of Chinese water torture?" Addison asked, sitting up in bed. He decided that the stock market was, for now, a closed book to him. And so he closed his book on the stock market. "A victim is tied down and water is slowly dripped onto their forehead. Drip . . . drip . . . drip . . ."

"Doesn't sound too bad."

"Not at first. But after minutes, hours, and days, the victim completely loses their sanity."

"You're going to drip water on Aunt Delia and Uncle Nigel?"

"Not water, Molly. Words. A casual mention here, a simple turn of phrase there. A pleading look, a subtle pout. It may take minutes, hours, or even days, but eventually, they will be driven completely out of their minds."

Molly slowly nodded. Addison had long since persuaded her not to question his powers of persuasion. "It could work."

••••••

Addison embarked on his campaign. Every morning he filled the kitchen flower vase with daylilies he liberated from Central Park. Every evening at dinner, Molly lit scented candles purchased with money Addison won hustling chess games in Washington Square Park. He sensed Aunt Delia and Uncle Nigel wavering in their resolve.

For his birthday on June 18, Addison was thrilled to finally receive the white linen dinner jacket he'd been hankering for, Roland J. Fiddleton's pocket-size *Asia Atlas*, and a copy of Sun Tzu's *Art of War* from his uncle Jasper in England. These were promising signs, signaling a thaw in aunt-nephew diplomatic relations. Addison decided the time was ripe to launch his final assault.

The next night, he and Molly took it upon themselves to cook dinner for Father's Day. They set a white tablecloth on the kitchen table and served Aunt Delia and Uncle Nigel linguini with a saffron-infused aioli sauce, lightly brushed with truffle oil. Addison and Molly were not gifted cooks, but Addison hooked up a secret work-for-food deal with Trastevere Restaurant on 47th Street and scored Uncle Nigel's favorite pasta dish premade. It was Addison's coup de grâce.

Uncle Nigel pushed back his plate and set down his fork. "Addison and Molly, I don't know how you did it. But this linguini is even better than Trastevere's."

Addison seized the moment and presented his case for

bringing Eddie and Raj to Asia. Uncle Nigel expressed some reluctance over bringing Eddie, who was in a never-ending growth spurt and seemed to eat his body weight in food every time he visited the Cookes. Addison countered that since he was not allowed to keep a dog in their Manhattan apartment, what with all the eating and fur shedding, the least they could do was allow him to keep Eddie. Besides, in addition to Spanish and Turkish, Eddie spoke Chinese, and that is the sort of thing that comes in handy when you are in a place like China. And so at last, with a reluctant sigh over a second helping of linguini, Uncle Nigel relented.

"You win, Addison," he declared. "Eddie and Raj may come with us to Asia."

Addison smiled and cleared the dishes from the table. Virtue was its own reward.

••••••

Having convinced his aunt and uncle to bring Eddie to China, Addison now needed to convince Eddie that he actually wanted to come. This required all of Addison's powers of persuasion and proved to be his greatest challenge, his Everest. Fortunately, with school out, Addison had full time to devote to this effort.

Eddie paced the floor of Addison's living room, scarfing down a bowl of cereal he had pilfered from the Cookes' kitchen. "It's out of the question," he declared for the seventh time. "My parents want to send me to music camp. I shouldn't even be in your apartment; I should be practicing."

"You're too high-strung," Addison said with genuine feeling. "A pleasant vacation will do just the thing. Picture the cooling countryside, the rolling green pastures, the beautiful vistas."

"I thought you said you're going to the Gobi Desert."

"We'll work on our tans."

"I can't tolerate heat."

"The Gobi is surrounded by mountains. We'll go skiing."

"The only skis I'm going near this summer are Tchaikov*sky*, Mussorg*sky*, and Kabalev*sky*."

"Are you trying to tell me you didn't have fun in South America?"

"Addison, we were almost killed seventeen times."

"The key word there," said Addison, "is *almost*."

Eddie paced into the kitchen to find a topping for his cereal. Rummaging through the backs of cabinets, he settled on sugar candy hearts left over from Valentine's Day. "I don't see what's so great about this trip."

Addison had read that the key to salesmanship is knowing what your customer wants. He watched Eddie shoveling cereal into his mouth and locked in on Eddie's puppet strings. "The food, Eddie. Think of it. If you want good Chinese food, where do you go?"

"Sam & Lucy's Chinese Bistro on 67th."

"Right. But if Sam and Lucy want good Chinese food, where do *they* go?"

Eddie considered this. "China?"

"Exactly. They go straight to the source."

Eddie was listening.

"Think of this trip as an all-expenses-paid culinary adventure. We'll be eating our way across the Asian continent."

"All expenses paid?"

Addison knew it was important to convince Eddie all the way so Eddie could set to work on the real challenge: convincing his parents to let him skip New England Music Camp. "I've already squared it with the museum. As research assistants, we'll be employees."

Eddie nodded slowly. He had only one more question. "Is Raj coming?"

At that moment, Raj burst into the living room by way of the fire escape window. He hit the ground, rolled, and sprang to his feet. He was dressed in his signature camouflage pants and clutching a survival backpack nearly twice his size. "Just finished packing. Is Eddie in?"

••••••

Museums are lumbering, bureaucratic beasts with slow reaction times. It was July when the museum finally green-lit the trip. Addison's group wasted no time boarding a transatlantic flight. They flew east into the rising sun, with brief layovers in London, Stockholm, and Kiev. The plane fast-forwarded through the hours of the day as earth's time zones rolled beneath its wings.

Addison sat with Molly in economy class. Aunt Delia and Uncle Nigel sat behind them, and Eddie and Raj sat in front, lowering their seats a little more than Addison would have preferred. Addison struggled to keep his newspaper out of his beef Stroganoff.

"Since when do you read *The Wall Street Journal?*" asked Molly, plucking the edge of the business section out of her rice pilaf.

"I'm checking stock prices."

"You don't own any stocks."

"Yet."

"Is this another one of your phases? Like the time you got interested in beekeeping and spent all your savings on a beekeeper suit?"

Addison folded his newspaper and regarded Molly philosophically. "I'm thinking about my future. I'm thirteen now. In many cultures I'd be considered an adult. I need to think about my prospects."

"You're going to become a stockbroker?"

"Molly, have you ever stopped to consider that archaeology is not a smart career choice?"

"Whoa," said Molly. "Who are you and what have you done with Addison?"

"I'm serious, Mo. You've seen how Aunt D and Uncle N are always struggling with money."

"Addison, you've wanted to be an archaeologist your entire life. Where is this coming from?"

"We go to school with people whose parents work on Wall Street. They always have plenty of money, and their parents never go missing unless it's to spend an extra day in the Hamptons."

"Wait. If you're having doubts about archaeology, why were you so adamant about coming to China?"

"Well, that's easy," said Addison, shrugging. "Free trip. Besides, it was that or math camp like last summer."

Molly looked at him skeptically. "Archaeology's sort of our family business."

"Exactly. We never chose it—it was chosen for us. But look where it got Mom and Dad. And a few months ago, look where it nearly got *us*."

Molly frowned, troubled by this new side of Addison. "Dad wanted you to become an archaeologist."

"Well, he doesn't get a say anymore, does he?" Addison picked the peas out of his pilaf with a spork. "We can't dwell in the past, Molly. It's not about where we came from, it's about where we're going."

"My kung fu *sifu* says you *are* your past. If you don't

know where you came from, how can you tell where you're going?"

Addison chewed that over for a while. He knew he loved archaeology, and he knew he loved the past. But he also knew he didn't want to see his family and friends in danger again.

About six hours into the long flight, he began to feel restless and punchy. Addison started singing "Summertime" by his favorite composer, George Gershwin. Eddie and Raj took up the tune. Soon, a few other jet-lagged passengers joined in. Addison got half the flight cabin singing before his aunt Delia put a stop to it.

It was midafternoon by the time they landed in Hong Kong. Addison unbuckled his seat belt and stretched luxuriantly. He had no idea he would soon be on the run for his life.

Chapter Three

The Hidden Tomb

SEARING TROPICAL HEAT AND a torrential down-pour welcomed Addison's group to the island city. As soon as they stepped out of the air-conditioned airport, monsoon rain drenched them like a dunking booth at a carnival. They high-stepped through puddles, leapt into a taxi van, and were whisked into the beating heart of Hong Kong.

Through windshield wipers, Addison's eyes feasted on the city. Banyan trees and towering eucalyptus competed for space with concrete towers and glass skyscrapers. Curving wooden balustrades adorned the sloping eaves of ramshackle shops selling teas, snakeskins, and herbal remedies. A sinewy man pulled tourists in a red-painted rickshaw while motor traffic screamed in all directions. Every surface was cluttered with signs and billboards drawn in the beautiful black, curving sword strokes of Cantonese script.

After the death-defying drag race through Hong Kong rush hour, the taxi dropped the woozy Cooke team in front of the Hong Kong Museum of Archaeology. The building sported a massive, pillared edifice like the Acropolis in Greece and was only slightly less run-down. They clambered up the concrete steps, made slick in the pelting rain.

"Here she is," Uncle Nigel exclaimed.

"The museum closes at five p.m., so there may not be anyone here to greet us," Aunt Delia called over a clap of thunder.

As if on cue, the front doors swung open, and a twinkly-eyed old man beckoned them in from the rain.

"Eustace, you old quack!" Uncle Nigel cried, his face breaking into a grin.

"Nigel, you ridiculous excuse for an archaeologist!" the man cackled, laugh lines crinkling the corners of his eyes. "Come inside before I have you arrested for loitering."

The group pressed their way indoors, stomping rainwater from their shoes.

Uncle Nigel clasped the old man's hand in two of his and shook it warmly. "I thought this museum was for archaeology—I didn't know they kept fossils."

"Well," said the man with twinkling blue eyes, "at least one old relic in this museum is genuine."

"Everyone," said Uncle Nigel with a grand sweep of his hand, "this is Eustace Goodworth Hawtrey III. The Hawtreys have curated here since Hong Kong became a colony of the British Crown in 1847."

"1842," corrected Eustace, "but who's counting?" He shook hands with Addison and Molly. "It's a pleasure to finally meet you both. Your father used to work with me here at the museum."

Addison reddened at the mention of his father. He never knew quite how to react.

Eustace turned quickly to Eddie and Raj. "Mr. Chang and Mr. Bhandari, I presume? Your reputations precede you."

Eddie and Raj nodded politely.

Aunt Delia gave Eustace a fond peck on the cheek. "Sorry we're late. We got bumped to a later connection in Kiev."

"So my sources informed me. I was notified the second your wheels touched down in Hong Kong." He guided them across the main atrium and into a replica of a sixteenth-century Japanese pagoda. He gestured for them to drop their luggage and take seats on the straw mat floor. "You are just in time for tea."

Uncle Nigel happily accepted a cup. Like Eustace, he was incorrigibly British, and not at all interested in leading a life that did not include tea. "Japanese green tea," he said, taking a grateful sip. "You remembered."

"You always said the British couldn't get the hang of green tea. I quite agree. And for the young people?"

"Earl Grey for me," said Addison.

"I'll take a soda," said Eddie.

"Do you have any protein drinks?" asked Raj.

Aunt Delia shook her head. "You can have whatever you like as long as it's water."

Eustace hefted a pitcher of water and poured glasses all around.

"Now," said Uncle Nigel, clapping his hands together, "what's all this about a Song dynasty fortress?"

Eustace beamed a thousand-watt smile. "There is none!"

"I'm sorry, Eustace," said Uncle Nigel, lowering his teacup. "It sounded almost as if you said there is no Song dynasty fortress."

"There isn't! I just fed your museum that line so they would fly you out here! What I actually found is far more important and far more secret."

A phalanx of janitors entered the main atrium with mops and began working their way across the floor.

Eustace lowered his voice conspiratorially. "There are spies everywhere—come with me, where we can speak openly." He leapt to his feet, surprisingly spry for a white-haired archaeologist. He beckoned Addison's group to follow him through the after-hours museum. They strode down a corridor lined with war masks from Papua New Guinea. "My office is ransacked, my phones are tapped, and people are following me. Hong Kong has a million eyes and a million ears."

Uncle Nigel looked at him skeptically. "Eustace, are you sure?"

"You've been followed since the airport. How do you think I knew the moment your flight touched down?"

Addison traded glances with Molly. The building rattled with a roll of thunder.

"Who are you worried about?" asked Uncle Nigel. "The Chinese gangs?"

"Absolutely," said Eustace, shortcutting through an armory of Samurai weapons, "but they are pussycats compared to the Russian gangs. Just last week, I had to fire a research assistant for selling secrets. The Chinese are following me. The Russians are following the Chinese. And I am following the Russians. We chase each other in a circle. Hong Kong has changed since you were here, Nigel. It is a vipers' nest."

Eddie listened nervously. "Raj," he whispered, "I thought this trip wasn't going to be dangerous."

Raj shrugged, hardly able to contain his grin.

Eustace guided them all into a massive atrium housing a reconstructed Burmese temple. "Now," he said, ducking behind the temple, "I will show you what I *really* found!" He checked both ways to make sure no one was coming and flipped open a security keypad concealed in a marble pillar. A few keystrokes, a hydraulic hiss, and he pushed open a secret door embedded in the wall of the museum.

The old archaeologist ushered them quickly inside. He flicked on his Zippo lighter and held the flame aloft to guide the way. The group squeezed down a hidden passageway hollowed inside the museum wall. "Three months ago, the Uzbeks decided to tear down a Nestorian church and put in a shopping mall. My team rushed to Samarkand to excavate before this priceless site was destroyed."

The passageway led down two dozen steps and fed into an underground chamber.

"We discovered an eight-hundred-year-old crypt hidden underneath the chapel in the church. And to our amazement, one of the coffins was carved with a coded message."

Eustace turned to face the Cookes and saw he had their undivided attention. "Would you like to see it?" He smiled innocently. He knew that an eight-hundred-year-old secret message was chum in the water for the Cooke family.

Uncle Nigel and Aunt Delia bobbed their heads.

Eustace hunched over another keypad recessed into the marble and typed a passcode. Addison marked the thick walls of the vault. Whatever was hidden down here,

Eustace did not want it stolen. The door unsealed, and he led them into a final chamber.

●●●●●●

Eustace clicked on a dim overhead light, revealing a vault packed with antiquities. There were parchment decrees from the Forbidden City, blood-encrusted bayonet rifles from nineteenth-century Mujahideen, and a Komodo dragon–tooth necklace from the island of Padar. But what most drew Addison's eye was the casket in the center of the room.

"Eustace, this coffin is incredibly well preserved," said Aunt Delia.

"Read the message on the lid." Eustace clasped his hands together with excitement.

Uncle Nigel and Aunt Delia both reached into their pockets to slip on glasses and plastic gloves. They bent over the casket like doctors preparing for surgery.

The coffin was oak, hardened by time. Uncle Nigel blew dust from the lid and lowered his eyeline until he caught the faint lettering scratched in the wood. "You said you found this in Samarkand?"

"I certainly did." Eustace's eyes glittered with merriment.

"But this writing is in medieval French."

"That," said Eustace, "is the first reason I brought you here."

"And the second?"

"Read what it says."

Uncle Nigel studied the ancient script and translated. "'Good Christian brother, inside my coffin lie the directions to . . .'" His voice trailed off. Uncle Nigel looked up at Eustace in wonder. "It's not possible."

"Keep reading," said Molly.

Uncle Nigel cleared his throat. "'Inside my coffin lie the directions to the tomb of Temüjin of Borjigin, son of Yesügei . . .'"

Aunt Delia peered over Uncle Nigel's shoulder. "Can it be? A map to the tomb after all these years?" She pored over the ancient text, her jaw slack in amazement. "Eustace, this could lead to a treasure greater than anything the world has seen in a thousand years."

Eustace smiled with delight.

"Who is Temüjin, son of what's-his-futz?" asked Molly.

"Temüjin was his birth name," said Uncle Nigel, straightening up. "You may know him by his nom de guerre . . ." He paused as monsoon thunder shook the earth. "Genghis Khan."

Chapter Four
The Khan's Treasure

EDDIE BROKE THE SILENCE that followed. "Okay, so there's a map to a grave. I don't see what the big deal is."

"If the legends are true, it's much more than a grave," said Eustace. He pointed to a parchment map hanging on the vault wall. "Genghis Khan conquered a quarter of the world, creating the largest empire in history. He looted every city from Beijing to Bukhara and carted all the treasure back to Mongolia, where it vanished. According to Mongol tradition, it was buried with the Khan."

"So why has no one found his tomb after all this time?" asked Molly.

"Legend claims the burial site was masked by ten thousand horsemen who trampled the earth to make it even. Then a river was diverted and a forest planted, hiding the tomb forever."

"Wow," said Molly. "Genghis Khan had trust issues."

"That isn't the half of it," said Eustace. "Mongol warriors killed the slaves who built the Khan's tomb. And when those warriors rode back to their camp, the army murdered the warriors, too. That way, no living Mongol knew the location of the Khan's tomb."

Raj let out a low whistle. It was a skill he had only recently mastered, and he tried to inject a low whistle into a conversation any time it seemed appropriate.

"The Germans, Japanese, Americans, Russians, and Brits have all led expeditions in search of the Khan's grave, spending millions of dollars. None have found anything. The location is one of the greatest mysteries in archaeology."

"So how are we supposed to find it?" asked Molly.

"We," said Eustace, "have a guide."

"Who?"

"This gentleman." Eustace tapped the wooden coffin. "Go ahead, open it."

Uncle Nigel and Aunt Delia stood at opposite ends of the coffin and slowly hefted open the oak lid.

"Are you sure the kids should see this?" asked Aunt Delia.

"We probably shouldn't," said Eddie nervously.

Addison waved his hand dismissively. "We saw thousands of skeletons in the catacombs in Colombia. This is just another day at the office for us."

Uncle Nigel and Aunt Delia set the heavy lid on the floor. Inside the coffin lay the skeleton of a medieval knight. His chain mail hung in loose folds over his dusty gray rib cage. Over his broad chest sat a circular iron shield.

Uncle Nigel dropped to one knee. He traced a reverent finger over the crest etched in the iron shield: an open eye in the center of a radiant sun. "He was a member of the secret order . . . A Templar knight."

"I thought you'd appreciate that," said Eustace. "From his gravestone, we know his name. May I introduce Sir Frederick Oeil-de-Boeuf."

"Oeil-de-Boeuf?" said Molly, struggling with the French pronunciation.

"It means 'bull's-eye,'" said Eustace. "And it's very fitting—he certainly had a bull's-eye painted on his back. Once he discovered Genghis Khan's tomb, half of Mongolia tried to kill him before he escaped the country."

Uncle Nigel peered closely at Sir Frederick's shield. "He's scratched a message into his shield. Delia, your French is better than mine . . ."

Aunt Delia knelt close to the ancient shield and read aloud. "'I am the Templar knight sent to explore the Kingdom of the Tartars. On the road to Zhongdu I met an old Mongol slave, covered in scars and dying of plague. I gave him water and all the medicine I could find in the wilderness, but I could not save him. On his deathbed, he confessed a secret . . .'"

The knight's words were etched around the shield's edge, spiraling in toward the center. Aunt Delia circled the coffin, reading Sir Frederick's tale. "'The slave helped build the tomb of Genghis Khan. Mongol warriors slaughtered them all, leaving them for dead. Only this slave escaped, crawling away under darkness, stricken with injuries. For years he lived in hiding until dying in my arms.'"

Addison felt the hairs on the back of his neck standing on end.

Aunt Delia shifted her glasses and studied the ancient text. "'I, Sir Frederick, followed his directions and uncovered the tomb of the Khan. I have held the golden whip . . .'" She stopped short. "Good heavens."

Addison saw she had tears in her eyes.

"I never dreamed it was possible," said Uncle Nigel, one hand against his chest. His glasses were fogging up as well.

"What?" Molly demanded. "Aunt Delia, what's the golden whip?"

"Just a second, Molly."

"Keep reading!" said Addison.

Aunt Delia read faster now. "'When I escaped the tomb, I was attacked by the Ghost Warriors—"

"He must mean the Black Darkhad!" Uncle Nigel cut in excitedly.

"Nigel, I thought they were only legends!"

"Wait," said Molly. "Ghost Warriors?"

"Molly, are you going to let us read this or not?" said Aunt Delia.

"C'mon," said Molly. "You can't just drop something like 'Ghost Warriors' and then leave us guessing!"

Uncle Nigel responded impatiently. "Some Mongols believe the Khan's grave is guarded by an army of ghosts."

"Oh, is that all?" said Molly.

Aunt Delia continued translating the tightly curving script. "'The Ghost Warriors wounded me in combat. They took me captive. After much debate, they released me. I did not know if I would live to see France again. So at each marker I passed on my return, I hid a secret message pointing the way to the Khan's tomb.'"

"A treasure hunt," said Addison.

Aunt Delia kept circling the coffin, deciphering the inner etchings toward the center of the shield. "'Three months ago I was ambushed by bandits who shot my horse out from under me. I took an arrow in the leg. Nestorians cared for me at their hospital along the Silk Road . . .'"

"My word," said Uncle Nigel in awe. "This knight limped from Kashgar to Samarkand with an arrow wound? He would have crossed the Altai Mountains of Kazakhstan at eighteen thousand feet."

"They were made of sterner stuff then," Eustace agreed.

Aunt Delia translated the final piece. "'The arrow wound gave me fever. I know I am to die, and cannot bear the Khan's treasure to be lost forever. My shield is the fourth and final marker. I pray a Templar knight will find my message.'"

"So there's a clue somewhere on this shield?" Uncle Nigel asked excitedly.

Eustace was about to answer when his eyes flitted to a security monitor mounted in a corner of the vault. A tall woman with black hair was entering the front doors of the museum, followed by a string of dark-suited bodyguards. Eustace grimaced. "Ladies and gentlemen, Madame Feng: the Casino Queen of Macau and our museum's largest donor. I must hurry upstairs to meet her. Whatever you do, do not tell her where I've hidden Sir Frederick!"

In a mild panic, he shooed the group out of the basement room. Before shutting off the lights, Eustace quickly pulled Addison and Molly aside. "I have something for you two. When your father passed, I had to clean out his office and couldn't bring myself to throw everything away. This is the curse of every archaeologist, I suppose—we cling to the past."

He heaved open an antique steamer chest and presented Molly with a leather shoulder pack covered with pockets, buckles, and carabiner straps. "Molly, this is your father's survival kit. He took it on all his adventures. It is filled with items that can save your life."

Molly shortened the strap and slipped it over her neck like a messenger bag. It was surprisingly comfortable.

Eustace handed Addison a worn, leather-bound book. "This is your father's copy of *The Secret History of the Mongols*. Genghis Khan's court recorded his life story nearly eight hundred years ago."

Addison cracked open the musty, faded book. His father's name, which also happened to be Addison Cooke, was penned in excellent cursive on the inside cover.

"Your father was an insatiable reader, fascinated by the Mongols. He dreamed of one day finding the tomb of Genghis Khan. He would be so excited by this discovery. You're going on this journey for him, Addison."

Addison nodded his thanks. He had done so much to forget his past. But even here on the far side of the world, he could not escape his father's ghost.

••••••

Eustace shepherded the group out of the secret passageway and behind the Burmese temple. They spilled into the main atrium and ran directly into a tall, striking woman with one hand cocked on her hip and one eyebrow arched in the air. Eustace gave a nervous start, collected himself, and then cranked up the charm. "Madame Feng, what a pleasant surprise."

"Eustace," said Madame Feng, peering suspiciously behind the Burmese temple, "you have more hidey-holes than a field mouse. One wonders what you are concealing."

Addison sized up Madame Feng. She wore a severe black business suit with her dark hair drawn up in a bun. Her black-painted nails put Addison in mind of a panther's claws. She possessed the coiled feline grace of a jungle cat who had learned to walk upright.

"Madame Feng has generously offered to sponsor our excavation," said Eustace. "And she is providing you with accommodations at her Hong Kong hotel."

Uncle Nigel took Madame Feng's hand. "Thank you for your hospitality. It is an honor to meet you."

"The honor is mine," purred Madame Feng. "I've heard all about your family's exploits in Peru. Finding the lost treasure of the Incas after five hundred years."

Uncle Nigel was incapable of taking a compliment. He blushed and stammered a few times.

Madame Feng smiled. "Asian history is my passion." She strutted a few steps closer to Eustace, her sharp heels clicking on the marble floor. "I've heard rumors among the museum staff that Eustace has unearthed an important clue to the location of Genghis Khan's tomb. Yet Eustace refuses to share it with me."

"I've told you, it's in storage, Madame Feng. It is a very fragile relic."

"So you say," said Madame Feng, taking a long-lashed glance behind the temple. "I'm sure it is very safe in one of your mouse holes." Madame Feng was flanked by steely-eyed bodyguards so serious and expressionless that Addison felt tempted to tickle them under their chins just to see what would happen.

"It is important to protect relics from thieves," Eustace said icily.

Addison looked from Eustace to Madame Feng and sensed an undercurrent of tension so strong, it could pull them all out to sea.

Uncle Nigel must have sensed it, too, because he clasped his hands together, laughed nervously, and changed the subject so abruptly Addison nearly lost his balance and tipped over. "I've chartered a bush pilot for our expedition: Dax Conroy. By coincidence, we're actually meeting him at your casino in Macau tonight."

"I will make sure you are given first-class service," said Madame Feng airily.

"Dax Conroy," said Eustace, wrinkling his nose. "The smuggler? He has less conscience than a pirate. He'll smuggle anything and look the other way."

"It's true," Uncle Nigel said, shrugging. "He's a liar, a brawler, a cheat, and a gambler."

"But he's a great pilot?" asked Addison.

"Oh, rather not. He's nearly gotten me killed numerous times. His plane is practically held together with Scotch tape, and his copilot is an absolute beast—fleas and all."

"So why use him?"

Uncle Nigel thought about it, as if for the first time. "Well, customer loyalty, I suppose. He knows the Gobi, and he's rather useful in a jam. Also, his rates are extremely reasonable."

"I will leave you scientists to make your plans," said Madame Feng. She turned to Uncle Nigel. "My Macau casino is just a short trip across the sea by hydrofoil."

"You have hydrofoils in Hong Kong?" Addison blurted out, deeply impressed.

"They run all night." Madame Feng seemed to notice Addison and his friends for the first time. She offered him a smile that showed all of her teeth and handed him a black poker chip embossed with the image of a dragon. "If you come to my casino, just show this chip and you will get anything you ask—food, drink, even a room for the night. Just do not wander far—Hong Kong can be a dangerous place."

Addison accepted the chip with a polite nod.

"I don't know if Addison will have time for much gambling," said Aunt Delia. "He's thirteen."

But Madame Feng had already turned on her heel,

strutting out of the atrium, flanked by her coterie of guards.

Eustace watched her leave and lowered his voice to a whisper. "Be careful of her. Madame Feng has friends in high places, but it's her friends in low places you should be concerned about."

"Oh?" said Uncle Nigel.

"Her casino business is protected by triad gangs."

"We'll be careful," said Uncle Nigel.

"Listen to me." Eustace spoke urgently. "Genghis Khan's treasure is so vast, it can rebalance world economies. Do you want that wealth and power in the hands of criminals?"

Uncle Nigel shook his head gravely.

"Madame Feng is ruthless. Whatever happens, Sir Frederick's clues must not fall into her hands."

Chapter Five

Code Red

THIRTY MINUTES LATER, A bellman led Addison's group into their massive penthouse suite on the top floor of the Feng Hotel. The golden sun was setting over the bay, and all the lights of Hong Kong glittered like a bed of diamonds. "This will do," said Addison, handing the bellman a few Hong Kong dollars for his bags.

The sprawling hotel suite was larger than the Cookes' Manhattan apartment. There was a spacious living room, a full kitchen, and a large bedroom with four single beds for Addison, Molly, Eddie, and Raj. Uncle Nigel and Aunt Delia were staying in their own suite down the hall.

"Finally," said Addison, "we get some proper accommodations. You see, Eddie? This is much better than South

America." He spread his arms magnanimously. "Molly, I shall let you choose whichever bed you want."

Molly rather preferred the setup they had in Manhattan. "Can we bunk them?"

"They may ding us for that on the bill," said Addison. "However, that's really Madame Feng's problem." He and Molly attempted to lift one of the beds, and found they could not. "Well," said Addison, "if you need the bunk bed experience, you could always sleep underneath my bed."

Raj busied himself figuring out the entertainment system.

Eddie cataloged and inventoried all the expensive foods in the minibar, though he was afraid to eat anything for fear of going bankrupt.

Aunt Delia poked her head in the door to suggest they all get to sleep early to combat their jet lag.

Addison readily agreed. He flopped down on a white upholstered lounge chair, cradled the hotel phone against his shoulder, and dialed the front desk. "*Ni hao ma*?" he said by way of greeting. "I would like a fresh start on the day tomorrow. Can you please send a wake-up call promptly at eleven forty-five a.m.?" He flipped through a hotel magazine with glossy shots of a Hong Kong golf course. In the back he found a Hong Kong map and studied it intently, memorizing what he could of the city layout. "Excellent," he continued breezily. "And a copy of the morning's *Wall*

Street Journal, English edition. And breakfast tea, also English. *Shie shie, ni.*" He hung up the phone, reclined the seat, and rested his feet on the ottoman.

"Addison, you're too young to drink tea," said Molly.

"And you're too young to tell me what to do."

"You read *The Wall Street Journal* now?" asked Eddie.

"I like to keep up on the markets."

"You don't own any stocks."

"So people keep telling me. Nevertheless, I want to be prepared for when my ship comes in."

Eddie stretched and yawned. "Man, I don't know why I'm so exhausted."

"Jet lag. It's one p.m. yesterday in New York and seven p.m. today in Hong Kong," said Addison. "Your body is stuck in yesterday, trying to catch up with today, and not realizing that today is tomorrow."

"Well, that clears it up," said Eddie.

"We skipped a day flying out here. When we fly home, we'll cross the international date line and lose a day. Then today will be yesterday again."

"Ugh, yesterday was awful," said Eddie. "I don't think I can do that again."

"Don't worry," said Addison. "Just because today will be yesterday doesn't mean everything that happened yesterday will happen again today. Otherwise, we'd cross the international date line again and the loop would go on forever."

"Addison, what are you talking about?" asked Molly.

"I have no idea. Ask me again tomorrow."

"You mean yesterday?" asked Eddie.

•••••••

Aunt Delia poked her head in the door after fifteen minutes and was reassured to see Addison, Molly, Raj, and Eddie each in their beds. "Good night," she said. "If you need anything, we'll be right next door."

After she softly closed the door, Eddie snapped on his sleep mask. "Well, g'night, everyone."

Addison stared at him, aghast. "Eddie, how dare you insult me!"

Eddie pulled off his sleep mask. "What did I say?"

"After all the years I've known you. You put a knife through my heart!"

"What did I do?"

"Do you really imagine for one split second that we're staying cooped up in this hotel room when there's an entire city to explore? I would think you'd know me better than that."

"But we got all ready for bed."

"No," said Addison indignantly. "We made a show of getting ready for bed, so that Aunt Delia and Uncle Nigel can go to bed." He swept aside his comforter, revealing he was dressed head to toe in his usual dress shirt, slacks, and British regimental striped necktie. He rose from the bed and donned his school blazer.

"But I'm exhausted from jet lag."

"Eddie, you can sleep when you're dead." Addison was already slipping on wingtips with his stainless-steel shoehorn. The shoehorn was a prized possession, purchased after he had spotted a first-edition Jules Verne novel at a flea market and sold it to the Palatine Antique Book and Map Shoppe for a cool eighty-five-dollar profit. "Raj, you ready?"

"Always." Raj jumped out of bed wearing his black T-shirt and camouflage pants. He tied on his red bandana with a ceremonial flourish.

Molly tugged on her running shoes.

Eddie pulled the covers over his head.

Addison reached for the door handle and sighed. "I'd prefer you did this willingly, Eddie. Don't make me call a Code Blue."

Eddie knew that resistance was futile. He tossed away his sleep mask and dragged himself out of bed.

······

Addison rode with his friends down the twenty-story glass elevator and was breezing his way across the main lobby when Molly called a Code Red, diving behind a large potted plant. On sheer instinct, Addison yanked Eddie to the ground behind a sofa. Raj somersaulted behind a pillar and stuck two fingers to his neck, checking his pulse; he was practicing keeping his heart rate low in emergencies.

"Mo, what is it?" Addison whispered from behind the couch.

"I saw Aunt Delia and Uncle Nigel leaving the hotel restaurant."

"Hannibal of Carthage!" said Addison.

"Hannibal of who?" asked Eddie.

"It's Addison's new shtick," said Molly. "When he wants to curse, he just names enemies of ancient Rome. It delights Aunt Delia."

Addison peered over the gilt rim of the sofa. He spotted Madame Feng's grim-faced bodyguards roughly escorting Aunt Delia and Uncle Nigel across the lobby. The A & U looked distressed, but he could not hear their words. He was quite sure his uncle was struggling against the bodyguards' tight grip. "Molly, this doesn't look good."

Molly curled a stray hair from her ponytail behind her ear and peeked through the palm leaves of her potted plant. The dark-suited bodyguards hustled Uncle Nigel and Aunt Delia out of the hotel and into a waiting taxi.

"Are we safe?" asked Eddie from behind the sofa.

"We are," said Addison, "but the aunt and uncle aren't."

"They look like they're in trouble," Molly agreed. "But, Addison, what if we're jumping to conclusions?"

"There's only one way to find out."

"Does it involve us going back upstairs and sleeping?" asked Eddie.

"Nope. We're going to follow them." Addison led his team through the lobby and out the front glass doors. He confidently approached the doorman, a thickset man with a taxi whistle, and offered him a five-dollar coin. "You didn't happen to hear where that last taxi was heading?"

The doorman stared at Addison with a face of chiseled granite.

Addison sighed and handed him another five Hong Kong dollars. "Maybe this will make you more talkative."

The man only frowned vacantly at Addison. It was like conversing with an Easter Island head.

Addison was about to burn a ten-dollar note before Eddie stepped in and spoke to the doorman in Cantonese.

Hearing Chinese, the doorman brightened and cheerily replied.

Addison grimaced; ten good Hong Kong dollars down the drain. "What's he saying, Eddie?"

"He says those men asked the cabdriver to take them to Edinburgh Place."

Addison nodded his thanks to the doorman and slid into the backseat of the next waiting taxi.

Molly hesitated. "We're not allowed in cabs."

"We're not allowed in *New York* cabs. Aunt Delia never said anything about Hong Kong cabs."

Molly felt this was stretching the rules a bit, but figured if anyone was going to get grounded for it, it would be Addison. She piled into the cab, followed by Raj.

Eddie climbed in the front seat and used his Cantonese to tell the driver to head toward Edinburgh Place.

"And tell him to step on it!" said Addison. He smiled. He'd always wanted to say that.

The car peeled out, heading north at speeds even more terrifying than usual for a Hong Kong cabbie. The bustling city was aglow with the dazzling lights of restaurants, cafés, and dance clubs, all reflected in vibrant colors in the glistening, rain-slick streets. Double-decker tramcars crept along brass rails, crisscrossing the intersections. Glass skyscrapers, rubbing shoulders with jungle foliage, sprouted high enough to disappear into fog. And people, everywhere people, from every nation in the world. Hong Kong was a tropical Manhattan.

Molly shifted in her seat. "What's the plan, exactly? Hong Kong is a big place, and all we have is a street name."

"We're not going to Hong Kong," said Addison calmly. "Edinburgh Place is where ferries leave for the other islands." He pointed ahead to a cab swerving through traffic and pulling up to the Star Ferry terminal. "You see, we're on the right track."

He watched closely as Madame Feng's bodyguards pried Uncle Nigel and Aunt Delia from the cab like shucking the meat from a stubborn clam. "You don't have to worry about Hong Kong, Molly. We're going across the harbor to Kowloon."

"Isn't Kowloon dangerous?" asked Eddie.

"Extremely." Addison smiled and patted him on the shoulder. "But so are we."

Chapter Six

The Alleys of Kowloon

ADDISON'S TEAM LOW-LINED THROUGH crowds of shoppers strolling the pier. Fishermen sold eels that slithered and writhed in their wooden buckets, and hawked wicker baskets of crawfish that clenched and flexed their tiny pincers. A wrinkled old lady sold wrinkled old peppers and deep-fried beef to deep-fried tourists.

The team sneaked into the ferry terminal, keeping a measured distance from Aunt Delia and Uncle Nigel. The ferry to Kowloon cost two Hong Kong dollars per person, but Addison got the boatman down to one fifty on a group rate.

They raced up the gangplank just as the ferry's engines cranked up, belching diesel and shaking the ship. The old boat shoved off into Victoria Harbor.

Molly kept a sharp-eyed lookout on Aunt Delia and Uncle Nigel as the bodyguards maneuvered them to the far end of the ship. She anxiously paced the deck.

Addison maintained a low profile, leaning against the gunwale on the starboard side and listening to the lonely sighs of a blind *erhu* player, bowing his python-skinned instrument and begging for change. The ferry crept across the channel with a rhythmic chug, sliding past the silent wraiths of three-masted Chinese junks whose fanned sails unfurled like the translucent wings of dragons.

The team disembarked in Kowloon, which Raj informed them was the most densely populated neighborhood in the world. Amid the throngs of people, Addison had to periodically hop into the air, trying not to lose sight of Aunt Delia and Uncle Nigel. He halfway wished for a periscope, but at least they had Eddie, who was tall and skinny enough to serve as one. They pushed north against the raging flood of foot traffic, fighting their way upstream like spawning salmon.

"This is triad territory!" Raj announced excitedly, pointing to several triangles spray-painted on the cracked walls of tenements. "The triads are the most powerful Chinese gang."

"That doesn't sound good," said Molly. "Also, why do you know that?"

"My favorite book, *Mission: Survival*, by Babatunde Okonjo, devotes several chapters to surviving encounters with Asian gangs."

Before Raj could unleash a tidal wave of data on Asian street gangs, Eddie halted the group with a warning palm of his hand. Up ahead, Madame Feng's bodyguards paused outside a restaurant called the Jade Tiger. They ushered Aunt Delia and Uncle Nigel inside, shutting the doors behind them. Two guards with square jaws, squared shoulders, and flattop haircuts blocked the doors, crossed their arms, and stared down any pedestrian who passed.

"Do we follow them into the restaurant?" asked Raj uncertainly.

"I don't think they're open," said Eddie.

"Addison, is this the part where you talk our way inside?" asked Molly.

Addison pursed his lips. Normally, he had boundless confidence with this sort of maneuver. Yet maybe it was the predatory stare of the guards, maybe it was the gun holsters protruding from their leather jackets, or maybe it was Addison's complete lack of Cantonese, but he just didn't see any percentage in this gamble. He made up his mind. "Back door."

They circled around to the rear alley and found the

restaurant kitchen door by dead reckoning. Addison crossed his fingers for luck and tried the handle, but it was locked.

"I brought my new lock-picking set! Bought it downtown on Canal Street." Raj eagerly drew a felt cloth from a side pocket of his camouflage pants and unfurled it, revealing a row of glittering picks and files. He cupped his ear to the lock, tongue out in concentration, and began inserting wires and pins into the keyhole.

Eddie and Molly kept a lookout.

Addison gave Raj a minute, then two, tapping his foot. "I could have sawed a hole through the door by now."

"Lock-picking is an art, not a science. It just takes time and patience."

"I have neither." Addison knocked loudly on the door.

"*What are you doing?*" Eddie yelped, leaping three inches into the air.

"This is how I pick a lock," said Addison. He heard someone unbolting the door from the inside. He turned quickly to his sister. "Mo, play dead."

Molly, trained by a lifetime of living with Addison, collapsed into Raj's arms, no questions asked.

Raj blushed red. He had no choice but to hold her up by the armpits, or she would fall into the alleyway, which was probably filthy. With one free hand, he did his best to gather up his lock-picking set.

The door scraped open, nearly tipping Raj over. "Eddie, don't just stand there, help me!"

Eddie scooped up Molly's legs. Her limp, lifeless body hung suspended between Eddie and Raj like a hammock.

A sullen man in a poofy white chef's hat stood backlit in the doorway, taking in the scene. A crooked trail of ash dangled from the cigarette wedged in his frowning mug. He was thick-necked like a bulldog and with the same jowled cheeks.

Addison stepped forward, straightening his tie. "Addison Cooke, pleasure to meet you."

The chef barked a few guttural words in Cantonese and set to slamming the door.

Addison quickly made his pitch. "Help us," he pleaded. "My sister is sick!"

Eddie translated and turned back to Addison. "He says, 'You think *you've* got problems—his stove is on the fritz.'"

Addison held up one of Molly's limp arms and let it drop to her side, dangling helplessly. "Please, she has so much life ahead of her. We just need to use your phone!"

The chef growled a few more words and pointed down the alleyway.

"He says there's an animal shelter three blocks away," Eddie translated.

Molly scowled, but the chef did not seem to notice.

Again, he tried to shut the door, but Addison stopped it with his foot, scuffing his prized wingtip.

Addison felt some tears might help sell his performance. He tried to think of a time he had lost a cherished childhood pet, but Aunt Delia had never allowed him to get one. This made him think of Aunt Delia's animal allergies, and Addison was able to approximate the teary-eyed look she gave after a cat-induced sneezing fit. "Please, sir. My sister barely has the use of her brain. She basically only cares about sports. We just want to use your phone!"

The chef shook his head firmly, but this time Addison did not trouble himself to listen. He marched through the back door and into the kitchen. Sometimes, it is better to ask forgiveness than permission.

Eddie and Raj waddled in after him, struggling to keep Molly's sagging body from dragging on the floor.

The chef threw his arms up in the air in defeat. He pointed to the phone hanging on the wall.

Addison turned to Eddie. "Well?"

"Me? You're the one who does the talking."

"Eddie," said Addison as patiently as he could, "only one of us speaks Chinese."

"Right." Eddie dropped Molly's legs abruptly and picked up the phone. "What's the number for emergency services in Hong Kong?"

"Eddie, she's not actually sick!"

"Oh, right."

"Just pretend to call someone!"

"Sure, got it." Eddie began plunking random numbers. The chef folded his arms and watched suspiciously.

Addison helped Raj hoist Molly onto a stainless-steel prep station, shoving aside chopping boards and measuring cups that clattered to the floor. He found a meat thermometer and considered poking it in Molly's mouth, but she cracked one eye open and glared at him. He made a show of feeling her forehead instead. "She's burning up!" He scanned the kitchen and spotted the walk-in freezer. He called to the chef. "Please, sir, do you have any ice? We've got to keep her temperature down or she'll get more brain damage."

Eddie cupped a hand over the phone he wasn't really using and translated.

The chef sighed and lumbered into the freezer room.

Addison took three quick steps and slammed the freezer door shut. He sealed the latch, trapping the chef inside.

The chef pressed his face against the window, hollering with rage and pounding his fists against the glass. But his shouts were barely audible through the sealed door.

"And that," said Addison, patting his hands together, "is how you sneak into a restaurant."

"Do you think he'll be okay in there?" asked Molly, returning to life.

Addison peered at the freezer thermostat and raised it to a balmy seventy-two degrees. "We'll let him out before we leave. He's in a room full of food—he won't starve."

Molly marched over to the kitchen doors and peered through the smudged circular window into the restaurant. Aunt Delia and Uncle Nigel were seated in the center table, surrounded by guards. "They're here!"

Addison found waiters' aprons in the kitchen closet and doled them out. He made Eddie tuck in his shirt and found a salad fork so that Raj could properly comb his hair.

"We're not real waiters," Eddie grumbled.

"Still," said Addison, fussing over Molly's apron knot, "I won't have you going out there looking like slobs. Not while I run this kitchen." He lined them up straight, examined their hands and fingernails, and nodded his approval. "It's showtime," said Addison, and pushed his way through the swinging doors into the restaurant.

Chapter Seven

Sir Frederick's Clue

THE JADE TIGER RESTAURANT was a feast for the eyes. Plush red couches were backed by thousand-gallon fish tanks that teemed with coral fish, manta rays, and the occasional circling shark. Underwater lights cast watery blue reflections across the patterned teak floors. Decorative jade tigers, mounted on pedestals, stood on their hind legs, baring their fangs.

Aunt Delia and Uncle Nigel sat at a center table, surrounded by Madame Feng's guards. The restaurant was closed, empty of customers, and eerily quiet.

Addison emerged from the kitchen and beelined for

the stairs to the balcony seating area. Dressed in waiter aprons, his team was practically invisible. Madame Feng's guards did not move their eyes from their captives.

"Addison, where are you taking us?" Molly whispered as they mounted the steps.

"Uncle Jasper gave me Sun Tzu's *Art of War* for my birthday present."

"So?"

"Sun Tzu was an ancient Chinese general. He says, *'Always occupy the high ground. It will provide a safe vantage point.'*"

The balcony seating area was dark and empty. Chairs were stacked up on tables for sweeping. Addison lay flat on his stomach and peered down through the banisters at the scene below.

Beaded curtains parted at the restaurant's entrance, and Madame Feng padded into the room with the coiled stealth of a black panther. She was flanked by thick-browed men with blue, green, and red tattoos peeking out from the starched white collars of their Italian suits.

"Triads," Raj whispered.

Addison watched, his senses on full alert.

Uncle Nigel stood up from his table, but was pushed back down by the strong arms of two triads. "Madame Feng, what is the meaning of this? Why force us from our hotel room and drag us all the way out here?"

"Privacy, Dr. Cooke," said Madame Feng. "Hong Kong has a million ears."

"I've heard that already."

"Then you prove my point." A guard pulled out a seat for Madame Feng. She perched primly on the edge, eyeing Uncle Nigel coolly. "People know me in Hong Kong. They know me in Macau. But in Kowloon, nobody knows anyone."

"These are triad headquarters, aren't they?" asked Aunt Delia.

Madame Feng only smiled.

"Let me guess," said Uncle Nigel. "You need our help because you want the Khan's treasure for yourself?"

"I do not care about the treasure," said Madame Feng, her eyes flashing. "I only care about one thing: the Khan's golden whip."

"The golden whip is just a legend," said Uncle Nigel.

Madame Feng rose and crossed to the fish tanks, admiring the grace of the hunting sharks. "A whip made of interlocking links of gold. Genghis Khan found it on the banks of the Tuul River in Northern Mongolia. It was a gift from the gods, a sign that he would rule the world." She wheeled suddenly to face the Cookes. "I am descended from the Khan himself! And I believe the legend of the golden whip."

"Lots of people are descended from Genghis Khan,"

said Aunt Delia. "And if the whip exists, it is invaluable to the Mongolian people. It's the single most important relic of their country—the symbol of their cultural heritage. You can't steal who they are."

Madame Feng smiled. "I possess many things that are valuable. But I covet things that are invaluable. The golden whip will be the prize of my collection."

"We work for the museum," said Aunt Delia firmly.

"You work for me now." Madame Feng signaled the triads, who unbuttoned their coats, revealing their guns.

"If we don't show up at the museum tomorrow, Eustace will notify the authorities."

"I've already handled Eustace." Madame Feng smiled. "He is on a slow boat to China."

"Literally?" asked Aunt Delia.

"Yes. By the time he reaches Beijing, it will be too late for him to interfere. I own the Hong Kong authorities. The local police will not want to see Asian relics fall into foreign hands."

Madame Feng folded her arms and stared down at Aunt Delia and Uncle Nigel. "Sir Frederick's tomb has been unearthed. A race has begun. The Russians are already hunting for the Khan's tomb. I cannot allow them to find it first."

"You don't need to worry," said Uncle Nigel. "Eustace hid Sir Frederick somewhere you will never find him."

"Oh, really?" Madame Feng snapped her fingers, and the beaded curtain parted. Two triads trundled in, staggering under the weight of Sir Frederick's coffin.

"You thief!" gasped Aunt Delia.

Madame Feng laughed delightedly. "Thanks to your visit today, I finally figured out Eustace's hiding place. Then it was just a question of persuading him to give us his access code."

"Did you hurt him?" Uncle Nigel demanded.

"He didn't break easily," said Madame Feng, by way of an answer.

Upstairs in the balcony, Molly whispered in Addison's ear. "We've got to do something."

"Well, we can't call the police," said Addison. "Madame Feng says she owns them."

"And we can't call Eustace—he's been kidnapped."

"I'll think of something." Addison chewed his lip in thought. "The Cooke brain is like a mighty steam engine. Sometimes slow to start, but nearly impossible to stop."

Molly blew the hair out of her eyes. It would never stay put in a ponytail. She either needed longer hair or shorter hair, she could never decide which.

Below, Madame Feng's bodyguards cracked open Sir Frederick's coffin and removed his iron shield. They flipped the shield over and set it down on a white tablecloth.

"You see? The clue is etched on the back of his shield," Madame Feng announced. "Translate it."

"No, thank you," said Aunt Delia coldly. "I'm sure you can find another translator."

"Really? Someone in Hong Kong who speaks Old French and just happens to have your expertise with antiquities?" Madame Feng impatiently tapped the shield with her black-painted fingernail. "Translate it."

"I'm afraid I can't help you," said Aunt Delia.

"I'm afraid you don't have a choice," said Madame Feng. "I have your kids. My men are snatching them from their hotel beds as we speak."

In the balcony, Addison turned to Eddie and whispered, "You see? Aren't you glad you came with us tonight?"

Eddie eyed the armed triads below. "The jury's still out on that."

At her table below, Aunt Delia turned white. "Let the children go. What could you possibly need with them?"

"They will motivate you to help me," said Madame Feng.

"Let me speak to them!"

"Only when you translate Sir Frederick's clue."

Aunt Delia hesitated. "How do I know you're not bluffing?"

"Do you really want to take that chance?"

Aunt Delia shared a long look with Uncle Nigel. He

nodded toward Sir Frederick's shield. She slipped on her tortoiseshell glasses and bent over the ancient text carved into the concave back of the shield. She began to translate.

> *"'Praise be to the Lord, my Rock,*
> *who trains my hands for war,*
> *my fingers for battle.*
> *God is my shield, my sword, my helm, and my lance.'"*

"What does that mean?" Madame Feng interrupted.

"It's a psalm from the Bible," said Aunt Delia. "Sir Frederick is just clearing his throat."

"Why is he writing all this in Old French? Why not Latin or Chinese?"

"Sir Frederick wanted only a member of his order to follow in his tracks," said Uncle Nigel.

"Ah yes," said Madame Feng. "This Templar business. Carry on," she said, with a wave of her hand.

In the balcony, Molly whispered to Addison. "Who *are* the Templars?"

"Later," Addison whispered. He drew his notebook from his blazer pocket and waited, pencil poised, for Aunt Delia's translation.

Far below, she traced the curving script with her fingertip and read . . .

"'There lies an oasis town on the Silk Road by the Dragon Desert
Where Nestorian Christians nursed me to health.
Know ye your Templar vows. Visit the sick and say a mass
for the dead. Pray for our sign and ye will know
the way to the Tartar's land.'"

Madame Feng leaned close to Aunt Delia. "Tell me what it means."

"I have no idea."

Upstairs, Addison furiously jotted down the clue as fast as he heard it.

"Does it rhyme in French?" Eddie asked.

"Why does everything have to rhyme with you? Sir Frederick was a knight, not a pop singer."

"We need to grab the shield, the aunt, and the uncle," said Molly urgently. "How is that plan coming along?"

Addison tucked away his pocket notebook. "Swimmingly. We just need a distraction. Something to divert the triads' attention."

Shouted Russian erupted from the restaurant below. Addison's team peered over the banister to see armed men in leather jackets burst into the restaurant. The triads aimed their guns at the Russians. The Russians aimed their guns at the triads. For several noisy seconds, the air was filled with the sound of guns cocking.

Molly turned to Addison. "You mean like that?"

"Yes, exactly like that."

In the restaurant below, a muscular crew-cut Russian sauntered into the room. Addison noted how the man oozed confidence; he ignored all of the guns trained on him and favored Madame Feng with a malevolent grin. He plucked a tulip from a centerpiece and handed it to her. "Hello, Eleanor."

Madame Feng accepted the flower in one clenched fist. She spoke through gritted teeth. "Boris."

"I've come for the shield," he said, still grinning.

"How did you find me here?"

Boris glanced at Sir Frederick's skeleton, lying exposed in his coffin, and crossed himself. He then appraised the iron shield with greedy eyes. "I've followed the Cookes all day. I've followed Eustace all month. And I've followed you, Eleanor, for years."

Addison watched, riveted. He desperately wanted to know who these Russian restaurant-crashers were. Judging from the guns and leather jackets, they were probably not from the Archaeological Society. But a sharp poke in the ribs from Molly reminded him it was time to swing into action. He marshaled his thoughts, hammering out a plan, and assigned roles in a low whisper. "Raj, you can be the diversion this time."

Raj pumped his fist and mouthed, *Thank you.*

"Make it count," said Addison. "Then rendezvous in the back alley behind the kitchen."

"Copy that," said Raj, beaming with pleasure.

"Mo, once Raj creates a diversion, you snag the A & U and rendezvous in the back alley."

Molly nodded, tightening the laces on her running shoes. She was ready.

"Can I stay up here?" asked Eddie.

Addison inventoried the mezzanine, cluttered with tables and chairs. "Yes, actually."

Eddie sighed in relief.

"Throw every piece of furniture over this balcony. Create mayhem down there. Meet us in the back alley when you're done."

Eddie gulped. He slowly nodded and rolled up his sleeves.

"Addison, what are you going to do?" asked Molly.

"I," said Addison, "am going to steal Sir Frederick's shield."

Chapter Eight
The Jade Tiger

RAJ KISSED HIS DOG tags for good luck. He climbed up on the banister, preparing to create his diversion, when he was struck by a sudden brainstorm. It all seemed so obvious. All he needed to do was leap to the chandelier, swing to the opposite pillar, slide down on top of an aquarium, and perform a cartwheel dismount. Then he could grab the shield, grab Uncle Nigel, *and* grab Aunt Delia. He examined the plan in his mind. Like a well-cut diamond, it was flawless from every angle. Raj saw it clearly: he would be a hero.

Down below, the tall Russian man smiled at Madame Feng. "My men outnumber you. We have the restaurant surrounded. Hand me the shield, Eleanor."

Madame Feng narrowed her eyes at the Russian and

gestured to Uncle Nigel and Aunt Delia. "Boris, the shield will be no use to you without the Cookes to decipher it."

"Are they loyal to you?"

"They should be—I have their kids."

Aunt Delia rose to her feet. "So you keep saying. Show them to me so I know they're all right!"

Madame Feng crossed her arms. "Do not try my patience."

A dozen armed men, fingers tensed on their triggers, nervously followed the exchange.

Aunt Delia squinted at Madame Feng, reading her expression. "You don't actually *have* the kids, do you?"

"Of course I do," Madame Feng hissed.

Aunt Delia was just hitting her stride. "No, I can tell that you don't. And you'll never catch them. Addison and Molly are far more clever than they look. You won't get within a million miles of them."

"Enough!"

"Addison and Molly were raised in the fever swamps of Cambodia," Aunt Delia continued. "They crossed the Mekong Delta in kayaks before they could walk. They've stamped their passports more times than a Swiss diplomat. They know every train and bus terminal from here to Calcutta. Those kids aren't dumb enough to stay in Hong Kong. They're probably halfway to the Ivory Coast by now!"

At just that moment, a piercing shriek split the air.

"BHAAAAAANDARI!" Raj screamed his war cry, took a running leap off the balcony, and flung himself through the air to grab the rim of the giant chandelier.

The chandelier chain snapped.

Raj's war cry petered out. He hovered in midair for an instant before he felt the chandelier, along with his plans, plummet, smashing down on the floor below.

Guards scattered, covering their heads. Thousands of glass beads spilled everywhere. Running men slipped, crashing to the floor on their backs.

Raj, grunting, rolled with the impact. He found himself belly up, staring at Uncle Nigel.

"Raj?" said Uncle Nigel, bewildered.

"It was Addison's idea!"

Up on the balcony, Addison was thrilled with Raj's distraction. "Eddie," he said, snapping his fingers, "mayhem."

"With pleasure," said Eddie, who set to work hurling chairs, tables, and floral centerpieces over the balcony, into the crowd below.

Addison grabbed Molly and sprinted for the stairs. He paused to toss one flower vase over the railing just to see how it felt. It landed somewhere below with a satisfying crash and an angry yelp from a Russian. Smiling, Addison raced down the steps and into the melee.

The Russians and Chinese quickly descended into a

full-on brawl. Addison had not seen so many flying Russians since his last trip to the circus. He ducked a soaring Slav, skidded sideways across scattered chandelier shards, and scuttled with Molly to the center table.

Uncle Nigel grabbed Sir Frederick's shield and charged for the exit, but was body-tackled by some Russians who clearly had wrestling experience. Aunt Delia scooped up the shield and Frisbeed it at a towering triad who blocked her path. It belted the man in the gut. The triad bent double, then triple, and then, somehow, quadruple. The shield rolled crazily around the floor, chased in dizzy circles by frantic tattooed triads.

Madame Feng's guards threw sacks over Aunt Delia and Uncle Nigel's heads, jerked their arms behind their backs, and hustled them to the front door. Molly struggled to reach them, ducking a barrage of whirling fists and kicking legs. Desperate to clear a path, she attempted a roundhouse kick on the kneecap of a passing triad. The hardened criminal turned to face her.

His ears were pierced, his nose was pierced, his lip was pierced, and he hit Molly with a piercing stare. In this moment, Molly learned a valuable life lesson: if you've only taken eight weeks of kung fu lessons, maybe don't pick a fight with a Hong Kong gang member.

The pierced man attacked. The only reason his first punch missed was that Molly was a foot shorter than the sorts of people he was used to punching. He wound up to try a kick instead.

Raj was chasing the shield around the room like a happy Labrador at the beach when he spotted Molly's predicament. "I'll save you, Molly!" He leapt up on a table, built up speed for a flying kick, slipped on the tablecloth, and crash-landed in a clatter of silverware.

The distraction gave Molly just enough time to crush a vase over the pierced triad's head. "Thanks, Raj," she said, pulling him to his feet.

Raj was not out of the woods yet. Any man with that many piercings must surely have a high tolerance for pain. The triad shook his head woozily and lunged with both hands. Raj bobbed and weaved, but was soon cornered in the elbow of a restaurant booth.

Addison saw Raj's danger. What Raj needed was a weapon to defend himself. "Heads up!" Addison snatched a heavy jade tiger from a nearby pedestal and flung it at Raj.

For a split second, Addison thought Raj might actually catch the flying jade tiger. For the next split second, Addison was terrified the flying jade tiger might catch Raj on the crown of his head, knocking his best friend out cold. In the next split second, the flying jade tiger missed Raj entirely and shattered the ten-thousand-gallon fish tank.

Addison watched the glass break as if in slow motion.

One moment there was a spiderweb of cracks spreading across the tank. The next moment a tidal wave of water swamped the restaurant.

The aquarium accomplished what no amount of brawling could. It knocked down every gang member in the restaurant. Addison was swept halfway across the room on the seething tide. Sharks flapped about on the floor like eggs in a frying pan. Russians picked seaweed out of their hair. A beached triad flopped on his back, gasping for air. Addison realized it was the pierced man.

Addison's favorite word in the English language was "cornobble," meaning "to slap with a fish." He had long wondered if he would ever be lucky enough to cornobble someone. At last, fate was lending a hand. Addison found a flounder floundering on the floor, took it by the tail, and walloped the pierced triad across the face with a satisfying smack. Addison smiled. He deplored violence, but he condoned cornobbling.

Struggling to his feet and silently mourning his soaked leather wingtips, Addison scanned the chaotic restaurant. Every violent gang member wanted a piece of him. The aunt, the uncle, and the shield were gone. Addison could see things weren't going exactly according to his plan. So he rapidly conceived a new one . . .

Run.

It was the simpler plans that were usually best. Molly

and Raj took their cue from Addison. They hightailed it into the kitchen, trailed by a team of ticked-off triads.

······

Addison burst through the swinging kitchen doors, gang members hounding his heels. His first order of business was opening the freezer door and releasing the angry chef, who was now wielding a frozen hanger steak as a weapon. Addison took a hairpin turn around a prep table and smacked the light switch, pitching the kitchen in pitch dark.

He listened to the satisfying music of Russians and triads crashing into everything. Overhead tongs and ladles smashed to the ground followed by loud grunts and metallic clangs. There was even the distinct rhythmic yelp of a triad being beaten with the raw hanger steak. It was a sweet symphony.

Addison and his team knew the general layout of the kitchen. He navigated through it at top speed, with the help of his shins, his elbows, and three surprisingly ill-placed garbage cans. He yanked on the back door and found it was locked. Addison jiggled the handle, but it would not give. "Hannibal Barca, slayer of Romans!"

He revised his itinerary. Addison dodged a few fumbling fists and burst back into the restaurant through the swinging doors.

The scene had changed remarkably in thirty seconds.

A candle had tipped over and ignited a tablecloth. Now several tables were sprouting flames. A triad was dunking a Russian in an unbroken fish tank until that fish tank broke as well.

Madame Feng spotted Addison from across the room. She rallied her men. "Stop those kids! We need them!"

Addison zipped up the stairs to the balcony, Raj and Molly at his side and two triads trailing behind.

Eddie was sopping with sweat and heaving the last potted bamboo over the railing. "Addison, this is a dead end!"

"Attila the Hun!" Addison shouted.

Triads pounded up the stairs. Addison saw only one option: he took a running start and threw himself out the window.

Chapter Nine

Tony the Triad

THERE ARE MOMENTS IN life when it is best to carefully consider one's actions. Choosing a college, choosing a career, choosing whether to throw oneself out the second-story window of a Chinese restaurant—these are all important life decisions, and not to be taken lightly. Addison considered himself a very thoughtful and conscientious person. He was as surprised as anyone when he chose to hurtle himself through a plate-glass window.

As he sailed through the window frame, he was struck by two important realizations. The first was that the window was already open.

This could mean either good news or bad news, Addison reflected. In the short term, it was very good news he wasn't opening a plate-glass window with his forehead. But in the long term, the open window might simply be hastening his express trip to the pavement. Addison decided it was a wash.

The second realization came quickly on the heels of the first. Addison considered himself a man of hard science, and was not quick to believe in signs or miracles. Yet every now and then, when life threw him a bone, it was hard not to ponder the handiwork of some divine providence. Addison, as he spiraled through the empty window, could not help but notice that the Jade Tiger restaurant was furnished with a front awning.

It was waiting for him like an old friend. It was red and stretched tight like a fireman's trampoline.

He bounced on it.

Molly, Eddie, and Raj bounced on it, too, in quick succession. They bounced to their feet, jogged a few sidesteps, and climbed onto the first-story roof of the building next door.

Several triads leapt out of the window after them. The triads, to their great misfortune, were full-grown adults, and therefore much heavier. They smashed right through the awning and were quickly acquainted with the pavement below. One of them would have to explain to Madame Feng how they had destroyed the awning of her restaurant.

More triads spilled out of the window like rats from a sinking ship. These gang members, learning by example, clung to the edge of the roof rather than plummeting through the yawning hole of the awning. Spying Addison's team, they sashayed along the sloping eaves, scattering roof tiles, and chased the New Yorkers across the building tops of Kowloon.

Addison checked over his shoulder. "This is the pig's whistle," he said in alarm. He wasn't sure if this was an actual expression, but he liked the way it sounded. "Pick up those feet, Eddie! They're gaining on us!"

Molly, always the fastest, scrambled up a service ladder onto the three-story roof of a rickety tenement.

Raj, Addison, and Eddie scampered after her, ducking linens on clotheslines and scaring up swarms of startled pigeons. The team skidded to a halt at the edge of a three-story roof. They stared down at the traffic below.

"Cornered by a street corner," said Addison.

Triads, fists pumping, galloped closer across the rooftops.

Raj pointed to the power lines stretching from building to building across the intersection. "We'll zip-line out of here!" He slipped off his waiter apron and slung it over the wire.

"Raj, are you sure you want to try this?" asked Addison, glancing nervously at the three-story drop.

"Of course he wants to try this," said Molly, who was pretty well acquainted with Raj by this point.

"What about electrocution?" asked Eddie.

"I'm only touching one wire—I'm not completing a circuit." Raj pushed off from the roof, gripping the apron in both fists as it slid along the wire. He dangled from the line, gathering speed as he swept high over the intersection.

Triads shouted as they drew close, branding guns and knives.

"Works for me," said Molly. She stripped off her apron.

Addison and even Eddie followed suit. They draped their aprons over the power line and leapt off the edge of the roof.

All things being equal, Addison felt pretty good about this decision. Granted, he possessed a healthy fear of heights, but he possessed an even healthier fear of knife-wielding criminals. He watched them slip away behind him as his zip line gathered speed. Cars and buses careened along the street below his flailing feet.

Addison was rather bullish about his prospects of reaching the far side of the intersection when he noticed his speed slowing down. The power line was bowing under the weight of four people.

Their zip line lost its zip. Raj reached the middle of the intersection first and slowed to a halt. Molly slammed into his back, with Addison and Eddie ramming her in quick succession.

"What now?" asked Eddie.

Addison was rarely at a loss for words; he usually ran at a surplus. But in this particular situation—the kind where one finds oneself dangling over a Kowloon street like a Christmas ornament on a breaking branch—he was unable to dredge even a few useful syllables up from his gullet. He could only stare at the heavy traffic rumbling ten feet below his wobbling wingtips. "Well, here we are," he managed.

The electric line strained and sagged under its groaning weight. The nearest telephone pole began to tilt like the leaning Tower of Pisa.

"And this seemed like such a good idea," said Raj wistfully. And it really was, all the way up until the line snapped in a shower of sparks.

Addison's team plummeted through the air.

••••••

Addison didn't have long to contemplate life choices before he landed hard in the bed of a passing garbage truck. He groaned, feeling his ribs bruised from the impact.

Raj, Molly, and Eddie crashed down beside him, instantly buried in food wrappers, nibbled bread crusts, orange rinds, and used Q-tips.

Addison struggled to sit up in the mounds of trash. "Alaric, king of the Visigoths!" He was pleased to be alive but not if it meant ruining his best wool slacks. He coughed a few times, which only hurt his ribs. "Let's get out of here," he croaked.

"I don't know," said Eddie. "At least we're safe in this truck."

The dump truck squeaked to a stop at a row of Dumpsters. Its hydraulic arm hoisted a Dumpster high in the air and turned its contents south. Addison's team was buried under a fresh mound of garbage.

"Okay," said Eddie, clawing a greasy clump of noodles from his hair. "Let's get out of here."

They wallowed through heaps of reeking trash and clambered over the iron tailgate of the dump truck. Surprised onlookers watched Addison's team emerge, perhaps wondering why anyone would throw away four perfectly decent American kids.

Addison shook trash from his clothes. He stood on the crowded Kowloon street and turned in a slow circle. He never thought he would regret climbing out of a garbage truck, but that was his immediate feeling. His ears were split by the roar of motorcycle engines closing in. Peering over the incoming high beams, Addison saw that each bike was piled high with triads. "Here they come!"

His ribs aching and stiff, he tried not to take deep

breaths. He led the group into a crowded Kowloon night market, weaving between food stalls heaped with shark fins and octopus, ducking past duck dealers in duck trousers hawking mallards dangling from strings.

Triads gunned their motorcycle engines, scattering crowds, catching up quickly.

Addison scooted under carts laden with pig heads, shortcutted through linen shops billowing with hanging fabrics, and sidestepped through incense shops reeking of scented oils. A tenacious triad throttled his motor, keeping pace behind them.

"Raj," Addison called, yanking a yard of silk from a display hook, "grab hold."

Raj took the other end and pulled the fabric taut.

The surprised triad, punching the gas, was clotheslined off his bike. He hit the ground on his back and lay there stunned and blinking.

Addison admired the sleek black racing bike lying toppled on its side, rear wheel spinning. He marked the roar of other bikes closing in. "Anyone know how to ride a motorcycle?"

"I've seen my cousin do it," said Eddie.

"Eddie, you are the Executive Vice President in charge of Not Driving Anything Ever."

"Can I be the president?" Eddie watched anxiously as another triad bike shoved its way closer through the throngs of shoppers. "Addison, there's four of us. We can't all ride one motorcycle!"

"Can't we?" Addison righted the motorcycle. It was surprisingly heavy. He climbed on. The forward pitch of the racing bike forced him low over the handlebars, like a jockey on a thoroughbred. "Okay, Eddie. You control the clutch because I have no idea how that works. But I'm steering."

Eddie was about to refuse, but the incoming motorcycles were so deafening that he knew his argument would be drowned out. He climbed on behind Addison.

Molly leapt onto the back—she was used to sharing a bicycle with Addison and didn't see how this was much different.

Raj perched on the front, feet balanced on the fork tube of the wheel.

A triad motorcycle burst through a neighboring stall, heading straight for them.

"Now!" shouted Addison.

Eddie gunned it.

The bike took off so fast, Addison felt his eyeballs pushed back inside his head. His first instinct was to shut his eyes. But he quickly discovered he could steer the bike far better with his eyes open. Hollering pedestrians fled from his speeding path. It filled Addison with a strange sense of power that he quite liked. "This isn't so bad," he said, over the sound of Eddie's screaming.

The trick was to stay one step ahead of the pursuing triads. This became increasingly challenging, what with all the local police brandishing nightsticks and blocking the way.

"More gas, Eddie," Addison shouted, taking a quick short-cut directly through a giant display of watermelons. He wiped juice from his shirt with his pocket handkerchief. He was not looking forward to his hotel's dry cleaning bill.

"Addison," shouted Molly, "now the police are after us, too!"

Addison drew deep breaths despite his aching ribs. He tried to remain calm. "First of all, there is no need to shout in my ear. Eddie already has that department covered. And second," he continued, "I see the police."

"Well," said Molly, "if we don't want the police after us, maybe we shouldn't destroy this Kowloon market."

"Look, it's not our fault someone put a market right here," said Addison, ramming a display of exotic birds, toppling their cages, and releasing several dozen cockatoos back into the wild. "Besides, Madame Feng already said the police were on her side."

"Addison, we need to stop messing around and get out of here if we're going to help Aunt Delia and Uncle Nigel."

"I'm working on it!" He steered left to avoid a police barricade and right to avoid an advancing triad. Up ahead, the market crowd grew too dense and he could drive no farther. Addison careened to a stop with the help of a row of mopeds, three pedestrians, two shopping carts, and an iron Dumpster.

Molly tumbled off the back of the bike, landing hard on her side.

Addison leapt off the bike. "Are you okay, Molly?"

She grimaced, clutching her elbow. "I skinned my arm."

"Hop back on! We can still lose them!"

A triad motorcycle skidded to a halt, closing off Addison's escape path. The triad flipped down the kickstand, dismounted, and swept off his helmet.

Addison sized up his opponent. The triad clutched twin trench knives, his fingers laced through the brass knuckles on each handle, allowing him to punch or cut. He was handsome with spiked hair, a black leather jacket, dark sunglasses, and a hint of a smile. Style went a long way with Addison, and he decided he rather liked the fellow. Granted, the man was about to attack him, but first impressions aren't everything.

"Listen," Addison began, backing up with his hands raised, "you seem like a reasonable man—"

"I doubt that," Raj interrupted. "He's a Green Diamond triad."

"A what now?" Addison leapt back to dodge a wild slash from the triad's knife.

"The most dangerous of the triad gangs! You can tell by his neck tattoo—a triangle of green swords."

Molly struggled to her feet. "Raj, how do you *know* this stuff?"

"In Chapter Seven of *Mission: Survival* by Babatunde Okonjo, he enumerates—"

"Guys," Eddie pleaded, "can we please focus on the matter at hand?"

Addison's group backed up slowly. They were cornered between a brick wall and a fishmonger's stall.

The triad took another mighty sweep with his knife.

Addison had nowhere left to retreat. He saw his moment and lunged to grab the gang member's blade.

The triad was too fast. Addison missed, collided with the triad's shoulder, and went down in a jumbled heap.

Raj seized an ice bucket from the fishmonger and walloped it at the gang member's head with all his strength. The man ducked. Raj missed entirely, scattering ice everywhere.

Molly, wincing from the pain in her arm, grabbed a heavy bottle of fish sauce from the fishmonger's stand. She swung it hard at the triad's jaw, looking for a grand slam.

The gangster stepped lightly backward, dodging the blow . . . only to slip on the ice, crack his head on the pavement, and knock himself out cold.

"Teamwork," said Addison.

"He was fast," Molly said, deeply impressed. "Who is that guy?"

"Tony Chin," said Addison.

"How do you know?"

"I took his wallet." Addison winked at Molly and held up Tony Chin's driver's license. "Little trick I learned in Bogotá."

More triads rushed closer, but it was a Hong Kong police officer who arrived first. Red faced with anger, he charged Addison, brandishing his billy club high. Winding up for the strike, he slid on the ice, went down sideways, and clobbered the street with his head. He lay there, dazed.

"Wow," said Addison, feeling invincible.

"We need to get away from this ice!" said Eddie.

A fresh tide of gang members flooded the market.

"Molly, can you still run?" asked Addison.

"It's my arm that's hurt, not my leg."

Addison's group feathered their way past the fishmonger's stall and fled.

Legging it through the Kowloon street, Addison made a quick inventory of Tony Chin's cash and, more important, the credit card situation. "American Express," he said. "I love the mileage points." Addison pocketed the wallet.

At last the alley opened up, revealing the pier and harbor beyond. Addison spotted the next ferry leaving the dock, sounding its deep horn across the bay.

The group ran, wheezing for breath. A few triads, marathon runners perhaps, still loped after them.

"We've missed the boat!" cried Eddie.

"This way!" called Addison, leaping down from the pier and onto a rickety Chinese junk. Three fishermen stared at the group in confusion until Addison whipped open Tony Chin's wallet and held up a fistful of yuan. The fishermen saw the running triads and grasped the situation. Then they grasped the yuan. They swung into action, unmooring and shoving away from the dock.

Raj lent a hand at the oars.

A single triad drew his gun, contemplating a shot that might spring a leak in the ancient ship. Crowds of travelers lining the pier made for too many witnesses. The triad slowly lowered his weapon.

Addison stood tall at the stern of the ship, the wind tousling his hair. He waved at the triads receding into the distance.

Chapter Ten

On the Run

THE ANCIENT JUNK GLIDED across Victoria Harbor, the dazzling city lights twinkling on the dark water all around them like constellations in a night sky. Addison and Eddie used wooden buckets to bail seawater from the leaky boat.

"Now I know why they call it 'junk,'" said Eddie.

The fishermen pulled hard at the oars, and soon they reached a strong current that carried the boat effortlessly toward the main island of Hong Kong. Only the wail of sirens carried this far out across the water. Otherwise, the chaos of Kowloon was far behind them.

Raj used his first aid kit to clean Molly's skinned arm. He padded it with gauze and wrapped it with a bandage.

"Aunt Delia and Uncle Nigel have a real talent for getting themselves kidnapped," said Addison.

"It should be called 'adult-napped,' not 'kid-napped,'" said Molly.

"Maybe it's not a coincidence," said Raj. "Madame Feng said she knew all about our trip to Peru. That could be how she got the idea of kidnapping them."

"Either way," said Addison glumly, "they've been shanghaied."

"But we're in Hong Kong," said Molly.

"It's an expression: 'shanghai' means 'to kidnap.' Sailors used to be knocked out and carted off to Shanghai. You can still get shanghaied in Hong Kong."

"The one place you can't get shanghaied is Shanghai," said Raj helpfully, "because you're already in Shanghai."

"If you're in Shanghai, you'd have to get Hong Konged," Addison agreed.

"What are we talking about here?" asked Eddie.

"We are talking," said Molly, "about the fact that Aunt Delia and Uncle Nigel are being shanghaied from Hong Kong, Eustace is being shanghaied to Beijing, and we can't shanghai ourselves home to New York because we have no plane tickets." She considered whether they had any shot of calling the Hong Kong police, and ruled against it. "Addison, we've never knocked out a policeman before."

"Well, there's a first time for everything." Addison paced

the deck. This was exactly the problem with archaeology: one minute you're packing for a pleasant dig in the Gobi and the next minute you're on the run from the Hong Kong police. It was not a stable career path. On the other hand, Addison knew he could not simply abandon his aunt and uncle. He thought about his father's obsession with the Great Khan. Pursuing the tomb felt like a way of sharing something with his father.

He turned to face Molly. "If only our family were stockbrokers. We wouldn't get into these messes."

She nodded sympathetically. "You know what we need to do, right?"

Addison sighed. He could see no alternative. "If we want to help the A & U, we need to find Sir Frederick's next clue." He had to admit, he was excited by the prospect. But he knew that great dangers lay ahead. Addison flipped open his notebook, squinted, and could only just make out his own hastily scrawled writing. "'*There lies an oasis town on the Silk Road by the Dragon Desert, where Nestorian Christians nursed me to health . . .*' Does that mean anything to anyone?"

Molly shrugged.

"The Gobi Desert is filled with dinosaur bones," said Raj.

"Thank you, Raj," said Addison. "Any other useful observations?"

Raj pressed his point. "Sir Frederick might call the Gobi

the 'Dragon Desert.' They didn't know what dinosaurs were in the Middle Ages. If Sir Frederick saw dinosaur bones in the Gobi, he probably thought they belonged to dragons. So: 'Dragon Desert.'"

Addison turned it over in his mind. There was a method to Raj's madness. The Gobi was near Mongolia, the home of Genghis Khan. And besides, they had already packed with the Gobi Desert in mind. He pivoted on his heel and faced the group. "All right, we're looking for an oasis town in the Gobi. We'll figure out the exact city as we go. All we need now is a way to get from Hong Kong to Northern China. All in favor?"

Molly nodded her agreement. Raj nodded eagerly as well.

Eddie stood up, shaking his head. "Oh, no. Absolutely not. I'm not going on a wild goose chase across Asia. We've been through this before. This will only end with us being killed or grounded."

"Eddie, we need you—we're going to China and you're our Chinese interpreter!"

"You're not talking me into this, Addison." He crossed his arms. "This may come as a surprise to you, but my idea of a fun summer vacation does not involve running from Hong Kong triads."

Addison knew from hard-earned experience how best to appeal to Eddie's better judgment. He took a deep breath and spoke calmly, using the sort of soothing voice dentists employ with nervous patients. "Eddie, when the Mongols sacked Beijing, it was the largest city in the world. The Mongols burned the city, killed the inhabitants, and stacked the skulls so high, travelers arriving across the plains thought they were seeing white, snowy mountains in the distance."

Eddie listened. He wasn't sure where Addison was heading with all this.

"Thousands of cartloads of treasure left the burning city for weeks, heading for Mongolia. The plunder of the richest city on earth. And think of it, Eddie: Beijing was just one of hundreds of cities the Mongols pillaged. The entire wealth of the medieval world was taken to Mongolia . . . and buried in Genghis Khan's tomb."

Eddie leaned against the gunwale, watching the flickering lights of Hong Kong shimmering like jewels.

"Gold, Eddie." Addison stepped close behind him. "Heaps and piles of gold."

Eddie gritted his teeth. His knuckles grew white, gripping the cleats of the wooden rail. He underwent an intense, internal struggle, like a kettle coming to a rolling boil. It was pointless to argue with Addison; it was like arguing with Mother Nature or Father Time. Addison was simply too great a force to be reckoned with. "All right, fine." Eddie let out a long sigh, like air escaping from a popped tire. "I'm in."

••••••

Addison's team crept into their hotel suite with all possible stealth. The door was hanging ajar, and clothes were strewn everywhere. The rooms had clearly been ransacked. Either that or the maid service had been inexplicably replaced by howler monkeys.

"Okay, only grab what you need," whispered Addison. "I want us out of this room inside two minutes."

Everyone set to work finding their clothes and filling their backpacks.

Addison selected a fresh pair of linen slacks packed neatly in his hanging bag.

"I thought we were only bringing necessities," said Molly.

Addison gestured to his clothes, soiled by the ride in the Kowloon garbage truck. "Well, I can't go find the Khan's treasure in these pants. Besides, looking sharp *is* a necessity!" Addison donned the blindingly white dinner jacket he had received for his birthday.

Molly was shocked. "Are you really wearing that?"

"I can wear white after Memorial Day," Addison said defensively.

"You look like a valet."

"Valets wear *red* jackets, Molly."

"Still, wouldn't it make sense for us to try to blend in?"

"I never try to blend in, Molly. You should know that by now." Addison fished around in his suitcase. "Since we know there are people out there who might hurt us, I'm also bringing this." He held out a butterfly knife.

"Where did you get that?"

"So many questions, Mo. I checked it with my luggage. It's from our old friend Zubov." Addison flicked and twirled the knife.

"You've been practicing," said Raj.

"Well, the twirling is fun. But I haven't had any practice in actually fighting anyone."

"That's for the best," said Molly. "You're not really planning on using that, are you?"

"Hey, this saved our lives in Peru."

"Yes, you used it to free us from rope, not hurt someone. Addison, you're a pacifist. You won't even show up to gym class—now you want to start a knife fight?"

"Well, I'm bringing it just in case." He carefully tucked it inside the pocket of his white blazer.

Addison led the team out of the suite and down the back stairs of the hotel. It was twenty flights to ground level, but at least they wouldn't be spotted.

"Where to?" asked Eddie, wheezing for breath.

"The Feng Casino in Macau," said Addison. "I want to try out one of these hydrofoils Madame Feng was so keen on."

"Isn't Madame Feng the last person we want to see right now?" asked Molly.

"Absolutely."

"Addison, I hate to state the obvious, but with you, it sometimes seems necessary."

"Go on."

"If we don't want to see Madame Feng, then isn't her casino the last place we should go?"

"Yes, but her casino is also the last place she'll expect us. Besides, we have no choice."

"Really? Because it seems like we have a choice."

"Au contraire, young Cooke. We need to go to Macau to hire Uncle Nigel's pilot, Dax Conroy. How else are we getting to Northern China?"

Molly frowned. Addison often had the annoying habit of being right.

He paused when they reached the bottom of the stairwell. "All in favor?"

Molly nodded grimly.

Eddie shrugged gloomily.

Raj gave an enthusiastic two thumbs up.

"Hang on, I've always wanted to say this." Addison dramatically pointed one finger in the air and shouted, "To the hydrofoil!" He rushed out of the exit door and into the shadowed alleys of the great city.

Chapter Eleven

Dax Conroy

ADDISON EXPECTED THE HYDROFOIL to be a bit more futuristic, but from the prow of the ship, it appeared no different from a ferry. It rose a little higher out of the water and it didn't rock with the waves, but otherwise Addison found the hydrofoil to be just a glorified boat. After a fifty-five-minute cruise through the nighttime harbor, his group set foot on Macau, the gambling center of Asia.

Spotlights slashed the air. Monstrous hotels were lit up like circuses. Every color of neon broadcast Chinese characters from the roofs of opulent buildings. Addison's team strode up wide boulevards decorated with pools, palm trees, and fountains that jetted plumes of water sixty feet in the air. Recessed lighting turned the cascading fountain water into lush greens, crimson reds, and lustrous golds.

Addison spotted the Feng Casino, its sign flashing so brightly, it might have been visible from space. He decided that the real winner in Macau's gambling scene was the power company.

The group approached the massive casino hotel, craning their necks to take it all in. It was several times larger than the New York Museum of Archaeology and many times gaudier.

"Are they going to let us in there?" asked Molly, gaping up at the red-carpeted steps. Guards with earpieces wired under their starched white collars lined the gilded doors.

"Molly," said Addison, "my thirteen years on this planet have led me to a single truth: you can get in anywhere if you're wearing a nice enough suit." Addison fluffed the white silk scarf he wore draped over his dinner jacket, and adjusted the matching pocket square tucked and folded in his chest pocket. He confidently climbed the steps and zeroed in on the main doors.

A well-muscled guard stopped Addison, planting one giant hand against his chest.

"I can't let you in here."

"Can't?" said Addison. "Or won't?"

"Both. How old are you?"

"Thirteen. But I read at an eighteen-year-old level."

"Then read this," said the guard, pointing to the sign that said "21 and over."

"I would prefer you read this," said Addison, peeling off a one-hundred-yuan bill from Tony Chin's wallet.

"I read you loud and clear, sir," said the guard, opening the door wide. "Right this way."

Addison was greeted by the din of ringing slot machines and enough flashing lights to flag down a UFO. Cocktail waitresses hustled to and fro, balancing giant trays of glasses. Men dealt cards, women rolled dice, roulette balls clattered and jumped along their wheels. The massive room had the manic energy of a record-breaking day on the New York Stock Exchange.

"There must be a thousand people in this casino." Molly scanned the crowded floor. "How are we supposed to find one pilot?"

"Deduction," said Addison. He deducted a fifty-yuan note from Tony Chin's wallet and handed it to a passing pit boss. "Can you point me toward Dax Conroy?"

"Dax Conroy?" The pit boss shuddered. "Over there at the blackjack tables. And tell him to pay his debts before we throw him out."

Addison thanked the man and beckoned his team. They wove through a football-field-size maze of slot machines until Addison sidled up to a lonely blackjack table curled in a quieter corner. A square-jawed, suntanned gambler sat perched on the catbird seat, one muddy boot cocked on the brass foot rail. He had the wary confidence of a man who's seen the wrong end of a shotgun and lived to tell about it. His rugged face was cut by a nose that had seen more than its fair share of bar fights. He chewed a stalk of wheat in his teeth and soaked the bruised knuckles of his right fist in a tumbler of ice.

Addison leaned one elbow on the green felt of the blackjack table. "I hear you know your way around the Gobi Desert."

Dax Conroy's eyes slowly rose from his drink. He wore a brown leather bomber jacket. His jaw was grizzled with stubble. His brow crinkled at the sight of a thirteen-year-old. "Get out of here, kid. I can't hear myself drink."

"You'll want to split those aces."

"Why don't you split? It's past your bedtime."

"You always split aces and eights," Addison persisted. "Especially when the dealer's showing a five."

Dax gave Addison a second look. "What are you, the Wizard of Odds?"

"Aces and eights," Molly put in helpfully. "Everyone knows that."

"Our uncle Jasper is in Gamblers Anonymous," Addison admitted.

"The management know you're in here?"

"Oh, Ms. Feng? She's a personal friend."

Dax gave Addison a third look.

The blackjack dealer tapped the deck against the felt tabletop impatiently, waiting for Dax's move.

Addison held Dax's gaze. "If I'm right, you'll buy me a drink and we'll talk."

"If you're wrong, I'm out five hundred yuan."

Addison turned to the dealer. "Split." He pushed Dax's entire pile of yuan onto the green felt.

Dax downed the rest of his drink and wiped his mouth with the back of his hand. "What do you figure the odds you can outrun me?"

Addison ignored this. "I'll be at the cocktail lounge," he said as the dealer flipped the next card. "You're buying." He turned and strolled to the bar.

Raj, Eddie, and Molly lingered behind.

The dealer laid down two kings. Dax stared at his two winning hands. Twenty-one and twenty-one. The dealer shoved a towering pile of yuan across the table to him.

The single stalk of wheat fell out of Dax's mouth.

••••••

Addison rested in a plush red booth in the cocktail lounge. His team piled in beside him.

Dax strode into the room clutching a fat wad of yuan. He nodded at the maître d', pointed a finger gun at the piano player, and dragged a bar stool over to the booth.

Addison signaled the waiter. "Arnold Palmer, no rocks." He lifted an eyebrow to Dax.

Dax grunted at the waiter and slid fifty yuan across the table. "I'll have what he's having."

The waiter nodded briskly and vanished to fill the order.

"Some bar snacks, too!" Eddie called after him.

Addison leaned closer to Dax and stated his business. "I need to charter a flight to an oasis town on the Silk Road in the Gobi Desert."

Dax studied Addison carefully, taking his measure. "I'm supposed to meet *Mr.* Cooke."

"I *am* Mr. Cooke," said Addison, handing over his business card.

"Kid, do I look stupid to you? Never mind, don't answer that," he said quickly.

"Look," said Addison. "You know the museum's good for the money. You might as well fly the plane."

"Kid, I ain't no babysitter."

Addison chewed on this. Dax was no pushover. "When I saw you stand up from the blackjack table without buttoning your jacket, I assumed it was because you're American. Now I can see it's because your button is missing. You need a gig, and our money's just as good as anyone's."

"I don't fly kids."

"Really? I hear you'll fly anything and look the other way."

"Kid," said Dax, reciting his motto, "the only direction a pilot needs to look is forward."

"But you still won't fly us?"

Dax leaned forward on his elbows. "The Gobi is not some giant sandbox. You'll need camels, water, and weapons. It's the largest desert in Asia. Most of it's not even sand, just rock. Like crossing the surface of the moon. It's a hundred and twenty-two degrees in the summer and minus-forty in the winter. Shifting sand dunes will bury a man in seconds. Snow leopards, brown bears, and wolves will eat you alive."

Raj leaned forward excitedly. He was rapidly developing an affection for Dax. Here was a kindred spirit.

Dax plowed on. "The Uyghur separatists carry out bombings and assassinations. The Hui people have a hatred of foreigners. If they'll slaughter a Uyghur or a Tibetan, they certainly won't think twice about carving up a westerner in a fancy dinner jacket. The Gobi is a thousand miles of the roughest country on earth. Kid, this ain't Disneyland."

"You're just trying to get a better price out of me."

Dax shrugged.

Addison didn't have all night to negotiate. He was in Madame Feng's casino, the heart of enemy territory. He decided to play his ace.

He fished in his pocket and held up Madame Feng's black dragon chip. Instantly, the maître d' appeared, quivering at his side, as if shot from a bow. Addison kept his eyes locked on Dax. "Forgive all of Mr. Conroy's debts."

"Immediately, sir."

Addison heard a buzz of excitement rippling through the lounge. Patrons had spotted his black dragon chip. He noticed one of the casino cameras, mounted on the ceiling, zooming in on him. He knew he had to hurry things along.

Dax held Addison's eye contact. "Three square meals a day, plus per diem for me and my copilot."

"You need a copilot?"

"I never fly without Mr. Jacobsen."

"Fine. Anything else?"

"When do you need me to start?"

Addison saw armed security guards converging on the cocktail lounge, drawing their riot sticks. "Right about now." He downed his Arnold Palmer.

Guards closed in.

Addison flipped his black dragon chip through the air, sending it skittering across the tiled floor. Patrons dove and fought for the valuable chip, slowing the advance of the security guards. Addison stood up from the table and smoothed the lapels of his dinner jacket. "Shall we?"

......

Addison did not like sprinting in his new blazer—it did not seem dignified. Still, running struck him as the most prudent course of action. He legged it for the front doors.

Dax seemed entirely comfortable running from casino guards, no questions asked. Addison got the distinct impression that Dax was quite used to exiting casinos at full gallop.

Addison reached the front doors and then jammed on the brakes.

A row of triads entered the casino. Tony Chin spotted Addison and smiled. In the blink of an eye, two trench knives were twirling in his hands.

Addison altered course, steamrolling a croupier, a card counter, and a cocktail waitress.

"I've seen him before," Dax called, checking over his shoulder as Tony quickly caught up. "Friend of yours?"

"Acquaintance," said Addison, vaulting onto a craps table and sprinting down its length.

"What does he want from you?"

"He probably wants his wallet back." Addison leapt off the craps table and hit the ground running.

"Who *are* you guys?!"

Addison slammed through an emergency exit door, nearly taking it off its hinges. Alarms blared throughout the casino.

Addison's team poured themselves down a set of concrete stairs, their ten feet flying faster than a speed typist's fingers.

Triads tore after them.

"They want us for bait," Molly explained to Dax as they wound their way down the dizzying staircase. "So Aunt Delia and Uncle Nigel will help them find Genghis Khan's tomb."

"You sure about that?"

"This has happened to us before," said Molly matter-of-factly.

"It's pretty much par for the course with us," Addison agreed.

Throwing knives sliced the air and drew sparks from the staircase wall.

"I would like to renegotiate my rate," Dax said.

Addison barreled through a second emergency door. The team found themselves in a back alley.

Dax spun around and shouldered his weight against the emergency door. Triads pounded against it from the inside. "Quickly," he said through gritted teeth, "wheel that Dumpster over here!"

Addison, Raj, Eddie, and Molly wheeled an alley Dumpster flush with the emergency door.

Dax kicked down the wheel lock, anchoring the Dumpster into place. Police sirens filled the night, echoing in from all directions. "The police, too?"

"Of course," said Molly. "They're on Madame Feng's side."

"I thought you were personal friends with Madame Feng!"

"So did we," said Eddie. "Turns out, she has a lot of sides."

The sirens grew deafeningly loud. "All right. Let's keep moving." Dax took off north up the alleyway.

Addison pointed south. "The airport's that way!"

"We're not going to the airport," Dax called over his shoulder.

"Mr. Conroy, I don't mean to tell you how to do your job," said Addison, "but I think you're going to need an airplane if you want to fly us to Northern China."

"My plane's not at the airport. I keep it in a garage and tow it to the airport."

"Ah," said Addison.

"Do you have any idea what the airport charges for hangar space?"

"What about your copilot?" asked Molly. "Do we need to call him?"

"Mr. Jacobsen sleeps in the plane."

Addison's team sprinted after Dax. He led them on bewildering shortcuts through crowded warehouses and busy loading docks, and down one fetid alley where they had to outrun a guard dog. They climbed over a chain-link fence and hid behind a hobo's shanty while police cruisers patrolled the neighborhood with spotlights. When the coast was clear, they ducked through an open culvert under some train tracks and loped along a potholed service road.

At last Dax rattled open the roll-top sheet-metal door of a mechanic's garage and waved them inside.

Addison saw a tiny six-seat twin-engine Apache airplane covered in a blue tarp. Tools were scattered everywhere. Sirens wailed closer.

Dax sealed off fuel lines and hurled loose wrenches and ratchets into the cargo hold. "Mr. Jacobsen!" he called.

A Great Dane appeared in the cockpit window and barked twice.

"We're leaving!"

Mr. Jacobsen bounded down out of the Apache and sniffed at Addison and Molly. He was a gigantic beast, nearly as tall as Addison and at least fifty pounds heavier. He had the dour jowls of an aged district judge and regarded Addison's team with a baleful expression.

"Hello, Mr. Jacobsen," said Molly.

"He doesn't speak English," said Dax. "He's Danish."

"*Godaften, Herr* Jacobsen," offered Eddie.

The dog barked a single profound woof.

"What is Mr. Jacobsen's first name?" asked Molly.

"I don't know," said Dax. "I don't speak Danish."

"Actually, Great Danes are from Germany," said Raj.

"I don't speak German, either."

"*Guten abend, Herr* Jacobsen," said Eddie.

The dog barked again.

"I think he's bilingual."

Dax hurled the tarp off the plane with the flourish of a magician completing a masterful trick and expecting thunderous applause.

Addison's heart sank. The battered old Apache was covered in rust. He thought Eddie looked more likely to take flight than this ramshackle hunk of used parts. "Does this plane even fly?"

"What else would it do? Tap-dance?" Dax climbed into the passenger hold, tossing blankets and empty food cartons out the window.

Addison formed the suspicion that Mr. Jacobsen was not the only one who slept inside Dax's plane.

"C'mon, hurry!" Dax called.

Addison's team clambered onto the plane, filling the four rear passenger seats. Mr. Jacobsen bounded on board and gave Addison a sloppy, drooling lick. His tongue was like a wet eel. Addison was mortified. He pulled out his handkerchief and began mopping his cheek. "Visigoths, Ostrogoths, and Huns!"

"What's his problem?" asked Dax, jerking a thumb at Addison. He settled in at the controls and pressed the starter. The engine kicked and the propellers whirled to life.

"Addison's germophobic," said Molly.

"Mysophobic," said Addison. "'Germophobic' is not a word."

"Either way, it's an irrational fear."

"It is extremely rational! Do you know what the Black Plague did to Europe? One-third of the population was wiped out!"

"That was seven hundred years ago. That's a long time to hold a grudge."

Dax steered the tiny plane out of the garage. "You guys always argue like this? You sound like you've been married for thirty years."

"We're siblings."

Dax nodded. It was all clear to him now.

The prop plane burst onto the service road, bouncing over rain-filled potholes. Immediately, roving police cruisers altered course, circling in. Dax yanked aviation goggles and two scarves out of the glove box. He wrapped one scarf around Mr. Jacobsen.

The big dog appeared to sense the danger of flying with Dax. He left his front passenger seat and climbed into the rear. He had conceived a fondness for Addison and promptly sat on him.

"He's enormous," Addison groaned. "Will the plane be able to take off?"

"It's not his fault he's a big dog," Dax called from the front seat. "He's a Great Dane."

"He's not that great—he can't stop licking me." Addison wiped more drool from his face. "He's a Mediocre Dane at best."

"Does he know any tricks?" asked Molly, who didn't mind dogs.

"He might know a lot of tricks, but only in Danish."

"German," Raj corrected.

Police cars caught up behind the Apache. Dax opened the throttle, gunning the plane up to forty miles per hour.

A phalanx of black Mercedes, crammed chock-full of triads, skidded around a corner, blockading the road ahead.

"Okay, slight detour," Dax shouted, braking hard and jerking the plane onto a busy Macau street. He merged left with no blinker and was rewarded with a chorus of horn blasts from an irate squadron of taxis. Cars honked and swerved around the airplane, dodging its outstretched wings.

"How do you normally take your plane to the airport?" Addison shouted, clutching an overhead handgrip to keep from tipping over.

"Normally, the service road isn't blocked by armed triads."

Gunshots rang out. Addison saw holes open up in the Apache's wing flaps.

Dax skidded the Apache down a side alley. They smashed through several clotheslines, the propeller mashing the laundry to pieces.

"Where did you learn to drive?" shouted Molly.

"You think this is bad, you should see my flying." Dax steered toward a busy intersection, police sirens flashing behind him. He leaned forward and kissed a plastic frog glued to his dashboard.

"Did you just kiss that frog?" asked Raj.

"Of course. It's good luck. You should kiss it, too, if you know what's good for you."

"I prefer not kissing frogs," said Molly.

"It's your funeral."

More gunshots punched the plane. Addison noted the holes inching dangerously close to the fuel tank. "All right, quit messing around, Dax. Get us out of here!"

"I get nose up at ninety miles per hour."

"So?"

"So, I need at least two hundred yards of runway to hit that speed!" Dax pointed at the traffic clogging the street. "Any ideas?"

A triad Mercedes pulled up next to the Apache and rolled down its windows. Addison's eyes widened at the sight of a gun muzzle. He reached forward and yanked the plane's nose wheel, steering the aircraft into oncoming traffic.

"What are you doing?!" Dax shouted, fighting for control of the wheel.

"Punch it!"

Bullets rattled the metal frame of the cabin. Dax didn't have any better ideas. He jammed the throttle wide open. The plane lurched forward, the engine roaring like a lion. Oncoming cars swerved out of their path. The Apache sped straight for the harbor.

"I'm not sure this is two hundred yards!" Molly yelled.

"Then you better kiss the frog!" shouted Dax.

Addison, Molly, Eddie, and Raj kissed the frog.

"Buckle up!" The plane packed on speed, mashing Addison's team back against their seats. The rickety aircraft reached the end of the street and smashed through the pier, wood splintering across the windshield. The plane dipped. The harbor rushed toward the windshield.

Addison's stomach took a sickening lurch. He shut his eyes, waiting for the crash.

It never came.

He opened his eyes. They were airborne. The city fell away behind them as the plane nosed toward the clouds. "Well, they will not remember us fondly in Macau." In his relief to be alive, Addison even gave Mr. Jacobsen a few pats on the head. "If anyone has plans to return here, consider changing them."

"They can keep this city," said Eddie, lying back in his seat, exhausted. "I'm through with it."

II

THE
EMPIRE
OF THE
KHAN

Chapter Twelve
The Silk Road

ADDISON HAD NEVER BEEN in a plane so small before. The cabin was about the size of Eddie's mom's station wagon. It was like flying a Buick Caballero ten thousand feet in the air. The plane shuddered and shook as it gained altitude. "Is this safe?"

"Define 'safe,'" said Dax.

"Are we going to crash?"

"Kid, I'm not a psychic." Dax seemed to realize this was not the answer his paying passengers were hoping to hear from their pilot. "Okay, the plane isn't one hundred percent safe. But it's a whole lot safer than flying China National Airlines."

"That is difficult to imagine." The plane climbed steeply,

pitched at a forty-five-degree angle. Addison's fear of heights was kicking in, so he avoided looking out of the windows. "Is China National Airlines publicly traded on the stock market?"

"I have absolutely no idea."

"Well, in any case," said Addison, "I will not be buying their stock."

"In *Mission: Survival II*, Babatunde Okonjo explains how to survive a plane crash," said Raj. "Let's say you fall out of an airplane without a parachute. You flatten out, glide, and aim for a body of water."

Dax frowned. "Water has surface tension, my friend. You fall from that height, it's like hitting concrete."

Raj was ready for this. "That's why you aim for white water—the waves break the surface tension. As long as it's deep enough, falling into white water is like falling into bed."

Dax considered this and nodded. He pulled a box of toothpicks from his center console, popped one in his mouth, and offered one to Raj.

Raj watched the way Dax's jaw muscles worked the toothpick. He squinted and followed suit. Raj didn't know why he needed to chew a toothpick, he just knew Dax made it look cool.

At last the plane leveled out. Addison chanced a glance out the window. China was spread out below him, its cities and streets teeming with a billion souls. Distant factories belched noxious gray smog clouds that Addison tried to imagine were rain clouds. Lit only by the silver moon, China was a land of shadows.

Addison carefully folded his prized white blazer and changed into his public school jacket, tie, and ivy cap. Molly wore a T-shirt, cargo pants, and rugged hiking boots. Raj swapped his forest camouflage pants for a desert pattern and topped it off with a tan T-shirt and his red bandana. Eddie wore his one pair of school slacks, which were a few inches too short for his long legs. They'd all been awake for more than a day. The roar of the engine became a soothing lullaby as they drifted off to sleep.

Dax refueled in Deqin, a smuggler's town where weather-beaten men offered to sneak Addison's team across the Tibetan border for five hundred yuan. Addison studied his pocket edition of *Fiddleton's Asia Atlas* and saw that the Wa headhunters, who worshipped the skulls that they captured, once lived just to the south, where they had occasionally battled the famous tiger hunters of Lanu. The air was cold and thin in the foothills of the Himalayas, and Addison was glad when they were airborne again, chased by the rising sun.

Calloused hands on the yoke, Dax banked the Apache north and west, ever closer to the Gobi. If he was tired from flying through the night, he didn't show it. "I think I should point out," he said at last, "that the Gobi Desert is five hundred thousand square miles. Where exactly in the Gobi are we flying to?"

Addison had not fully considered this. "That's a decent question." He cracked open his notebook and read Sir Frederick's clue aloud for the team.

"'There lies an oasis town on the Silk Road by the Dragon Desert
Where Nestorian Christians nursed me to health.
Know ye your Templar vows. Visit the sick and say a mass
for the dead. Pray for our sign and ye will know
the way to the Tartar's land.'"

"Can you make anything of it, Molly?"

"Not even a little bit."

"You and me both. I would give my kingdom for an Arnold Palmer to get the synaptic juices flowing." He closed his eyes to relax his mind but then quickly realized he might fall back to sleep. Instead, he decided to employ his usual strategy, which was to simply start talking. "Well," he began, "Sir Frederick was buried in Samarkand. And the clue said he was unhorsed three months earlier."

"So?"

"So wherever we're going must be three months' walking distance from Samarkand."

"Addison," said Molly, "you're jumping to conclusions so hard, you're going to throw out your back."

"Mo, stick to me like dryer lint. Imagine you're Sir Frederick. You're galloping along the Silk Road, minding your own business, when you're ambushed by bandits. They kill your trusty mount and you take an arrow in the leg. It becomes infected and you don't have penicillin because it's the Dark Ages. What do you do?"

"Well, he said he found a Christian hospital."

"So for a few days, you're sweating out your fever in the hospital. You have no more horse and you think you're going to die."

"You find a place to hide a clue," Eddie piped in.

"Right. Because you can't bear the thought of dying with your secret. You want your fellow Templar knights to find their way to the Khan's treasure."

Molly picked up the thread. "When Sir Frederick gets better, he manages to walk another three months before he finally croaks in Samarkand."

"Exactly."

"That means our next clue is three months' walking distance along the Silk Road from Samarkand," said Molly.

"Precisely."

"How far is walking distance?" asked Eddie. "He could be a power walker."

"I don't think so," said Addison. "He was dying of an arrow wound. Plus he had to climb those eighteen-thousand-foot mountains Uncle Nigel was talking about." Addison flipped through his pocket-size edition of *Fiddleton's Asia Atlas*, found Uzbekistan, and stabbed a finger in Samarkand's general direction.

"Raj, how many miles do you reckon a wounded man can walk in a day?"

"With armor? And climbing mountains? Five miles, tops."

"Mo, how many days are in three months?"

"Ninety."

"Just for kicks, let's say Sir Frederick spent ten of those days belly-up in the hospital. So he had eighty days to hike five miles a day, which means he walked . . ."

"Four thousand miles," said Eddie.

"Four *hundred*," Molly corrected.

"Oh, right. I added too many zeroes," said Eddie, embarrassed.

Addison studied the map, tracing a four-hundred-mile line east along the Silk Road trading route from Samarkand. His finger arrived on a city. He smiled. "We're going to Kashgar."

Dax gave a thumbs-up and made a small westerly adjustment to his flight path. The sun rose higher in the sky, and the miles fell away beneath them.

Molly practiced tiger punches and eagle claws, drilling her kung fu exercises into her muscle memory. Eddie practiced piano scales on his armrest. Addison devoured his father's copy of *The Secret History of the Mongols*, learning of Genghis Khan's stunning journey from enslaved orphan to warrior king.

Dax refueled the Apache in Kathmandu, leaving Nepal before lunch to skirt the mountains of Pakistan. By two p.m. local time they were wheels down in Kashgar.

••••••

The airport was little more than a clearing in the sand. Addison stretched his aching legs and used the sun to find his bearings. To the west, the snowcaps of the Tian Shan Mountains guarded the wilderness borders to Kyrgyzstan and Tajikistan. To the east, the desolate wasteland of the Taklamakan Desert spread to the curving horizon. To the south lay Kashgar, a chaotic warren of brown brick buildings scattered and stacked in all directions.

Dax led the team into the heart of the town. Mr. Jacobsen, panting with the heat, padded at his heels on the dusty road. "What exactly are you looking for?"

"Food," Eddie answered immediately. He had already spotted a kebab vendor grilling chicken on a rotating spit.

"Eddie, we've barely been here five minutes," said Molly. "Besides, you ate four sticks of beef jerky on the plane."

"Those were my emergency rations," Raj grumbled.

Weary donkeys, heads bowed, hauled creaking carts of carpets, silk, and copper teapots up the rut-pocked street.

"We," said Addison, picking up Dax's thread, "are looking for a Christian hospital where a certain Sir Frederick convalesced after meeting the business end of an arrow."

"And when did Fred stay at this hospital?" asked Dax.

"Oh, about eight hundred years ago."

Dax gave Addison a long look. "Shouldn't be too difficult."

The road opened onto a cobbled market square, choking with foot traffic. Buryat traders with broad faces and pointed bear-fur hats peddled baskets of cardamom, cloves, figs, and dates. Uyghur tribesmen with striking blue eyes lighting up their weather-tanned faces grilled chestnuts over open mulberry wood fires. Hui herders in white skullcaps shook wooden crooks and goaded their goats through the open market.

"So how do you find this hospital?" Dax called over the din of traders and shopkeepers.

"There's nothing to it," Addison said confidently. "In the Middle Ages, hospitals were run by churches. So all we need to do is find the right church, and Bob's your uncle."

"Well, good luck with that, kid."

"What do you mean?"

"Look around you." Dax spread his arms wide to the bustling bazaar where bearded men in embroidered *takiyah* skullcaps bartered with women in colorful head scarves. "Kashgar is a Muslim city. If there are any churches left, they've been converted into mosques."

"I like a challenge."

"A challenge?" said Molly. "Addison, we're not even sure we're in the right city. Kashgar was kind of a guess."

"An extremely well-educated guess. It was the Harvard PhD of guesses," said Addison, with a confidence that brooked no argument. "Kashgar was a hugely important city for caravans traveling the Silk Road. Molly, haven't you read Marco Polo?"

Molly had not, so she assumed Addison knew what he was talking about.

"Right, then," he said, clasping his hands and scanning the crowded market. "We're just going to do a bit of reconnaissance. We're going to turn Kashgar upside down, shake it, and see if a church doesn't fall out." Addison flipped open Tony Chin's wallet, peeled off a fresh hundred-yuan note, and tucked it into the chest pocket of Dax's leather bomber jacket. Then he tore a sheet of paper from his notebook. "Here is a list of provisions we shall require."

Dax regarded the list listlessly. "You want me to buy you eight climbing axes . . . sixty feet of nylon climbing rope . . . six pounds of dynamite . . . twelve blasting caps?" He crumpled the note into his pocket. "Sure. I'll get right on this. Just as soon as I make a pit stop." He turned down a crooked side alley, Mr. Jacobsen loping after him.

Addison noted that Dax did not appear to take direction well. He jogged after him. "I don't mean to micromanage you, Dax, but I'm not sure you are likely to find provisions by *leaving* the market."

"All Mr. Jacobsen and I require is an upscale establishment where we can enjoy a relaxing beverage and a civilized game of cards."

"You said Kashgar's a Muslim city. I don't think you're likely to find either beverages or cards."

Dax held up Addison's one-hundred-yuan note. "Where there's a bill, there's a way."

The alley darkened under the looming shadows of teetering tenements where flint-eyed cats spied from drooping balconies and the curling eaves of clay-tiled roofs. Dax strode past a restaurant with bullet-shattered windows and turned his nose up at a smoking den where a one-eyed man threw daggers against a target on the wall. Finally, he reached a noisy saloon ringing with raucous laughter, shouts, and the occasional bloodcurdling scream.

A man hurled out of a second-story window crashed to the ground at Dax's feet. His hat was thrown out after him. The shaken man struggled to his knees and spit three teeth into the dust.

"This'll do," said Dax, and pushed his way through the saloon doors. Mr. Jacobsen trotted after him, wagging his tail.

Addison's team stood in the dusty street, flummoxed.

"Maybe you shouldn't have handed him all that money," said Molly.

"Do you think we'll ever see him again?" asked Eddie.

"Of course," said Addison, lathering his voice up with confidence. "Uncle Nigel has the utmost faith in Dax. He always comes through in the end. We will meet him back here after our reconnaissance."

Addison, keen for a high vantage point, led them up the spiraling steps of an ancient minaret. They gazed out at the mud-brown sprawl of Kashgar.

"Are you sure we're in the right city?" Molly asked again.

"Without a doubt," said Addison, who was not at all certain. He was rapidly getting up to speed on Mongol history, much of which seemed to involve butchering staggering numbers of people. "Genghis Khan's generals conquered Kashgar in 1219. They chopped off the prince's head and paraded it through the town."

"That must have ticked off a few people."

"Not really." Addison shrugged. "Nobody really liked the prince. Genghis was hailed as a conquering hero. It would make sense to hide a clue to his tomb here." He gazed out at the myriad minarets, steeples, and spires stuck in the cityscape like candles in a birthday cake. "The question is, which church? You can't throw a rock in Kashgar without hitting one. Not that I condone throwing rocks at churches," he hastily added.

"It could take us weeks to search all these buildings," said Molly.

"The solution to any problem is to be found in a book." He dipped into his blazer pocket, drew out his pocket-size edition of *Fiddleton's Asia Atlas*, and handed it to Molly. "How many churches does the good Mr. Fiddleton list in Kashgar?"

Molly thumbed through the index. "There are forty-seven churches, mosques, and churches that have been turned into mosques."

"How many of them existed eight hundred years ago?"

Molly scanned the ages listed next to each building. "Only three."

"You see, Mo? Books are the answer to life's questions."

"Do you trust Fiddleton's numbers?"

Addison stepped backward in shock, a hand fluttering to his chest. "Roland J. Fiddleton is a world traveler, polar explorer, fisherman, trapper, polo champion, gourmet chef, bon vivant, holder of five patents and seven world records, and the treasurer of the London Explorers Club. If Roland J. Fiddleton says there are only three medieval churches left in Kashgar, then we must take Mr. Roland J. Fiddleton at his word."

The team wound their way south, deeper into the city.

Every wide street was a tent-covered bazaar. Leather-skinned merchants sold dates, saffron powder, and pistachio nuts from Persia. Laughing women in head scarves hawked frankincense, aloe, and myrrh from Somalia. Addison spotted sandalwood from India, handblown glass from Egypt, and dried fruit from as far away as Saudi Arabia.

"We're almost at the first church on our list," he said, consulting the atlas.

"How will we know if it's the *right* church?" asked Eddie.

"Easy," said Addison. "Our church will be the one crawling with Madame Feng's triads." He didn't know if this would actually be the case, but he also didn't know if this wouldn't actually be the case, and he figured that what he didn't know couldn't hurt him, so he put his faith in the first option.

"You better hope we're in the right city, Addison," Molly grumbled, dodging land mines of cattle droppings in the potholed street.

"Molly, my youngest Cooke, lowest branch on the family tree," said Addison, "I am absolutely positive we're in the right city."

"If the next clue is in the first church we check," said Eddie, "this will be pretty easy."

"Why would you say that, Eddie?" Molly sputtered. "You'll jinx us!"

"What, I'm just saying."

Eddie was about to turn the corner when Molly grabbed him by the jacket collar and tugged him back. "Okay, I take it back."

"Triads!" she whispered.

The team peeked around the corner of the alley to a crumbling stone church across the cobbled square. The whole building was swarming with triad guards in dark suits and darker sunglasses.

"Not so easy, is it, Eddie?" Addison beamed.

"Well, don't look so happy about it," said Molly.

"I'm relieved," said Addison.

"Why?"

"Until this moment, I had no idea if we were in the right city."

Chapter Thirteen

The Triad Guards

ADDISON'S TEAM LOW-LINED ACROSS the alleyway and ducked behind a row of hay bales. Molly sneezed once, then twice, then two more times to keep the first two sneezes company. When she finally finished her sneezing fit, they peered over the wiry clumps of hay to survey the church.

Generations of pigeons roosted in the tower belfry, the wrought iron bells long since melted down for cannons. Great doors of rotted oak hung ajar in the porticos of Gothic arches. Sections of slate roof were crushed inward by the heavy hands of time.

"Sun Tzu says you must begin every battle by gathering information," said Addison. "'*Know thyself, know thy enemy. A thousand battles, a thousand victories.'"* He turned to Raj. "How many triads do you count?"

Raj counted the triads covering every door, watching the square, and patrolling the high parapets along the buttressed roof. "Seven. But if there are as many guards on the other side of the church, that makes fourteen."

"They must be really worried about us finding them," said Eddie.

"They're not losing sleep over us—they're worried about the Russians." Addison grimaced. The guards had every square inch of the church covered. He was having trouble finding a silver lining to this thundercloud. He plumbed the depths of his mind, but no ideas bubbled to the surface. He tried taking a few deep, meditative breaths, but that only resulted in him, too, sneezing from the hay. That made Molly sneeze twice for good measure. At last he shook his head. There was only one solution. "I need an Arnold Palmer."

The team slunk across the far end of the square to the outdoor patio of a mahogany wood teahouse. A group of Mongols sipping tin mugs of horse milk in the shadows grew silent and watchful as the New Yorkers entered.

A Tajik man with a wizened beard and a goatskin vest greeted Addison in broken English.

"Good afternoon," said Addison, sinking into a cushioned seat. "Arnold Palmer, please."

The Tajik man blinked and looked around the establishment. "He is not here."

Addison saw that the man's English was not much better than Addison's Chinese. "I am not asking for Arnold Palmer, the famous golfer. I just want his drink."

"You wish to have Arnold Palmer's drink?"

"Precisely."

"My friend, neither Arnold Palmer nor his drink have ever set foot in this restaurant."

"I don't need Arnold Palmer the person," said Addison patiently. "I just need Arnold Palmer the drink."

"If this Arnold Palmer is not here, how can he have left his drink?" The waiter was losing his patience.

Addison saw they were rapidly reaching an impasse. "Please fill a glass with tea and lemonade. Put some ice in it and we can forget all about Mr. Arnold Palmer."

The waiter nodded.

"Do you have orange chicken?" Eddie asked.

"Our chickens are regular colored."

"Do you have General Tso's chicken?"

"I do not know General Tso, and I do not have his chicken. Is General Tso a friend of Mr. Palmer?"

"Okay, fine," said Eddie. "How about moo shu pork?"

"No pork, Eddie," said Molly. "We're in a Muslim city!"

"Why don't they have Chinese food in China?" cried Eddie. "Is that too much to ask?"

Once the team finally ordered, their food arrived quickly. They shared a cauldron of mutton stew so spicy, Addison broke out in a sweat. He could not decide if the stew was delicious or he was just ravenous with hunger. The team had barely eaten in a day.

Addison discovered his Arnold Palmer was a strange concoction of tea and pomegranate juice, inexplicably doused with a mound of curry powder. He rather liked it. He was enjoying a few thoughtful sips when Molly spotted movement on the parapet of the church across the street.

"Aunt Delia and Uncle Nigel!"

Addison squinted his eyes and, sure enough, spotted the A & U being prodded along the tower roof by Madame Feng and Tony Chin. They appeared to be searching the outer wall of the belfry.

"If the aunt and uncle have led Madame Feng onto the roof, you can be sure the clue is down in the deepest basement," said Addison. "They'll be doing everything in their power to slow her down." He drummed his fingers on the table. "We've got to get inside. Somewhere in that eyesore of a church is the next clue to the Khan's treasure."

"Any ideas?" asked Eddie, fanning his mouth from the steaming heat of a second helping of stew.

Addison concentrated. He'd taken this lunch break to observe the guards. He was hoping they'd rotate shifts, leave for coffee breaks, take naps, or perhaps grow old and retire. But it appeared these triads were professionals and they weren't lowering their guard any time soon. The one advantage Addison could find was that he did not recognize any of the door guards' faces. If they were recruited locally, they would not recognize him, either.

He downed the remainder of his Arnold Palmer, or whatever it was, and shivered from the dregs of curry powder at the bottom of the pewter cup. He rolled up his sleeves.

••••••

"Do you have a plan?" asked Molly, hurrying to keep up as Addison strode toward the church.

"Sun Tzu says, *'The supreme art of war is to subdue the enemy without fighting.'*"

"Um, that's great, Addison. But I think it might be a little bit better if we had a plan."

"I don't think they speak English, Addison," Eddie put in.

"I'm counting on that."

"Well, it's just that I think I'm with Molly on this one," said Eddie. "We need a plan."

"Here's a plan." Addison gestured to a row of mules parked at the hitching post by the church's front entrance. "Hide behind that fig cart and wait for my signal to walk inside the church."

"What's your signal?"

"The signal is when I tell you, Molly, and Raj to walk inside the church." Addison selected an apple and two eggs from a pushcart vendor and slipped the merchant a few yuan. He unfolded a large insert map of Kashgar from *Fiddleton's Asia Atlas*. Then, to his team's horror, he strode right up to the armed triad guards, who quickly moved to block the church door.

The triads barked in Chinese. Addison didn't know what they were saying, but it did not sound friendly. They pointed for him to leave.

"Hello," he said genially. "Does anyone speak English?"

The guards looked at each other. "No English."

Addison pointed to his map and spoke very slowly. "I'm creating a diversion so my friends can sneak into this church. Can you help me?"

The guards grunted more orders in Chinese. The shortest triad, who seemed to know a few words in English, stepped forward. "You go now!"

"Here," said Addison, "take this apple and hold it over your head, like so." Addison demonstrated and pressed the apple into the short triad's hand.

The triad took it, baffled.

Addison pointed to the map, then pointed to the apple. He motioned for the triad to hold the apple directly over his own head. The triad, thoroughly confused, did so.

"Now you," said Addison, turning to a tall, skinny triad.

"Hold these two eggs directly over your eyes." Addison demonstrated before handing the eggs over to the triad.

The triad covered his eyes with the eggs. Addison showed his map to the third triad, round and muscled. "This is your church on the map." Addison pointed at it insistently. "My friends are going to sneak in while you stare at my finger."

The short triad had no idea why he needed to hold an apple over his head. He slowly lowered the apple.

"No!" said Addison firmly, gesturing with his hand. "Keep that apple high."

The short triad snapped the apple back into position over his head. The tall triad kept the eggs planted in front of his eyes. The round, muscled triad stared closer at Addison's map in confusion. The language barrier was too high for him to scramble over. Across the square, more guards took interest. They moved in, surrounding Addison.

A large triad with a rifle slung over his shoulder gestured to Addison. "No English. You go now!"

"Do you know the Chinese word for 'diversion'?" Addison repeated himself slowly and carefully. "Di-ver-sion."

The large triad looked to the dozen soldiers now flanking him. He struggled to pronounce the English word. "Diversion?"

"Yes, diversion. You know, like when a magician gets

you to look in the wrong direction while they perform a trick?"

"No English!" said the guard again.

Addison led the triads a few steps away from the shadow of the church door and tilted his map to the sunlight. He pointed adamantly at the map. "Molly, Eddie, and Raj," he said in the same tone he had been using, "walk inside the church now."

The guards stared at him in confusion. The skinny guard dared to peek from behind the eggs he was holding in front of his eyes.

Addison risked a quick glance over the large triad's shoulder to where Molly stepped uncertainly from behind the fig cart, tiptoeing toward the church.

Raj ninja rolled past her and scuttled up the church steps on all fours like a beetle.

Eddie stepped into the open and stood there blinking. Molly and Raj beckoned him toward the church door, but Eddie seemed to have lost his nerve.

The large triad seemed to sense movement behind him and turned to look.

Addison hiked his map up in front of the triad's eyes. "I just need you to stare at this map a few seconds longer because my friend Eddie is very slow."

Molly grabbed Eddie and hauled him bodily up the church steps.

Addison sighed as they safely skirted past the heavy oak door. He turned to the large triad. "So you have no idea what a diversion is?"

The guard shook his head.

"Clearly not," said Addison, folding up his map. He patted the guard reassuringly on the shoulder and took the liberty of straightening the lapels on the man's jacket. "I thank you gentlemen. Here is my card if you ever need anything." He handed the large triad his business card with a flourish.

The guards pressed close to study the card with confusion. They did not read any more English than they spoke.

"Have a pleasant afternoon."

The guards watched him leave. The short triad slowly lowered the apple from over his head, staring after Addison in befuddlement. The skinny triad obediently kept the two eggs covering his eyes until the large triad smacked him on the back of the head.

Addison strolled around the far side of the church, admiring the Nestorian architecture and tipping his cap to an incense vendor. When he reached the narrow alley behind the ancient building, he heard a whisper just over his head.

"Up here!" Raj and Eddie reached their hands from the empty shell of a shattered stained-glass window. Addison gripped their wrists and they pulled him inside.

Chapter Fourteen

The Nestorian Church

ADDISON TOUCHED DOWN IN the nave of the ancient church, its wooden pews long since rotted into the dust of centuries. Yellow light lanced the shadows where mice and voles built their cities in the cracks of crumbling masonry. The great domed roof of the apse was crumpled inward like a fallen soufflé, its time-faded painted angels vanishing into the past.

Molly shushed Addison before he could comment on the décor. *"Listen!"* she hissed. Madame Feng's purring voice wafted down from the rafters, the staccato tap of her high heels strutting along the belfry high above. Molly could also make out Aunt Delia and Uncle Nigel's voices as the pair paced across the roof. "They're okay!"

"Excellent," Addison whispered. "Now let's move quickly, before we're spotted inside this church." He cracked open his pocket notebook and reread Sir Frederick's clue. "'*Know ye your Templar vows. Visit the sick and say a mass for the dead.*'"

Grains of sand and masonry cascaded from the ceiling as Madame Feng's triads clambered around on the roof. Addison cast a nervous glance upward. "Pretend there's a tornado. That's how badly we need to find the basement."

The group split up, scouring the stone-tiled nave for any sign of a staircase, a ladder, or even a ventilation shaft.

"Who were the Templars?" asked Molly, checking the pulpit for trapdoors.

"A secret order of knights from the Middle Ages," said Raj. "They were once so powerful, they controlled entire governments and pulled the strings of power throughout Europe."

Everyone looked at Raj in surprise. History was more Addison's domain.

"I love secret organizations." Raj shrugged. "Freemasons, Skull and Bones, the Illuminati . . . I would join any of those groups if I knew how to get invited."

"So what happened to these Templars?" asked Molly.

"They grew too powerful. The governments of Europe hunted them down and killed them off."

"Are any left? Can you still join?"

"They were driven extinct centuries ago."

The group froze as the handles turned on the front doors of the church. *We're going to be driven extinct now,* thought Addison. The doors swung open. The group fled behind the main altar and ducked into the sacristy.

"It's a dead end," Molly whispered.

Triad voices echoed from the church nave, drawing closer.

Addison searched the narrow sacristy. Candlesticks, crosses, and a curious collection of cricket carcasses. At the far end of the room stood a locked door. It was not the door that caught his eye. It was the Latin inscription carved into the masonry above the door: *Hospes.*

"Hospital," Addison whispered. "This is it." He pressed a hand against the heavy oak door. "*'Know ye your Templar vows. Visit the sick.'* This is where Sir Frederick stayed."

The triad voices sounded closer, along with the tread of heavy boots.

"I can use my lock-picking set!" Raj dropped to his knees and unshouldered his pack in one fluid motion. He riffled through tourniquets, razor wire, bear spray, a vial of battery acid, and what appeared to be a snakeskin.

"We could just use the keys," said Addison, producing a ring of rusted iron keys from his blazer pocket.

"Where did you get those?"

"Nicked them from the door guard when I straightened his lapels."

The triads' shouts reverberated in the domed chapel just a few feet away. Addison quickly fed each key into the lock of the *hospes* door until he found the one that fit. Biting his lip with concentration, he carefully pushed the door inward, slowing each time he sensed an impending squeak. His team slipped quietly through and closed the door with a soft click just as the triads stormed into the sacristy.

Addison's group found themselves in the hospital ward of the ancient church. The low-ceilinged hallway was lined with brass braziers filled with sandalwood ashes long since grown cold. Nestorian monks in brown cassocks tied with hemp-rope belts had once bustled along this corridor, tending their patients in the adjoining rooms.

Addison, Molly, Eddie, and Raj split up to search the rooms in the hospital ward and met up at the far end of the hallway.

"Anyone happen to discover an eight-hundred-year-old clue?" asked Addison.

"I found an eight-hundred-year-old spiderweb," said Eddie, blinking and waving his hands spastically in front of his face.

"I found a fully intact mouse skeleton," said Raj, beaming.

"I found something," said Molly, waving them into the last windowless cell in the ward. She pointed to a low wooden door, just big enough for a man to crawl through. Unfortunately, it was shut tight.

Addison read the inscription above the door. *"'In perpetuum.'"* He broke out in a smile. "Excellent work, young relative. *'Know ye your Templar vows. Visit the sick and say a mass for the dead . . .'"* He turned to face the group. *"In perpetuum* is what Christians write outside a cemetery."

"Great," said Eddie. "Can't we go anywhere without visiting a cemetery?"

"Eddie, our whole mission is to find the Khan's grave, so you might as well get used to the idea of visiting cemeteries."

A harsh pounding boomed across the hospital ward. Triads were smashing down the *hospes* door. "Only one way out for us," said Addison. He drew his stolen key ring and opened the tiny door.

The team ducked into the low chamber. Addison hoped his eyes would adjust to the gloom, but it was pitch-black.

"I have a military-grade flashlight," said Raj, rustling around in his backpack. "Fully waterproof, one thousand candlepower, and good for up to seventy-two hours. Cave divers use this very model. Nothing can beat it." There were a few clicks and scratches in the darkness, but no light.

"Well, where is it, already?" asked Molly.

"I forgot the batteries."

Addison fished his own flashlight from his messenger

bag. In the total darkness, his penlight seemed as bright as a rising sun.

The team followed its glow down a sheer flight of narrow steps, curving into the earth like the threads of a screw. The spiraling staircase opened onto a low hallway carved into the sandy bedrock. Dozens of wooden caskets lay stacked on shelves hollowed into the rock.

"Look at all these coffins," said Raj, his eyes gleaming in the frail light.

"I guess their hospital wasn't very good," said Molly.

Eddie glanced nervously around the room. "Addison, if I see one single skeleton down here, I'm going to have a bone to pick with you."

Addison stepped to the center of the chamber, scanning the walls for any secret message, passage, package, or clue.

"What's our next move?" asked Molly. She kept a careful ear craned to hear if Madame Feng's triads discovered the door to the burial chamber.

"We visited the sick and the dead," said Addison. "The next line of the clue says, *'Pray for our sign and ye will know the way to the Tartar's land.'*" He stroked his chin as he'd seen his Uncle Nigel do. The burial chamber ended in a round chapel carved into the end of the tunnel. Ornate rugs and tapestries had long since decayed into the earth, leaving nothing but dust. All that was left in the chapel was a cedarwood altar and an iron cross.

Raj tugged at the cross and searched behind the altar but found nothing.

Addison got down on his knees and joined his hands before him. "We've followed Sir Frederick's instructions to the letter. The last step is to pray for a sign to the Tartar's land. C'mon, everyone kneel."

Molly frowned. "You don't really think this will work, do you?"

"It couldn't hurt."

Molly couldn't think of a better alternative. She, Raj, and Eddie knelt beside Addison and clasped their hands together in prayer.

"Anyone getting anything?" asked Addison after a minute.

"Hungry," said Eddie.

"We're missing something." Addison closed his eyes in concentration. "'*Pray for our sign and ye will know the way . . .*'"

"It's not just any sign," said Molly. "Sir Frederick specifically says, pray for *our* sign."

"You're right." Addison's eyes flicked open. "The Templar sign." He took the flashlight from Molly and bowed low before the cross, as if praying. And there, near the ground below the altar, he saw it. The Templar symbol from Sir Frederick's shield was carved into the stone wall. "Raj, a little help."

He and Raj dragged the heavy cedar altar away from

the rock. "Careful," said Addison, setting the altar down. "It's an antique."

They squatted low to examine the Templar symbol: an open eye surrounded by rays of spreading light. Addison flipped open his butterfly knife and scratched at the mortar latticework of the stone wall. Flakes of dry mortar crumbled loose. Soon he and Raj had pried the Templar stone from the wall. Raj became fixated on the task and quickly removed a second and third rock as well. They felt the cool draft of a hidden chamber. A few stones later and they had opened a tunnel large enough to squeeze through.

"Dibs," said Molly, taking Addison's flashlight in her teeth and climbing in headfirst.

"Will there be booby traps?" asked Eddie.

"Absolutely not," Addison assured him. "Remember, Sir Frederick was only in this hospital a week or two. He didn't have time to build anything too elaborate. I predict whatever is in this chamber will be extremely safe."

Eddie narrowed his eyes suspiciously, but followed Addison, Raj, and Molly through the hole in the wall. They crawled on all fours for a few feet before the tunnel dropped steeply downward. Slipping and sliding on skittering rocks, they scrambled for footholds. The chute descended thirty feet before opening into a massive chamber with tunnels branching in all directions.

"Wow," said Eddie, brushing himself off and rising to his feet. "Sir Frederick must have been a fast worker."

Addison wiped dirt from his knees, careful to preserve the carefully ironed creases of his slacks. "I don't think so." He shook his head in amazement. "I think this took centuries."

Molly played the flashlight around the gloom. Hundreds of caskets lay stacked in nooks in the walls—floor to ceiling—as far as the eye could see in the darkness.

"More dead people?" asked Eddie, astonished at his poor luck.

"That small crypt upstairs was just a decoy," said Addison. "I'll bet the monks hid the real catacombs down here to protect them from grave robbers."

Raj pulled his toothpick from his chest pocket and tucked it in the corner of his mouth. "How did they squeeze all these coffins down Sir Frederick's tiny chute?"

"There may be other entrances," said Addison, peering down the closest tunnel. "Though they could all be sealed off by now."

"There must be thousands of bodies down here," Eddie said, his voice tremulous in the stifling dark.

"Let's say the church buried a hundred people a year," said Molly, doing the math. "That's ten thousand people every century."

Eddie shivered.

"We've got to keep moving," said Addison. "The triads could be right behind us."

Molly shined the flashlight down one tunnel and then another. "Each path looks the same. We go too far, we may get lost."

"We'll leave a thread of Ariadne," said Addison. "Like Theseus when he faced the Minotaur."

"You've lost me," said Molly.

"I think he might be having a stroke," Eddie agreed.

"A stroke of genius," said Addison. "C'mon, don't you know your Greek mythology? A long thread is how you find your way out of a labyrinth. Raj, how many feet of fishing line do you have?"

"A six-hundred-foot spool," Raj answered immediately. "That's standard for deep-sea bluefin tuna fishing."

Raj's answer seemed to beg more questions than it answered—namely, why Raj saw fit to travel to the Gobi Desert while fully equipped for deep-sea fishing. Still, Addison knew better than to lick a gift horse in the mouth. Or was it look a gift horse in the mouth? Either way, Addison had no time for horse's mouths at the moment, so he tied Raj's fishing line to a heavy stone and unspooled the reel behind them as they stepped warily down the first chamber.

When it dead-ended, they looped back and tried a side chamber, taking a left and a right through the maze. Wrapping around a hairpin turn, Eddie snagged his foot on a trip wire and tumbled to the ground. An awful grinding sound cut the darkness. Raj and Addison yanked Eddie backward as a one-ton rock plummeted into place, sealing off the passage.

The giant crash echoed into the darkness long after Eddie's heart had decided it was safe to start beating again. "Addison, you said no booby traps!"

"I say a lot of things. It's not my fault there's a booby trap!"

"I have other friends in school," said Eddie, brushing off his hands. "And when I hang out with them, I am almost never crushed to death by booby traps."

Addison surveyed the massive stone blocking their path. "It doesn't make sense," he declared. "Whoever built this booby trap, it wasn't Sir Frederick. He was only here a short time, and he would have been half dead from an arrow wound."

"So who set the trap?" asked Eddie.

Before Addison could offer a theory, Molly shushed him. The distinctive purr of Madame Feng's voice carried along the echoing walls of the stone tunnels, followed by the low grunts of triads.

"They'll have a hard time catching us in this maze," said Eddie hopefully. "Not even *we* know where we are."

"We'll be easy to find," said Molly, holding up Raj's fishing line. "We're leaving a trail everywhere we go."

"Well, we can't ditch the thread," said Addison. "We need to be able to make a fast exit." He frowned, thinking. "Sir Frederick wanted a fellow Templar knight to find his clues. So which direction would a Templar knight go?"

"The Templar symbol," said Molly. "The rays of the sun go in all directions, but the eye is at the center."

Addison took his flashlight back from Molly and shined it down the passageway, illuminating the next thirty feet. "You think all these passageways meet in the center, like the spokes of a wheel?"

Molly shrugged. "It's just an idea."

Addison heard triad voices down the tunnel behind him. "Well, it's the best idea we've got." He set off down the corridor. Every time a smaller tunnel branched left, Addison chose the larger tunnel branching right. The tubes grew progressively bigger. Every so often, Raj would point out a trip wire and they would step carefully over it. At last they arrived at a large junction where all the passageways met in a central terminal. "Not too shabby, Mo."

Molly was not one to rest on her laurels. She was already scanning the mica-speckled walls. "There it is—an eye scratched into the stone!"

Addison pointed his flashlight at a staring eye carved into the side of a pillar. "The eye is looking this way," he said, pointing to the opposite wall. He crossed to a casket nestled in a rocky nook. "It's level with this coffin. C'mon, quickly!"

Raj was at Addison's side, heaving at the coffin's sealed lid. Addison wedged his butterfly knife under the wooden planks and pried upward. The long-rusted nails squeaked, splitting from the ancient timber.

"There could be a dead person in there!" said Eddie, astonished to see how quickly his friends had turned into grave robbers.

Raj gripped the coffin lid and put his back into it, dead-lifting with all his strength. He was only five foot two and ninety pounds. With a creak and a groan, the lid yielded to Raj's willpower. Raj overbalanced and toppled over.

Addison set the wooden lid on its side. When he cast the flashlight beam inside the musty casket, his breath caught in his throat. He stared reverently into the coffin, his expression filled with wonder.

"Who is it?" asked Eddie.

"What is it?" asked Molly.

"The sword of Sir Frederick," said Addison. "Hidden for eight hundred years."

Chapter Fifteen

The Crusader's Sword

ADDISON PASSED HIS FLASHLIGHT back to Molly. He clasped the hilt of the crusader's long sword in both hands and hefted it out of the coffin. The blade flickered and gleamed in the light.

"High-carbon steel," said Raj, his eyes wide in the darkness. "The twin fullers add strength to the blade."

The two-handed grip was nearly a foot long to the tang, and the blade was another four feet on top of that. All told, the heavy sword was nearly as tall as Addison. He set it down on the ground to examine it carefully under Molly's light. The front was unadorned, so he turned the sword over on its back. He spotted a few stanzas of Old French carved into the withered leather hilt. "The next clue." He grinned.

Madame Feng's voice grew suddenly louder as she turned a corner in the maze, her stiletto heels clicking closer down the rocky tunnels.

Addison had lost enough relics in his day to make a habit of copying down clues as soon as he found them. He flipped to a blank page in his notebook, set a pencil on its flat edge, and traced a rubbing of the clue.

"Faster! They're almost here!" Molly whispered.

The triads seemed to be closing in from two directions. Addison realized they were already out of time. "Everybody get inside a casket!"

Raj wasted no time in prying the lid off a fresh coffin. It was as if he'd been waiting his whole life for someone to order him inside a casket. He shoved aside a dusty skeleton and dove in next to it.

Addison heaved the long sword back inside its empty coffin and climbed in after it, Molly squeezing in beside him. They were used to sharing a bunk bed, and Molly figured a casket wouldn't be too big a transition.

Only Eddie balked. He stood in the passageway, hopping from foot to foot.

Addison maneuvered his coffin lid shut. "Eddie, stop messing around!"

"I'm not getting in a casket with a skeleton."

"Get in the casket or *you'll* be the skeleton."

Madame Feng's trilling laugh grew louder down the stone passageway.

Eddie scrambled into Raj's coffin headfirst. "This is the worst summer vacation of my life!" he hissed before Raj slid their coffin lid closed.

Addison lay still in his coffin, controlling his breathing and hoping Molly wouldn't sneeze from the dust. His aunt Delia had often warned him that his antics would put him in an early grave, but this was all happening much sooner than he'd expected. Through knotholes in the wood, he followed the conversation in the passageway.

"There it is!" Madame Feng's voice rang in the stone chamber. "The All-Seeing Templar Eye, scratched into the rock. I must thank whoever left this fishing line. I might never have found this clue on my own."

Inside his coffin, Addison received a sharp elbow in the ribs from Molly. He grimaced.

"The next clue must be here somewhere," Madame Feng continued.

Addison perked up at the sound of his uncle Nigel's voice. "The All-Seeing Templar Eye is a deception. The Templars are trying to trick you."

Addison knew his uncle was a mediocre liar at best, but he was better than Aunt Delia. "It might not be the

All-Seeing Eye at all," she offered. "It might just be ancient graffiti."

"Nonsense," said Madame Feng. "The eye is staring directly at that coffin." She called to two of her triad body-guards. "Hu and Wen, open that casket."

Addison heard a few hesitant shuffling steps, followed by an angry screech from Madame Feng. "Don't be super-stitious cowards! Open the coffin and look inside!"

It was at this point that Addison began to question his wisdom in hiding inside the very coffin Madame Feng was searching for. He heard heavy boots trudge close. Rough hands seized the wooden lid. Even in the darkness, Addison could see Molly's eyes darting back and forth in a panic. He thought about mentioning the fact that this was a sticky wicket but thought better of it. His mind raced. He vaguely remembered Sun Tzu saying something pithy about the element of surprise. He decided to give it a whirl.

The coffin lid jerked open, and several faces appeared over the rim: Madame Feng and two gang members.

Addison leapt up screaming and waving his hands demonically.

The two gang members sprang backward in horror. Even the cold-blooded Madame Feng was momentarily frozen in shock.

Addison jumped out of the casket and landed on the

floor in a crouch. Before the gang members could recover their cool, Molly sprang from the coffin, screaming like a banshee.

"Eddie! Raj! Code Red!" Addison shouted.

Raj and Eddie burst screaming from their coffin, following Addison's example. Raj adopted more of a zombie-like moan, while Eddie's screams appeared to simply be genuine fright.

Addison spun toward Aunt Delia and Uncle Nigel, who seemed to have dislocated their jaws in astonishment. "Run for it!"

When neither moved, Addison realized that each relative was handcuffed to the wrist of a triad. Escape was impossible.

Madame Feng, recovering her wits, yowled with anger. "Catch these brats!"

The triads, still jittery from their shock, swung their fists at Addison and Molly, but Aunt Delia and Uncle Nigel yanked their handcuffs backward, stalling each punch.

Hearing the commotion, more triads thundered down the tunnels, closing in.

"Addison, Molly, get out of here!" Aunt Delia called.

"We're not leaving without you!" said Addison.

"It's too dangerous for you!"

Addison ducked a wild haymaker from the triad handcuffed to Uncle Nigel.

"Addison Herbert Cooke, I order you to leave!" Aunt Delia shouted.

Her stern voice had an instant effect on Addison, who knew better than to cross his aunt when her blood was up. He hauled the heavy sword from the coffin. "Give us a hand, Mo!"

Molly took the sword, almost tipping over from its weight.

Addison dodged a leaping triad and scooped up the fishing line. "Run!" he shouted to his friends. He took off sprinting without looking back. He hurtled down a long passage, scooping up thread, hand over hand, and trying not to trip on it. He knew if he gathered all of the thread, Madame Feng would lose time finding her way back out of the labyrinth. He banged a left and another left, the shrinking tunnels signaling the edge of the maze. Addison could hear his compatriots galloping after him. "Almost there!"

He turned the next corner and slammed straight into a triad. Addison sprawled on the hard stone floor. The triad held the other end of the thread in the air and smiled.

Addison looked up in shock. "Tony Chin!"

To his surprise, Tony spoke clear English with only the faintest whiff of a Hong Kong accent. "Addison Cooke. I have been waiting for you."

••••••

Tony the triad whipped out his trench knife, beckoning Addison to fight.

Addison clambered to his feet. He drew his butterfly knife, flipping it open with an elaborate flourish.

Tony laughed and shook his head.

Eddie took a few steps backward. "Addison, do you have any idea what you're doing?"

"Of course. And thank you for that vote of confidence, Eddie. Here, hold this so I can see what I'm doing." He tossed his flashlight to Eddie, who fumbled it.

Light danced around the cavern, throwing crazy carnival shadows across the walls until Eddie managed to scoop up the rolling flashlight. By the time Addison could see what was happening, Tony was right on top of him. Addison made a few panicked swipes with his knife.

Tony ducked and sidestepped, effortlessly dodging Addison's blows. The triad twitched his arm and knocked the butterfly knife from Addison's hands. It clattered uselessly to the ground.

Tony stood back to let Addison retrieve the knife. Addison realized he was being toyed with.

"Do you want help, Addison?" Molly asked.

"In a sec," said Addison. "I'm finding his weaknesses."

Tony laughed again and immediately smacked the butterfly knife out of Addison's grasp. Again, he paused to let Addison pick up the knife. "May I give you a tip?"

"Only if it's not a knife tip."

"When someone attacks you blade up, you know they've never been in a knife fight. Hold your blade down, like this." Tony demonstrated.

Addison adjusted his grip.

"Good," said Tony. "Now jab with your full arm. Fast, like a cobra strike."

Addison whipped his arm toward the triad, the blade singing through the air.

Tony blocked the strike with a clash of steel. He smiled, pleased. "That's better. Very good."

"Thank you, Tony," said Addison. "You seem like a decent fellow. I don't suppose you'd like to let us go."

"I would love to. But orders are orders: I'm supposed to capture you. I hope you understand, it's nothing personal."

"I understand completely," said Addison. "No offense taken."

"Also, I apologize," said Tony, gesturing to Molly, "but I'm going to need to take that sword."

Molly barely registered his words before he was lashing at her with two trench knives. She retreated, attempting to parry with the massive weapon.

Eddie, who was covering his eyes, was not doing a spectacular job of lighting the cavern with the flashlight.

Molly could hardly see Tony's strikes in time. She was quickly backed against the rough-hewn wall of the passage.

Raj sprang into action. "I'll save you, Molly!" He dove for Tony's knees, attempting to knock him over. Tony held strong, and Raj simply clung to the triad's legs like a tenacious koala bear.

Molly dropped the sword and ducked out of the corner. She managed to drag Raj away from Tony a split second before he would have connected with a well-aimed swat.

"Thank you, Molly!" Raj gasped.

She turned to square off with Tony. She was weaponless.

"Use your kung fu!" Addison called.

Molly didn't love taking orders from Addison, but he had suggested a sensible course of action. After all, what was the point of spending the past two months drilling kicks and punches? She visualized herself in class, on the blue mats, calling out each move in unison with the other students. "Roundhouse kick!" she shouted, and launched a leg at Tony.

He dodged it easily.

"Tiger claw!" she shouted louder, striking her hand at Tony's throat.

He bent backward like a limbo dancer, sliding out of her reach.

"Dragon fist!" she cried a bit desperately. She struck out with both hands, but Tony had already sidestepped.

The triad was smiling. "If you want my advice, you shouldn't announce each move before you do it. Sort of tips your hand."

Molly gulped. He made a decent point.

Addison heard more triads moving closer through the dark maze, homing in on his team. They needed to pick up the pace if they hoped to escape. He pocketed his butterfly knife and scooped up the long sword. "Tony, I hope you understand, this isn't personal."

The great sword was too heavy for Addison to wield. When he wound up for a home-run swing at Tony, Molly and Eddie had to duck to avoid the inconvenience of having their heads lopped off. Addison swung and missed. Strike one. His momentum carried him right around in a circle. He tried for a second swing at Tony and missed that, as well. Strike two.

Addison didn't imagine it was possible to be worse than Molly with the sword, and yet here he was. Tony would surely have skewered him by now if he hadn't been laughing so hard. Addison's heart sank; he'd read so many swash-buckling adventure books, and apparently none of them had rubbed off. As good as Ludwig van Beethoven was at playing a piano, that's how bad Addison was at swinging a sword. He came extremely close to decapitating Raj, and even himself. Out of options, he attempted a direct poke at Tony's ribs.

Tony deflected this with a trench knife and grabbed the handle of Sir Frederick's sword. It happened as quickly as a sleight-of-hand trick. To Addison's amazement, Tony now held the sword, admiring it in the gleam of Eddie's flashlight. "It's much safer for your team if I hold on to this."

Addison had to agree. Besides, he felt the vague inkling of a plan coming on, tickling at him like an impending sneeze. Madame Feng's men were only a few chambers away, working their way closer in the gloom. Addison spotted Raj's spool of fishing line lying on the cavern floor. "Eddie, pass me the fishing line."

Tony swung the long sword in a wide, flashing arc.

Eddie pressed his back against the wall. "I think I'm going to pass out."

Addison danced backward from one of Tony's swipes. "You can pass out when you're dead. Toss me that line!" He knew Tony was attempting to stall them until the rest of Madame Feng's triads arrived. "Eddie, now!"

Eddie stared at the slashing sword, transfixed. "This isn't happening," he muttered. "I am at home in my bed. Mother, is that you? I've finished piano practice. May I go downstairs to Restaurant Anatolia for some shawarma?"

"Snap out of it, Eddie!"

Eddie turned to blink at Addison. He had the blank, confused look of a basset hound trying to read the editorial page of *The Washington Post*.

"Eddie, fight! We have eight hands and he only has two!"

"I have delicate hands! And they are made for piano keys!"

"Fine," said Addison. "Just turn off the flashlight!"

This, Eddie could do. The tunnel plunged into darkness.

Addison ducked Tony's sword and dove for the reel of fishing line, grasping it in the pitch black. He found Tony's ankle and wound a few loops of line around it before rolling from the path of the striking sword. Sparks shot up from the cave wall where the metal struck. "Eddie, turn the light back on!"

In the dark tunnel, the flashlight was so bright, it hurt Addison's eyes. "Mo, hot potato!" He tossed the reel to Molly, who passed it to Raj, who threw it back to Addison. Tony was soon snagged in a growing web of fishing line . . . line strong enough to reel in an eight-hundred-pound bluefin tuna.

The team kept passing around the fishing wire until Tony was hemmed in like a caterpillar in a cocoon. "Ha!" said Addison.

Tony dropped the sword and drew his trench knives. He slashed the cords, freeing his arms. "Ha!" said Tony.

Addison was not too proud to admit when he was beaten. Tony could fight, but for at least a few more seconds, he could not run. Addison turned and fled headlong down the tunnel.

Molly kept pace at his side. Eddie and Raj were somewhere behind. They were easy to track in the dark, what with Eddie's screaming.

"Nice work with that sword," Molly called to Addison.

"Thanks, Molly. I love sarcasm."

"No, you don't," said Molly.

"I know," said Addison. "I was being sarcastic."

Molly paused to let Raj and Eddie run past. After all, Eddie still held the flashlight. She counted three Mississippis and then yanked a trip wire, triggering a stone door to slam down, blocking the tunnel after her. She listened for the satisfying thwack of Tony the triad running smack into the door in the dark.

Up ahead, Raj and Eddie took a hard corner in the tunnel and collided with an unsuspecting triad, sending the gang member sprawling. By some rare miracle of physics, Raj and Eddie were uninjured. The triad lay flat on his back as if he had recently played chicken with a wrecking ball.

Raj realized he had just bested a gang member in single combat, even if it was by accident. This was, perhaps, the single greatest moment of his life. "Yeah, New York City! 86th Street!" Raj pounded his fist against his chest.

He stopped shouting when a crowd of fresh triads rounded the corner at a fine clip. Raj's eyes bulged from their sockets.

Addison grabbed him by the sleeve. "C'mon, Raj, before they eighty-six *us*."

The group bounded down the final passage, their leg

muscles burning. Molly had the presence of mind to trigger one last stone door, slowing their pursuers.

Addison's team scrambled up the narrow chute, darted through the secret crypt, hurtled across the hospital ward, tore out of the sacristy, and exploded onto the chaotic streets of Kashgar.

They hid behind a cartload of cardamom. Eddie put his head between his knees, sucking oxygen. After a minute he remembered to turn off Addison's flashlight to save the batteries.

Molly sighed. "After all that, the triads have the sword of Sir Frederick."

"On the bright side," said Addison, "at least we don't have to lug that thing around."

Chapter Sixteen

The Russian *Vor*

ADDISON'S TEAM RACED THROUGH the alleyways of Kashgar, checking over their shoulders for pursuing triads. They burst into the filthy saloon where they had last seen Dax. Scanning the establishment, Addison saw two Tajiks dancing on the billiard table and a capuchin monkey swinging from the chandelier, but no sign of Dax.

It was Molly who spotted Mr. Jacobsen sharing a few links of Russian sausage with some Uzbek traders at the poker table. The Great Dane was lapping from a water bowl and appeared to be the toast of the bar.

Addison was not entirely surprised to find Dax lying underneath the table. He slapped him a few times across the face. "Dax, the triads are after us. We gotta hop!"

"No hello, how are you, how was your day?" Dax rubbed his jaw gingerly. His face was scratched and bruised.

"What happened to you?"

"I met one of your friends. They asked if I was your pilot."

"You got beat up?" asked Molly, spotting a nasty welt over Dax's eye.

"That's putting it a bit strong."

"You *look* beat up." Addison and Molly helped Dax to his feet.

Dax took a sip from the first glass he could reach at the bar. "He got in *one* lucky hit to my jaw," Dax said defensively. He took another sip of his drink. "Followed by six lucky hits to my head, three lucky hits to my stomach, and seven or eight lucky kicks after I hit the ground." Dax shrugged. "What can I say? He was a lucky guy."

"How did the gambling go?" asked Eddie.

"Not so hot." Dax grimaced. "My Chinese isn't the best. I asked the dealer to hit me, and he took it literally."

"How many people hit you today?" asked Raj, his voice full of glowing admiration.

"Including Addison just now?"

"Never mind all that," said Addison, keeping things on track. He eyed the room for triads. "We need to get to your plane."

"Yeah, about that," said Dax. "Your Russian friend took

my keys. Sometime after he kicked my ribs in and before he poured his drink on me."

"We have a Russian friend?" Molly asked.

Addison frowned. "Dax, you're saying I've got a pilot with no plane?"

"Think how *I* feel."

"Dax, armed men are hunting us."

"That does not surprise me."

"What's that supposed to mean?"

Dax looked down at his bruised knuckles. "Kid, before I met you, I had two good fists, one good plane, and zero black eyes."

"I wouldn't say you had a good plane; it was okay at best," said Addison.

"She was better than nothing, which is what I've got now."

"C'mon," said Addison, forcing Dax to down a fresh glass of water. "We're going to the airport. How hard can it be to find an airplane? It's not like they can just up and fly away." He patted sawdust from Dax's leather jacket and waved a warning finger before the pilot could respond. "Dax, losing airplanes is not acceptable. I want to let you know that I am seriously reconsidering our employment situation."

"So am I, kid. So am I."

......

Addison tore through the dusty, winding streets of Kashgar. Cutting through the market, he spotted triads combing the crowd. Mr. Jacobsen, tongue flapping in the wind, had no trouble keeping up with Addison's team. Dax, on the other hand, kept pausing to clutch his ribs and wince.

It was when Addison was sidestepping between vendor stalls that he caught a glimpse of the ancient Mongol.

Addison's brain could not make any sense of it. Here he was, running through the present day, and there—across the alleyway—stood a vision of the thirteenth century. The Mongol wore plate mail, a full quiver of arrows, and a tangled beard. His hair was a long black ponytail on the top of his head. In his right hand he gripped a spear. His coal-black eyes stared directly at Addison. Addison did not make a regular habit of being spied on by ancient Mongols, and he found this sight particularly arresting. He skidded to a halt and backed up a few steps to take a second look. But by the time he had disentangled himself from a sprinting Molly, the Mongol had vanished. Addison blinked and rubbed his eyes. He had no time for a psychological evaluation. Clearing his head with a few quick shakes, he powered back into a sprint.

Triads shouted across the market square and began shoving their way through the crowds. Addison raced past carts selling nuts, roots, spices, and Persian carpets; stalls selling sweets, knives, musical instruments, and Uyghur hats; street hawkers shilling Tajik garments, honeys, tamarinds, and kitchen utensils; herders auctioning sheep, donkeys, goats, horses, camels, and yaks. What Addison really needed was a bicycle, but nobody had one of those.

Addison spotted the potholed road leading to the airport. He took the turn at full tilt and found himself with a face full of Russian belly. He staggered back a few paces to see Boris, the crew-cut gangster from the Jade Tiger restaurant, folding his brawny arms across his broad wrestler's chest. Addison was getting altogether fed up with racing around corners and smacking into people, but his manners had not yet deserted him. "I beg your pardon."

"Addison Cooke," spat the Russian. "You vile, pathetic son of a donkey."

"Present," said Addison.

"You are the impish kid who finished off Vladimir Ragar, trapping him in that Incan treasure chamber."

"Vladimir Ragar? That vile, pathetic son of a donkey?" said Addison. "Why would anyone care what happens to him? I would expect you to thank me."

"He was my brother."

"Ah." Addison removed his ivy cap, rotating it a few times in his nervous hands. "Right, then. My condolences." He had missed the basket but still thought he could grab the rebound. He was not necessarily afraid of tall, angry, muscle-bound men, per se. But Boris was just a tall, angry, muscle-bound man in the same way the Sahara was just a rather large beach. "Listen, I think we may have gotten off to a bad start," he began.

"You're going to get off to a worse end," said Boris.

Apparently, Addison thought, cooler heads were not going to prevail. The rest of his team caught up behind him, assessed Boris's intimidating physique, and maintained a healthy distance. Addison thought that with Dax's help they might be a match for Boris. But when he caught the wary look in Dax's eye, he realized Dax had already fought Boris enough for one day.

"How," said Addison, searching for a fertile topic of conversation, "did you find your way to Kashgar?" He steeled himself for a fight and was pleasantly surprised that Boris seemed to prefer to continue chatting.

"My team tracked Madame Feng's flight to Kashgar. We decided to let her find the clue. We've surrounded the airport. She will have a hard time escaping."

"Well," said Addison, finding himself on firmer ground, "we don't have the clue. What do you need us for?" He did not particularly feel like a stop-and-chat. He would really have preferred to keep running straight for the airport. The thing of it was, he couldn't help but notice Raj uncoiling a climbing rope from his backpack and clipping it firmly to a fence post with a carabiner. He figured it was best to keep Boris talking until he knew Raj's angle.

"I am under special orders to capture you," said Boris, taking a step closer to Addison.

"Orders from whom?"

"Vrolok Malazar."

Addison's blood froze at the sound of the name. "When you say Vrolok Malazar, you don't by any chance mean the same Vrolok Malazar who hired Professor Ragar to kidnap my aunt and uncle?"

Boris nodded, feeling he was finally making some progress with Addison.

"The same Vrolok Malazar," Addison continued, "who has a strange vendetta against my entire family?"

"The very same," said Boris.

"I see." Addison did not think they could be talking about two different Vrolok Malazars. He was now extremely invested in the conversation, but saw Raj clip a second carabiner onto Boris's rearmost belt loop. Boris was now, unknowingly, tethered to a fence post. Addison decided their conversation had run its natural course. Besides, a few triads were now scouting the opposite courtyard. He cocked two fingers to his cap in a polite salute. "Well, tell Vrolok Malazar that Addison Cooke says hello."

Addison turned and fled. He wasn't proud of this; it just seemed like the right thing to do.

Boris raced after him. The big Russian made it twenty feet before the slack ran out of Raj's rope and snapped taut.

Boris, unfortunately, had poured on a good head of steam. When the rope stopped short, Boris ran right out of his pants.

There was a violent tearing of fabric. Boris, surprised to find himself suddenly in his underwear, took a few uncertain steps, unsure whether to maintain his pursuit.

A crowd of women in head scarves, carrying buckets from the well, tittered and pointed at Boris. A goat herder joined the laughter.

Boris decked the goat herder in the jaw and set to work trying to steal the man's pants. The goat herder's brothers joined the fray, fighting to keep the man's pants on their rightful owner. A fierce tug-of-war ensued.

Addison knew this was the perfect moment to exit stage left, but he couldn't resist doubling back to where Boris's pants dangled on the end of Raj's rope. He relieved the pockets of their contents. Before Boris could spot him, he sprinted after his team, heading for the Kashgar airport.

Chapter Seventeen

Escape from Kashgar

ADDISON'S TEAM BARRELED TOWARD the airfield like they were outrunning a cattle stampede. Molly spread her arms wide and halted the group, beckoning everyone to duck low behind the fueling station. "Triads," she whispered, gulping for breath, "everywhere."

Addison scanned the perimeter of the airfield. One by one, he spotted gang members, carefully concealed behind tractors and trailers and lying prone on the roofs of the hangars. The triads had the airport completely covered.

"It's a good strategy," said Raj. "Easier to watch the airport than to search the entire city."

Addison nodded. "What they don't know is that the Russians are watching the airport, too."

"So how do we get out of here?"

"We've got to take Dax's plane from the Russians."

"That's stealing!" said Molly.

"They stole it first! If you steal something that's stolen, that's the opposite of stealing—that's un-stealing! We're un-stealing his plane!"

"Okay, fine. But if we're going to un-steal an airplane, don't we need the keys?"

"Way ahead of you, Mo." Addison held up the keys he'd stolen from Boris's pants.

"Who *are* you guys?" asked Dax.

Nobody bothered to answer him. Molly pointed to Dax's Apache parked far away across the dusty airstrip. "The plane is totally exposed. We'll be spotted running to it."

"Okay," said Addison. "We sneak into the airport from the north end. It's a no-brainer."

"Only because you haven't got one," said Molly. "The Russians are up there."

Addison studied the north side of the tarmac and glimpsed leather-jacketed mobsters crouched behind the wheels of parked cargo planes. "Alaric the Visigoth!"

"Who?" asked Eddie.

"Enemy of Rome," said Molly, blowing the stray strand of hair from her eyes. "We need a decent plan."

"All right, Mo," said Addison. "What do you suggest?"

"Mayhem." Molly riffled through the gear in her father's survival kit. She flicked a butane lighter and tossed it at the airplane fueling station. The same fueling station, it should be noted, in which they were currently hiding.

Addison, Dax, Eddie, and Raj, all popped their mouths open in shock. Even Mr. Jacobsen seemed to sense that this was an apocalyptically bad idea.

A puddle of spilled fuel ignited, sending flames racing toward the giant gas tanks used to fill the airplane engines.

Addison had already done his fair share of running for the day. He would never have guessed his tired legs were capable of the burst of speed that propelled him out of his hiding place and across the tarmac. A human sneeze travels at forty miles per hour. A human voice travels at seven hundred miles per hour. And a thought can travel from neuron to neuron across a brain at one hundred miles per second. Addison beat all of these speed records in his race from the burning fuel tanks.

Molly chased after them. She assumed there would be an explosion. She had no idea it would be only slightly larger than a volcanic eruption. A blast of heat and sound raged behind her as if she were being chased by a dragon. The pressure wave nearly knocked her to the ground. All she could do was continue running for her life as chunks of asphalt and concrete rained down from the sky. She glanced back to see a fireball rising into the air from the torn wreckage of the airstrip. She felt a twinge of guilt about destroying the airport, until she remembered that the airport had been in pretty bad shape to begin with.

Once Addison realized he had outrun the specter of death, he was immediately overwhelmed with pride for his sister. "Fine work, Molly!"

Triads were diving for cover across the tarmac.

Dax loped up to the group, wiping soot from the back of his neck. "Who *are* you guys?"

Addison allowed himself to briefly wrap a proud arm around Molly's shoulders. "We're Cookes!" He turned back to the airstrip. "C'mon, let's get that plane!"

The group ankled it along a row of parked airplanes. Addison began hearing loud pops and noticing chunks of metal tearing from metal fuselages in angry blossoms of sparks. He was an eternally optimistic person, yet he could not help but form the distinct impression that he was being peppered with bullets. "Is that gunfire?"

"Of course it's gunfire!" Dax shouted, covering his head with his arms.

Addison felt there was no need to take that sort of tone, particularly when one is already dealing with being fired upon.

"The Russians are aiming at the Chinese," Dax growled. "We're in their cross fire."

The gunfire on the tarmac was growing a bit too hot. Addison waved the team into an airplane hangar, where they squatted low to the ground.

"We need to hunker down in a bunker!" Eddie shouted. "We need a bunker hunker!"

Mr. Jacobsen whined softly.

"What we need is a new plan!" Molly called over the din of gunshots.

Addison gasped for breath. "This is the pig's whistle." Bullets hammered the corrugated walls of the hangar like baseball bats on a steel drum. He could still hear the roaring flames of the burning fuel depot and the shouts of men fighting the fire. He tried to think, but his brain had the clarity of three drunken bears fighting in a bouncy castle. Also the bears were wearing tutus. And party hats. One of them strummed a ukelele. What was he supposed to be thinking about? Ah, yes. A plan.

He crawled to a parked equipment truck, opened the door, and was relieved to find the keys in the center console. Sometimes Providence drops a few pennies in your tip jar. Addison turned the ignition, laid a spud wrench down on the accelerator, and shifted the truck into gear. It set off across the tarmac at a jaunty five miles per hour, aiming vaguely for Dax's plane.

"How does this help?" shouted Molly.

"We run beside it, sheltered from bullets!"

Addison trotted alongside the moving pickup. His team hurried after him. Unfortunately, the truck continued to pour on speed, and they were soon sprinting to keep up. "Nothing like a refreshing jog to restore the spirits," he gasped.

The truck pulled ahead and was building a distinct lead. Addison began to have his doubts.

"I don't think this is a very good idea," said Molly. "The truck could crash into Dax's plane. It could head to the wrong plane entirely. If it gets hit by a bullet, the tank could explode. This is extremely dangerous!"

"Hey, you don't have to convince me," said Addison. "I think this is a terrible plan."

"Well, then, why are we doing it?"

"I couldn't think up anything better!"

Fresh bullets winged overhead. Addison was finding it difficult to maintain his normally cheerful outlook on life. The truck began charting its own course, heading off the tarmac and on toward Uzbekistan. "Run for the airplane!"

Molly did not feel Addison was in a position to offer direction at this point. "Don't give me any more orders!"

"Is that an order?" asked Addison.

"Run on the other side of me," shouted Molly. "I want you to get shot first!"

Addison turned to Raj, sprinting alongside him. "Sisters, am I right?"

"Tell me about it," said Raj. "I have *three* of them."

More gunfire erupted.

Addison was no great runner. It might be said he was a better swordsman. But somehow, in the chaos of dodging gunfire, it was Addison who reached the Apache first. He unlocked the door, leapt inside, and jammed the keys into the ignition. The twin propellers roared to life. Addison released the wheel brake and the plane began to roll forward. "Get in, Dax! I don't know how to drive this thing!"

Dax was pinned down by gunfire, crouching behind the wheel of a Cessna.

Eddie launched into the cockpit next, sailing in horizontally and crashing into Addison. Addison was forced into the passenger seat. Eddie found himself alone behind the wheel of the moving plane.

"Don't let Eddie drive anything!" Molly shouted, remembering the time he had crashed a limousine into an Ecuadoran fountain. Sprinting alongside the moving aircraft, she and Raj managed to leap aboard the wing runner and clamber inside the cabin. "Great! Everyone's on board except the one person who knows how to fly!"

Mr. Jacobsen hopped aboard in a great bounding leap. He favored Addison with a great, slobbering lick from nose to ear. "At least we have a copilot," said Addison.

The plane, picking up speed, was drifting farther and farther from its pilot. Eddie grabbed the nose wheel and steered the plane into a U-turn. Dax, still stiff from his bar fight, limped across the runway.

A few triads raced across the Apache's path, brandishing weapons, but Eddie guided the plane straight toward them, its whipping propeller blades chasing the triads right off the tarmac. Eddie laughed maniacally, mad with power.

Dax ducked raking gunfire and reached the plane as Eddie was taxiing onto the one runway not completely gutted by Molly's fuel explosion. A bullet grazed past Dax's head and struck the Apache's dashboard, obliterating the plastic frog.

"Frog down!" shouted Addison.

Eddie slithered into the backseat.

Dax scrambled on board, sealed the cabin door, and seized the controls. He stroked the broken plastic frog with one finger and gnashed his teeth. "That's not good."

Triads stormed the runway.

Addison spotted his Aunt Delia and Uncle Nigel hunkered down next to Madame Feng. They were hiding by an equipment shed as Russians raced past.

Dax opened the throttle, and the plane bucked forward like a sprinter at the starter pistol. The plane bounced and rattled down the pocked and gutted airfield. Triads took potshots before diving out of the plane's speeding path.

"Why aren't we taking off?" shouted Molly.

"There's no frog on this dashboard," said Dax.

"If the plane blows up, the way to survive a fire is by—"

"Not now, Raj!"

The runway bumped and jerked the plane, shaking them like a can of spray paint. Addison fastened his seat belt. "Can't you fly better than this?"

"What can I say, my copilot's a dog!" Dax clutched the throttle and gritted his teeth. Everyone was a critic. The edge of the runway raced toward the windshield. Bullets pegged the tail rudder. With only feet to spare, the Apache's nose cleared the ground. The plane vaulted into the sky, Kashgar sliding away into the distance.

"Do you guys ever leave a city without everyone trying to kill you?" asked Dax.

Molly shrugged. "This is pretty much how we leave every city."

Chapter Eighteen

Good News and Bad News

ADDISON REMOVED HIS SCHOOL blazer and settled back in his seat. He was dismayed to find his dress shirt—one of his favorites—drenched in sweat. He cast a sidelong look at Dax. "My uncle says you have a knack for coming through in a pinch, but that was cutting it a bit close."

"Hey, that wasn't easy what I just did!"

Addison decided to let the matter rest. The gentle sloping dunes of the desert were spread out beneath them like the folds of a blanket. The early evening sky was a darkening blue with amber glowing at the sunset edges. It was a decent world, Addison decided, as far as worlds went.

"This is beautiful and all," said Dax, cutting in on Addison's thoughts, "but where am I going?"

Addison was not at all sure. "Head toward Mongolia," he suggested.

"Can you be more specific? Mongolia's a big country, and I like to know what I'm aiming at."

Addison decided it would be prudent not to keep flying in the wrong direction at one hundred and fifty miles per hour, so he pulled his notebook from his blazer pocket and handed it back to Eddie. "Eddie, take a whack at Sir Frederick's clue."

Eddie stared at the cursive script Addison had traced from Sir Frederick's sword. "I can't read French."

"You can read *Chinese* and you can't read a little French?"

"Addison, I can't read *all* the languages."

Molly sighed. "We nearly killed ourselves getting this clue and we can't even read it."

"Do you want my help?" asked Dax.

"I think you've helped enough," said Addison curtly.

"Even if we could read the clue, it's hopeless," said Eddie. "The triads have guns. The Russians have guns. We can't do this on our own. We should get back to civilization and alert the authorities."

"Which authorities?"

"I don't know—the US embassy. Maybe the CIA or the Chinese police."

"Eddie's right," Molly put in. "I'm worried sick about Aunt Delia and Uncle Nigel—we have to do *something*."

Addison shook his head. "The Chinese police are on Madame Feng's side. And even if the embassy decided to help us, they wouldn't have any better idea of how to find Aunt D or Uncle N than we do."

"Well, we're in a plane full of bullet holes, and we have no idea where we're going."

"We will just as soon as we crack this clue."

"Do you want my help?" Dax cut in again.

"Dax, I appreciate your willingness," said Addison. "But we've established that languages are not your strong suit. You don't know Chinese, you don't know Danish, and your own dog knows more German than you do." He sat back in his seat and crossed his arms crossly. He felt bad for digging into Dax. Addison liked to maintain impeccable manners, and right now he knew his manners were extremely peckable.

Dax flew for a few moments in silence. "I'll get us into Mongolia. We'll land at the first big city we reach and figure it out from there. In the meantime, you can all get some rest."

Night fell as they soared over the ancient ruins of Gaochang in the Mutou Valley, a gorge nestled deep in the Flaming Mountains. Raj patched up Dax's cuts and bruises with his first aid kit. Eddie ate the remainder of Raj's emergency rations.

Addison read his father's copy of *The Secret History of the Mongols* until his eyelids grew heavy and his head began to nod.

Toward midnight, once Eddie and Raj were asleep, Molly leaned across her seat and whispered to him. "Addison, do you think the Black Darkhad are real?"

"You mean the Ghost Warriors Uncle Nigel talked about?"

Molly nodded.

"If you're asking me if I think the Khan is guarded by eight-hundred-year-old ghosts, the answer is: probably not." He thought back to the vision he'd seen earlier in the alleyway . . . the Mongol with fiery eyes, a messianic beard, and tangled black hair streaming down his back. "Out of curiosity, why do you ask?"

"No reason," said Molly. "It's just that I thought I saw something on the street today in Kashgar."

Addison frowned, but his jet-lagged brain was too addled to pursue the thought much further.

......

It was three a.m. when Addison woke to see Dax nervously tapping the instrument panel. He did not like to see a pilot nervously tapping an instrument panel. "Engines running okay?"

"The engines are running great," said Dax.

Addison sighed in relief.

"It's the rest of the plane I'm worried about."

Addison contemplated this for a moment, but soon found himself drifting back to sleep. He awoke a few minutes later to the sound of the port engine coughing and sputtering.

"Buckle up," said Dax.

Addison did so. He also buckled the special seat belt for Mr. Jacobsen and fastened on the dog's goggles.

The tiny plane bucked like a bronco, one engine wheezing asthmatically.

"Talk to me, Dax," Addison shouted over the wind whistling through the windshield's bullet holes.

"All right. Do you want the good news or the bad news?"

"Let's start with the bad news."

"The bad news is there's no good news."

"Well, then, what was the good news?"

"I just told you there's no good news."

"Well, then, what was the bad news?"

"That there's no good news!"

"Dax, what are you trying to tell me?"

"We got an engine out."

Addison looked out the port window. "I thought you said the engines were fine."

"They are. But they stop working when there's no fuel."

"We're out of gas?" Addison exclaimed.

The starboard engine popped, stuttered, and sputtered out.

"The tank's full of gas, but it's not getting to the engines," Dax shouted over the wind. "The fuel line was rusted through last time I checked."

"Why didn't you fix the fuel line?"

"Maintenance is the copilot's job."

Mr. Jacobsen lolled his tongue and lapped at Addison's cheek. "How were you going to fly a plane with a busted fuel line?"

"I was going to buy a new one with the money you paid me to fly the plane."

"That sounds like circular reasoning."

"Circular reasoning is still reasoning," said Dax.

Addison considered this. "Wait a second: I paid you when we landed in Kashgar. You gambled away our fuel line money."

"Listen, there's no need to point fingers, there's plenty of blame to go around."

"What did I do?" asked Addison.

"You got me beat up by gang members before I had a chance to win our money back!"

The plane drifted into a nosedive. Addison realized the situation was getting serious.

Dax fought hard on the tiller. "To be fair, getting riddled with bullets probably didn't help the fuel line any."

"Can you get us down?" Addison called over the howling wind.

"You think I don't know how to crash-land a plane?"

"I think that's the *only* way you know how to land a plane!"

"Hey, listen! I may not be the best pilot . . ." Dax trailed off.

"Was there a 'but' in there?"

"No, I was simply stating a fact!"

The plane lost altitude fast. Addison saw the desert rising up to meet them.

"Are we going to die?" Eddie shouted from the backseat.

Addison did not have time to formulate a response. "Dax, tell me you have parachutes!"

"I do . . ." Dax gripped the yoke with grim determination. "But they're stowed in the cargo hold. Sorry about that."

Addison tried to find the right words to express his anger. The ground was hurtling closer. He bitterly regretted that Dax was going to get in the last word.

Dax smiled. "Don't worry, kid. This isn't my first rodeo."

The Gobi Desert raced toward the windshield at one hundred and fifty miles per hour. Addison shut his eyes tight to the sound of tearing metal as the plane crashed.

Chapter Nineteen

The Camel Trader

ADDISON THOUGHT HE WOULD see his life flash before his eyes, but instead it was mostly just sand and airplane parts. Dax clipped the crest of a dune, slowing their speed, before slamming into the next dune. One wing sheared off completely as they carved a deep furrow through the sand. Addison realized that the good thing about having no fuel reaching your engines is that they do not explode when you crash. He was quite pleased to find the bright side in all of this.

He wiped sand from his eyes and kicked out the emergency exit window. He crawled from the wreckage, patting himself to make sure he still possessed 206 bones and hadn't divided any in two. "Is everyone alive?" he asked, coughing through a throat full of sand.

He heard a series of groans as everyone hauled themselves out of the flattened Apache. Addison struggled to his feet, fixing his rumpled tie. He tried to look unflappable, but really he was quite flapped. His fear of heights was not altogether pleased with the past few minutes. "Right, then. Nothing like a small plane crash to make one appreciate the smaller things in life."

Dax was last to heave himself out of the wreck. He stared at his crumpled plane and cradled his head in his hands. Mr. Jacobsen offered him a tentative lick, but Dax was inconsolable.

"At least we're alive," said Molly.

Addison gazed at the endless sands of the Gobi. "For now."

"I've never lost two planes in one day before," said Dax. "This must be some kind of record."

"You only lost one plane," said Molly, trying to comfort him.

"But I lost it twice."

Addison turned in a slow circle, surveying the distant moonlit horizon. "If we knew which direction to head, we could at least go after the next clue." He turned to Eddie. "You're fluent in Spanish. Spain is *right next* to France. You're sure you can't take a crack at deciphering the clue?"

"There are thousands of languages in the world and only one Eddie. I'm sorry I haven't learned French!"

Addison needed a place to vent his frustration. He

wheeled on Dax. "My aunt and uncle are out there some-where and we're stranded in the Gobi Desert with a one-winged airplane. I want you to know, you will not be getting any referral business from me!"

"You've known me for twenty-four hours, kid. What do you know about me?"

"I've seen enough."

Dax brushed sand off his stubbled chin and stood up. He towered over Addison, anger flickering in his eyes. "Yeah, kid. You've seen me get nose up on one hundred and fifty yards of runway in a firefight. Twice. You've seen me hold my own against a giant Russian *vor* who attacked me by surprise in Kashgar. You've seen me go thirty-six hours without sleep since you hired me in Macau. But ever since we met, you've treated me like I'm useless. Your uncle seems to think I'm good for something; why don't you?"

"As far as I can tell, the only things you're good for are getting beat up and crashing airplanes."

"Well," said Dax, shifting the toothpick from one side of his mouth to the other, "at least I can read French." He pulled his toolbox out of the cargo hatch and headed to the starboard engine.

Addison stared after him. He was nonplussed, but quickly slingshotted back to being plussed. He walked around to the starboard wing. "French?"

Dax loosened lug nuts with a spanner and opened the engine. He drained water from the coolant system, filling his canteen. "When I was a bush pilot in Algeria, I spent eight months in a French prison for a fistfight with a Moroccan loan shark."

Addison raised his eyebrows. "I didn't know you spent eight months in a French prison for a fistfight with a Moroccan loan shark."

"You never asked." Dax drained the remaining coolant from the engine, filling a second canteen with water.

......

Dax squatted in the desert sand, studying the clue in Addison's notebook. "This French is medieval." He held the page to the crescent moonlight. "Luckily, the prison where I learned French was pretty medieval, too." Dax squinted his eyes, jaw muscles working his toothpick, and slowly translated.

> "'Praise be to the Lord, my Rock,
> who trains my hands for war,
> my fingers for battle.
> God is my shield, my sword, my helm, and my lance.'"

"Sir Frederick said that already," said Eddie.

"It's important," said Addison. "We've found Sir

Frederick's shield and sword. My guess is the next clue will be his helm."

Dax read farther.

> *"'In the city of the son of the Khan*
> *Lies a sanctuary for the idol worshippers of Buddha.*
> *One hundred seven will watch over you.*
> *Pray at the one that will show you the way.'"*

Dax flipped the notebook shut and tossed it back to Addison. "Mean anything to you, kid?"

Addison nodded and gazed across the open waste. He had already finished reading *The Secret History of the Mongols* and knew the city of the son of the Khan. "Karakoram."

"Karakoram? That place is a ghost town. There hasn't been anything there for centuries."

"Can you get us there?"

Dax slowly nodded. "If we travel by night and don't meet any bandits, it's possible. First things first, we need to find a nomad camp with water and food, or else the Khan won't be the only one dead in a tomb."

Addison retrieved his messenger bag from the wreck. "Pack light," he called to his team. "Take only what you need!"

Dax filled a few more canteens with water from the portside engine. Addison pocketed the flare gun he found in the glove box. Raj helped Dax slice parachute cords for rope and bottle engine grease for fuel. Dax cut canvas from a parachute and wrapped it around his head like a turban to shield him from the coming day's sun. Addison lightened his pack, reluctantly parting with his prized white dinner jacket.

"Here," Dax said as they readied for their march north. "I siphoned water from the radiator. We can share." He took a plug and handed it to Addison.

Addison balked, waving him away with a shudder.

Dax turned to Molly. "He doesn't like sharing?"

"He doesn't like germs," said Molly, wiping the lid and taking a pull.

"Well, he won't like dying of thirst, either."

The group set off across the desert in the deep of the night.

· · · · · ·

Even though he was missing a second night's sleep, Dax's pace never slowed. He was eager to put miles behind them before the merciless sun crested the edge of the world. Addison's group hustled to keep up with Dax's long strides.

After an hour of hiking, Eddie fell far behind. Eventually, he collapsed under the weight of his bags. Circling back to help him, Addison discovered Eddie had packed way too much. He and Raj riffled through Eddie's bags.

"The complete Beethoven sonatas?" said Addison, pulling out two heavy volumes.

"I thought maybe I could practice if we ran across a piano."

"In the Gobi?" Addison tossed the books into the sand. Eddie couldn't bear to watch. After Addison dumped out a metronome, a portable desk lamp, and several pairs of loafers, they were back on their way.

Raj zigzagged across the group's path, foraging for food in the desert waste. Toward five a.m. he began shouting and waving excitedly. When the group caught up to him, he proudly produced a handful of grubs from under a rock. "I found us some breakfast!"

"Slugs?" asked Molly.

"They're filled with protein!"

"Raj, we've only been in the Gobi for two hours," said Addison. "We're not starving to death."

"More for me." Raj gave one grub a tentative nibble and elected to stick the rest in a pocket for later.

The sky was already lightening in the east. Addison joined Dax at the top of a ridge. The pilot pointed to the fourth star of Cassiopeia and drew a line to Polaris, the North Star. "We need to keep heading northeast."

"How far is Karakoram?"

"Hard to say without a landmark. Maybe sixty miles."

"Sixty miles!" said Eddie, readjusting the straps on his backpack.

"The Gobi's five hundred thousand square miles. Sixty miles isn't that much."

"It's enough to kill us!"

"The icy-fingered grip of death," said Raj solemnly.

Dax shot him a quizzical look.

"Sixty miles!" Eddie said again. He stared at the vast expanse of desert. "Outer space is fifty miles up. We're literally closer to outer space than we are to Karakoram!"

They traveled through false dawn, the deep sands sucking at their footfalls and slowing them down. Near daybreak, Raj emitted an excited yelp. He ran a few steps, threw down his pack, and dropped to his knees.

Addison assumed he had discovered water. Instead, to his horror, Addison saw that Raj was hunched over a large, steaming pile of dung.

"Isn't it wonderful?" Raj cried. He closed his eyes and inhaled deeply. "It's fresh! I'm an expert in animal spoors," he said, by way of explanation. "An amateur scatologist." He beckoned the team closer. "Camels. A whole team of them." He took another deep breath, snatched up his pack, and began following the hoofprints east.

Dax nodded. "If there's a caravan out here, we could barter for supplies."

The team followed after Raj.

The sun came up like a slap across the face. Within an hour, everyone was dripping with sweat. It was midmorning before Molly sighted the camel train over the next dune. With eager shouts, they flagged down the nomad trader and his five camels.

Addison shucked his shirtsleeves from his jacket cuffs, tightened his tie, and smiled pleasantly at the leather-skinned Uyghur man. "Addison Cooke, good to meet you. I was wondering if we might take a look at your camels?" To his surprise, the trader replied in English.

"I have magnificent camels for sale, the finest in the Gobi. You are American, yes? I love blue jeans and cowboys and doughnuts. Also baking soda—a marvelous invention. Look at these beautiful creatures!"

Addison looked up at the cud-chewing, two-humped beasts in their shaggy wool coats. "Beautiful" was not the first word to cross his mind, but he was pleased the trader was open to making a sale. "What do you think of these camels, Dax?"

"Bactrian camels," Dax said grimly. "Ornery and difficult. They bark, spit, and reek like a sweaty armpit. But they can last a week without water and a month without food."

The trader nodded a yellow-toothed grin and stroked the mangy mane of the nearest camel. "Each of these miraculous animals provides five kilograms of wool per year! And up to six hundred liters of milk!"

"What's your price for three camels?"

"Ten thousand yuan."

Addison frowned. He'd never bought a camel before, and he wasn't entirely sure what yuan were worth, but ten thousand sounded a bit steep. He thought about checking a camel's teeth, but when he got close to one, the camel snapped at him. He figured that meant the camel's teeth were plenty healthy. "Dax, talk to me."

The pilot circled the shaggy beasts, shadowed closely by Raj. "You can tell the health of a camel by its humps," said Dax. "A firm hump means a healthy camel. A droopy hump means a thirsty camel."

Addison thought the camels looked a bit deflated. He turned to the trader. "Two thousand yuan. For three camels."

The trader was aghast. "Each of these marvelous mammals creates two hundred and fifty kilograms of dung per year! Highly valuable for fuel! Their meat is tough to chew, but very nutritious!"

"Two thousand," Addison repeated.

"Nine thousand yuan. It's an incredible price."

"Can't do it. Two thousand or we walk."

"Five thousand! You are eating all my profit. My wife will never speak to me again."

"Two," said Addison. "C'mon, guys. Let's go." He shouldered his messenger bag and turned to hike across the limitless Gobi, the sand stretching to infinity. His team, sweltering in the heat, watched him in shock.

"But . . . camels," said Eddie.

"It's no good, Eddie. This gentleman doesn't want to offer us a fair price."

Addison tromped onward across the dune. One by one, his group reluctantly followed.

The camel trader pulled at his beard and ground his teeth. He couldn't believe he was losing this trade. "All right, fine! Three thousand yuan!"

"Two," called Addison across the desert waste. He had to walk another fifty paces through the sand before the camel salesman broke. Addison took three camels for an even two thousand yuan. When he offered to pay by credit card, the trader offered him the pointy end of his knife.

"But I get points on the credit card," said Addison.

"I'll give you points," said the trader, gripping his horn-handled blade.

Addison forked over the cash.

The camel trader insisted on shaking hands to seal the deal, which Addison regretted. He knew it would be many miles before he found a sink where he could wash.

Dax watched the trader—muttering and cursing—lead his two remaining camels away over the next dune. He turned to Addison. "How did you know you could get his price down?"

"I didn't," said Addison. "I'd just rather die than overpay for transportation."

Chapter Twenty
The Gobi Desert

DAX GRABBED EACH CAMEL by the hackamore and dragged it down to sit on its haunches. "Always approach a Gobi camel from the left, kid. That's how they're trained. You approach from the right and they might rear."

Addison mounted the first camel, with Molly climbing up behind him. The camel stood up hind feet first, pitching them precariously forward before righting itself.

"This doesn't look safe," said Eddie doubtfully. "Maybe we overpaid for these."

"Eddie, you don't have to be a rocket scientist to ride a camel," said Addison. "And luckily, we're not rocket scientists."

Raj mounted the next camel, with Eddie clambering on behind him.

"Don't pull back on the reins," Dax cautioned. "The camel will turn around and spit at you."

Eddie laughed.

Dax gave him a warning look. "The spit is so caustic, you'll need a doctor if it gets in your eyes." He climbed onto the final camel and reined it north. "Whatever you do, never turn your back on a camel. They'll bite, given the chance."

Mr. Jacobsen tried to lick Addison's camel. The camel spit at the Great Dane, nailing him squarely on the head.

"You see, Mr. Jacobsen?" said Addison. "Now you know how it feels to be covered in slobber. That's called karma."

Mr. Jacobsen shook himself off and bounded along ahead, seeming to have no conception of saving his energy for the trip ahead.

They set off across the barren desert. Perched high off the ground, they could see the broad panorama of the distant dunes. The camel saddles were nothing but blankets—very itchy blankets. Addison noticed the camels walked with both right feet followed by both left feet. He grew used to the unusual rocking sway.

"Do you think Madame Feng is already in Karakoram by now?" Molly asked. "While we're stuck in this desert, she could be getting a huge lead on us."

"Maybe," said Addison. "The last we saw, she was ankle deep in Russians. For all we know, she's having a tougher time than we are."

"I hope Aunt Delia and Uncle Nigel are okay."

"They can handle themselves. They have plenty of experience being kidnapped."

Addison decided to focus on the perilous journey ahead. "Raj, is there anything in this desert that wants to kill us?"

"You mean besides the sun and the complete lack of water? Oh, absolutely!" Raj was so excited by the topic, he nearly choked on the slug he was chewing. "For poisonous snakes, you have the Central Asian pit viper, the Halys pit viper, the European adder, and the steppe rat snake. You also have the Mongolian death worm. It's up to five feet long and spits acid."

"How deadly is a Mongolian death worm?" asked Molly.

"Well, if it doesn't kill you or paralyze you, it will certainly put a dent in your afternoon plans."

"Raj, is there any chance you can tell us something pleasant about the Gobi?"

He racked his memory. "Well, there are lots of dinosaur fossils."

"Great," said Molly. "Not even dinosaurs could survive this desert."

By noon, Addison's head felt as heavy as an anvil with the sun hammering relentlessly down on him. The camels toiled along the crest of a mesa, and Addison could see for miles. He was a single speck in a galaxy of sand. He began to daydream about water. Waves of heat rose off the desert floor, distorting the shapes of the camels and riders.

Eddie kept up a steady chatter, doing his best impression of Addison. "Hey, Eddie, let's go to China for summer break. The desert is just a giant beach. Like Coney Island but less crowded. We can all work on our tans."

Addison quietly wished for a break from the pitiless sun, and his wishes were soon granted.

It was afternoon when the sandstorm hit.

Molly spotted it first, squinting over her shoulder at the winds kicking up in the west. A wall of dust billowed toward them, hundreds of feet in the air, swallowing everything in its path.

Dax lashed the camels into a loping gallop. "Get to high ground!"

The howling storm overtook them, instantly turning day into night. Addison couldn't breathe—couldn't even open his mouth. Pelting sand stung his face. His eyes were red and burning—he clamped them tight.

Dax leapt off his mount and pulled all three camels to the ground. The group huddled on the lee side of the furry beasts, whose long snouts and fuzzy eyelashes protected them from the whipping sand.

Addison watched their day's tracks quickly scatter with the winds. Dax anchored his riding crop in the sand, pointing true north before he lost all sense of direction in the shifting desert.

"Is this bad?" Raj asked Dax, shouting over the raging gale.

"This is nothing! I once saw three members of a caravan team buried alive in the Sahara."

"You were in the Sahara?" asked Raj, deeply impressed.

"I've been all over Africa like a bad rash. Now grab an extra shirt and wrap it over your head like a turban."

Raj pulled an extra T-shirt from his pack. Dax moistened it with his canteen before he had Raj wrap it around his face. Dax repeated the procedure for Addison, Molly, and Eddie, and they were all pleased to discover they could suddenly breathe. Mr. Jacobsen nuzzled close to a camel and shut his eyes.

Addison rested his back against his camel's rump. He was deciding between naming him Hump-rey Bulgart or Alexander Camilton when he spotted something in the midst of the sandstorm. It was the dark-clad figure of a Mongol rider, turban blocking his face, tugging a reluctant horse through the sand. Addison peered harder, but before he could elbow Molly, the vision had vanished in the swirling dust.

He thought about the legend that Genghis Khan's tomb was guarded by Ghost Warriors. Addison considered himself a man of science. He did not believe in ghosts, let alone thirteenth-century ghosts in the middle of a sandstorm. He chalked his vision up to dehydration and finally accepted a drink from Dax's weathered canteen.

••••••

They traveled at dusk when the storm abated. Dax kept them moving late into the night, navigating by starlight. Addison was glad for the jet lag that allowed his body to stay on such a confusing schedule. Rationing their remaining water, Dax did not allow them to rest for long. They crossed miles of desert the following day, the plodding hooves of the camels churning the sands in a rhythmic beat that threatened to send Addison drifting off to sleep. Each time his chin nodded against his chest, he jerked awake, slapping his cheeks to stay alert.

On the evening of their second day, Dax guided the camels to an oasis. The group dug three feet into the sand before striking mud, and finally water. Dax insisted the camels drink first, which Addison didn't consider very sanitary. But it was only fair; as Raj pointed out, the camels were not riding the people across the desert.

Dax filled the last canteen with muddy, brackish water. The landscape was shifting from sand to scrub to crabgrass. He plucked a sprig of millet and chewed it thoughtfully, worrying it from one side of his mouth to the other, his tanned face squinting at the dry horizon.

Raj liked the look of it. He plucked a stalk, cocked one boot up on a rock, and chewed as well.

"Few more clicks and we'll make Karakoram," said Dax finally. "We'll rest here for the night."

They laid their packs by an old mining camp. Nothing but a cluster of desolate wooden shacks with doors creaking on their hinges in the lonesome wind. Dax and Molly broke up wood to make a fire.

Raj foraged through the abandoned shacks searching for canned food, but anything of value had long since been picked clean.

Dax struck a match against his unshaven chin. He coaxed the old firewood to light with the help of engine grease from the downed Apache and a pile of camel dung that Raj had saved especially for this purpose. By dark they had a roaring fire to cover the sound of their growling stomachs. Addison decided a little reading would help take his mind off his hunger. He had already finished his paperback copy of *Numerology* by Lily Wakefield and zipped through his well-thumbed copy of *The Girl from Jupiter* by Isaac Clarke. So he borrowed Raj's copy of *Mission: Survival* by Babatunde Okonjo. "Raj, which is the section where I can bone up on Asian street gangs?"

"Chapter Twelve: 'Gangs of the Far East,'" Raj answered immediately. "It's right after the chapters on sinkholes, typhoons, and gray wolves."

Addison flipped through the pages. "Before or after landslides?"

"Before."

He settled into that most pleasant activity, reading by firelight, but kept losing his place. He found the mining camp vaguely creepy and could not shake the feeling he was being watched.

The first time Molly foraged for fresh firewood by the outhouse, Mr. Jacobsen barked a few times for no reason. Other than that, there was nothing particularly eventful to report on. It was on her second trip to collect firewood that Molly saw the ghost of the Mongolian warrior.

When she turned the corner of the outhouse, she saw the dark figure silhouetted against the starry night. In one smooth flicker of motion, the figure advanced on Molly, raising a hand to strike.

Molly was the sort of person who, when faced with a Mongolian ghost outside her camp, paused to consider all the possibilities and choose the most sensible course of action. One could flee, one could attack, or one could shut one's eyes and hope the problem somehow resolved itself. Molly chose the first option: she bolted.

● ● ● ● ● ●

"Did you know," said Addison, looking up from his reading, "that if a Japanese Yakuza offends a fellow gang member, he must cut off his own pinky?"

Raj's eyes gleamed in the darkness. "Awesome."

"Seems a bit harsh," said Eddie. "What if he plays piano?"

Molly sprinted back to the campfire. Her cheeks were flushed, and she gasped for breath. "I was attacked by the outhouse!"

"How," asked Addison, setting his book down wearily, "were you attacked by an outhouse?"

Molly described the Mongol warrior as best she could. Addison was somewhat concerned for his sister's sanity, but also somewhat concerned for his own. She was describing the same Mongol warrior he had seen a thousand miles away in Kashgar, which may or may not have been the same Mongol warrior he had glimpsed in the middle of the sandstorm. None of this made a tremendous amount of sense to Addison, but it was worth investigating.

He, Raj, Eddie, and Dax armed themselves with brands of firewood and searched behind the outhouse. They found no trace of a Mongolian warrior. Raj, squatting on all fours, could not even find footprints.

"I'm telling you, there was something here," said Molly.

Addison wondered if Dax would say something

dismissive at this point. Instead, Dax was staring at the hairs standing up on Mr. Jacobsen's shoulders. The Great Dane peered intently into the night, working his giant nostrils like a blacksmith's bellows. "We'll sleep in watches," Dax said.

They settled in around the fire, piling it with enough wood to burn brightly for hours. The fire still smelled faintly of camel dung, but there was nothing to be done about that.

Raj had a million questions for Dax. "When you were in Africa, did you ever see a king cobra?"

"Yup." Dax lay in the shadows, eyes shut, resting his head on the Great Dane.

"How about a full-grown male lion?"

"Sure."

"Fire ants?"

Dax opened one eye. "Kid, you want to know the scariest thing I saw in Africa?"

"Um, yes?"

"Malaria. I've been stalked by hyenas, stalked by leopards, and stalked by guerrilla fighters in the Congo. But all it takes is one mosquito bite to cash out your chips."

Raj nodded. He dragged his bedroll around the fire so he could sleep next to Dax. He rested his head on his backpack. "Good night, Dax."

But Dax was already out.

Molly took the first shift, followed by Raj. Addison took the two a.m. shift and watched the stars spin around Polaris. No one saw or heard anything in the night. Yet when they woke in the morning, their camels, their water, and all their provisions had vanished.

Chapter Twenty-One

Karakoram

IT WAS ADDISON WHO discovered the theft. He woke early in the morning and set to work brushing every last grain of sand from his shirt, tie, slacks, and blazer until they were spotless. Between the sandstorm and the sleeping arrangements, there was sand everywhere. The entire cleaning operation took ten minutes.

Molly woke next and began stretching for her morning kung fu practice. She could already do front splits without trouble. It was the side splits that needed attention.

Eager to get a start on the day, Addison circled the wooden mining cabins, looking for the camels, and was surprised to discover there weren't any. He was quite sure there had been three camels the night before. He thought about retracing his steps from the prior evening, but couldn't think of anywhere he might have misplaced one camel, let alone three.

When he returned to the smoldering campfire, he found Raj, Eddie, Dax, and Mr. Jacobsen stretching and yawning. "Fine morning, isn't it?" Addison began pleasantly.

The tired group mumbled their agreement.

"Oh, by the way," he continued, "I couldn't help but notice all our camels are gone."

Dax jumped to his feet.

Raj liked the look of that and jumped to his feet as well.

They searched the mesa for telltale footprints, but night winds had swept the area clean of tracks.

"Some watchdog," said Molly, turning an accusatory eye on Mr. Jacobsen. "Dax, your supposedly *Great* Dane didn't bark once."

Dax frowned and shrugged. "He's not a guard dog, he's a copilot."

Addison shook his head at the ungainly dog. He preferred smart dogs that could fetch or perform tricks. Panting and drooling seemed to be the warp and woof of Mr. Jacobsen's personality.

"All right," said Addison, keeping things on track. "We'll just forage for some breakfast and be on our way."

"Addison, we're in the middle of a desert!" said Eddie. "You think food just grows on trees?"

"Some food grows on trees. Apples, for instance."

"Well, we haven't got any apple trees!"

"Save your energy for walking. We'll find food in Kara-koram." Dax turned up the collar on his bomber jacket.

Raj saw the move and did the same with his rain poncho. He liked the idea of foraging for food, but the slugs he had eaten the previous day hadn't sat well with him. The key was to make it to Karakoram and hope they had decent takeout.

The team shouldered their packs and trudged north.

The scrub gave way to desolate grassland. Addison tried not to think about water, so he pictured his favorite place—the New York Museum of Archaeology. He pictured the Aztec temple it housed, surrounded by a reflecting pool with a fountain of cool, refreshing water. Water so deep you could dive in and drink for hours. Addison shook his head and pictured his second-favorite place in the world: Bruno's Fossil Emporium on West 47th Street. Aisles of fossils captured in sedimentary rock, formed by eons of running water. Sweet, rejuvenating, thirst-quenching water. Addison frowned and thought of his third-favorite place in the world: Frank's Pizza on 23rd and Lexington. The perfect meatball slice, just a little salty—perfect with a tall glass of ice-chilled, life-giving water. His stomach growled and Addison growled with it. "Does anyone know any good stories?"

Raj piped up. "Did I ever tell you about the time I dared my sister to drink an entire gallon of water?"

Addison frowned and kept walking.

After a few miles of listening to Raj's stories about his sisters, Dax requested that they hike the next few miles in silence. By midmorning, the ancient Mongol capital was rising out of the empty plains like a mirage. Surrounded by crumbling mud walls, it contained a few scattered ruins overgrown with centuries of grass. Addison insisted on reconnaissance, so they climbed a hill overlooking the once great city.

"Karakoram," said Addison with a grand sweep of his arm, "the 'Black Prison.' Once the capital of the Mongol Empire. Founded by Ögödei, the son of Genghis Khan."

Molly looked at the shantytown of tin shacks, surrounded by lumpy ruins of broken bricks. "Not much now, is it?"

"You try starting a capital," said Addison. "See how it looks in eight hundred years."

He thumbed through *Roland J. Fiddleton's Asia Atlas* and pointed out the city as Marco Polo once saw it. The Muslim quarter, the Christian quarter, and the twelve pagan temples. Now the only ancient structure still standing was the Erdene Zuu Buddhist Monastery.

Molly glassed the monastery using Raj's binoculars. She yelped when she spotted Tony Chin parking a large passenger van by the rear entrance. Tony slid open the suicide door and helped Madame Feng out. She was followed by Aunt Delia and Uncle Nigel, bound in handcuffs. Triads then poured out of the van in an endless stream, like clowns from a clown car.

Addison crawled to the edge of the hilltop to take a closer look. He lay on his belly peering through the binoculars. He spotted Boris's Russian team parking a fleet of silver Mercedes-Benzes on the far side of the monastery. He passed the binoculars to Molly. "The A&U are leading the Chinese on a wild goose chase. And the Russians are falling for it."

"Why do you say that? Sir Frederick's clue said a Buddhist sanctuary in the city of the son of the Khan. And that is clearly the best and only Buddhist sanctuary around."

"Well, it's not the Buddhist sanctuary we're looking for. According to Roland J. Fiddleton, the Erdene Zuu Monastery was built in 1585. Sir Frederick was here three hundred years too early."

"Let me see if I've got this straight," said Eddie. "We just crawled across a desert with no food and water in order to find a Buddhist sanctuary that isn't here?"

"I've got some good news," said Dax, borrowing the binoculars and squinting at the tin huts of the shantytown. He pointed to the hitching post of a grubby cantina. "I just found our camels."

......

Dax led the group down into the desolate shantytown, weaving past broken tractor parts to reach the forlorn cantina. It was built of hammered scraps of corrugated tin. Addison recognized their camels tied at the hitching post, particularly when one of them tried to spit on Mr. Jacobsen. Next to the camels stood a row of sturdy Mongolian horses with wild manes and forelocks.

"The only thing worse than a camel thief is a horse thief," said Dax. From the disgust in his voice, he seemed to be speaking from a great deal of personal experience.

Addison marched up to the cantina. A piece of black tarpaulin was hung for a door. He pushed his way inside and allowed a few seconds for his eyes to adjust to the gloom. A few hardened herdsmen leaned against the bar. What they lacked in personal hygiene they made up for in facial hair.

Addison spotted the camel trader by his bowlegs and whip. He wore an ugly scowl on an uglier face, and unlike math, Addison did not think that multiplying two negatives made a positive. "Normally, I would politely introduce myself. But I'm tired from walking all day because you stole our camels."

The trader drew himself up to his full height. "You call me a thief? I purchased these camels just this morning."

"Right," said Addison, unimpressed by this story. "We need them back."

"That," said the trader, "will cost you ten thousand yuan."

Addison took a deep existential sigh. He hadn't eaten for days. And for once, he found he just didn't have the energy. "My friends and I are going to eat some food. And then we can negotiate the cost of buying back our stolen camels."

The team dined on steamed dumplings and barbecued beef. Dax thought the beef might actually be horsemeat, but Addison thought it was one of the best meals he'd ever tasted. He drank seven glasses of water straight, barely pausing to breathe. He was astonished when the total bill came to only fifty yuan; the price was so reasonable, he searched his soul from stem to stern and felt no urge to negotiate.

The cantina owner, excited to find customers pleased with the way he cooked horsemeat, wanted to make conversation. "Have you come to see the Erdene Zuu Monastery?"

It was an understandable question. There was almost no other earthly reason to visit Karakoram. Yet Addison eyed the owner closely. Ever since Madame Feng's betrayal in Hong Kong, he didn't want to make the mistake of trusting anyone. If he revealed his plans to this shopkeeper, the shopkeeper might squeal if interrogated by triads. "Yes, we're here to see Erdene Zuu," Addison lied. "What's left of it."

The cantina owner scratched his scraggly goatee and nodded wistfully. "There were once sixty temples, three

hundred *gers*, and one thousand monks at the monastery."
He drew a hand-rolled cigarette from behind his ear and lit
it off a kerosene lamp that hung from the low tin ceiling.
"The Communists destroyed all but three of the temples.
They killed ten thousand monks across Mongolia. Our
monks were some of the few to escape."

"Where did the monks hide?" asked Addison, intrigued.

"The Thousand Buddha Caves."

"Are they close by?"

"They are hidden in the dunes of Elsen-Tasarkhai."

Addison leaned forward with interest. "How old are
these caves?"

"One thousand years old."

"And why are they called the Thousand Buddha Caves?"

"Because there are so many Buddhas carved into rock."

Addison arched one eyebrow at his team. The tingling
on the back of his neck told him they had just found Sir
Frederick's Buddhist sanctuary. He tipped the cantina
owner an extra twenty yuan.

······

They hiked out of the valley to the dunes of Elsen-
Tasarkhai, where cliffs rose hundreds of feet from the
desert floor. Addison had attempted to purchase their
camels back from the trader, but ultimately decided that
walking was cheaper. He regretted that choice the farther

they trudged into the desolate wasteland. Mr. Jacobsen bounded ahead of the group, chasing any sand plover or sandpiper that dared to show its face. After another half mile, it was Molly who rounded a bend and spotted the thousand-year-old monastery carved into the stone edifice of a cliff.

The group scaled treacherous rocks and reached a narrow parapet that zigzagged up the yellow limestone gorge. Stone Buddhas, a dozen feet high, presided over the mountain path. The monastery was like a fortress, impregnable to attack. For the price of a hundred-foot climb in searing heat, they reached the carved entrance to the cave monastery.

Mr. Jacobsen celebrated the occasion by marking his territory.

"Dax, your dog just relieved himself on a thousand-year-old temple," said Addison.

"Mr. Jacobsen ain't interested in archaeology, kid. Just old bones."

"Is he a bark-aeologist?" tried Molly.

Dax squinted at her and said nothing.

She shrugged. It was worth a try.

"That joke was only a *ruff* draft," said Addison.

The team surveyed the dark entrance to the cave monastery. It carried the musty cobalt smell of centuries. Wind whistled eerily in the opening, as if the cave mouth were moaning. Sir Frederic may have considered it a place of sanctuary, but Addison found the cave a bit too sinister for his taste.

"You sure you want to go after the clue?" asked Dax. "We can still get out of here before the triads arrive."

Addison shook his head. "We have to keep moving forward. Sun Tzu says, *'Attack is the secret of defense.'*"

"Sun Tzu also says, *'He will win who knows when to fight and when not to fight.'*"

The whole group turned to look at Dax, impressed.

Dax shrugged. "What, like I can't read books?"

"Thanks, Dax. But we're doing this. We can't allow the triads to find the next clue. They'll steal the Khan's treasure if we give them the chance." Addison took an anxious glance back toward Karakoram, wondering how long Madame Feng would be delayed. "If you can find us a fast way out of here, that could save our lives."

"Don't worry, kid. I can find a way in and out of any situation." Dax whistled for Mr. Jacobsen and headed back down the cliff walkway.

Addison and his team marched through the entrance of the Thousand Buddha Caves.

Chapter Twenty-Two

The Hidden Temple

THE CAVE MOUTH WAS low and dark. After a few paces, the ceiling rose dramatically to reveal a large open cavern. Rows upon rows of Buddha statues were carved into the limestone, stacked one above the other like stadium seating. It was as if a crowd of ten-foot Buddhas was filling a movie theater. The room appeared to dead-end. Addison was worried this was going to be a very short treasure hunt.

"How many statues do you think there are?" asked Molly, taking in the strange sight. The Buddhas stared down at them impassively.

"One thousand," said Eddie. "It's the Thousand Buddha Caves."

"I don't know," said Molly. "There are definitely a lot of Buddhas, but nowhere near a thousand."

Eddie saw she was right. "False advertising."

"There are one hundred and seven Buddhas," Raj declared.

"Are you just guessing?" asked Molly.

Raj shook his head and quoted Sir Frederick's clue. "*'One hundred seven will watch over you. Pray at the one that will show you the way.'*"

"I don't see why they have the nerve to call it the 'Thousand Buddha Caves' if they only bothered to put in one hundred and seven Buddhas," said Eddie.

Molly saw that the statues were arranged in nine rows of twelve. She did the math. "There are one hundred and *eight* Buddhas here, not one hundred and seven."

"Does that mean something?"

Addison cupped an elbow in one hand and thoughtfully tapped his finger on his chin. "*'One hundred seven will watch over you. Pray at the one that will show you the way.'* One of these hundred and eight Buddhas is not like the others."

Molly stared at the crowd of statues. "So which Buddha are we looking for?"

"The only one at which a Templar can pray," Eddie blurted out. "I've got it! I know the answer!"

"I don't follow you," said Addison, not wishing to dampen Eddie's fire. "At all."

But Eddie was already bounding across the floor like a Labrador after a tennis ball. He scanned the crowd of Buddhas and pointed to the fourth row, second from the end. "That one! That's the Buddha we're looking for."

Addison followed his finger to the forty-seventh Buddha. Its stone face was completely crumbled with time—it no longer even resembled a person. "That one? It's the worst Buddha of the lot. It's basically just a lump of stone."

"Exactly!"

Eddie insisted they take a closer look. Addison didn't have any better ideas, so Molly removed a twenty-foot coil of rope from her father's survival kit and they scaled the stone edifice, level by level. Along the way, panting for breath, Eddie tried to explain his hunch.

"The key is in the clue. What did Sir Frederick call this room?"

"A Buddhist sanctuary," Molly answered.

"Almost," said Eddie. "He called it a sanctuary for the *idol worshippers* of Buddha. That's the key."

Addison frowned. "You've lost me, Eddie. I'm stranded at sea."

"Sir Frederick is a Christian knight," Eddie tried again. "And I go to church every Sunday with my mom."

Addison could follow this so far, but had no idea how Eddie was going to connect these dots to the forty-seventh Buddha.

"You memorize the Ten Commandments in Sunday school. The second commandment says a Christian can't worship idols." They reached the fourth level of statues. Eddie strode along the narrow aisle, swiveling sideways each time he had to sashay past a statue. "A Christian Templar knight would be forbidden to pray at a graven image. Sir Frederick cannot pray before one hundred and seven of these Buddhas." Eddie reached the broken, crumbling, faceless Buddha, and turned dramatically to address the group. "This is the only one where a Christian knight can pray."

"Fine work, Eddie." Addison nodded, impressed. "Let's pray you're right." He winked and dropped to his knees. He bowed low as he had done in the Kashgar chapel, and was immediately rewarded with the sight of the Templar crest etched into the base of the rock. "Hallelujah," he said. He rose back to his feet. "Sir Frederick says this Buddha is supposed to 'show us the way.' Any ideas?"

Raj hunted for any loose brick they could pry from the base. Eddie tried pushing the Templar seal like a button. Molly checked the statue's sightline, but that simply led back out of the cave. Addison pushed on various parts of the Buddha, looking for a secret trigger mechanism. He tapped on the remains of the nose and the belly, and even rubbed the Buddha's bald head.

Finally, more from frustration than hope, Addison gripped the Buddha in a bear hug and shoved with all his might. The entire statue swiveled on its base, revealing a staircase leading down into the mountain.

Addison, caught by surprise, nearly tumbled right down the staircase. He clung to the Buddha, his feet dangling helplessly in space, before Eddie and Raj pulled him to safety by his elbows. He straightened his shirt cuffs and, after the jitters had passed, regained his sense of dignity. He examined the dust that powdered the hidden staircase. "Raj, what do you make of this? Are we the first ones to enter in eight hundred years?"

"Not by a long shot." Raj squatted low to the ground and indicated footprints in the sand.

"Well," said Molly. "The cantina owner said monks hid here from Communists."

"That was years ago. These footprints seem fresh."

"You think people are already inside?" Molly dropped her voice to a whisper.

"Hope for the best, prepare for the worst," said Addison. He scooped his flashlight from his messenger bag and led the way down the stone staircase into the mountain.

•••••••

After two flights the staircase opened onto a massive arcade the size of a cathedral. Shafts of light lanced down from holes cut in the mountain, filling the hall with golden light. Addison shut off his flashlight to save the batteries.

For a solid minute, the group stood with their heads craned back and their jaws dangling open. There were carved stone Buddhas everywhere. Large and small, skinny and fat, they filled the room.

"So this is why they call it the Thousand Buddha Caves," Eddie breathed.

"Search for any place Sir Frederick might have hidden something." Addison knew he was being vague, but he had no idea how to pin things down. They'd already used up all four sentences of Sir Frederick's clue. He strode through the cavernous room, taking it all in. He saw the remains of cots, mattresses, cook pots, and books. "This must be where the monks hid from the Communists."

Raj pointed to faded murals sketched on the pale rock walls. They depicted hundreds of monks, hunted by soldiers as the monasteries of Mongolia burned. "Think of it. All the monks who yielded their last, desperate gasp of life before embracing eternity."

"It's a tragedy," Addison agreed. He didn't quite understand Raj's obsession with death, but somehow, in some twisted way, he felt Raj's heart was in the right place.

"Over here," Molly called. She waved them to the exact middle of the circular room and pointed, triumphantly, to a Templar symbol carved into the floor. "The eye is always in the center."

Addison discovered the floor tiles were not mortared

to the rock. Gaining purchase with his fingertips, he and Raj were able to lever a few square tiles out of the floor, revealing a dark, gaping hole.

Before they could take a vote, Molly had already taken Addison's flashlight, clamped it in her teeth, and begun climbing down into the darkness. Raj and Eddie lowered themselves in after her.

Addison took one last look around the shrine and suddenly shivered, overwhelmed by the feeling of being watched. He lowered his legs into the chute and hurried after his team.

He found himself in a square shaft. Wooden pegs, driven into the wall, allowed precarious handholds and footholds. In some places the pegs were so sparse, it was difficult to find any safe route down; in other places the pegs were so dense, it was difficult to wriggle through.

Addison saw Molly's flashlight glowing some ten feet below him. He had no idea how deep the shaft ran or how far he would plummet if his dress shoes lost their slippery grip on a wooden peg. His arm muscles were shaking with fatigue when he finally heard Molly's triumphant call as she reached the bottom. A few more rungs and he stretched a tentative toe south until it tapped gratefully against the rocky earth. He touched down with both feet and then lay on his back for a minute until the world stopped spinning.

By the time he sat up, Raj was already exploring the narrow tunnel ahead. Molly aimed the flashlight at a series of signs painted in several languages across the limestone wall. Addison recognized Mongolian, Chinese, and Cyrillic text.

"It's a warning." Eddie read the Chinese aloud. "'The Khan is guarded by Ghost Warriors. Turn back or face death.'" He weighed the two options. "I vote for turning back."

"It said we'll 'face death,' not that we'll die." Addison squeezed past Eddie in the narrow hallway. "We've faced death lots of times, Eddie."

"Yeah, but not from ghosts."

"In all history, no scientist has ever proven a haunting."

"Sure, but have any of those scientists conducted their experiments here in this cave in Mongolia?"

Under normal conditions, Addison would have argued the point. But he still felt as if he were being watched, and his memory kept conjuring images of the Mongol visions he'd seen in the past few days. He set his jaw with determination and took his flashlight back from Molly. The hallway ahead was guarded by twenty-foot statues of Mongol warriors that cast long shadows in the beam of the flashlight. "The signs warned us fair and square. Expect traps. Nobody touch anything."

They inched forward in silence, eyes peeled for any sign

of a booby trap. A quarter of the way down the hallway, Addison was beginning to feel confident. But it was halfway down the hallway that a heavy rock sailed out of the darkness and smashed only inches from his head. He ducked on instinct, splinters of rock dusting his cheek.

"Eddie, what did you touch?"

"Nothing! I was getting my inhaler out of my bag. I doubt Sir Frederick wired any booby traps to my inhaler."

Three more rocks crashed on the floor, inches from their feet. The team ran forward a few steps and ducked. Smashing rocks followed their progress. "This is no booby trap!" said Raj. "The aim is too good." The rocks appeared to be coming from the stone statues, but it was impossible to know for sure in the dim glow of the flashlight.

"Run," said Addison. "It's our only chance!"

The group sprinted headlong down the hallway and into the next chamber. They paused to collect their breath and their wits.

"What caused that?" asked Molly. "The Black Darkhad? The Ghost Warriors?"

Addison shook his head. "Something's down here with us, and we need to keep moving." He approached the next passageway, a low tunnel decorated with the carved, howling faces of ghosts. He aimed his flashlight into the gloom.

Raj inspected the passage. "I don't see any traps."

"We didn't see the last ones, either." Addison stepped

carefully over the white granite stone that marked the threshold. He ducked into the tunnel, Raj and Molly following close behind. "Nobody touch anything. I'm looking at you, Eddie."

"I'm not touching anything!" said Eddie, his hands in the air. "C'mon, Addison. Give me some credit!" Eddie stepped directly onto the white granite threshold rock. It sank with an ominous click. A stone door grumbled shut behind him, sealing them into the passage.

To Addison's horror, the ceiling began dropping, inch by inch, like the clamp of a vise, threatening to crush them. Addison's feet began running of their own accord, and his upper body sailed after them. "Hurry," he called. "Get to the end of the tunnel!"

They reached the far end of the passage, only to discover that it was not, in fact, the end of the passage. The hallway took a hard left, followed by a hard right, and then just kept on going. Addison kept right on running and the ceiling kept right on dropping. He found it was hard to sprint when bent double, and was soon scrambling forward on all fours. With a deafening grind, the ceiling was now only a foot from the floor. Addison dropped to his knees and elbows, crawling like a lizard for the end of the tunnel.

"We'll never make it!" shouted Eddie.

"Not with that attitude!" Addison gasped, squirming

on his belly. The ceiling was ten inches from the floor, and then nine.

Molly was slightly shorter and slightly faster. She squeezed through the final stone door just as it slammed shut.

"Molly," Addison shouted, "look for a switch, a lever, something! Anything that might trigger the trap to stop!"

The ceiling was now six inches from the ground. Eddie was trapped, squished flat like a bug. Addison felt his ribs compressing, the air being crushed from his lungs. "Molly," he wheezed, "stop lollygagging and save us!"

Molly must have found something, because just when Addison was ready to throw in the towel on this whole staying-alive business, the ceiling ground to a stop. Addison wanted to cheer but could not inhale a breath. Slowly, millimeters at a time, the cave ceiling ground its way upward and the tunnel door lifted open.

"Thank you, Molly, you wonderful Cooke." Addison filled his lungs with air and felt oxygen return to his brain. "That was absolute torture."

"You think that was bad," said Molly. "The release lever was inside one of these stone ghost skulls—I had to stick my hand in there!"

Addison made no argument. He, Raj, and Eddie scraped themselves off the floor and crawled into the final chamber.

••••••

Addison made the steep climb to his feet and teetered there, remembering how to balance. They were in a circular chamber with cliff walls soaring above them on all sides.

"Up there!" said Molly.

Addison followed her eyeline to a spur of stone that jutted one hundred feet directly into the air. He cranked his neck farther and farther back until he could see the top, where a single stone Buddha sat cross-legged, eyes half closed in meditation. A hole cut in the cliff illuminated the Buddha with a single shaft of light. And there, on the Buddha's lap, a steel object glinted. "The helm of Sir Frederick!"

The team tittered excitedly until Molly lifted a finger for silence. Somewhere, far behind them, came a sound like shouted Russian.

Addison felt his stomach drop. "C'mon, let's snag this clue and skedaddle." He made it sound easy, but the group stared doubtfully up at the enormous pillar of stone.

"Do we climb it?" asked Raj.

"I don't have that much rope," said Molly.

Addison weighed the problem. "Buddha does not go to the mountain, the mountain comes to Buddha."

Eddie looked at him quizzically. "Say what?"

"We don't have to get to the helmet, we make the helmet come to us."

"How, telekinesis?"

"The Mongols were excellent bowmen. Maybe the idea is to plunk the helmet with an arrow and knock it all the way down."

"I thought Sir Frederick hid these clues for Christians to find, not Mongols."

"Maybe," said Addison. "But this all seems too elaborate for Sir Frederick to construct while he was fleeing Mongolia for his life. I think there's more to this story."

"Okay," said Molly, thinking practically. "Anybody have a bow, an arrow, and incredible aim?"

Addison frowned in thoughtful silence. Molly, as was her habit, made a decent point. He thought of the flare gun tucked in his blazer pocket, but didn't think it'd be accurate enough to hit a small target at one hundred feet. "If only Dax had bought that dynamite I asked for, we could set a charge and knock down this pillar."

"That might collapse the whole cave and bury us," said Molly. "Plus, what kind of archaeologists would we be if we blew up an ancient monastery?"

Addison did not appreciate Molly being right so often. He heard more shouted Russian from somewhere deep inside the caves. Time was running out. He stared at the rocky pillar and shook his head. "Dad could solve this." Addison turned back to Molly. "What's in Dad's survival kit?"

Molly threw open the satchel. She tossed aside a

magnifying glass, a water purifier, and a braided hemp rope. She kept searching, half hoping a bow and arrow would magically pop out. Either that or a giant magnet to attract the metal helmet. What Addison discovered was significantly better.

"Beautiful!" Addison picked up the braided hemp rope. He unraveled it and stretched it taut.

"Addison, that rope's two feet long. I don't think it will reach."

"This isn't a rope. It's one of the deadliest weapons in history."

"A leash?" asked Raj.

"A belt?" asked Eddie.

"It's called a sling. This is how David killed Goliath." Addison pointed to the pouch sewn halfway along the rope. "You pack a stone in this pocket, swing the sling around your head, build up some speed, and whip the rock at your target."

"Sounds kind of primitive," Molly said doubtfully.

"It's lethal. A good slinger fires a stone ninety miles per hour."

This was good enough for Raj. He found a few chunks of stone and selected the most evenly rounded piece. He whirled the sling over his bandanaed head and launched a rock ninety degrees in the wrong direction. Everyone ducked as the stone smashed against the wall by their heads.

Addison tried the sling next and managed to wing himself in the head. He sat down, slightly dazed.

Everyone agreed that since they valued their lives, and still had much to live for, Eddie should not have a turn.

Molly tried the sling last. She twirled the sling over her head like a lasso, building up speed, and flung the stone high in the air. It blasted sand from a rock two feet to the left of the Buddha statue.

Addison shushed the team before they could cheer too loudly. With Russians searching the caverns, it was best not to reveal their location so easily.

Molly tried a few more stones, getting a feel for the ancient weapon. "I feel bad launching missiles at the Buddha. He's a symbol of peace." Her next stone clanged loudly off Sir Frederick's helmet, but did not dislodge it. Still, the helmet skittered a few inches across the Buddha's lap, and that was encouraging. Her sixth and seventh stones were also encouraging, but it was her seventeenth stone that sent the helmet clattering off the precipice and clanging to the ground.

"Molly, you're a natural," Addison proclaimed.

Molly held the sling proudly in her hand. She felt she had made a new friend.

Addison scooped up the helm and brushed it off with the backs of his fingers. Eight hundred years ago the helm had crowned Sir Frederick. Now it was in Addison's hands.

Turning it over, he discovered the next clue scratched on the inside of the helm, just above the visor. "Bravo, Molly."

"It's *'brava,'*" said Eddie, who understood a little Italian.

Molly was not paying attention. She was craning her ears toward the door. A few seconds passed before they heard the sound of crashing rocks and a shouting Russian.

"Someone's coming through the haunted hallway." Addison started for the exit.

"Addison," said Molly, "we have to copy the clue!"

"We'll copy it on the run. We're trapped here if we don't move quickly. All in favor?"

Addison's team voted with their feet. They ran.

Chapter Twenty-Three
The Pig's Whistle

ADDISON RUSHED BACK TO the collapsing corridor. He paused to stretch his hamstrings and limber up. "Everybody ready?"

Molly, Raj, and Eddie nodded somberly.

Addison stepped into the chamber and nothing happened. "Excellent. Maybe the trap can only be triggered on the other side. Still, just to be safe, nobody touch anything."

Halfway through the tunnel, just when it took a sharp left turn, they heard an awful rumbling and the ceiling began its slow descent. Addison broke into a sprint.

"I didn't touch anything!" Eddie shouted.

"Then who did?" Addison rounded the next turn and skidded to a halt.

Boris Ragar stood in the passage, staring in bewilderment at the lowering ceiling. Addison noted that Boris was wearing new pants. Scruffy, wool pants.

"Somewhere in Kashgar there's a shepherd who wants his pants back," said Addison.

The second Boris laid eyes on Addison's team, he seemed to forget about the ceiling problem entirely. He attacked with a growl of rage.

Addison saw no way around Boris—the broad-shouldered man blocked the passage entirely. Addison turned and fled back the way they had come, Raj, Molly, and Eddie scurrying ahead of him. To his horror, he saw the final stone door grinding its way closed. Only Eddie managed to escape through the door before it slammed shut.

Ducking low, Addison wheeled to face Boris. As much as he loved exploring archaeological sites, Addison discovered that there were any number of places he would rather be than trapped in a homicidal hallway with a raging psychopath.

Boris, seeing the passage door sealed shut, seemed to have his first inkling that something was horribly wrong. He was already bending double under the lowering ceiling, his head crooked at an odd angle. He bellowed and charged at Addison like a feral boar.

Somehow, Addison got the distinct impression that Boris blamed him for the collapsing ceiling. He ducked and dodged Boris's bearlike paws in the narrow tunnel, but with each passing second, he had less and less room to maneuver. "Eddie! Pull the lever!"

Eddie's voice traveled back through the stone door. "I can't! It's inside a skull!"

"Please, Eddie! Get us out of here!" Addison did not like to issue orders, or even raise his voice, but desperate times, desperate measures.

"I can't see what's inside this skull! If a spider bites my fingers, I can't practice piano!"

"If I get out of here," shouted Addison, *"I'll* bite your fingers!"

"Well, then, why would I free you?!"

Addison crouched on all fours as the ceiling clamped down on him like a garlic press.

Realizing he had bigger problems than assassinating Addison, Boris shoved hard against the ceiling with his broad back, trying to slow its descent. He strained his muscles so that his neck veins stood out like harp strings. He might as well have tried bench-pressing a battleship.

"Eddie, do it now!" screamed Addison. He gave up on all fours and lay flat on his belly as the cave ceiling bore down on him.

"When you shout at me, it makes me not want to help you."

"Eddie, pretty please, with sugar on top, *OPEN THE GATE!"*

"Not until you apologize!"

Finally, Boris filled his lungs with one last gasp of air and shouted. "Pull the release or I will skin you alive!"

After a moment's silence, Addison heard the release switch click into place. The ceiling stopped its dreadful march. With a grinding and scraping, the ceiling lifted upward, inch by inch, until the wind returned to Addison's lungs.

The door slid open, revealing Eddie, smiling proudly.

"Thank you, Eddie," said Addison weakly.

"Don't say I never do anything for you." Eddie marched into the chamber, absentmindedly stepped on the pressure sensor, and immediately triggered the death trap again.

••••••

The team hurtled for the exit. Addison appreciated that Boris decided to run in the same direction this time. What he did not appreciate was when Boris grabbed Addison by the leg, sending them both crashing to the ground. He watched the rest of his team safely escape the chamber. The ceiling continued crushing down, with the stone door grinding shut. Addison kicked his leg but could not detach himself from Boris. He had only seconds left before the door was sealed tight. In desperation, Addison took Sir Frederick's helm and tossed it down the tunnel, past Boris. The big Russian released Addison and lunged for the relic.

Addison, now in possession of both his legs, scrambled through the closing door. It clamped on his back like a pair of jaws. Raj, Molly, and Eddie grabbed Addison by his arms and yanked him out like a loose tooth. He rolled free, and the great stone door ground shut.

Addison dusted himself off. He was going to thank everyone, but was distracted by Boris Ragar's screams from beyond the stone door.

"The helmet!" said Molly. "Addison, we don't know the clue yet, and it's about to be crushed into scrap metal."

Addison was aghast. "Molly, you're not suggesting we let Boris out of there?"

"Of course I am! We're archaeologists, not murderers!"

"We've already killed one Ragar brother," Eddie pointed out.

Addison wasn't sure how many Ragar brothers he needed on his conscience. He listened to the Russian's desperate shouts as the passageway slowly crushed him. Addison grimaced. He stepped firmly onto the white granite threshold and the trap reversed course, opening the stone door and releasing the *vor* gang member.

Boris crawled out of the corridor, clutching Sir Frederick's helm. He passed a few seconds on his hands and knees, catching his breath. Once his hands stopped shaking, he clambered to his feet, rising to his full height. "Okay. Now I'm going to kill you."

"But we just saved your life!" said Molly.

"That's your mistake, not mine," said Boris. For such a big man, he moved with the light grace of a ballet dancer and was now blocking Addison's group from escaping the chamber.

There was no way past him, and Addison was not keen on stepping back into the death trap. Boris closed in. Addison had nowhere to move his feet, so he moved his mouth instead. "How did you find these caves?"

Boris stretched his arms wide, filling the tunnel, and circled in on Addison. "For twenty yuan, a camel trader told me he saw you in the cantina. Then I questioned the cantina owner with these two fists." Boris held up his two fists, for clarity.

Addison felt he had a score to settle with this camel trader, provided he could survive his present conversation with Boris. "What does Malazar want with the Khan's treasure?" he asked, just to keep Boris talking.

The gang member continued bobbing and weaving, waiting for Addison to slip within striking range. "Malazar does not care about the treasure. He'll sell it for profit. He only cares about the golden whip."

"Why?"

"'The last Templar wins the prize.'"

"What prize?"

"The prize, boy. Hasn't your uncle told you the prophecy?"

Addison was now thoroughly confused. He had heard about this prophecy from Ragar's brother in Peru, and it hadn't made any sense to him then, either.

"Here's a prophecy," said Raj, popping up behind Boris. "You're about to get hit on the head." Raj swung his backpack at Boris and put his full weight behind it.

Unfortunately, Raj's full weight wasn't all that much. When Boris ducked easily, the momentum of Raj's backpack sent him sailing off his feet.

Boris swung out with his left hand, the one that happened to be clutching Sir Frederick's steel helmet. He walloped Addison in the stomach so hard, it knocked the wind out of him.

This is it, thought Addison, since he could not speak. *I'm about to be pummeled to death by a man wearing stolen pants.* He waited for an earth-shattering punch that would reorganize the general layout of his face. It never came.

Tony Chin dashed into the corridor at full speed and attacked the big Russian with a blinding flurry of kicks and punches. Stunned, Boris retreated, raising his fists to shield his head.

"Tony, I could hug you," gasped Addison.

"Don't even think of it," said Tony. He rained punches down on Boris so rapidly, Boris barely noticed when Tony stole the helmet.

Unfortunately for Tony, Boris was thick-boned, milk-fed,

and extremely difficult to injure. Tony seemed to realize he might have better luck beating up a dump truck. Boris lowered into a wrestler's crouch and charged, mashing Tony against a rock wall and nearly flattening Eddie in the process.

Tony discovered that holding Sir Frederick's helmet meant he could only fight one-handed. And fighting Boris, like eating lobster, was an activity that required two hands. Tony set the helm down on a rocky ledge to deliver a two-fisted punch to Boris's concrete jaw. When he turned back to pick up the helm, it was gone.

Chapter Twenty-Four
Mr. Jacobsen

ADDISON SPRINTED DOWN THE haunted corridor, clutching the helm like a rugby ball, his team racing after him. He expected rocks to be hurled from the shadows of the Mongol statues, but none came. Addison fancied his luck was finally changing until Eddie shouted that Tony was now chasing them and catching up quickly.

"Eddie, I promised you Asia would be an exciting adventure!"

"Please. If I wanted to be filthy, claustrophobic, and afraid for my life, I would have stayed in New York and ridden the F train."

Addison arrived at the climbing chute and reached for a wooden peg. He realized there was no way he was going to climb out of this chasm faster than Tony Chin. Particularly while holding a heavy steel helmet.

"Let's go," shouted Molly. Tony was running at her heels.

"No, I'm going to fight Tony." Addison tossed Sir Frederick's helm to Molly. She caught it with both hands. Addison figured it was high time for Molly to copy the clue into his notebook, so he tossed his notebook and pencil at her as well. Molly was holding the helm in both hands, so the notebook and pencil bounced off her forehead.

Addison turned to square off against Tony. He just needed to buy Molly time. He flicked out his butterfly knife and beckoned Tony forward.

Tony paused, rolled up his sleeves, and nodded approvingly. "You're holding your knife point down. I'm impressed." Tony twitched his wrists, and the trench knives were suddenly in his grip.

Addison lunged and Tony parried.

Tony lunged and Addison parried.

Molly was desperate to watch the fight, but remembered she needed to copy Sir Frederick's clue into Addison's notebook.

Addison circled and struck with his knife. It met one of Tony's in a clash of metal.

Tony grinned broadly. "Good. You're improving!" He danced around Addison, flipping the trench knives so they glittered in the dark passage. "Now, we need to work on your footwork. Always keep your balance. When you lunge, you're overextending."

Addison lunged and Tony knocked him over easily. Tony stepped back, letting Addison return to his feet.

In an instant, Tony knocked him down again. "Balance, Addison! Keep your feet spread apart and no one can knock you down."

Addison tried it and immediately felt sturdier. Before he could lunge at Tony, Madame Feng's voice screeched from somewhere high above. "Quit playing around down there! I haven't got all day."

Tony shrugged at Addison. "Duty calls."

Addison saw a blur of motion followed by his butterfly knife sailing out of his hand. Tony caught the knife in midair and tossed it back to Addison. He grinned. "Keep practicing."

Tony swiveled to face Raj and Molly, tripping one and clotheslining the other. He caught Sir Frederick's helmet as it flew from Molly's grasp. He needed to free his hands to climb out of the cave, so he simply popped the helmet on his head. Within seconds Tony had scaled the wooden pegs up the chute, disappearing into the darkness above.

Molly shook her head. "He's really good."

"Let's hurry," said Addison. "Maybe we can still get the helmet back."

The group climbed from peg to peg up the shaft. Their

progress was slow until Boris appeared at the bottom of the chute and began climbing up after them. Addison found this to be extremely motivating. He raced up the climbing pegs like a cat up a tree.

When they hauled themselves up into the cathedral-size room, they spotted Tony, completely outnumbered by Russian gang members. One large Russian punched Tony so hard, the helmet flew off his head. It bounced across the stone floor, clanging like a dinner gong, and rolled right into Addison's hands. "Goes around comes around," said Addison.

The Russians continued to attack Tony, knocking the trench knives from his grasp. Addison, wishing to keep things sportsmanlike, slid his butterfly knife across the stone floor to Tony, who scooped it up and kept the Russians at bay. Boris crawled out of the pit and joined the fight against Tony, backing him up against a wall.

"Tony's in trouble," said Addison. "And I think he's a pretty decent guy."

Molly tugged at Addison's sleeve. "We can't help him. We've got to run."

Addison's conscience nagged at him. "You're right, Molly. We can't help him. But maybe Madame Feng can." Addison charged up the hidden steps under the forty-seventh Buddha and burst back into the first cave. His team followed, leaping down each row of Buddha statues. Addison sprinted to the entrance tunnel of the cave and found Madame Feng standing guard over his aunt and uncle.

●●●●●●

Madame Feng spotted the helmet under Addison's arm and gestured to her bodyguard Hu. Hu was a thickset man with a face like a slab of mutton. "Hu, stop him."

"No, I need your help," said Addison. "Boris is going to kill Tony!"

Hu paused. Madame Feng frowned in confusion. Apparently, she was not one to be troubled to know the names of her employees. "Boris is going to kill who?"

"Whom," said Addison.

"I don't know, that's what I'm asking you."

"Yes, but you mean 'whom,' not 'who.'"

"Who is going to kill Hu?"

"No one is killing Hu!"

"That's it," said Madame Feng, stepping forward. "Hu and me are going to kill *you*!"

"Hu and *I* are going to kill you," said Addison, thoroughly exasperated.

Hu screamed and attacked.

Addison retreated from Hu, and, to his team's consternation, fled back inside the cave. He saw that Tony had somehow fought his way past the doorway of the forty-seventh Buddha. Boris was busy shaking Tony around like a bulldog with a chew toy. Addison whistled to snag Boris's attention and tossed him the helm.

Boris unceremoniously dropped Tony and caught the helmet with pleasure.

Addison was pretty sure he had just saved Tony's life. But before he could savor the moment, Hu slammed Addison to the ground and pinned him. For the second time in ten minutes, Addison mentally prepared to have the entire map of his face redistricted. He looked up at Hu's face, which could have benefited from its own redistricting, and was surprised to see a dog peering over Hu's shoulder. "Mr. Jacobsen?"

Hu turned his head and was startled by the sight of the giant, slathering beast.

"Get him, boy!"

The Great Dane cocked his head and bent one ear, confused.

Hu held one clenched fist hovering over Addison's nose, ready to punch. He hesitated, eyeing the massive dog.

"C'mon, boy!" said Addison. "Attack!"

The giant dog only panted.

Hu laughed. He wound up to punch Addison an even larger mouth.

"Mr. Jacobsen, attack!" Addison shouted.

Mr. Jacobsen leapt onto Hu, rolled the triad onto his back, and began licking him.

Hu wiggled and squirmed, trying to escape the slobbering Dane.

This was all the distraction Addison needed to escape. He jumped to his feet and sprinted for the exit.

Mr. Jacobsen loped along after him, tongue lolling out of his mouth.

Addison caught up with Molly as they raced toward freedom.

"Some dog that is," she said, pouring on the speed.

"Hey, he just saved my life."

"By accident."

"I'll take it."

Addison's team reached the final tunnel that led to daylight and skidded to a halt. Madame Feng blocked the cave mouth. Two triads were still handcuffed to Aunt Delia and Uncle Nigel.

"Let my aunt and uncle go," Addison said firmly.

Madame Feng looked down her nose at Addison and emitted a full, ringing gale of laughter. "You're just kids! You have nothing to bargain with. Go, run into the steppe. You have no horses or camels. No water for five hundred miles. Go and die in the Gobi!"

"Addison, we'll handle this," said Aunt Delia. "You guys get as far away as you can!"

Several triads were already rushing closer across the cave floor.

Addison, Molly, Raj, and Eddie sidestepped Madame Feng and fled down the final tunnel. Daylight glimmered at the far end.

Russian gang members ducked into the opening, sealing off the escape. Addison spun and saw triads closing in from behind. They were trapped in a criminal sandwich.

"We're going to die!" shouted Eddie.

"Eddie, you can die when you're dead!" said Addison. He reached behind his blazer and drew Dax's flare gun from his belt. He aimed it at a rushing Russian and fired.

The flare struck the man square in the chest, blasting him backward. It lit up the tunnel like a giant red firework, ricocheting off the tunnel walls and showering everyone in sparks. The triads, eyes accustomed to the dark gloom of the cave, were blinding by the dazzling light. The *vori*, coming in from the daylight, could not yet see in the tunnel.

Addison's team charged through the fiery chaos and into the light. They sprinted a hundred-yard dash down the mountain path. When they turned back to look, the flare still burned and fizzled red in the tunnel where triads fought *vori*. Addison gazed down at the flare gun, still clutched in his hands. "What an excellent product. I must buy their stock."

Mr. Jacobsen, for lack of a better word, embarked. He bounded past the group and greeted Dax at the base of the hill.

Dax wrapped an arm around the Great Dane. "Good work, Mr. Jacobsen!"

Molly was nonplussed. "What did *he* do?"

"I told Mr. Jacobsen to go find you." Gunfire rocked the cave above. "What exactly did you do up there?"

"It's a long story."

Dax shrugged. He was getting accustomed to the amount of chaos Addison's team could generate if left to their own devices for an hour. "C'mon, I found transportation."

He led the team around a bend in the pass. And there, to Addison's amazement, was a string of Mongolian horses.

They were beautiful animals. Addison stroked one by the mane. "Where did you get them?"

"Stole them from that camel trader." Dax winked and mounted a chestnut mare. "Told you I can get you in and out of any situation."

Addison's team climbed onto their horses and kicked them into a gallop, escaping into the wilderness of Mongolia.

Chapter Twenty-Five
The Next Clue

SPROUTS OF FEATHER GRASS and millet showed through the dunes, quickly thickening into grassland. Soon, the horses were galloping across the open steppe. Molly spotted black-tailed gazelles leaping in the distance. The hills rose like storm-driven swells on a turbulent green sea. The wild manes of the horses flared in the stiff wind.

Dax trailed a string of extra mares behind him, their hackamores tied to a catch rope.

"Why'd you take so many horses?" Molly called over the blustering prairie breeze.

"Spite, mostly."

"We can use them as spare mounts, like the Mongols," shouted Addison.

Mr. Jacobsen bounded alongside the horses, tongue lolling, taking frantic detours to pursue every marmot in Mongolia without success.

This was only Addison's second time on a horse, the first being a mare he had stolen in Central Park in April while evading the New York Police Department. Addison loved Central Park in April. And to be fair, the horse was eventually returned. Cantering across the ancient steppe, he found he rather had the rhythm of it. He was pleased to have his own mount, instead of sharing one with Molly. The horse was a fly magnet, but it beat walking.

Eddie bounced along on his gelding, constantly on the verge of falling off. Addison counted it a near miracle Eddie was staying on at all. The overall impression was of a ping-pong ball being bounced on a paddle while hurtling over rough terrain.

Whipping across the high plateaus, the grass passed beneath them in a green blur. Dax taught them that "*chu*" was the Mongolian word that made the horses go faster.

"What's the Mongolian word for 'stop'?" shouted Eddie.

"There isn't any," called Dax.

They rode until the horses were lathered in sweat and the sun was swan diving into the western horizon. Dax found an abandoned stable with a rusted water pump. He dismounted and worked the iron hand pump, filling the water trough for the horses to drink. The sunset was a brilliant orange and pink. "We'll rest here for the night," he declared.

Addison scanned the empty basin and the rolling primordial hills. "Will the Russians find us here? Boris really seems to have it in for us."

"He'd have to be one ace of a tracker," said Dax, scanning their back trail. "Mongolia is a land of nomads. You'd be hard-pressed to find a road or a fence within a hundred miles."

Dax hobbled the horses and left them to crop grass on the mesa. Raj and Molly scavenged wood, scrub, and dried moss to feed the fire. Addison found the tarnished key that unlocked the barn doors. He and Eddie gathered old straw for bedding.

They relaxed by the campfire, drinking well water and dining on dried apples and sheep jerky Dax found in the horses' saddlebags.

Addison kept trying to train Mr. Jacobsen to stop licking, but the Great Dane kept at it with dogged persistence. "I wish he'd give the licking a rest. He thinks I'm ice cream."

"Hey," said Molly, "his licking may have saved you from Hu."

Addison sighed. Molly had been making a lot of good points lately. "Okay, Mr. Jacobsen, lick away."

The summer constellations blossomed overhead: Sagittarius, Aquarius, and Lyra. Addison was used to seeing only two or three stars at night in Manhattan, where every skyscraper shimmered with light. But here in the Mongolian steppe, there seemed to be millions of stars to speckle the sprawling sky.

"Let's have a look at that clue," said Dax, chewing a fresh sprig of millet. Addison handed over his notebook, and Dax tilted it to the firelight.

> *"Praise be to the Lord, my Rock,*
> *who trains my hands for war,*
> *my fingers for battle.*
> *God is my shield, my sword, my helm, and my lance."*

"Guy really likes saying that, doesn't he?" said Dax, looking up.

"He was writing in the Dark Ages," said Addison. "They started everything with a prayer. What does it say next?"

The dried crabgrass crackled in the fire, sending up small bursts of sparks. Dax crinkled his brow and read.

> *"At the palace of Prestor John*
> *I bested his top warrior in single combat;*
> *He swore to keep my sign forever hanging*
> *Among the weapons in his trophy room."*

"Again, not big on rhyming," said Eddie.

"He was too busy battling Mongol warriors," said Raj.

"It'd be a crime to rhyme all of the time," said Addison. "It'd hardly be sublime," he added.

Molly brought things back on track. "Sounds like all we have to do is find the palace of Prestor John. And then poke around in his trophy room."

"I've read about Prestor John. He was a Mongol lord named Wang Khan. It was the Christians who called him John." Addison flipped through the index of his copy of *The Travels of Marco Polo*. "Marco visited Wang Khan's palace in the Black Forest by the sacred Tuul River. Now, where is the Tuul River . . ." Addison dug his copy of *Fiddleton's Asia Atlas* out of his messenger bag.

"Addison, how many books are you carrying in that bag?" asked Molly. "I thought we were only supposed to carry necessities."

"Books *are* necessities." He thumbed through the index of *Fiddleton's Asia Atlas* and peered at the map of central Mongolia. "The capital city of Ulaanbaatar. That's where we'll find Wang Khan's palace."

"Ulaanbaatar is east of us," said Dax, shaving fresh kindling into the fire with his bowie knife. "There are no roads on the steppe, so the horses can take us straight there. There are mining villages every ten miles or so, but we can steer clear of them."

Addison studied Dax thoughtfully. He felt he had misjudged the man. His uncle Nigel had said Dax was useful in a scrape, and Dax had proven that in the past few days. "When did you first meet my uncle?"

"When I was flying intelligence missions for the navy."

"You were a spy?" Raj asked. He didn't think his admiration for Dax could soar any higher, but Dax kept raising the bar.

The pilot shrugged. "I just marked the locations of bunkers and silos and tried not to get shot down." He poked the fire with a stick and fresh sparks drifted up into the night. "Your uncle requested an airdrop behind enemy lines. Some archaeological relic he needed to save."

Addison could not picture his uncle Nigel parachuting, but he supposed it was a long time ago. "What country was it?"

Dax shook his head. "Still classified."

"Did he get the relic?" asked Molly.

Dax nodded.

"What happened to you, Dax?" asked Addison. "How did you go from navy pilot to smuggler?"

Dax leaned back, crossed his hands behind his head, and stared up at the starry night. "I became a bush pilot in Tanzania. My job was to follow the elephant herds across the Serengeti and hunt for poachers."

"So you were a poacher poacher."

Dax nodded. "I liked the work. I tried hard. Soon I was poached by a rival wildlife agency."

"You were a poached poacher poacher?" asked Addison.

Dax nodded again. "They moved me to Zimbabwe to track white rhinos. There, I met a beautiful Danish girl and fell in love."

"Here we go," said Eddie.

"One night I got back from a sortie and she was gone."

"Someone poached her?"

Dax shrugged. "I only know she took my car, half my pride, and all my money." He patted Mr. Jacobsen. "All she left me was her Danish dog."

"German," corrected Raj.

"After that, my luck ran south. I couldn't seem to win back my money at the blackjack table. I kept trying and dug a deep hole. Don't ever go into debt, kid."

"Do you ever think of going back to Tanzania?" asked Addison. "You were happy there."

Dax's eyes settled on the middle distance as he gazed back into the far reaches of his memory. "I think about it sometimes. There were mornings I'd go up in my Cessna Skyhawk—a beautiful plane—and glide into the golden dawn. I'd see the morning mist rise off the Serengeti and swear I'd gone back in time. I'd swear I was the first man in the world."

"You could go back, you know. There's nothing stopping you."

Dax shook his head, returning to the present. "You can

never go back, kid." He stood up and kicked the dust off his boots. "The only direction a pilot needs to look is forward."

When Addison was drifting off to sleep, he heard the horses whinnying and stomping on the mesa. He, Raj, and Molly roused Eddie out of bed and crossed behind the barn to investigate. They found Dax saddled up and leading the string of extra mares. "Where you going?" asked Addison.

"Reconnaissance," said Dax, reining the horses east.

"He's going to sell those extra horses so he can gamble in the next mining town," said Molly in a low voice.

Dax's face was hidden in the dark. His horse chewed its bit and sidestepped until Dax shook the reins. "I'll be back before you wake." He kicked the horses into a trot.

Addison watched him gallop away.

"Why does he do it?" asked Eddie.

"Because he's unhappy," said Molly.

Addison suddenly felt very alone on the open prairie, the eerie wind whistling through the barren land.

••••••

They assigned watches to guard the remaining horses and prepared to go to sleep. Molly gathered firewood behind the barn, and Addison went to fetch fresh water from the well pump. So they were in two completely different locations when they both saw the shadow of a Mongol warrior slipping through the night.

Addison and Molly sprinted back to the campfire and were confused when they both blurted out the same story.

Raj crossed his arms and crinkled his brow. "So what you're saying is, there are Mongolian ghosts hanging out behind the barn."

"You all heard Uncle Nigel talk about the Black Darkhad," Addison insisted. "Legend says Genghis Khan's tomb is guarded by ten thousand Ghost Warriors!"

Raj frowned. "If there was such thing as ghosts, I'd be flabbergasted."

"You mean you'd be flabberghosted," said Eddie.

Addison insisted that the group set a trap. "If it was just me who saw it, I would assume I was crazy and leave it at that. But Molly saw it, too. And what are the odds we're both crazy?"

"Well," Eddie reasoned, "you *are* related."

"Guys," said Addison, "I don't know how else to say this. Code Blue."

They stuffed their sleeping bags with straw to make them look occupied and left them in the half-light of the dying fire. Addison gathered the remaining horses and corralled them inside the barn. He, Molly, Eddie, and Raj climbed up the barn ladder and hid in the hayloft. They waited for the Mongol to appear.

Chapter Twenty-Six

The Black Darkhad

ADDISON'S TEAM STAYED UP late into the night, carefully concealed under a half foot of hay, with Molly heroically suppressing her sneezes. Palest starlight cast the hills in black and white, a photo negative of the world. Under the great black dome of the sky, the grasslands were a dark ocean, unnavigated. Sometime around midnight, Molly pricked up her ears and shook Addison back to full alertness. Two figures appeared in the calico shadows of the campfire's embers and made their way stealthily to the barn doors, stepping inside.

In the moonlight, Addison saw two cloaked Mongolian warriors. Dark turbans covered their heads and faces. Only their eyes glittered in the darkness. They moved with the silent grace of wraiths, soundlessly opening the stalls to steal the horses. Eddie watched in terror, but Addison only smiled. The Mongols had taken the bait.

Raj waited until the Mongols were in place before springing his carefully constructed trap. He toppled a heavy iron plow out of the hayloft. It yanked a rope over a pulley, hauling up a tarp Raj had hidden under the hay-covered floor. The Mongols were scooped up into the tarp and dangled from a crossbeam.

"Yes!" Raj exclaimed, pumping his fist. Addison had told him his trap wouldn't work, and here it was working perfectly.

The tarp immediately snapped under its weight and fell to the ground with a crash. The Mongols rolled free and sprang to their feet.

"Bummer," said Raj, completely deflated.

Addison was already shimmying down the hayloft ladder. He dashed to the barn door and slid it shut, preventing the Mongols' escape.

Molly ran straight for them, attacking head-on with a blistering flurry of punches and kicks. Kung fu was a Chinese martial art, and Molly was pretty sure the Mongols wouldn't know anything about it.

She was profoundly mistaken.

The Mongols deflected every strike before turning on Molly with terrifying force.

Molly saw only a whirling tornado of fists and feet from which she desperately tried to escape, weaving in and out of the horse stalls and through the horses' legs. One blow caught her on the chin and another above her eye.

"I'll save you, Molly!" Raj valiantly joined the fray, providing the Mongol warriors with a second punching bag.

In the midst of the chaos, Molly scored a single roundhouse kick on the smaller of the two Mongols, and had the satisfaction of hearing the Mongol grunt. She immediately regretted it, as the kick seemed to whip her attackers into a deadlier state of fury.

The larger Mongol slipped past Raj and tried to jerk open the barn doors. To the warrior's astonishment, the doors were chained and locked. The warrior rattled the chains and kicked angrily at the door. He delivered a sharp sidekick to Addison's ribs that sent him sprawling to the ground.

Addison winced and clutched his side. He could not believe his ribs had been bruised twice in the same spot. He swallowed his pain and stood shakily to his feet. As calmly as he could, Addison smoothed the lapels of his school blazer and removed a stray piece of hay from one sleeve. "There's no way out, you know."

"Give us the key," the larger Mongol growled in slightly accented English.

"I don't have it. We're locked in here."

"What?" said the Mongol.

"What?" said Molly, Eddie, and Raj.

"Why would you do that?" asked the smaller Mongol.

"We're trapped in here with these things?" asked Molly.

Addison rubbed his aching ribs and addressed the taller Mongol. "It was the only way to ensure you couldn't escape. If I had the key, you could just take it."

The Mongol looked down at the padlocked door. "Well, where is the key?"

"I threw it out the hayloft window. Dax can unlock us in the morning when he sees we're not at breakfast."

"You're assuming Dax will even come back," said Molly angrily.

The Mongols looked at each other uncertainly.

"I have my lock-picking set," Raj volunteered.

"That's great, Raj," said Molly. "We'll be trapped in here for months."

Addison turned on his flashlight. In its beam, the Mongols didn't look quite so tall or intimidating. One of them was Addison's height. The other was shorter.

"If you're ghosts," Raj reasoned, "you should have cleared out of here by now. You know, melted through a wall or something."

The Mongols said nothing.

Addison sighed. "Frankly, I'm disappointed. If we had really captured two ghosts, we would be famous throughout the scientific community. *Finally*, I could be in *National Geographic*."

The larger Mongol struggled against the door again and gave up. He turned to Addison, defeated.

Addison smiled. "Well, then. If we're going to spend the night together, we might as well get acquainted." He extended his hand. "Addison Cooke. Pleasure to meet you."

•••••

The larger warrior took off his helmet and unwrapped the black turban that hid his face. He was a Mongolian boy, about sixteen, with a suntanned face. "My name is Khenbish."

Addison tried to wrap his tongue around the strange Mongolian pronunciation. "*Khen-bish?*"

"It means 'Nobody,'" said the boy.

"Your name is Nobody?" Raj blurted out.

"The evil spirits cannot find me if I am Nobody," Khenbish explained.

Addison nodded. He had to remind himself he was six thousand miles from Manhattan and that not everything was going to make perfect sense. In fact, things often didn't make sense in Manhattan, either. "So when you go to the library and check out a book, Nobody checked out a book."

"Yes."

Addison rarely had to reach far to find a response. But in this instance, he was thrown off his balance entirely. "Wow," he said finally. "For days we've been followed by Nobody."

"Explains why we didn't find any tracks," said Raj.

Addison noticed that both Mongols wore swords strapped to their backs, but neither had chosen to use them. He took this as a good sign. "Okay, then," said Addison, turning to the shorter Mongol. "What is your name?"

The shorter Mongol was still crouched in a fighting stance. Reluctantly, the warrior relaxed, pulling off both helmet and turban. To Addison's astonishment, the warrior was a girl, long black hair spilling from her helmet and streaming down her back. She was about fourteen and looked at Addison with haughty resentment. "I Don't Know."

"You don't know your own name?" Raj was astounded.

"I *do* know my name: Medekhgüi."

"What does Medekhgüi mean?" asked Addison.

"I Don't Know," said the girl.

Addison was a little out of his depth, but still felt he could make his way back to shore. "So if you call a friend on the phone, and they ask who's calling, you say, 'I Don't Know.'"

The girl nodded impatiently. "My name is very common in Mongolia."

Addison wanted to make sure he wrapped his mind

around this. "So your dad turned to your mom and said, 'What should we name her?' And your mom said, 'I don't know.' And your dad said, 'Sounds good!'"

The girl nodded. "Mongolians are superstitious people. My name confuses the evil spirits."

"I can see how," said Addison, who was thoroughly confused.

"Did you follow us all the way from Kashgar?" Molly cut in.

"What? No. That's impossible," said Nobody. "We're not *actually* ghosts."

"Well, I saw you in Kashgar," said Molly, "and I'm not *actually* crazy."

"There are many of us, spread throughout the Khan's empire. We have radios, a whole network of outposts. You must have seen another member of our order in Kashgar."

"We've been following you since the Gobi Desert," said the girl.

"How?" asked Addison. Somehow, he found everything she said utterly fascinating.

"We knew your plane escaped Kashgar. But it never landed in Karakoram. My brother and I patrol the Gobi. We're young, so they give us the patrols no one else wants."

Molly planted her fists on her hips and squinted at the girl. "It was *you* who stole our camels and sold them to a trader in Karakoram."

Neither Nobody nor I Don't Know answered.

"We could have died out there!" said Eddie.

"And you were trying to steal our horses again tonight!" said Molly.

Nobody and his sister suddenly seemed very skilled at not talking.

"We've got all night," said Addison.

"We did not mean to harm you," Nobody said at last. "Our duty is to prevent you from discovering the Mongols' secrets."

"You say you don't want to harm us," said Molly, "but you tried to kill us in the Thousand Buddha Caves today."

"We did not hit you with any rocks. We were only trying to frighten you away."

"Are you Black Darkhad?" asked Addison.

Nobody bowed. "We are descendants of Muqali and Bo'orchu, the renowned generals of Genghis Khan. When the Great Khan died in 1227, our clans were tasked with guarding his tomb. Our families have kept this vigil for thirty-eight generations. We are the Black Darkhad, the Ghost Warriors."

Raj's mouth hung open. He had never met a Ghost Warrior before. He had never even known he wanted to. And now here there were two of them—an embarrassment of riches. He found he had only one burning question. "How come your English is so good?"

Nobody shrugged. "TV."

"So," said Addison, getting down to business. "Where is the tomb of Genghis Khan?"

"I don't know," said I Don't Know. "None of our clan has ever tried to find it."

"Then what are you guarding?"

"We guard the clues that lead to the tomb. It's safer if we don't know the actual location—then we cannot be tortured for information."

"But the site is invaluable to archaeology!" Addison exclaimed.

"It's invaluable to our people," Nobody countered.

"How can it be invaluable to your people if none of your people have ever been there?"

"It is safer this way," Nobody said again. "And that is why we cannot allow you to continue on your journey."

"Look," said Addison, who sensed an opening for negotiation. "Do you want Madame Feng to find the Khan's tomb?"

"Of course not," said I Don't Know.

"We don't want the Russian *vori* finding it, either," Nobody added.

"So that makes us allies," said Addison.

The Mongol boy watched Addison with his dark eyes, considering.

Addison continued. "We're going to Ulaanbaatar to

find the next clue before the triads or the *vori*. The surest way to stop them is to find the next clue and hide or destroy it. Join us." He reached out his hand. "We're on the same team."

The Mongol boy shared a glance with his sister. Slowly, he reached out and shook Addison's hand. "For now."

Addison reached inside his pocket and produced the padlock key. He unlocked the barn door. "Let's get some rest. We have a big journey tomorrow."

Chapter Twenty-Seven
The Grasslands

DAX RETURNED AT DAWN. He was somewhat alarmed to discover the two Mongol warriors sleeping by the campfire. "Who are these people?" he demanded.

"Nobody," said Addison. "And I Don't Know."

Dax nodded slowly. "I need more coffee."

"We haven't got any," said Eddie.

"Why," said Dax, "does Molly have a black eye?"

Molly smiled proudly. "Does it look good?"

Dax had only been with the Cookes for five minutes this morning and he was already exhausted. He lay down by the fire and shut his eyes for a catnap. Addison couldn't help but notice that Dax had returned with far fewer horses than he had left with the night before.

As the sun blossomed over the horizon, Molly stretched and started her morning regimen of kung fu practice, launching a barrage of high kicks into a crooked fence post.

I Don't Know tied her long black hair into a ponytail and watched Molly with a critical eye. "You have the kick of a horse, but you lack discipline. You can train with me if you like. I will teach you Mongol-Zo."

Molly stood for a few seconds, catching her breath. "I've been taking kung fu for eight weeks now. I'm not sure if I should switch to a new martial art so quickly."

I Don't Know nodded. She lashed out with her foot, hooking Molly's ankle.

Molly landed hard on her back before she knew what was happening. She groaned. "Okay, we can learn your way."

The Mongolian girl tossed her ponytail over one shoulder and helped Molly to her feet. "You have no balance, no core strength, and no technique. But before anything, we need to start with your roundhouse kick." I Don't Know drilled Molly for an hour with the help of her brother, Nobody. Finally, Dax woke, readied the horses, and pointed the way to Ulaanbaatar.

Addison was a bit sore from the previous day's ride, but he found it was good to be back in the saddle. The fresh wind rippled the sage and barley that whispered past his legs as the horse cut a trail through the boundless fields.

The world was two bands of color: the vibrant green of the grassland and the low blue shell of the sky that seemed just inches out of reach. In Manhattan, surrounded by the buildings and lights, Addison felt tall and important. But here in the highlands, each vista revealing the curve of the planet, he felt like a dust mote clinging to the edge of the world.

"Picture it," he called over the prairie wind. "The Mongol Empire stretched across five thousand miles of steppe. The warriors were trained to fire their bows mid-gallop, while their horse's hooves were off the ground. They carried a hundred and fifty arrows in their quivers and fired twelve arrows per minute. Fifty thousand Mongols could launch enough arrows to blot out the sun." And for a while, thundering across the plains on their galloping horses, they could really picture the terrible might of the Mongol Horde.

There was no food left in the saddlebags, so they skipped lunch and slowed to a walk to rest the horses. Addison rode alongside Nobody. Molly rode beside I Don't Know, hammering her with questions. "I don't get it. Is serving the Black Darkhad your full-time job? How do you make a living at it?"

"We can hold other jobs, but we must fulfill our duty to guard the Khan's tomb. Our family swore an oath of honor."

"You didn't swear that oath," Molly pointed out. "One of your relatives did eight hundred years ago. Why should you care about Genghis Khan?"

Nobody's eyebrows shot up. "Genghis Khan conquered more land than any one person in history. He allowed religious freedom. He didn't tax the poor. He was probably the greatest general who ever lived."

Addison could not help himself. "He also butchered forty million people."

"I never said he was perfect."

Addison frowned. "He slaughtered more than a million Persians at Nishapur because they killed some diplomats."

"He had an incredibly rough childhood. What do you expect?"

"I had a rough childhood, and you don't see me burning down any villages," said Molly.

"Rough childhood? Genghis's father was murdered, his wife was kidnapped, and he was thrown into slavery—all before he was sixteen."

"Lots of people have rough childhoods," said Addison. "Genghis Khan reduced the world population by *eleven percent*."

Molly turned to I Don't Know. "The man killed more people than the Black Plague. Why devote your life to protecting his grave?"

"Because your past is who you are."

"I think your future is who you are," said Addison. "But I take your point."

••••••

At night they slept on the open plains. The prairie was infested with wolves, and their howls filled the night. Eddie was terrified, but Addison found the wolves' songs as beautiful as anything he'd ever heard. Apparently, Mr. Jacobsen enjoyed it as well, because he tilted his head back and began howling along until Dax shushed him.

After midnight, summer rain pounded the countryside in a torrential downpour. Nervous about flash foods, Dax insisted they move camp to higher ground. Nobody and I Don't Know warned that horse thieves still operate on rainy nights, so they helped split the night watch, allowing Addison to get more sleep than usual.

The next morning, everyone woke up starving. Molly practiced martial arts with I Don't Know, but they were each too hungry to perform with gusto. Fortunately, the horses found no shortage of grass, so the team mounted up and kept right on moving toward Ulaanbaatar.

By midmorning Eddie was driven to the verge of madness by the Mongolian mosquitoes. Raj advised eating garlic as a natural mosquito repellent, but nobody, not even Nobody, had any garlic.

Addison would periodically infuriate Eddie by pausing

to wonder aloud at the majestic beauty of the passing scenery. Eddie would then wonder aloud at the majestic beauty of regular meals and central air-conditioning.

"This is nothing," Nobody cut in. "The ancient Mongols were taught to sleep in the saddle and live for days without rations."

"What would they eat when they ran out of rations?" Eddie asked.

"They would eat their own dogs. Or even wolves or rats."

"What if they ran out of rats?"

"They would puncture their horse's neck vein and drink the blood as they rode."

"What if they ran out of horse blood?"

"Then the Mongol army would eat the lower-ranking soldiers."

Eddie stopped asking questions.

In the late afternoon, Ulaanbaatar rose over the next hill like a mirage. Addison found the industrial smokestacks and concrete factories jarring to the eye after so many days on the open prairie. By nightfall the hooves of their horses clattered onto the paved streets of the city.

Chapter Twenty-Eight

Ulaanbaatar

DAX LED THE GROUP down worm-rotten wood steps to an unlicensed tavern in the cellar of an abandoned coal warehouse. The tavern keeper grunted at Dax and slid warm bowls of mutton stew across the bar top. Everyone eagerly tucked in with tin spoons. Addison ordered Arnold Palmers all around. Dax ordered his strong, with extra iced tea. He needed the caffeine.

Shadowy figures whispered from the dark corners of the cellar, traded dark looks, and slipped away into the dark shadows. Addison was too exhausted to take much notice. Even the Great Dane looked dog-tired.

"Talk to me, Dax," said Addison, swiveling in his stool to face the pilot. "You've barely said a word for fifty miles."

Dax tipped back his glass, finishing his Arnold Palmer. "You were nearly killed in Karakoram. The journey's too dangerous, Addison. I don't know why you need to keep going with this."

"I don't know why you have to ask."

"I don't know why you're willing to endanger yourself."

"I don't know why muffins have wrappers," said Addison.

"It's so you can get them out of a muffin tin," said Eddie, sitting next to Addison at the bar.

"Chicken pot pie is cooked in a tin—you don't have chicken pot pie wrappers. Pies are cooked in pie tins—why aren't there pie wrappers?"

"I don't see what this has to do with the Khan's tomb," Dax cut in.

"It has everything to do with the Khan's tomb. It's an analogy!" said Addison. "I don't have to know why muffins have wrappers—I just know I'm supposed to eat the muffin!"

"What are we talking about?" asked Molly.

Dax threw his hands up in the air. "I'm done. I've been robbed, beat up, and shot at too many times for one week. I'm out."

"What do you mean?" asked Addison. "We need your help to get to the Khan's treasure."

"I'm not going to help you get yourself killed. You've been lucky so far, but you have to know when to cash in your chips and step away from the table. Besides, you don't need a pilot without a plane."

Addison drew a fresh credit card from Tony Chin's wallet. "We'll score you a new plane."

Dax shook his head. "I crashed the plane, that's on me. Keep your money. Use it to buy yourselves a flight back to the States."

"We're not leaving Mongolia without my aunt and uncle," said Addison firmly.

"What do you hope to accomplish? I don't know if you've noticed it, kid, but you're up against two of the deadliest criminal gangs in the world. And you're *twelve*."

"Thirteen."

"Same difference. You want to do your aunt and uncle a favor? Get home safely. They chose this life; you didn't."

"I thought you were their friend."

"I am. Doesn't mean they'd want me to die for them."

Addison frowned. "Dax, you're not the type of person to turn tail and run. You're better than this."

"Kid, you don't know anything about me."

Addison inched his bar stool closer to Dax. "I know from the navy badges under your bomber jacket that you've seen combat, which means you're braver than you pretend to be. I know you chew toothpicks when you're tense because you gave up smoking, and that means you've got willpower. And I know from Eddie that the Chinese character tattooed on your forearm means 'loyalty.' So yes, I do know something about you. And I know that underneath all your questionable qualities, you're actually a decent man."

Dax stared at the bottom of his empty stein and said nothing.

Addison stood up from his stool. "Poaching poachers in Africa is noble work. Brave, too. Sooner or later, Dax, you're going to have to face the fact that you're a good person." He handed the pilot one of Tony Chin's credit cards. "I'm sorry your plane crashed, but you should be thanking me."

"Why?"

"Your plane wasn't that great, anyway." Addison polished off the dregs of his Arnold Palmer and swirled the ice cubes in the pewter mug. "Get yourself a new one. Maybe that Cessna Skylark you were talking about."

"Skyhawk," said Dax.

"Same difference. As long as it has a faster liftoff." He patted Dax on the shoulder and signaled the tavern keeper. "Get him another AP, and make it a double."

Addison snagged a business card from a stack on the bar top. The tavern was called the Muddy Duck. He gestured to the phone behind the bar. "Dax, I'm going to find my aunt and uncle. And I'm going to stop the triads and the *vori* from raiding the Khan's treasure. When I need to reach you for an extraction, I'll contact this bar." He pointed to the triad credit card in Dax's hands. "There's a pretty high limit on that card. You could start over with a new plane or you could gamble the money away. I know which one I'm betting on."

He ushered his team out the door. Before Addison pushed through the beaded curtain, he took one last look at Dax. The pilot sat nursing his drink, staring at the credit card, turning it over and over in his hands.

••••••

Addison's group found lodging for the night in a ramshackle stable they shared with their horses. Nobody and I Don't Know proved adept at negotiating with the stable owner in Mongolian. Eddie was not thrilled with the accommodations, but Addison was thrilled with the price. He was running low on Tony Chin's cash, and wasn't sure when he would find another opportunity to pickpocket a triad.

He woke the next morning to the sight of Molly and I Don't Know balancing on the wooden posts of a horse stall, practicing jump kicks. He didn't know much about martial arts—absolutely nothing, in fact—but he rather thought Molly's form was improving. After several minutes of meticulously picking all the straw from his blazer, he herded the group out into the capital to search for Sir Frederick's next clue.

Ulaanbaatar was a grim, soot-stained city of concrete,

smog, and smokestacks. Addison did not find much to recommend it, although he did admire the brand-new museum of archaeology. The city was papered with colorful fliers advertising the newest exhibit. With such attention to archaeology, Addison figured the city could not be all bad.

The group breakfasted on sheep cheese, ground millet, and lamb jerky that Addison wangled from a street-side vendor. Eddie complained that it was disgusting and also that there wasn't enough of it.

Armed with his compass and *Fiddleton's Asia Atlas*, Addison set off in search of Wang Khan's twelfth-century palace. "We've found Sir Frederick's shield, his sword, and his helm. So we know the next clue is his lance, because that's the next item in the psalm he keeps repeating."

Consulting the address in his atlas, Addison circled the coordinates of the palace on his map and jigsawed his way through the chaotic grid of city streets. A bloodhound, hot on the scent, his excitement was reaching fever pitch. "Genghis Khan's father was blood brother to Wang Khan. The Great Khan stayed in this palace before attacking the Tangut people in 1226." He turned a corner and spread out both hands. "And here we are, the palace of Wang Khan!"

There are times when life wildly surpasses all expectations. There are also times when the opposite is true. Addison realized he was pointing directly at a shopping mall. He double-checked his directions.

"Is it conceivable," Molly said cautiously, "that Roland J. Fiddleton got the address wrong?"

Addison fixed her with a withering look.

"Sorry I asked."

Addison looked from the map to the shopping mall to the map to the street signs to the map to Nobody to the map and back to the shopping mall. He was still befuddled so he repeated the sequence, but it didn't help.

I Don't Know read a placard by the mall entrance, engraved in traditional Mongolian script. "This shopping mall was built last year on the former site of Wang Khan's palace."

Addison's jaw fell open like a broken tailgate.

"Can they do that?" asked Molly.

"Of course," said Addison. He felt his face growing hot with anger. "It happens all the time. The Chinese bulldozed every Ming dynasty building in Kunming to put up new chain stores. The government of Belize knocked down a hundred-foot-tall Mayan pyramid so they could run a highway through it. In Peru, developers dynamited a four-thousand-year-old pyramid to put up a luxury apartment building!"

"Well, what did they do with Wang Khan's palace?" asked Molly.

"I don't know," said I Don't Know. "I guess they paved over it."

Addison sat down in the middle of the mall parking lot, defeated. "We crossed the Gobi Desert, fought Hong Kong triads, dodged a hundred bullets, and someone paved over our palace?"

Molly sat down next to Addison. He was normally an irrepressible optimist; she was not used to seeing him like this.

"Is that it?" asked Raj. "Do we just give up, after all that?"

Addison ran his hands through his hair. He repeated the clue he had memorized.

"At the palace of Prestor John
I bested his top warrior in single combat;
He swore to keep my sign forever hanging
Among the weapons in his trophy room."

He sighed. "It made perfect sense . . . Sir Frederick's lance would best a Mongol in single combat; the Mongols didn't have weapons that long. Then Prestor John hung the lance in his weapons room, commemorating the battle. We solved the clue perfectly. We were just a year too late."

"Maybe Dax was right," said Eddie. "We should just go home."

"We still need Aunt Delia and Uncle Nigel."

Molly saw the faraway look in Addison's eye that meant gears were turning in his brain. "What are you thinking?"

Addison wasn't listening. He stood up and sat down. Then he stood up, paced in a circle, and sat down again. "Julia Aurelia Zenobia, queen of Syria and scourge of Rome!"

"Is he having another stroke?" asked Eddie.

"I know where the lance is. We've been staring at it all morning!" He laughed excitedly.

Molly watched him nervously; possibly the strain of travel was finally causing him to crack.

Addison spoke quickly. "The Mongolians wouldn't just pave over the ruins of a palace. Not when they have a perfectly good archaeology museum!" He leapt to his feet and crossed to one of the many museum ads that papered the lampposts of Ulaanbaatar. He pointed to the Mongol script. "I Don't Know, what does this sign say?"

"It's an ad for the opening of a new museum exhibit."

"What sort of exhibit?"

I Don't Know read the sign and smiled. "Relics of the Wang Khan palace."

Addison studied the collage of images on the poster. One photo in particular caught his eye. "Wang Khan's Weapons Room." He turned to show the group, jabbing his finger at the picture. And there, front and center on the museum wall, hung a knight's lance.

The team gathered around to take a closer look.

"You think so?" asked Molly.

"Absolutely." Addison's face was suddenly solemn. "Molly, do you realize what this means?"

Molly was already shaking her head. "Don't even think it, Addison."

"What? What does it mean?" asked Eddie.

"Addison, I'm warning you . . ." said Molly.

"We have no choice." Addison turned to face the group. "We're going to do the one thing Uncle Nigel told us never to do in our lives: the worst imaginable crime."

Addison Cooke took a deep breath. "We're going to rob a museum."

Chapter Twenty-Nine

The Gala

ADDISON STRODE THROUGH THE city streets, zeroing in on the museum. His team hurried after him, struggling to catch up with his pace and his logic.

"You mean like, a heist?"

"Yes, Raj. Poke your eyes back inside your head. I need your full wits."

"Can't we just copy the clue from the lance and leave?" asked Eddie.

"What, and leave the lance for Madame Feng to find?"

"Can't we just borrow the lance?" asked Molly. "Or explain the situation to the authorities?"

"Sure, we'll talk to the authorities," said Addison. "Then the Khan's secret will be out and Madame Feng has the police in her back pocket. Boris Ragar has the police in his pocket, too, if he's anything like his brother."

Addison arrived at the museum, all modern glass and steel. "Raj, what do you figure the security's like in a new building like that?"

"State of the art."

Addison agreed, but he kept his hopes up. He crossed to the plaza in front of the museum to begin his location scout and immediately smelled opportunity. He noticed policemen erecting barricades in front of the museum and closing off downtown streets. "Nobody, what's going on here?"

"The festival of Naadam begins tonight. The city celebrates all weekend. There will be wrestling and archery and a carnival. Then the big horse race will go straight through the city. This is the biggest festival of the year. The Naadam horse race is our Super Bowl."

Addison approached the front of the museum and found that security guards had closed off the main pavilion. A red carpet was being rolled up to the front doors. Catering trucks were unloading mountains of lobsters, crab, and crushed ice.

Nobody translated the sign posted on the barricaded front walkway. "The museum is closed today."

Molly shook her head. "Great. Now how do we get in?"

Nobody continued reading. "It is closed for the opening

night gala celebrating the new Wang Khan exhibit." He nodded, pleased. "They timed the opening gala with the Naadam festival to celebrate Mongolian culture."

Addison smiled. "A high society gala. It's perfect! Fewer alarms for us to bypass."

"I think high society galas require an invitation," said Eddie.

"Nonsense. They only require panache."

"So how do we get in?"

Addison sized up the museum. He was not entirely sure yet.

"I do have my lock-picking set," said Raj optimistically.

Addison counted the security guards: too many. He counted the security cameras: dozens. He imagined the motion sensors, pressure sensors, and heat sensors that could guard a museum of this immense size. "Well, it's like they say. Go big, or go home."

"We can't go home, Addison," Molly said grimly. "Not yet."

"Then I guess we have to go big."

......

Addison's first order of business was a trip to the bank. They were going to need to buy a few supplies if they wanted to pull off a successful heist. He pulled out Tony Chin's last two credit cards and kissed them for good luck.

"We're pretty lucky the triads haven't canceled these credit cards yet," said Molly.

"They're gangsters, Mo. They don't have the best accountants."

Addison strutted out of the bank a few minutes later, his pockets bulging with cash. "Money here is called tögrögs," he explained, a fresh spring in his step. "The exchange rate is excellent. I asked the bank to change five hundred dollars and now I'm a millionaire in tögrögs!"

"Thank the gods," said Eddie. "We can finally get some real food!"

"Soon, Eddie. First, we have a museum desperately in need of a robbing. We require provisions."

"What sort of equipment are you thinking?" asked Raj, rubbing his hands together with anticipation. "Rappelling ropes? Grappling hooks? Glass cutters? Mirrors to redirect laser trip wires?"

Addison shook his head. "Our first stop is that shopping mall. We need decent attire." He sized up the Black Darkhads' sword sheaths and Raj's camouflage pants. "No one's going to let you into a formal gala dressed like two assassins and a commando."

••••••

The group was significantly spruced up when they arrived back at the museum that night. Addison was pleased that it had taken only a matter of hours to update the Black Darkhads' wardrobe by eight hundred years. Nobody wore a sharp, black suit with a black tie and a black pocket square. I Don't Know sizzled in a black dress, with all of the hay and road dust brushed out of her hair. When Addison saw her with her hair up for the first time, he stared for so long that Molly swatted him on the back of the head.

They joined the line of partygoers heading toward the gala. Addison fussed over Raj and Eddie's unbuttoned shirt cuffs and uncombed hair. "You are disheveled and I need you sheveled!" It amazed him how Eddie could memorize an entire Beethoven sonata and still have no idea how to tie a Windsor knot.

Limousines pulling up to the red carpet disgorged all the glitterati of Mongolia. The mayor of Ulaanbaatar posed for photos with TV actors, CEOs, and foreign dignitaries. Addison smoothed his hair, buttoned his blazer, and strolled up the red carpet, beckoning his crew to follow.

"Addison, this party's filled with important people," Eddie whispered. He eyed the guards at the museum entrance who were double-checking every guest's name against a list. "I bet it's a crime to go in there."

Addison beamed for the flashing cameras. "Eddie, it'd be a crime not to."

Eddie tugged at Addison's sleeve, but Addison did not

slow his casual pace along the carpet. He winked and waved at local celebrities and spoke to Eddie out of the side of his mouth. "How much food have you eaten in the past week?"

"Barely anything."

"And do you know what they have inside, Eddie?"

"Food?"

"No, something better than food."

"What," asked Eddie, "is better than food?"

"*Free* food."

They drew closer to the security guards checking names at the entrance. Eddie was sweating with nervousness. His blazer was two hours old and already needed a trip to the cleaners. "How are you going to talk us inside, Addison?"

"I'm not. You are."

"Me?"

"I'm counting on you, Eddie."

Eddie shook his head desperately. "No, absolutely not."

"Your mouth is telling me no. But your stomach, Eddie, your stomach is saying yes."

"But Addison . . ."

But Addison was already at the door. The security guard held up his guest list and eyed them suspiciously. He addressed them in English. "Your names?"

"Our names?" Addison pointed at Eddie indignantly. "Do you know who zis is?" For no reason Eddie could fathom, Addison was speaking in an exaggerated French accent. "Zis is zee prime minister's son!"

The security guard looked at Eddie Chang, not believing it for a second. He barked at Eddie in Mongolian.

Eddie turned to Addison desperately. His pleading facial expression served up a combo platter of fear, anger, and bewilderment.

Addison sighed with exasperation and turned to the security guard. "He is zee *Chinese* prime minister's son." China did not technically have a prime minister, but the guard did not know that, and neither did Eddie.

The guard rattled a string of questions at Eddie in Mandarin Chinese, and to Addison's pleasure, Eddie fired right back. Eddie took on a tone of righteous indignation, puffing up his chest and shaking his fist at the guard.

The security guard bowed to Eddie in apology. He returned his unibrowed gaze to Addison. "All right, if he's the prime minister's son, who are you?"

"I," said Addison, drawing himself up, "am zee French ambassador's son. Zis is my sister, Moliere."

"Moliere?"

"*Oui,*" said Molly.

"These are our Mongolian interpreters." Addison gestured to Nobody and I Don't Know.

"And who are you?" asked the guard, pointing at Raj.

"I'm Raj," said Raj.

This seemed good enough for the guard. He unclipped the velvet rope, and Addison's team strode into the black tie gala.

"Addison," said I Don't Know, squeezing his arm nervously in one of her silk-gloved hands, "you are one of the most unusual people I've ever met."

"Thank you," said Addison, his cheeks flushed with color.

The party was in the large entrance foyer to the museum. Floor-to-ceiling glass and steel opened the atrium to the stars overhead. Indoor trees grew to thirty feet. One wall was hung with oversize photos of the annual Naadam horse race. Women in opulent dresses clinked champagne glasses by an elegant fountain. High society gentlemen in sharp suits eyed priceless archaeological artifacts displayed on pedestals. Addison even spotted the prime minister of Mongolia, with a boy who Addison figured was the prime minister's actual son.

Eddie beelined to the buffet and scoped out the food like a cat burglar in a jewelry store. "Kebabs, just like the ones at Restaurant Anatolia! And Addison, you were right. This is a *free* buffet!"

"That's my favorite kind of buffet." Addison stabbed a shrimp with a toothpick and dipped it in some cocktail sauce. His voice quavered as he savored the flavor. "Free is the best spice."

Eddie heaped a plate with hors d'oeuvres, appetizers, and amuse-bouches, and began shoveling them all into his mouth like an engineer piling coal into a steam engine. He did not find the Ulaanbaatar food exquisite. He thought the fish tasted like chicken and the chicken tasted like fish, but as long as he was getting both chicken and fish, he didn't much mind the order in which the flavors arrived.

"Eddie, don't eat so much—you'll kill yourself," said Molly.

"I want to die doing what I love."

Addison decided it was time for reconnaissance. He found a museum directory on a dais by the fountain and studied the map. "Excellent. Wang Khan's Weapons Room display is on the second floor."

"There's just one problem," Molly said, pointing. The grand staircase was sealed off by a velvet rope. A quick glance at the second-floor balcony revealed a locked door. The rest of the museum was off-limits for the night. Only the downstairs was open for the party.

Raj assessed the situation. "We could beat up a guard and take his keys?"

Addison shook his head. "Too violent. It lacks finesse."

"We don't have to knock the guard out, we could just tie him up. I have twenty feet of new climbing rope wrapped around my torso." Raj held open his blazer to show everyone.

"No wonder your cummerbund keeps slipping," said Addison, buttoning Raj's jacket. "I appreciate your enthusiasm, Raj, but I don't think we can beat up and hog-tie a guard without changing the mood of this party."

Nobody eyed the branches of a tall indoor poplar tree that leaned close to the lip of the second-floor walkway. "If I climb up to that balcony, I can open the security door from inside. Then I let you all in."

"How are you going to climb up there without everybody watching?" Molly asked.

Addison smiled. "With a distraction." He straightened his pocket square, adjusted his necktie a micron, and headed for the bandstand.

The evening entertainment was a set of ancient Mongol monks in even older robes engaging in *Khöömei* throat singing. Addison wanted to fully appreciate Mongolian culture, but to his ears, throat singing sounded like the groaning of dying bullfrogs. Bullfrogs who were probably dying from having to listen to throat singing. Addison looked out at the stilted party and felt the need to liven things up. "Eddie," he called. "Your fingers itching for some piano practice?"

"Always!" said Eddie, looking up from the buffet table he had just ravaged.

Addison pointed to the baby grand on the stage. "Tickle those ivories and give me a bouncy C."

"What's a bouncy C?"

"Okay, give me a fox-trot swing in the key of G."

"Can you be more specific? How about an actual song?"

"Okay, fine. How about that old evergreen, 'Keep Your Eyes on Me,' by Ira Frankfurt."

Eddie nodded.

"And Eddie?"

"Yeah?"

Addison straightened his tie pin so it glittered in the stage lights. "Make it classy."

Chapter Thirty

The Heist

EDDIE CLIMBED UP ONTO the stage, rolled up his shirt cuffs, and took a seat at the baby grand. A flashy arpeggio, and the audience was paying attention.

Addison slipped the throat singers a ten and told them to take five. He grabbed the microphone and suddenly felt at home in the world. "Eddie Chang on the black and whites, ladies and gentlemen." There was a smattering of applause as Eddie lathered a bit of schmaltz into the intro of the jazz standard. Addison leaned over the mike and crooned. He was not a gifted singer, but he could work a crowd like da Vinci worked a paintbrush. A few winks and finger guns at the audience, and he was off and running.

"Keep your eyes on me
I realize there are other guys
And some of them might mesmerize
But darling keep your eyes on me . . ."

Addison tracked Nobody at the back of the room. The tall boy, in suit and tails, had climbed onto a buffet table and was slowly grappling his way up the poplar tree. Addison knew he had to hold the crowd riveted, and that was just fine by him. A few security guards roamed the room, but so far they were enjoying this impromptu performance.

"Who is that singer?" Addison heard the prime minister say from the front row.

"That is the French ambassador's son," a woman replied. "And his piano player is the son of the prime minister of China."

"What a rare treat!"

Addison threw in a bit of soft shoe while Eddie took a solo. A quick spin, some jazz hands, some spirit fingers, and a "Shuffle Off to Buffalo."

Nobody was now halfway up the tree, in full view of anyone in the crowd who might happen to look over their shoulders.

Addison needed to keep the whole room laser focused on the stage. He threw all the topspin he could into the next verse.

"Keep your eyes on me
Lots of guys may tantalize
And hypnotize with tender sighs
But darling keep your eyes on me"

Nobody reached the lip of the high balcony and pulled himself up. He teetered for a moment, on the brink of falling, but somehow willed himself over the parapet. Addison breathed a sigh of relief into the microphone, and then sold it to the crowd as a musical flourish. They ate it up.

Eddie paid off the big finish with a heart-stopping glissando up and down the ivories. Addison didn't love a show-off, but he had to admire Eddie's skill. The audience certainly did, roaring their approval. Addison basked in the applause and was genuinely reluctant to leave the stage, ignoring the shouts for an encore. The audience was visibly angry when the throat singers returned to the stage to resume groaning.

Addison and Eddie worked the crowd as they carved a path to the back of the atrium. They even shook hands with the prime minister of Mongolia. At last, already exhausted by their newfound celebrity, they ducked behind a museum display. Molly tugged at Addison's sleeve and led them under the velvet rope and up the grand staircase. As long as they crouched low, they were protected from view by the elaborate stone balustrade. They joined Raj and I Don't Know at the second-story landing.

"What did you do with the money?" I Don't Know whispered to Addison.

"What money?"

"The money your parents gave you for singing lessons."

Addison frowned.

I Don't Know grinned.

"Moment of truth," said Raj. "We'll find out if the door is alarmed." He gave a thumbs-up to Nobody through the glass door.

Nobody pushed open the security door, and nothing made a sound. Addison's team piled into the dark second floor of the museum.

••••••

The sounds of the party faded away behind them. The team crept silently down the long corridor, past galleries of medieval Mongol art, Buddhist frescos, and Chinese pottery. Unfolding a museum map, Addison led the way to Wang Khan's Weapons Room. Raj, fearful of triggering security alarms, held out his arms to prevent anyone from setting foot in the gallery.

A great medieval lance hung on the far wall of the exhibit, just as in the museum posters. Addison smiled.

"That must be the lance of Sir Frederick. Mongols didn't use lances like that—only Europeans."

Raj studied the way the great spear was mounted on the wall. "We're definitely going to trip some kind of alarm when we take it. Motion sensors, at least."

Addison had anticipated this. "We'll send two decoys to opposite sides of the museum. If we trip an alarm here, the decoys both trip alarms on the far sides of the museum. That will split the security guards into three groups and make it easier for us to escape."

Raj nodded. It seemed sensible enough.

"Who can take the east wing?" asked Addison.

"I Don't Know."

"Perfect. And who can cover the west wing?"

"Nobody."

"Excellent." Addison knew he needed to cover his back trail. "Eddie, you guard the balcony door."

"Why me?"

"The guards think you're the prime minister's son. If they find you, they're not going to give you a hard time. Just yell at them in Chinese."

Eddie nodded nervously. "I can do that."

"Whatever you do, do *not* leave your post. If you see triads, *vori*, or security guards—anything—give us a signal."

"How about I whistle a bar of Beethoven's *Appassionata* Sonata?"

"Okay, fine," said Addison. "And if I hear a bar of any other sonata, I'll know it's some other eighth grader impersonating you."

Eddie, Nobody, and I Don't Know trotted off to their positions. Addison's group turned to the weapons room.

Raj dropped to his knees, removed a can from his blazer pocket, and spritzed a thick cloud of hairspray a few inches above the floor. "This will show if there are hidden laser sensors."

Addison coughed, waited for the cloud to clear, and strolled right into the gallery.

Molly followed.

"Wait! There could be heat sensors! Or infrared!" Raj whispered.

"It's an archaeology museum, not a CIA bunker," said Addison calmly. "Look, I'm counting on the chance that we might set off an alarm or two. We just need to do this quickly and have a good escape planned."

"Did you plan a good escape?" asked Molly.

"I do my best planning at the last second."

Molly frowned at this.

"I could find a utility closet and shut off all the circuit breakers in the museum," Raj volunteered. "When the power goes out, we'll have an easier time making our escape."

Addison thought this sounded like overkill, and possibly dangerous. But Raj was quivering with excitement.

Addison nodded his assent, and Raj somersaulted out of the gallery.

Addison took a deep breath and smoothed his hair, settling his nerves. It was now down to him and Molly to pull off this heist. They crossed the marble tiles of the gallery and stood beneath the giant lance. Ten feet long, tapered to a hard point, and scarred by a dozen battles. Two metal brackets cradled it to the wall.

He leaned close to the lance and examined the wall brackets. "Pressure sensors," he declared. The devices were very simple. Once the lance was lifted from each cradle, a spring would lift and sound an alarm.

Molly's fingers were smaller than Addison's. She plucked the black hair tie from her ponytail and pinched down one bracket cradle with a thumb and forefinger. A single drop of sweat beaded on her forehead and rolled down her face, but she ignored it. Addison carefully took her hair tie and double-looped it to clamp down the spring action of the bracket.

"Have any more of those?" he whispered, hardly daring to breath.

Molly plucked a spare hair tie from the collection she kept on her wrist.

Addison repeated the procedure on the second wall clamp. Satisfied, he nodded to Molly and took a deep breath. "Here goes."

Together, very gently, they lifted the great lance off the wall mount. It was like lifting a baby from its crib without trying to wake it. No alarms sounded.

"This might actually work," Addison whispered.

They carefully set the old, battered lance on the floor. Addison found French words scratched into the iron shaft. "We did it, Mo. This is the lance of Sir Frederick!"

Before he could celebrate, a Russian voice spoke up behind him.

"Well done. Now hand it over."

Addison turned and saw the gloating face of Boris Ragar. As was his habit, Boris was blocking any possible retreat. Addison checked his memory bank and was pretty sure he hadn't heard any whistled refrains from the *Appassionata* Sonata, or any other Beethoven sonata, for that matter. He glared at Boris. "What did you do to Eddie?"

"Who?"

"Our lookout."

"I didn't see any lookout."

"Did you come up the main staircase from the atrium?"

"I did."

"And you didn't see a tall, skinny kid with black hair and a raging metabolism?"

"Nope."

"Huh."

"Can we return to the issue at hand?"

"Well, actually I'm a bit concerned about Eddie."

"Hand over the lance, Cooke!"

"Right. About that," said Addison, who had no interest in turning over the lance. His plan was to keep stalling until he could think up a good diversion. "The thing is . . ."

At that moment, an earsplitting blast rocked the museum.

Chapter Thirty-One

The Lance of Sir Frederick

ALARMS BLARED THROUGHOUT THE museum. Screams erupted from the gala on the first floor. Boris Ragar, perhaps suspecting an air raid, dove to the ground and covered his head.

There are times, Addison reflected, when life wildly surpasses all expectations. And times when the opposite is true. This was one of the former. Addison had no idea what caused the deafening blast that rattled the teeth in his gums. He didn't much care.

Addison and Molly, both clutching the lance like firemen with a tall ladder, legged it for the exit. They nearly collided with Raj in the hallway. His hair looked a little darker than usual, and his eyes a little wilder. His clothes looked a bit singed, and he smelled like an egg that'd been forgotten on the fryer. He was trailing smoke.

"Raj, what happened?"

"It wasn't my fault!" Raj said defensively. "I couldn't find the utility closet to shut off the power, so I thought I would just cause a short circuit."

Addison, to his horror, saw flames licking from the balcony. He shouted over the din of fire alarms. "Raj, what did you do!"

"I tore out all the electrical wires in the radiator. I destroyed the heating system. Sure, it seems like a bad idea now, but at the time—"

"Never mind," said Molly, checking nervously over her shoulder. She pulled her half of the lance toward the nearest exit sign. "We've got to run!"

"No," said Addison, jerking his half of the lance and stopping Molly in her tracks. "We can't have a fire in a museum. We have to stop it!"

Nobody and I Don't Know dashed in from an opposite hallway. "We heard your alarm and set off our own alarms," said the Mongolian girl.

Addison realized that if firefighters arrived, they wouldn't know which direction to find the fire. He began to wonder if perhaps he should have spent more time formulating an actual plan. His thoughts were interrupted by the unwelcome sight of Boris Ragar bounding toward them like a bull in a cape shop. "Molly, Nobody, and I Don't Know—you guys know how to fight. Can you slow down Boris?"

The Black Darkhad were all business. They leapt into Boris's path and assumed fighting stances. Boris smiled. It was Molly who sailed in from the side and scored a punishing kick to Boris's shin.

Addison spotted Eddie rushing toward them, his cheeks bulging with chicken kebab. "Eddie, you're okay!" Addison did not wait for any explanation. He struggled awkwardly with the heavy lance. "Help me with this thing!"

Eddie jumped to his aid, and together they hobbled toward the balcony exit. Addison cradled his half of the lance in one arm while the other fished for his pocket notebook and pencil to trace Sir Frederick's clue.

"What do I do?" asked Raj, pivoting in a confused circle.

"You're going to put out that fire you started!" Addison reached the balcony and saw it in flames. Reaching the exit door without getting singed was going to be the pig's whistle.

Raj yanked a fire hose from the wall box in the hallway and cranked the spigot. The massive pressure of the hose jerked him off his feet. He clung to the hose like a bull rider, blasting jets of water in all directions except toward the fire.

Black-tie guests in the gala below screamed as they were drenched under the sudden deluge. Raj's fire hose knocked over trash cans and blew the exit signs off of walls.

Addison realized Raj was causing far more damage than he was helping. "Raj, remind me to never allow you in a museum again!"

"It's not my fault!" Raj yelled, holding on to the flailing hose for dear life.

Addison and Eddie dropped the lance as carefully as they could and dove to capture Raj's hose. Russian *vori* were pounding up the main staircase. Addison directed the fire hose, blasting the Russians back down the stairs before turning the stream to douse the flames. Revelers in the gala below were showered by overhead sprinklers and occasional jets of freezing water from the fire hose.

Molly and the Black Darkhad had their hands and feet full fighting Boris. He seemed incapable of experiencing pain; it was like picking a fight with a Viking berserker.

Boris focused all his attention on Molly. "This is for what you did to my brother!" He swung hard at Molly, who barely rolled out of the way in time.

I Don't Know could kick only so high in her black dress and heels. But Nobody kicked and punched at Boris as hard as he could. He might as well have been swatting a rolled-up newspaper at a bull rhinoceros. Each time

Boris bellowed and charged, they could only scramble out of the way.

"Who is this guy?" Nobody asked.

"Russian Mafia," Molly gasped. "He is not fond of us."

"What did you do to his brother?"

"We kind of locked him up in a room."

"That doesn't sound so bad. You did the same thing to us."

"Well, the room filled with sand and suffocated him."

"I see."

"To be fair," said Molly, "he was trying to kill us."

Molly ducked a punch from Boris that shattered the drywall an inch above her head. As she wiped Sheetrock dust from her eyes, she realized two things. One: she was not going to win this fight. And two: she didn't need to. All she needed was to lure Boris far from the lance, giving Addison a chance to escape. She decided to make like a wild goose and lead Boris on an epic chase.

Molly called to the Darkhad, "It's me he wants—he hates Cookes!" She fled across the balcony and downstairs into the center of the party. Boris barreled after her. To her annoyance, she realized she couldn't maneuver in the panicked crowd. Ragar's *vori* surrounded her, gripping her arms in their fists. Boris closed in, rolling up his sleeves.

From the balcony, Raj saw Molly being dragged across the atrium. He cupped his hands to his mouth and hollered,

"Hang on, Molly!" He estimated the length of the fire hose and the distance to the floor and figured the hose would stop him before the floor did. He leapt up onto the balcony railing and thundered his war cry: "Bhaaaaaandari!!!"

Gripping the hose, pirate-style, Raj leapt before Addison and Eddie could intervene. The pressurized hose snaked over the balcony, and to Raj's credit, it may have slowed his fall a tiny bit. It didn't really matter. Raj was aiming for the great fountain, and he nailed it. Addison gave the jump a perfect ten. The splash drenched tuxedo-clad onlookers, the press, and the prime minister of Mongolia. The mayor, diving for cover, hit the corner of a buffet table, flipping it over. Koi from the fountain flopped around in a puddle of shrimp cocktail sauce, getting their first taste of freedom, and horseradish.

Boris's men were so astonished by Raj's leap, they momentarily forgot about Molly. She slipped their grasp, ducked through the legs of a diplomat's wife, and managed to fish Raj out of the fish fountain.

Addison and Eddie jogged down the balcony steps, cradling the colossal lance. It jostled in Addison's arms as he frantically attempted to trace the French clue into his notebook. It was not his best work. He and Eddie galloped through the gala with the ungainly ten-foot object, smashing and knocking over flower vases and the occasional politician. Every time they turned to adjust course, high society guests were forced to duck or be walloped. The lance was knocking down more opponents in one night than in Sir Frederick's entire jousting career.

"Eddie," said Addison, searching for a clear path to the front door. "You had one job: don't leave your post."

"That's true."

"And yet, what did you do?"

"I left my post."

"The first moment you had the chance."

"Well, it's like this," said Eddie, lifting his end of the lance to avoid clotheslining a fleeing throat singer. "When I get nervous, I get hungry. I didn't want to leave my post. I didn't set out to leave my post."

"And yet?"

"There I was, looking at the kebabs on the buffet table. And I thought, *Eddie, don't go to the buffet table for a kebab.* And I said to myself, *I know, I'll go to the buffet table for a kebab.* And here we are."

"Eddie, the next time we rob a museum, I will tell you to *leave* your post at all costs. Then you will almost certainly fail to leave your post."

"That is a good idea. So what you're really saying is, it's your fault."

"Yes," sighed Addison, "I suppose it is."

They were almost at the door, excruciatingly close to their freedom, when Boris stepped in the way. He grabbed the heavy lance with one hand and Addison with the other. He gripped Addison by the tie and proceeded to shake him like a paint mixer.

Addison was not too proud to ask for help when he needed it. He reverted to his French accent. "Help! Zis monster is attacking me!"

A museum security guard clutched Boris's arm. "Don't hurt this boy! He's the ambassador's son!"

Boris punched the security guard with the closed fist that held the lance. The security guard collapsed, knocking Eddie off his feet in a chain reaction.

"*Sacré bleu!*" said Addison.

A second security guard rushed to the scene, astonished. "Are you crazy? His father's the prime minister of China!"

Boris punched out that guard, too. Addison seized the opportunity to try one of the roundhouse kicks he'd seen Molly practice a hundred times. It was harder than he imagined and accomplished precious little besides upsetting Boris's rather delicate sensibilities. Addison decided that violence was not always the answer. The Russian gripped him by the throat. "You must want to get hurt bad."

"You mean bad*ly*," Addison corrected.

Boris stared at him blankly.

"It's an adverb," Addison added helpfully. "It modifies a verb or adjective."

The *vor* punched Addison squarely in the stomach. "You must be real stupid."

Addison groaned and doubled over. "*Really* stupid."

Boris wrapped one giant paw around the back of Addison's neck and pulled him close. "Remember the prophecy."

"I don't know the prophecy! Nobody's bothered to tell it to me!" said Addison in frustration.

Nobody overheard this, working his way through the crowd, and was momentarily confused.

"The last Templar gets the prize," said Boris. He hefted the lance in his paw and strode out of the gala, followed by his men. Addison, gasping for breath, watched him go. There was nothing he could do.

······

The Ulaanbaatar fire brigade rushed into the gala carrying ladders. They were immediately followed by the Ulaanbaatar police, who arrived just in time to completely fail to stop Boris. The police assessed the chaos of the party with slack-jawed amazement. They had no experience with this sort of situation and had no idea whom to arrest. They had a rapid conversation in Mongolian with various gala guests.

Addison couldn't quite follow the thread, but one by one he noticed guests pointing at him, Eddie, Molly, and especially Raj. He also noticed Nobody and I Don't Know slowly slinking out of the gala, turning tail, and running.

Before Addison could do the same, police tackled him to the ground, yanking his arms behind his back. "Zis is an outrage," said Addison in his questionable French accent. "Zis is an act of war against zee great nation of France!"

"You are under arrest for bombing this museum," said the police lieutenant. "We will take this up with the French embassy."

Addison had no interest in provoking a Mongolian-French international conflict; he just wanted to talk his way out of his handcuffs. Molly, Eddie, and Raj were hand-cuffed as well.

"This can't get any worse," said Eddie.

Madame Feng stepped into the gala, followed by her coterie of guards.

Addison groaned like a throat singer.

"Let them go," she announced.

Addison pricked up his ears.

"Impossible," said the police lieutenant. "These animals nearly destroyed the museum."

"Arrest them and book them if you must. I shall make their bail. In fact," Madame Feng said, pulling out her checkbook, "why don't we just cut out the middleman?" She signed a personal check and handed it to the portly museum director.

The museum director was a short-statured man with a high-stature job. He glared at Madame Feng indignantly before deigning to read the check. He saw a one followed by so many zeroes, he nearly fainted. The museum director had his scruples, but he also had his price.

"Do you wish to press charges against these kids?" asked the police lieutenant.

The museum director picked the nearest cocktail glass off the buffet table and downed it. He chased it with a second glass before finally finding his voice. "The museum does not wish to pursue charges against these children," he said at last.

The police lieutenant sighed, defeated. And he was so close to making his quota this month.

"Excellent," said Madame Feng. "The children are coming with me."

Addison could not help but admire Madame Feng's efficiency. Within seconds his handcuffs were gone and he found his wrists clamped in Hu's viselike grip. "I want to thank everyone for a lovely party," said Addison, before he was hauled out of the gala.

He still couldn't see Madame Feng's angle. Addison doubted she had suddenly become a Good Samaritan. She enlightened him as her triads marched his team toward her waiting passenger van. "The Russians have the lance, but I know you saw it first. I know the next clue is rattling around in that little Cooke brain of yours. And you are going to give it to me."

"I'm afraid I have no idea what you're talking about, Madame Feng," said Addison smoothly. "My friends and I were just here to enjoy the throat singing."

"We'll see whose throat sings last." Madame Feng pivoted on her high heel and climbed into the front of the van.

Addison gave her last comeback a B-minus at best, but she did manage to get the last word in. Hu duct-taped Addison's wrists together and moved on to Molly.

"I don't want to say I told you so," said Molly, "but we probably should have come up with a stronger plan."

Addison watched Hu duct-tape Raj and Eddie as well. "Molly, everything is working out perfectly. They're taking us to wherever they're holding Aunt D and Uncle N."

"Fantastic. We'll get to share a cell with them," said Molly.

"Molly, relax. Sooner or later you're going to realize that I have everything under control." The guards tossed Addison into the back of the van and slammed the doors. The van sped off into the dark streets of Ulaanbaatar.

Chapter Thirty-Two

The Templar
Medallion

THE VAN RUMBLED DEEPER into downtown, passed through a security gate, and entered the private garage of an enormous mansion. Hu left Addison's team locked in the back of the van for an hour before finally releasing them. He hustled across the palace grounds. Addison admired the beautiful sloping eaves of the buildings and the tastefully manicured gardens that hemmed the perimeter wall. He realized this was an old estate and that the modern city had simply grown up around it.

Hu guided the group through the palace foyer and into a magnificent great room where Madame Feng reclined on a couch and sipped tea by a roaring fire. Addison could not imagine the need for a roaring fire in the middle of July, but then, he could not really imagine the need for living in a palace either. Still, the room was magnificent, with Manchurian weaponry, Mongolian tapestries, and Ming dynasty vases.

"I love your home," said Addison, with genuine feeling.

"Thank you." Madame Feng sipped her oolong. "I love Mongolia and keep this as my summer home. My family traces its lineage all the way back to Genghis Khan, so I feel a great affinity for this country. Besides, I have many business interests in Ulaanbaatar."

"You mean with the triads? I've read there are plenty of gangs operating in this city. Are you familiar with Babatunde Okonjo's *Mission: Survival*?"

Madame Feng fixed Addison with a stare so cold, it risked freezing her steaming tea. "In the morning, I am taking your aunt and uncle north. The Russians have the lance, and my spies are trailing them." She leaned forward on her sofa, addressing Addison like a close friend. "Addison, neither one of us wants to see Boris get his hands on the Khan's treasure. If there is anything you can tell me about Sir Frederick's latest clue, you must tell me now."

"I'm sorry," said Addison, who would sooner remove his own appendix with a rusted spoon than share information with Madame Feng. "We don't know anything."

Madame Feng's feline eyes narrowed. "Can I trust you to tell me the truth?"

"Absolutely." Addison gave her a "trust me" grin that would make a used-car salesman blush.

Madame Feng held her teacup out for a servant to refill. The fire crackled and roared as a log collapsed in a spray of sparks. "Genghis Khan trusted Inalchuq, one of the governors of Persia. He sent his diplomats to visit the country with a caravan of gifts. Inalchuq executed the entire caravan."

Addison was not entirely sure where Madame Feng was going with this, but he loved a good story.

She sipped her tea and continued. "Genghis Khan did not suffer fools gladly. He traveled to Persia at the head of his army. He burned every city to the ground. When he reached Nishapur, he slaughtered two million Persians in a single day. His warriors built pyramids out of the skulls and laid them where the cities once stood. When Genghis finally captured Inalchuq, he murdered him by pouring molten silver into his eyes and ears."

It was not the best story Addison had ever heard, but he sensed Madame Feng was winding up to her point.

She carefully set her antique teacup down in its saucer and rose to her feet. "This palace contains a dungeon. You will stay there until you tell me everything you know about Sir Frederick's clue. If you do not talk by tomorrow morning, I am going to pour molten silver down your lying throats."

Addison gulped with his lying throat.

Molly used hers to speak. "You talk about trust. But you lied to Eustace and lied to my aunt and uncle. You kidnapped them, and they didn't do anything to you. Madame Feng, you are shifty, underhanded, and two-faced."

Madame Feng's eyes glittered. "You say that like it's a bad thing."

"You know, I think you really are related to Genghis Khan."

"Thank you."

"Wasn't a compliment," said Molly.

Addison wasn't sure whether Molly should be provoking their captor. Perhaps Madame Feng had the fire roaring in case she felt a hankering to start melting down some silver right away. He took a step forward. "Madame Feng, I will consider your request. But first I must speak to my aunt and uncle."

Molly was shocked. "Don't tell her anything, Addison!"

Addison kept his gaze locked on Madame Feng.

She smiled, showing her perfect teeth. "I see you do have information to share after all. Very well, Addison. You may spend a few minutes with one of them, but only one."

······

To Addison's pleasure, it was Tony Chin who walked him down to the dungeon. They followed winding stone passages through the kitchen and down into a cellar. Once out of the earshot of Madame Feng, Addison peppered Tony with questions. "Is she really going to torture us, Tony?"

"Probably," Tony admitted. "She'll do whatever it takes to find the Khan's tomb."

"Do we have any chance of getting out of here?"

"Not really. I'm sorry, Addison."

"Well," said Addison, feeling the need to get one up on Tony, "we've been using your credit card."

"Of course you have. How do you think we tracked you to Ulaanbaatar? You used a credit card three blocks from the museum."

Addison frowned. Now he understood how the triads had found him. "Why do you help her?"

"When I was a teenager, I swore an oath to the triads. Madame Feng controls a branch of our group. She's very powerful."

"I read about the triads. Hundreds of years ago, before the triads were criminals, they were freedom fighters. They wanted to overthrow the Qing dynasty. Do you remember the oaths you took?"

"Of course. I vowed loyalty, honor, justice, fealty, and respect."

"Tell me," said Addison, "did you vow to rob and beat up children? Is that in your code of honor?"

Tony hesitated. He ducked through a cellar door and into the low stone hallway that led to the dungeon cells. "You started it when you took my wallet."

"You started it when you took my aunt and uncle."

Tony lit a candle, melted some wax with the match, and stuck it in a wall sconce carved into the rock. He guided Addison into an empty cell and locked the iron grill shut. He looked at him through the bars. "You saved my life at the Thousand Buddha Caves. Why?"

In the dim light, Addison could see that Tony's face was still swollen with bruises from his tangle with the Russians. "I live by a code as well."

Tony nodded. "I will give you a minute alone with your uncle." He reached into his pocket and handed Addison his butterfly knife. "Thank you for saving my life." He turned away, leaving Addison in the flickering candlelight of the dungeon.

· · · · · ·

"Is that you, Addison?" came a familiar voice from the neighboring cell.

"Uncle Nigel!" Addison reached out through the bars and

clasped his uncle's unseen hand. He held it for a minute. He couldn't help but notice how frail and tired his uncle sounded. "Is Aunt Delia all right?"

"She's holding up. They're keeping us in separate cells to break our morale. How are you? How is Molly? Eddie and Raj?"

"Everyone's fine. Eddie's even getting in some good piano practice. I negotiated to see you because I need your help. We have to work quickly—I don't know how much time Madame Feng will give us together." Addison used his pencil to bookmark a page in his notebook. He passed both around the bars to his uncle. "It's Sir Frederick's next clue. I need your help with the French."

"You found the lance of Sir Frederick?" cried Uncle Nigel.

"Oh yes." Addison was careful not to mention anything about setting fire to a museum.

"So Sir Frederick left his lance in Ulaanbaatar, his helm in Karakoram, his sword in Kashgar, and his shield in Samarkand . . ." Uncle Nigel laughed. "It's a good thing he didn't make it all the way back to Europe, he'd have arrived naked." He uncrinkled the notebook page and held it out to the candlelight. He translated aloud for Addison.

> *"'Praise be to the Lord, my Rock,*
> *who trains my hands for war,*

my fingers for battle.
God is my shield, my sword, my helm, and my lance.'"

"I've got that part," said Addison.

"Right. But since you've found the lance, that makes this Sir Frederick's final clue! My Old French is not as strong as Delia's, but I shall do my best." He bent his gaze to the notebook.

"'In the land no living Mongol may pass, I climbed the eagle cliff.
I swam beneath a river, and crawled under a
mountain to the city of the dead.
Know the Khan to open the tomb; know thyself to escape.'"

Uncle Nigel scratched away in the dark, translating the clue into Addison's notebook. He slid the notebook and pencil back through the iron bars.

Addison tucked them inside his blazer pocket. It was not an easy feat, as his wrists were still duct-taped together.

"I don't know if we will make it out of here," said Uncle Nigel's voice in the darkness.

"Madame Feng told me she's taking you and Aunt Delia north tomorrow."

"I don't think she intends to let us survive. We know far too much about her and her crimes." Uncle Nigel took a long sigh. "Oh, Addison. There is so much I need to tell you."

"You mean about the prophecy?"

"Yes. There is a prophecy."

"And it involves killing Cookes?"

"It does," said Uncle Nigel. "And there is a very dangerous man named Malazar who believes this prophecy. Some call him the Shadow, because few people have ever seen his face. He will stop at nothing. I did not want to put your aunt Delia at risk. You remember, of course, our separation this past year?"

Addison nodded. "A trial separation. But you're back together now."

"We are." Uncle Nigel sighed again in the darkness. "Do you understand now why I tried to separate from Aunt Delia? Men are trying to kill off our family to fulfill the prophecy. I thought if I could leave Delia, it would save her life. And maybe yours as well."

Addison's thoughts were swimming. "Drowning" might be the better word.

Uncle Nigel continued. "I wasn't separating from your aunt because I don't like her. I was doing it because I love her!"

Addison swallowed hard but could not rid himself of the lump swelling in his throat. It tugged at the corners of his cheeks, it pulled his lips into a stiff frown, and it wetted his eyes.

Uncle Nigel spoke faster. "You and Molly are in grave

danger—you always have been. If anything ever happens to me—"

"No," said Addison. "You and Aunt Delia are going to be fine!"

"If anything ever happens to me," Uncle Nigel continued, "you and Molly must find your uncle Jasper in England. He will know how to keep you safe."

Addison shook his head. "It's because of archaeology, isn't it? This prophecy—it involves some secret from the past. It's this obsession with the past that puts us in these situations. If we didn't care about dusty old relics, we'd be home, safe in New York."

"That's not what you really want, is it, Addison? To give up on the past?"

"I don't want to lose you and Aunt Delia like I lost my mom and dad! I wish we were a family of stockbrokers."

"I need to show you something. It's the medallion I wear around my neck."

Addison heard a scrape of metal across the stone floor. He reached through the cell bars and lifted a bronze medallion into the air. It twirled on its chain in the candlelight.

"This is who you really are."

Embossed on the polished surface, Addison saw an eye in the center of the rays of a bright sun. "But this is the symbol on Sir Frederick's shield . . ."

"We are an ancient order. He was one of us, Addison."

"One of who?" For the first time, Addison noticed five Latin words surrounding the rays of light. He did not yet know enough Latin to translate.

"I think you know," said Uncle Nigel.

"My father, too?"

"And your uncle Jasper."

Addison watched the medallion twirl on its bronze chain. He wondered how long it had been in his family. He wondered about the prophecy of the Cookes.

"Did you read your Sun Tzu?"

"I did."

"*If you know the enemy and know yourself, you need not fear the result of a hundred battles.*'"

Addison tried to hand the medallion through the metal bars, but his uncle pushed it back.

"You must take it, Addison. It may save your life."

Addison took a deep breath. He heard footsteps approaching in the passage. "I'll hold on to it for you, until we all escape together." He fed the locket and chain into his inside blazer pocket.

Hu stepped into the chamber, unlocked Uncle Nigel's cell, and hauled him toward the exit.

Addison was startled by the sight of his uncle, stooped over with his hands chained to his feet with manacles. Uncle Nigel's face was haggard and his beard spotted with gray. He looked at Addison with tired eyes. "Remember who you are, Addison. Always remember who we've taught you to be."

Hu dragged Addison's uncle away.

A few minutes later, Madame Feng appeared in the chamber. "Have you had time to think?"

"Yes." Addison rose to his feet.

"Tell me the clue."

"I will do you one better. Madame Feng, if I deliver you the golden whip, will you release my aunt and uncle?"

Madame Feng smiled, bemused. "I hate to tell you this, but you are on the wrong side of these bars."

"Let me worry about that. I deliver you the whip and you have everything you want. We'll be of no more use to you. The whip for my family's freedom." Addison thrust his duct-taped hands through the bars and held them out for Madame Feng to shake.

Madame Feng's smile was as straight and flat as a guillotine. "I don't make bargains with prisoners. I'll let you spend the night in here. In the morning I will give you one final chance to talk."

Addison reached out and gripped her hand. "Promise me. The whip for my family's lives."

She snapped her hand away. "I will have both: the whip and your family's lives." Madame Feng strutted out of the chamber, blowing out the candle, leaving Addison in darkness.

III

THE
TOMB
OF THE
KHAN

Chapter Thirty-Three
Raj's Mistake

IT WAS A DISHEVELED Addison Cooke who awoke the next morning to the sound of the ancient cell door scraping open. Hu shoved Molly, Eddie, and Raj inside the windowless cell and locked the door shut again. Addison fished his flashlight from his messenger bag in the dark and checked the time on his watch. Eight a.m. He fixed his hair and straightened his tie. "Where were you guys?"

Molly groaned. "They locked us all in a tiny supply closet in the kitchen. And Raj still smells like a radiator explosion. Sort of a gassy smell."

"It was horrendous," Eddie agreed. "They only let us out when the cook arrived to make breakfast and threw a fit that he couldn't open his pantry." Eddie scanned his new surroundings and found them lacking. He gripped the iron bars and shook them as hard as he could. They did not budge. "Every morning I wake up and tell myself, *Eddie, don't get stuck in a Mongolian prison.* And so far, I've been pretty good at not getting stuck in a Mongolian prison. And yet, here we are."

"I'm glad you're back." Addison flicked out his butterfly knife and began sawing the duct tape from everyone's wrists. "Madame Feng wanted to keep me alone to lower my morale. And I have to admit, it was working."

"There is always room for hope," Raj announced, beaming with pleasure, "because I have my lock-picking set!" He held it proudly in the air like an Olympic torch. He set to work on the padlock of the iron cell door.

Addison settled in for a long wait.

Molly, tired of being cooped up, practiced her roundhouse kick. Her muscles were sore, but she felt she was sticking it now. All she needed was someone in need of a proper kicking. "Where do you think Nobody and I Don't Know are? They just abandoned us last night."

"It was the smart move," said Addison. "We should have done the same thing. We're just not as smart." He thought about I Don't Know—her black eyes, black hair, and black dress. He hoped she hadn't blackballed or blacklisted him. Sure, she was a horse thief, but she was his kind of horse thief.

Molly turned to face Addison. "So what did you tell Madame Feng? Are we getting murdered with boiling silver this morning, or did you sell out to her?"

"Which would you prefer?"

Molly wasn't sure.

"I didn't tell her anything. I just needed to see Uncle Nigel so he could translate the next clue."

"Do you have it?" Molly asked excitedly.

Addison cracked open his notebook and read his uncle's scribbled translation.

"In the land no living Mongol may pass, I climbed the eagle cliff.
I swam beneath a river, and crawled under a
mountain to the city of the dead.
Know the Khan to open the tomb; know thyself to escape."

"This one sounds like a doozy," said Eddie. His fingers were drilling piano scales on the concrete bench. The drumming of his fingers was slowly driving Addison crazy.

"Any ideas?" asked Molly.

Addison shook his head. He studied the map of Mongolia in *Fiddleton's Asia Atlas*. "We know the Russians went north. But there's nothing but wilderness up there on the map." He sat down against the cell wall, his feet splayed out before him. "Archaeology. It's caused nothing but trouble for our family."

Raj threw down the lock-picking set in disgust. "This thing is impossible! I want my money back."

Eddie covered his ears in the echoey stone cell. "Please don't shout. I have sensitive ears."

Molly snapped. "Eddie, all you care about is your delicate fingers and sensitive ears! Can we just focus on the fact that we're trapped in a cell and about to be tortured?"

Addison saw that his team's nerves were fraying. He needed a solution, he needed to lead, but he saw no ray of hope. His hand sought the medallion in his jacket pocket and held it for luck. He placed the chain around his neck and hid the medallion under his shirt, close to his heart. Somehow, he felt calmer. Eddie's thumping on the concrete bench no longer bothered him. Addison watched him thoughtfully. And then, in a moment of clarity, he suddenly smiled. "Eddie, what are you practicing?"

Eddie looked up from his imaginary piano. "Scales."

"Practice this, instead." Addison picked up Raj's lock-picking set from the floor and handed it to Eddie.

Eddie regarded it doubtfully. "I keep telling you, Addison. These fingers are for piano keys."

"Maybe they're meant for a different kind of keys."

Eddie's entire face seemed to clench with thought. He selected a pin in one hand and a pick in the other. He turned them carefully in his long, thin fingers. "I suppose it couldn't hurt to try." He knelt down by the padlocked door, fed his hands through the iron bars, and quoted Sir Frederick. "'Praise be to the Lord, my rock, who trains my hands for war, my fingers for battle . . .'"

He pressed his ear to the lock, carefully inserted the pick, and nudged it a millimeter. A beatific calm spread across his features, like a saint at prayer. "Wow," he whispered. "I can hear the spring click when the tumbler locks into place."

Addison held a hand in the air, signaling the group for complete silence. They watched Eddie in fascination. It was like watching Mozart sit down at a piano for the first time in his life.

"I've got a second tumbler," Eddie whispered, his eyes shut in concentration. "And a third. Just one more, I think . . ." The padlock sprang open. Eddie opened his eyes and pushed the cell door ajar.

"Amazing," said Molly.

"There's nothing to it." Eddie shrugged. "You just need delicate fingers and a sensitive ear."

Raj rose to his feet, a solemn expression on his face. He rolled up his lock-picking set and handed it ceremoniously to Eddie. "You should have it, Eddie—you've earned it. You've found your calling."

A slow smile spread across Eddie's face, and he nodded his thanks.

Addison wanted to spare his flashlight batteries, so

they crept out of the dungeon chamber in darkness, traced their fingertips along the cold stone walls of the wine cellar, and climbed the steps into the morning light of the kitchen.

Ducking the short cook pulling a frozen duck from the short freezer, Addison Cooke pulled up short, froze, and ducked. His team crawled into the dining room and crossed into the great room where the glowing embers of last night's fire still crackled in the fireplace. They listened to the boot steps of a triad guard making his early morning rounds upstairs.

"We're almost out of the palace," said Molly.

"Not so fast," said Addison. "If we're lucky, we have a chance to find where they're keeping the A & U."

Molly nodded her agreement. They glided silently down the wooden hallway until they reached a closed door. Eddie carefully opened it and discovered a room full of triads. They were sleeping on a sofa, with a few in sleeping bags on the floor. Struggling to avoid a heart attack, Eddie carefully clicked the door shut. "They're not in there," he reported.

The group crossed through a den with a magnificent bookshelf. Addison admired the leather-bound first editions of the complete works of Rosie M. Banks. Molly had to tug Addison's sleeve before he got too distracted.

When the group reached a second closed door, Eddie

refused to open it. So Molly carefully twisted the handle and eased the door open. They stepped inside to find a storage room piled high with ivory tusks. Some of the larger ones were ten feet long. Addison's face darkened. "These triads are monsters."

"Why?" asked Eddie.

"They're trafficking illegal tusks. Poachers kill endangered elephants in Africa and sell the tusks throughout Asia."

"That's not all Madame Feng's trafficking," said Raj, pointing to the far end of the storage room.

There, Addison saw boxes of rifles, crates of bullets, and even barrels of gunpowder. Addison had not thought he could like Madame Feng any less, but he kept discovering new things to dislike about her. It was like the opposite of a love affair.

Molly guided them out of the room. "We have to keep moving. The sun is up, and Madame Feng will come looking for us."

Raj tried the next door in the hallway: a utility closet with buckets and brooms stacked next to the hot water heater. "Perfect!" Raj unscrewed the supply hose from the gas line, so methane gas hissed into the room. "This ought to slow them down."

Addison leapt back a foot. "Raj, what are you doing? That's dangerous!"

"The gas will leak into the house and put everyone to sleep."

"They're already asleep. Besides, gas is highly flammable! Raj, put it back the way it was."

Raj shook his head and sighed. "Okay." He twisted the spigot rod, but it wouldn't budge. He twisted it harder, and it snapped in his hand. More gas spewed loudly from the main.

"Honestly, Raj," said Addison, in a rising panic. "You're one of my favorite people in the world, but sometimes you have a real genius for stupidity."

"So, what you're saying is, I'm a genius."

"The gas is spreading fast," said Molly.

"This is the pig's whistle," said Addison.

The group took wing like a flock of birds spooked from a tree. There was no debate—they simply ran, searching for a rear exit from the palace. The group took a wrong turn into a bedroom and doubled back.

"Wait a second," said Addison, skidding to a halt. "What about Madame Feng's fire?"

"Oh, right," said Raj, his eyes widening. "Sorry about that."

The gas explosion that followed was many decibels too loud for Eddie's delicate ears. The center of the house erupted like a rocket launch. A concussion of hot air blasted the team off their feet, sending them sliding down the polished wood floor. A fireball surged down the hallway, incinerating everything in its path.

"Raj," Molly shouted. "Can't you go ONE DAY without burning down a building?"

......

The group sprinted away from the spreading flames. Addison flung open each doorway they passed, searching for Aunt Delia and Uncle Nigel. Glass shattered across the palace as triads leapt from the windows. Madame Feng's voice screeched above the din, shouting frantic orders.

"On the bright side," Addison called over the roaring inferno, "this fire is the perfect cover for our escape!" He quickly realized he had spoken a bit too soon. A trio of triads burst from a side door, hunting for an exit. They spotted Addison's team and raced toward them like three dogs chasing the last four squirrels on earth.

Molly attempted her Mongol-Zo roundhouse kick, but her balance was off. She airballed it, missing a triad and somehow landing on her back. It didn't matter. The raging fire was racing up tapestries and chewing the wood-paneled walls. The triads quickly reassessed their priorities in life. Although they were dying to catch Addison's group, they didn't want to *actually* die catching Addison's group. So instead, they ran for their lives, fleeing the burning house. The three triads did not trouble themselves with doors, they simply crashed headfirst through the windows.

"If you can't beat 'em, join 'em," said Addison. He took a running start and dove out of a window after the triads. He was getting rather used to diving headfirst out of windows. Molly, Eddie, and Raj followed suit.

It was when they were leaping rock to rock across one of Madame Feng's koi ponds that the roaring fire must have reached the storage room . . . the storage room that was filled with gunpowder. The entire palace exploded as if struck by a missile.

Addison's team covered their heads as floorboards and shards of Ming dynasty vases rained down around them. One of Madame Feng's porcelain teacups shattered at Addison's feet.

Safe from the blast radius, they turned and watched the burning ruins as chunks of mortar and wisps of charred wallpaper fell from the sky. No one spoke for a long moment. "Can we all agree," said Molly at last, "to never, ever tell our parents or guardians we blew up a palace?"

Everyone silently nodded.

Triads ran in circles on the far side of the lawn. A few were trying to rescue elephant tusks from the flaming wreckage. Fire engines clanged in the distance. To Addison and Molly's intense relief, they spotted Aunt Delia and

Uncle Nigel—alive and well—being herded by triads to the safety of a koi pond.

"Can we rescue them?" asked Molly.

Addison counted the number of triads guarding his aunt and uncle. He then counted the number of triads furiously charging directly toward him. Addison's math was not spectacular, but it was good enough. "The A & U will have to fend for themselves a little longer. We have our own problems to sort out."

Chapter Thirty-Four

The Naadam Horse Race

ADDISON PUSHED OPEN THE estate's main gate, and the team escaped into the chaotic streets of downtown Ulaanbaatar. They fought their way upstream against a river of pedestrians. Addison was shocked by the crowds. Streets were barricaded from vehicle traffic, and cheering throngs waved Mongolian flags.

Molly spotted a tidal wave of triads pouring from Madame Feng's compound. They pointed at Addison's group and shoved their way through the crowd.

"Hurry!" cried Molly. She tried to squeeze her way through the press of bodies, but there was no way past the police barricades. She wrung her hands in frustration. "Why are all these streets shut down?"

"The horse race!" Addison shouted over the noise of the crowd. "Nobody said this is a national holiday." He gestured for everyone to duck low as the triads scanned the teeming legions of people. The barricades marked the route of the horse race, and none of the Mongolians wanted to give up their front-row spots. "We're not getting anywhere on foot—we need transportation." Addison did most of his best thinking aloud. "We know the Russians went north and there are no roads in the wilderness. If we want to follow Sir Frederick's clue, we need horses."

Molly feathered her way through the masses of Mongolians. It seemed less crowded as they approached the starting line of the race. All the action would be happening at the finish line. "Where are we supposed to find horses?"

Addison slowly smiled.

Molly began shaking her head vehemently. "No, Addison. Absolutely not."

But he was already on the move, heading straight for the race stables.

Addison's team had no choice but to follow, keeping one step ahead of the triads.

Molly eyed the security guard manning the stable entrance. She didn't need to read Mongolian to understand the "Do Not Enter" signs. "Addison, we're not allowed in there."

Addison did not break his stride. "Good. That means Madame Feng isn't allowed in there, either."

"At least tell me you have a plan this time."

He reverently quoted Sun Tzu. *"'Let your plans be dark and impenetrable as night, and when you move, fall like a thunderbolt.'"*

"You have no idea what you're doing, do you."

"I'm improvising!"

Addison waved to the guard manning the entrance. The young man was reclining on a chair, his feet propped on a porch railing, his legs blocking the doorway. He wore a New York Yankees cap and was reading a horse-racing magazine. Both were in English, so Addison felt he was on good footing. "Good morning. We're just popping in to the stables for a quick look around."

"No, you're not," said the guard.

"Look, I hate to name-drop," said Addison, pointing to Eddie, "but this is the prime minister's son. We need to check on the prime minister's investment."

The guard licked a thumb and turned a page of his magazine. "Uh-huh."

Addison could see he was dealing with a rather intelligent security guard. Judging from the guard's taste in magazines, he knew a thing or two about horse races.

Addison just needed to lure him onto that topic. He baited the hook. "All we need is a minute with the jockeys."

"I can't let you enter. How do I know you're not doping horses?"

Addison had never been mistaken for a horse doper. He had not considered this angle. He sensed an opportunity and folded his arms across his chest. "If we were horse dopers, that would be valuable information to you."

"Yes, so I could throw you in jail."

"You could throw us in jail. But that wouldn't put money in your pocket."

The guard squinted up at Addison, looking at him for the first time.

Addison could see that he finally had the man's attention. "I can't tell you which horse is going to win. But I can guarantee you which four horses are going to lose. There are people who would pay a lot of money for that information."

The guard scratched his chin. "I work for the stable—I can't gamble on the race."

"Of course not," said Addison, reeling in the hook. "But your friends can. And your friends can share the wealth. Let us in and you'll be up to your ears in tögrögs."

The guard returned to his magazine, but he slowly lowered his legs from the railing, allowing Addison's team to pass. They percolated past the porch and into the stable.

In the nick of time, thought Addison, spying Hu searching the stable yard.

Inside the stable, Addison's nose was greeted with a bouquet of cigar smoke, horse sweat, and dung. The smell was so intense, he forgot about Raj's odor entirely. He led the team into the locker room where all the jockeys were strapping on their boots for the race. To his surprise, the Mongolian jockeys were all young, probably for their small size. One girl looked young enough to be in elementary school. The cigar smell was so strong, someone might as well have lit a skunk on fire. Taking the temperature of the room, Addison sensed the jockeys were a disgruntled lot, and not too pleased about the upcoming event. He sidled up to a boy who looked to be his own age. "Sounds like a tough race."

"Yeah, fifteen kilometers," said the boy, in surprisingly good English.

"And dangerous?"

"Are you kidding? Every year kids get thrown and injured. Half the horses cross the finish line without riders." He turned to spit on the dirt floor.

"Don't you wear helmets?"

"Of course not."

"They must not have many liability lawyers in Mongolia," Eddie put in.

"Well," said Addison, favoring the jockey with a

sympathetic eye, "I guess they give you a lot of money if you win?"

"No, nothing," said the jockey bitterly. "We're just kids."

"Well, at least credit?"

"No. The way they see it, the horse did all the work."

Addison saw that several of the jockeys were listening now. They were getting worked up. He continued stirring the pot. "So you're risking your lives for what? Just to entertain some fanatical grown-ups?"

The jockeys considered this. The thirteen-year-old finished lacing his boots and cocked an eye at Addison. "What's your angle here?"

"I have a proposition."

"I'm listening."

"Instead of getting paid zero tögrögs to risk your life, how about I pay you fifty thousand tögrögs to skip the race."

"No good. Someone will notice we're missing."

"Not if we're riding your horses."

The jockey sized up Addison's team, mulling the idea. He waved over three of his comrades. "Fifty thousand tögrögs. Each."

Addison did the math in his head. Fifty thousand tögrögs was about twenty-five dollars per horse. In America, horses cost thousands of dollars. Twenty-five dollars was a 99 percent discount. Normally, Addison would negotiate, but this was the deal of a lifetime. "Done."

The jockeys stripped off their jerseys and boots, showed Addison's group to the stalls, and helped them mount up. The thirteen-year-old grinned up at Addison. "If anyone asks us, we'll say you jumped us and stole the horses."

"Fair enough." Addison handed over the last of his cash and saluted with two fingers. Trainers guided their horses out of the stable, across the yard, and up to the starting gates.

······

The crowd greeted Addison with a delightful medley of cheers, boos, and what he was pretty sure were death threats. He looked down at his red jersey. Whichever district of Mongolia he was representing, it wasn't a popular one.

He shifted on his mount, trying to get comfortable. It was Mongol custom to ride bareback, so there was no saddle to cushion his ride except a thin horse blanket.

Trainers locked each horse into its starting gate. Molly whispered from the stall next to Addison's. "What is the plan?"

"The street barricades will give us a clear path right out of the city."

"Everyone in Mongolia watches this race!" she hissed, noting some TV cameras. "Don't you think we'll get noticed?"

"We're hiding in plain sight!" Addison had no sooner spoken than several triads in the front row of spectators began leaping, shouting, and pointing at him. They called for the racing officials but couldn't be heard over the din.

"They've found us!" cried Eddie. "We're done!" When the starter pistol fired, Eddie clutched his heart, convinced a triad had shot him. Luckily, the horses knew their business and leapt out of the gates.

Addison suddenly knew how a bullet feels when it's shot from a gun. One moment, you're minding your own business, and the next, you're hurtling through space at the speed of sound. Addison's hands clung to his horse by the withers, but his stomach was left a hundred yards behind at the starting gate. He reminded himself that the horses were carefully chosen from around the country, and were quite possibly the twelve fastest in Mongolia. Addison had only a few days' experience on horseback. He felt like he was taking driving lessons on a Ferrari.

The horses galloped past the VIP stand. Addison saw the mayor of Ulaanbaatar and the prime minister of Mongolia pointing at him. "Hey! That's the French ambassador's son!"

"Bonjour!" Addison waved as he charged past. Checking over his shoulder, he was alarmed to see the mayor shouting directions at the police lieutenant. He didn't like where this was going. He called to Eddie and Raj behind him. "Pick up the pace a bit!"

The more experienced riders were pulling ahead.

Addison leaned low over his horse's neck, streamlining his body. Police officers on walkie-talkies stepped into the racecourse ahead and attempted to grab Addison's reins as he careened past. He swatted at them with his riding crop.

Addison swiveled his neck to see a police car burning up the racecourse behind him, flanked by two police motorcycles. They caught up to Eddie's mare. One of the motorcycle riders stretched out a gloved hand to snag Eddie's reins. Eddie managed to swerve out of reach at the last minute. The crowd, who had a lot of tögrögs riding on this race, loudly booed the police, showering them with rotten fruit.

A police motorcycle pulled up close, spooking Addison's horse with its roaring engine. The policeman drew his baton and jabbed between the horse's ankles, trying to trip the galloping animal. Addison decided things were getting out of hand. It was time to take these horses off-roading. "Follow me!" he cried to his team, and steered his horse straight for the nearest barricade.

He assumed his mare would leap the barricade, but instead she crashed right through it. The crowd screamed and dove for cover. After his experiences in the Hong Kong night market, Addison was quite used to the sight of crowds diving for cover. His horse, however, was not. The panicked mare flailed her hooves, and Addison struggled to control her as they galloped clear of the thick press of the crowd and into the wide streets of downtown Ulaanbaatar.

••••••

Addison checked to see if his group was keeping up and heard the roar of hundreds of angry Mongolians. They were tearing up their race tickets and shaking fists at him for wrecking the most important horse race in the country. Addison had upset a few people in his day, but never an entire city. He found he quite liked the attention. Dozens of enraged spectators began chasing him down, hungry for blood. Addison was thrilled he could now say he'd been chased by a horde of Mongols.

The New Yorkers cantered ahead of the angry throng. Weaving through side streets, they found the rest of downtown Ulaanbaatar somewhat empty.

Addison opened his mare up to a full gallop. Behind him, Mongolians vented their rage on every shop and food cart they passed, tearing open storefronts and looting the city. Ulaanbaatar was descending into a full-scale riot. Addison was not proud of this, but he thought it might help keep the police occupied.

He was mistaken.

The full might of the city police department cruised in from all directions, patrol cars skidding to barricade intersections. They may have been riding the fastest horses in Mongolia, but they were no match for the fastest police cars in Mongolia. With each street blocked off, Addison felt himself being hemmed into the maze of the city.

"Addison, where are we going?" called Molly.

"I don't know and I'm not stopping for directions!"

He pulled *Roland J. Fiddleton's Asia Atlas* from his pocket, craning his neck, and turned the map in all directions as they galloped from north to west to south and back to west again.

"The police are boxing us in!" called Molly. They galloped into an intersection and found all their exits walled off by police cars.

Addison spurred his horse down a side alley. *"Chu! Chu!"* he shouted, and the horse kicked into a higher gear. A police car roared down the alleyway behind them. Addison was sure they were going to be mowed down. There was no escape.

Looking forward, Addison caught a sight that stopped the breath in his throat. Two Mongol warriors at full gallop, swords drawn, black hair streaming behind them as they barreled toward him. Before Addison could react, the warriors swept past him, past his team, and swung their swords down at the police car, slashing all four tires.

The police car's rims struck the raw concrete in a shrieking shower of sparks. It skidded to a stop, wheels grinding against the pavement. A conga line of police cars rear-ended the first car, clogging up the alley like plugging a dike. The Mongols reined their horses and reversed course, catching up with Addison's crew.

"Who are these guys?" asked Eddie, astonished.

"I Don't Know!" shouted Addison. "And Nobody!"

The Black Darkhad unwrapped the scarves from their faces and smiled at the New Yorkers.

Addison recognized their horses and remembered they had stabled them by the Muddy Duck. "How did you find us?"

"You're kind of hard to miss!" said I Don't Know.

Addison couldn't help but admire the way I Don't Know's long hair tumbled across her shoulders, but before he could get too distracted, he heard fresh sirens bearing down from the east. "Can you get us out of this city?"

"We want to go north," said I Don't Know, "but there's a race in the way."

Addison cut a path due north. A horse race is not an obstacle when one is on a horse. He knew he was heading in the right direction when the crowds grew so thick, it was hard for the police cars to follow. He steered directly for a course barricade, and this time his mare made the leap.

He touched down on the racecourse, expecting to be loudly booed or pelted with fruit. After plowing around a few curves, Addison noticed the crowd was actually cheering him. Somehow, his team had taken a massive shortcut and they were suddenly in the lead. Addison had never entered a national horse race before, but his competitive instincts kicked on like a stadium floodlight. "C'mon," he urged his excited horse. *"Chu, chu!"*

Molly's gelding pulled within a horse's tail of Addison before they galloped over the finish line, snapping the yellow racing tape. Addison was showered in confetti. Champagne bottles popped and the crowd cheered. The horses slowed, enjoying their moment, but Addison spurred them to keep right on running.

Nobody grinned radiantly. "All my life, I've dreamed of competing in the Naadam Horse Race. I never thought I would someday cross the finish line."

"Stick with me, Nobody," said Addison.

Police cars closed in on Addison's left hand and his right. They skidded into place, walling off escape routes. A few squad cars crept up on Addison's rear. The team's horses were laboring hard, heaving for breath.

Addison was not worried. "Nobody, have you ever seen a 'spinning duck'?"

"What's a spinning duck?"

"Just a little trick we learned when we were chased by the *policia* in Ecuador. First you spin . . ." They galloped their horses around the blind corner of an intersection. Following Addison's lead, they reined into a crowded horse paddock. "Then you duck!" They jumped down off their mounts and lay flat, hiding among the crowd of horses.

Addison peered through the wooden fencing and counted seventeen police cars that thundered past at full speed, red and blue sirens blaring, before disappearing around the next bend.

The team walked their horses through alleyways and backyards, keeping off the main roads until they reached the perimeter of the city. It wasn't until they'd crossed an empty highway and climbed into the cover of the wooded foothills that they paused to look back. From the shouting and police sirens, at least half of Ulaanbaatar was embroiled in a riot. Smoke still rose from the heart of the city where they had blown up Madame Feng's palace.

Molly shook her head. "We're running low on cities we haven't completely wrecked."

Addison shrugged, admiring their work. "Plenty of fish in the sea, Molly."

Chapter Thirty-Five

The Forbidden Lands

ADDISON'S GROUP WALKED THEIR horses along the crest of a hill, high above the coal heaps and slag pits of Ulaanbaatar.

"Where to?" Nobody asked.

"To *'the land no living Mongol may pass,'*" said Addison, quoting Sir Frederick's last clue.

Nobody and I Don't Know shared a dark look.

"What?" asked Addison. "Does that mean something to you? A land where Mongols are forbidden to go?"

Nobody stopped his horse and turned to Addison. "You speak of the Ikh Khorig, the Great Taboo. At its heart lies a sacred mountain called Burkhan Khaldun, guarded by the Darkhad. Any person who trespasses there is punished by death."

"Why?" asked Molly.

Addison surprised the Darkhad by knowing the answer. He had read *The Secret History of the Mongols.* "When Genghis Khan was young, the Merkit clan tried to assassinate him. He hid in the Burkhan Khaldun and believed the mountain saved his life. He declared the mountain sacred and decreed that his children and grandchildren should pray to the mountain every day of their lives."

I Don't Know nodded, impressed.

What Addison did not say was that ideas were now bouncing around in his brain like popcorn in a microwave. It made sense that Genghis would want to be buried on the mountain he declared sacred. And the fact that no Mongol would set foot there went a long way toward explaining how the Khan's tomb had remained hidden for eight centuries.

"No one is allowed in the Great Taboo except the Black Darkhad," said I Don't Know, as if reading Addison's thoughts.

"Then I know we'll be safe."

"Not that safe. The penalty is death."

"Protecting a mountain is more important to you than human lives?" asked Addison.

Nobody nodded firmly. "The golden whip is the symbol of the Khan and of our country. If it exists in these mountains, it is more precious than a human life."

Addison wasn't entirely sure if there was anything more precious than a human life, but he let the matter slide. "Can you lead me to your fellow Darkhad so I can negotiate?"

"We can. But they will kill you for entering these lands."

Addison turned to I Don't Know. "Do you believe in these rules?"

She shrugged. "The Darkhad have been this way for eight hundred years. They're sort of set in their ways."

"We've come this far. I want to finish this." Addison looked back at Ulaanbaatar, filled with a million Mongols who were more than a bit peeved with Addison's team for setting fire to a museum, blowing up a palace, ruining their horse race, and causing a riot. "I think it's best if we go to the one place in Mongolia where no Mongolians can get their hands on us."

••••••

Austere mountain peaks presided over the foothills. I Don't Know spurred her horse along a trail that wound into a deep forest. "Stay close behind me. This a wild land, filled with wolves and hunting eagles. There are brown bears in the mountains, as well as wild boar, lynxes, wolverines and . . . " She stopped short. "Is your friend okay?"

Addison turned, and to his horror, saw Raj wiping himself with a handful of horse dung like it was a bar of soap. "Raj, what are you doing!?"

"Clearly," said Raj, looking at Addison as if *he* were the weird one, "I am masking my scent from predators."

The forest opened up on a crystalline lake, reflecting the mountain peaks in a pristine way that reminded Addison of the Swiss Alps. The air was cool and clean here, untouched by man.

Nobody sat his horse and scanned the forested foothills. He drew an ibex horn from his belt and blew a long, low signal that echoed across the valleys. He clicked his tongue, spurred his horse, and kept riding.

In the afternoon they reached a crag in the mountain where boulders rose up on either side of the path. Addison's first thought was that it was the perfect site for an ambush. His second thought was to wonder if he'd been reading too much Sun Tzu.

Nobody reined his horse again. He drew his ibex horn and blew another low, trilling call. He slid down off his mount in one fluid motion. He allowed the mare to crop grass while he sunned himself on a rock.

"Wait," said Molly, shielding her eyes. "I thought I saw movement in those trees."

"It's the Black Darkhad," said I Don't Know, dismounting like her brother. "They've found us."

"I don't see anything," said Eddie.

Addison felt a tingling on the back of his neck. He scanned the impenetrable woodlands just beyond the boulders.

In a single flicker of movement, two dozen bowmen stepped out from the rocks. One moment there was no one. The next moment there were twenty-four iron-tipped arrows poised on bowstrings, ready to rip Addison's team to shreds.

I Don't Know called out to the Darkhad in her native dialect.

A thick-browed man whom Addison took to be the chieftain barked a harsh word at I Don't Know, driving her to silence.

"Um, excuse me," Addison began in his most reasonable voice. "Perhaps I should introduce myself."

Armed men tore Addison off his horse and threw him to the rocky ground. Addison winced, arching his back in pain. He was pinned down, a knee on his stomach. A twelve-inch steel dagger was pressed to his throat. He looked up into the midnight black eyes of the thick-browed chieftain.

Addison swallowed hard and managed to croak, "Addison Cooke. Nice to meet you."

The Darkhad bared his nicotine-stained yellow teeth. "You are on sacred ground. The penalty is death."

"We're friends with Nobody and I Don't Know."

"No one can know our names! That penalty is death."

"Is that your answer for everything?"

The man pressed his blade harder against Addison's neck.

"I will take that as a 'yes.'" Addison found that the key to negotiation was discovering what the other person wanted. But in this case, the only thing the Darkhad seemed to want was to kill Addison, and Addison was not willing to make that deal. "I have information," he said, desperate to find wiggle room to negotiate. "I know the Chinese triads and Russian *vori* who are coming to trespass on your land and rob the tomb of Genghis Khan!"

"We do not mention the tomb of Genghis Khan!" hissed the warlord. "That penalty—"

"Let me guess," said Addison. "Is death."

Strong hands pinned his arms to the ground. His tie was loosened and his collar torn open, exposing his heart. Addison shut his eyes.

The Darkhad warrior straddled Addison's chest, clutched his dagger in both hands, and raised it high over his head to strike.

Chapter Thirty-Six

The Darkhad Camp

ADDISON WAITED FOR THE blow. The suspense was killing him. He had never been a very patient person to begin with. He had to know how things turned out. Finally, out of curiosity, he opened one eye and then the other.

The Darkhad leader was staring, transfixed, at the medallion around Addison's neck. He dropped his dagger in the dirt and muttered what Addison took to be a prayer.

Other Darkhad warriors gasped in astonishment. They released Addison and stepped back in superstitious awe.

At last the chieftain spoke. "How did you come to wear this medallion?"

"My uncle gave it to me. It belongs to my family."

"Please, I beg your forgiveness." The Darkhad chieftain bowed low, pressing his forehead to the earth.

"That's more like it," said Addison, standing up and patting himself off. Nearly every single person he'd met on this summer vacation had seemed intent on murdering him. It was nice to finally get some proper treatment.

······

The chieftain mounted his warhorse and guided them up the steep slope and through the forest to the hidden Darkhad encampment. It was a circle of huts, a few cook fires, and some mountain pasture where the horses could graze. Addison studied the hard lines etched into the faces of the nomads. In the cooler high country they were bundled with sable and fox furs. Their broad shoulders were strapped with weapons.

"Welcome to our camp," said the chieftain. "I am Not a Human Being."

"I beg your pardon?"

"That is his name," said I Don't Know. "Khünbish." She pointed to a one-eyed warrior who carried a hunting eagle on his gloved arm. "And that is Not a Person." She pointed out a few other men in the encampment. "That is Not This One, and that is Not That One. No Name is the one brushing Nobody's horse."

Addison nodded. This was all becoming quite

reasonable. He pointed to a scarred bowman who walked with a limp. "What's his name?"

"Ganzorig. It means 'Steel Courage.'"

"Wait, how come he gets to be named Steel Courage?"

I Don't Know shrugged. "Just lucky, I guess."

The chieftain led Addison's team to his *ger*, a circular tent of stretched wool, covered with animal pelts and cinched together with horsehair ropes. Addison ducked inside and stared at the tent intently. It was decorated with weapons, hanging slabs of mutton, and a horse-head fiddle.

Nobody steered the males to the left side of the *ger*, while I Don't Know led Molly to the right. "Men sit under the protection of the great sky god, Tengger," Nobody explained. "Women sit to the east, under the protection of the sun." The chieftain took his seat at the rear of the *ger*, by the family altar, which was covered in small idols. Addison sat by a wooden tent pole and rested his back against a pile of saddle blankets.

I Don't Know served everyone cups of horse milk. She then stirred a large pot of stew on the cook fire in the center of the *ger*.

The chieftain spoke for a while in the Darkhad dialect before turning to Addison's group. "My niece and nephew tell me you escaped Ulaanbaatar."

Addison looked in surprise from the chieftain to Nobody and I Don't Know. He did see a family resemblance.

"I am not a city man myself," the Darkhad leader continued. "How did you like it?"

Addison realized, to his amazement, that the chieftain was making friendly small talk.

Molly answered before Addison could reply. "Ulaanbaatar was so-so. We blew up a museum and burned down a palace."

The chieftain slowly nodded. Addison knew that small talk was not Molly's best department.

"Here, have some *makh*," said I Don't Know, ladling some stew into a bowl and handing it to Eddie.

"Thanks, I'm starving! What's in it?"

"Boiled sheep parts. You know, bones, fat, organs . . ."

Eddie stared into the pot and watched a sheep's head bubble to the surface. Out of politeness, he tried to hide his gag reflex with a cough.

"There's sliced potato in there, too," I Don't Know said helpfully.

Raj held out his bowl to try some.

"What else are you cooking?" Eddie asked.

"Oh, lots of things. We have mutton broth, mutton dumplings, and mutton pancakes."

"Do you have anything that's not made out of mutton?"

I Don't Know held up a shriveled black creature skewered on a stick. "Blowtorched marmot. A delicacy in the steppes."

Eddie sipped his mare's milk and kept quiet.

Addison had been gazing into the fire, deep in thought, and finally looked up at the chieftain. "Sir Frederick met the Black Darkhad hundreds of years ago. He called you Ghost Warriors. Your tribe nearly killed him, but decided to let him live." Addison leaned closer to the fire, fixing the chieftain with a knowing smile. "You know about Sir Frederick's clues. That's why there are Darkhad as far away as Kashgar. It was the Darkhad who built those booby traps!"

Not A Human Being nodded. He bit the crispy arm off a burned marmot with evident relish. "You caught us off guard in Ulaanbaatar. We would have done a better job protecting Sir Frederick's lance, but honestly, we had no idea you would rob a museum."

"I don't get it. If you want to protect the Khan's tomb, why protect the clues? Why not destroy them?"

"As Darkhad, we can neither follow the clues to open the tomb nor bring ourselves to destroy them. They are our only link to the prize we've guarded for eight hundred years." The chieftain opened the collar of his tunic, revealing an embroidered bead mandala hung around his neck. It was the Templar symbol—an eye in the center of a radiant sun. "Your knight found the tomb and the Darkhad tried to kill him. He told the Darkhad that if we did not know where the tomb was, or if it even existed, one day our people would forget their vows and the Khan's legend would fade from the earth. By remembering our history, we remember who we are. So we protect the clues and we honor your knight."

"And now that I've appeared, with the same medallion as Sir Frederick?"

The Darkhad leader shook his head. "I cannot allow you to go after the tomb. It guards the golden whip. And that is sacred to Mongolians."

Addison frowned. "How big is the Great Taboo?"

"Two hundred forty square kilometers."

"And how many Darkhad are left to guard it? Twenty-five? Fifty?"

The chieftain maintained a stony silence.

Addison pressed his point. "You can't defend an entire mountain. The smart move is to find where the tomb is hidden. The Russians have the clues and the Chinese are not far behind. They *will* find the tomb. They *will* find the golden whip. Our only chance is to find it first and bury it somewhere else in the wilderness. Somewhere where there are no clues." Addison saw I Don't Know nodding in agreement.

The chieftain's jaw muscles tightened so that veins pulsed in his temples. "This is impossible. No Darkhad may approach the tomb. We have taken vows for centuries."

"Your vow is to protect the tomb and its treasure. You must find the tomb now in order to protect it."

The chieftain rose to his feet. "No. It is forbidden by our laws." From his stern expression, it was clear that his decision was final.

• • • • • •

Outside the *ger*, Addison's team found their horses fed, watered, and groomed. Addison admired how the Darkhad trimmed their horses' forelocks short and left the bridle path unclipped. Already sore from the morning's race, he mounted up.

The chieftain pointed south to the foothills. "In memory of your knight, I will spare your lives. Nobody and I Don't Know will escort you safely off our sacred land." He handed Nobody a two-way radio that Nobody handled like a religious artifact, tucking it carefully into his pack.

Addison guided his horse to the mountain path, carpeted with pine needles. "If you see my aunt and uncle on your land, please don't kill them. They're being held against their will." He lifted the bronze medallion from his shirt so that it sparkled in the light.

The chieftain raised his hand in farewell.

• • • • • •

As soon as they were on the trail, Molly, Eddie, and Raj pelted Addison with questions about his bronze medallion. Addison explained it as best he could.

"Are the Cookes descended from Templar knights?" asked Molly.

Addison really had no idea. Somehow, he couldn't quite picture his uncle Nigel swinging a sword around. And he knew from experience that he wasn't particularly talented with swords himself. He would have to rescue his uncle if he hoped to learn more.

They reached a fork in the mountain path. One route led downhill toward civilization. The other wound higher into the dark forest, disappearing around a steep bend. Addison reined his horse and faced the Darkhad. "I Don't Know, you liked the plan I told your uncle in the *ger.*"

I Don't Know quietly nodded. "We have a better chance of defending the tomb if we actually know where it is."

Addison turned to her brother. "Nobody, what do you think? We find the tomb and alert the Darkhad." He gestured to the radio in Nobody's pack. "Then the Darkhad can defend the right spot instead of patrolling this entire wilderness."

Nobody hesitated. He chose his words carefully. "It's not that I'm disobeying my uncle, it's that I'm following my vow to protect the tomb."

Addison nodded. Whatever helped Nobody sleep at night.

Nobody guided his horse to the steep path up the mountain. "There is a river near the mountain peak. My whole life, our uncle has never let us go near. I've always wondered what is hidden beyond. I believe it is a good place to start."

Addison recalled the river mentioned in Sir Frederick's final clue. "It works for me," he said.

The horses labored uphill through the late afternoon. Moss hung from the trees like witches' hair. Molly spotted a roe deer in the midafternoon, but they did not see another living creature for the rest of the day. Occasionally the fairy-tale forest parted to reveal the mystical landscape below. The sweep of the valleys, cloaked in blankets of mist; the faint brushstrokes of the mountains.

Addison consulted *Fiddleton's Asia Atlas* and gasped in astonishment. "My God, this has never happened before!" He held out Fiddleton's map for all to see, stabbing it excitedly with a finger. "We're in uncharted land! There's just a blank green spot on Fiddleton's map that says, 'forbidden.'" He shook his head, amazed. "Roland J. Fiddleton rounded Cape Horn in a kayak. He rescued three Sherpas from the summit of Mount Everest. If Roland J. Fiddleton hasn't mapped this mountain, it really is forbidden!"

The dense forest thinned, giving way to rolling hilltop fields. The horses crossed beds of red, yellow, and purple wildflowers. Vultures, falcons, and steppe eagles hunted the slopes.

Nobody guided them to a cairn of rocks piled at the

crest of a barren hill and signaled a dismount. "This is an *ovoo*. Mongols pile stones on top of high hills to serve as altars to the gods."

On foot, I Don't Know bade them circle the *ovoo* stones three times clockwise for luck on their journey. She took a splash of mare's milk from her canteen and spritzed it in the air with her fingers for the sky gods. She then plucked hairs from their horses' tails and added them to the rock pile. The horses didn't like having their tails plucked. Molly had her own ponytail, so she could relate. Out of sympathy, she plucked one of her own hairs and placed it on top of the *ovoo*.

Nobody dropped grains of rice in the stone circle, announced his family name, and placed a white pebble on top of the pile of rocks. Last, he and I Don't Know made Addison's group take off their shoes and lie on the ground to absorb the good luck of the holy site. Addison wasn't sure if this was all a waste of precious time, but he knew they needed all the luck they could get.

Chapter Thirty-Seven
The Shaman

THE SKY GREW DARK when a rainstorm broke over the mountains. Addison became a bit annoyed with the sky god at this point, but kept his feelings to himself. They were quickly drenched. The horses' hooves kept suctioning into the mud, slowing their pace.

At last the path became too steep and rocky for the horses. Nobody released them into the mountains, saying simply, "They will return to the Darkhad."

The massive thunderstorm shook the steppe. The wet group trudged along the backbone of a forlorn ridge, with no trees to shelter them from the pounding deluge. Nobody led the way to an overhanging rock jutting from the side of the mountain. They ducked underneath and shook water from their clothes.

At the crease of the rock was a shallow cave, and inside burned a crackling fire. An old man with wiry eyebrows and a laugh-lined face sat wrapped in a horsehair blanket, poking the fire with a stick. Nobody crawled into the cave and asked permission for Addison's team to spend the night under the overhang.

Nobody emerged a moment later and gestured to Addison and Molly. "The shaman wants to speak with you."

"With us?" asked Addison.

"He asked for the boy with the bronze necklace, and his warrior sister."

Addison frowned. There was no way the old man could know he was wearing a medallion under his clothes.

Nobody beckoned him to the cave. "It is a great honor. The shaman speaks the sacred language."

Addison and Molly shared a glance and crawled into the cave.

• • • • • •

The old man greeted them with a cracked-tooth smile. He poured tea from a tin pot hung from a stick. The cook fire glowed yellow and orange on the cave walls.

He flicked some tea in the air to honor the sky gods and gestured for Addison and Molly to drink. The tea tasted of moss and pine needles. The strange little man wrapped a cloth around his head, blindfolding himself. He began pounding a deerskin drum and singing an ancient tune, almost without melody. After a few minutes he set the drum aside and smiled pleasantly.

Addison was, by this point, completely mystified. To his immense relief, the old man began speaking in English. Addison had been worried this was going to be a very short conversation.

"Your legs are tired from the horse."

"Yes," said Addison. It wasn't riveting conversation, but it was a start.

The old man swiveled his head to Molly. "Your legs are tired from kicking."

Molly's mouth opened and shut. "Have you been following us?"

"I can't," said the old man. "My legs are too tired." He broke into a cackling laugh.

Molly looked at Addison and back at the old man. She eyed him suspiciously. "Who are you and what do you want?"

"I am Not Here . . ."

Addison and Molly nodded: this much made sense.

". . . and I want to talk to you."

"Well, have at it," said Molly.

Addison reminded himself that small talk was not Molly's forte. "We would be honored to hear anything you wish to tell us."

The old man rocked his body from side to side. "I see

much pain in your past, my son. And green in your aura, for healing." The fire kicked up smoke that had trouble escaping the hollow. It filled the small room, blurring Addison's vision and watering his eyes.

"We lost our parents when we were young," Addison found himself saying.

The shaman nodded as if this were old news to him. "The ones who did this to your family are hunting you . . ."

Addison's brow furrowed. "What can we do?"

"Ah . . ." When the shaman's blindfolded eyes aimed at the smoking fire, it seemed to burn brighter. "Your family is old and full of secrets. Like this world, it is not as modern as it seems. Your life's work is the past. The past is who you are. Ancient secrets are everywhere, waiting to be revealed."

Addison could not make heads or tails of this, but he listened, entranced.

The crackling fire lit every wrinkle in the shaman's face. The man leaned forward, lowering his voice. "There are many trials ahead. Things will become harder than you can bear. And then they will become even harder. I see a catacombs under a great city, I see your sister held prisoner on an island. I see a perilous journey through a hostile desert. I see a prophecy. You will feel alone in the world, but you have powerful allies you do not yet realize."

Addison's head was swimming. He wondered if it was

the smoke or just exhaustion. He did not believe in magic or voodoo, yet he found himself believing the mystic visions of the old man.

The shaman leaned back, smiling. "I know what you seek on the mountain."

"Will we find it?"

"The only way to find something is to seek everything. The only way to find everything is to seek nothing."

"So . . . is that a yes or a no?" asked Molly.

The shaman only giggled his reedy, gap-toothed laugh. "You will find more on this mountain than you came looking for. But it will cost you dearly."

Addison leaned forward, spilling his doubts to the old man. "Should we continue on our journey? Should we even be here? Should we just go back to New York?"

"There is no cheating your destiny." The shaman's expression changed to sadness. "If you do not face your problems in this lifetime, my son, you will only have to face them in the next."

It was hours before Addison finally found sleep. He spent the night under the outcropping, wrapped in a blanket of bearskin he borrowed from Nobody. The thunderstorm rocked Addison's dreams with visions of his past and his future. In the morning, the rains were gone, and so was the old man, vanished without a trace.

Chapter Thirty-Eight

The Cliff and the River

ADDISON'S GROUP BREAKFASTED ON jerky Nobody had packed for the journey. Molly performed her morning martial arts practice with I Don't Know. They sparred on top of the rocky outcropping as morning light filled the valleys below. Molly was pleased to land a kick.

"You've been practicing," said I Don't Know, rubbing her hip where Molly had clipped her. I Don't Know was older and taller than Molly, with a longer reach. She did not expect Molly to slip anything through her defense. She smiled. "You're strong; I can tell you're a soccer player. But you need one more ingredient before your kicks have true power."

Molly was all ears.

"Don't hold your breath. You'll move faster when you exhale. Whether you swing a sword, a punch, or a kick— always breathe out. Your life force is in your breath."

Molly tried her Mongol-Zo roundhouse kick, this time with a sharp exhale. It felt smooth and effortless. She was improving. She smiled at I Don't Know.

Addison's team spent the morning hiking north through a white birch forest. After a few miles, the woods deepened into Scotch pine, and finally towering Siberian larch that blocked out the sun like high-rise apartment buildings. At last, Nobody found the forbidden river that spilled down the side of the mountain. Over millennia it had cut a deep gorge. White waters raged a thousand feet below, but high in the cliffs, the sound was peaceful.

Addison took out his notebook and reread Sir Frederick's final clue.

"In the land no living Mongol may pass, I climbed the eagle cliff.
I swam beneath a river, and crawled under a
mountain to the city of the dead.
Know the Khan to open the tomb; know thyself to escape."

Addison turned to Nobody and I Don't Know. "We need to find this 'eagle cliff.' Is there a cliff in this mountain range shaped like an eagle?"

Everyone scanned the bluffs on either side of the gorge. There were jagged rock formations in all directions, but none that resembled an eagle. For an hour they hiked south along the gorge, keeping their eyes on the summits of the mountains. At over seven thousand feet, Addison's group was huffing for breath from lack of oxygen.

Addison felt his thoughts wandering and sensed his exhaustion. His tired feet plodded along the uneven rock, each step an unpleasant jolt on his aching limbs. He wondered if they were even in the right part of Mongolia. He was beginning to have thoughts of giving up.

Eddie put his hands on his knees and bent double, gulping for breath. "This is hopeless! This mountain range goes on forever. We keep climbing and climbing, and I don't see any cliff that looks like an eagle!"

Addison tried to think of something positive to say, but found he happened to agree with Eddie.

"We've just been guessing! We don't even know if we're within a hundred miles of an eagle cliff!" In frustration, Eddie picked up a rock and chucked it hard across the narrow gorge.

When it struck the opposite bluff, the entire face of the cliff erupted in motion. A hundred golden eagles took flight, their mighty wings pounding the air. They circled overhead, shrieking, their seven-foot wingspans casting dark shadows that sped across the landscape. After a minute of eardrum-piercing squalls, the eagles gradually settled back into their ancient aeries along the cliff wall.

"Eagle cliff," said Raj, dumbfounded.

"Sometimes," said Eddie, "I am happy to be wrong."

......

The team hiked along the rim of the chasm, searching for a place to cross. The eagles seemed to roost only upon the south-facing side, where they enjoyed the most sunlight. At last Raj, scampering ahead, found a spot where the gorge narrowed. A single spur of stone jutted most of the way across the precipice.

The gap was a six-foot jump. One by one they took running starts and leapt over the thousand-foot drop. Raj insisted on going first, followed by Molly. The Darkhad went next, making the jump seem effortless. Addison and Eddie, dreading a fatal plunge, went last.

Soon they were all clinging to the lip of the eagle cliff. They edged along the promontories, using cracks and handholds to maneuver their way higher. The eagles regarded them suspiciously from their perches. Addison had gotten a bit better about his fear of heights, but he still had a healthy interest in not dying. All in all, climbing up the precipice was not among the brighter spots of his day.

Raj navigated his way up the steep rock until he reached the level plateau. He shouted instructions, encouragement, and suggestive criticisms to the team until they all crested the cliff and lay flopped beside him, catching their breath. A flat field spread out before them, bursting with wildflowers.

The team lunched on the remains of Nobody's mutton jerky. They crossed the field and found a river where they refilled their canteens. "This may be the route Sir Frederick took," said Addison, examining the lay of the land. "He said to cross the eagle cliff and swim beneath a river."

He had barely finished his sentence before Raj tore his shirt off and plunged into the frigid mountain stream. Despite his shivering, Raj swam back and forth across the river, dipping his head under the clear water. "I don't get it," he called at last. "I'm swimming beneath the river and I don't know what I'm supposed to be looking for."

Raj climbed out of the water, dripping wet, and lay down on a sunny rock to dry.

"Wow, you're finally clean!" said Molly.

Raj frowned, a bit disappointed. He preferred not to attract wolves with his freshly clean scent. He wondered if his prized can of bear spray would also work on wolves.

Addison paced in a circle, quieting his mind, working over the puzzle of the river. He thought back on everything he had read about the Khan's burial. He pictured the funeral procession: Genghis Khan's body draped in white robes and bundled with sandalwood to prevent insects from devouring the remains. Addison spoke his thoughts aloud because that had often helped him in the past. "Legends claim the tomb was hidden by ten thousand horsemen who trampled the earth to make it even. Then a river was diverted and a forest planted over it, burying the site forever."

"Do you believe it?" asked Molly.

Addison stared at the river, thinking. It was a young river, nowhere near as old as the one that carved the thousand-foot gorge in the mountain. In fact, thought Addison, judging from the shallow banks, the river might be only a few hundred years old. He arrived at a decision and headed upstream. "Genghis Khan moved heaven and earth to hide his tomb. We have to move heaven and earth to find it."

"What are we doing?" asked Raj, jogging after him.

"Diverting the river. If the Mongols moved it here, we need to move it somewhere else. It's the only way we can truly see what Sir Frederick saw beneath the river." Addison did what he always did when he needed to cause a large amount of destruction. He turned to Raj.

"I'm on it!" Raj eagerly scrambled up the hillside until he found a massive boulder overlooking the river. His plan was to shove it loose and send it rolling downhill to block the waterway. Raj nearly gave himself a hernia pushing on the giant rock, but it did not budge.

Frustrated, Raj found a large stick, levered it under the rock, and heaved. The stick snapped.

Losing patience, Raj climbed higher up the hillside, searching for a bigger stick. In his haste, he tripped over some creeping vines and landed hard on some loose shale. The shale rocks skittered downhill, kicking loose a few large rocks. Soon, boulders tumbled downhill, pushing even larger rocks ahead of them.

Addison's team looked up in horror to see a full-scale avalanche thundering straight toward them. They turned and ran.

An entire hillside worth of stone and dirt crashed into the river, blocking it entirely. The river water backed up, overfilled its banks, and found a new course down the mountainside. Addison marveled at Raj's astonishing capacity for destruction; even Mother Nature was no match for him. "Good work, Raj!"

Raj emerged from the woods, weaving unsteadily, blanketed in dust. He gave Addison a weak thumbs-up.

••••••

I Don't Know performed a ritual to appease the *nagas*, or water spirits, for disturbing the river. The group fanned out along the drained riverbed, searching for any symbol or clue left among the debris. The wet earth was soggy, muddy, and clogged with leaves.

Nobody searched for a spot deep enough to fill his canteen. Climbing down among rocks once hidden deep underwater, he shouted for Addison's team to come look. When they all gathered near him, he pointed.

In the smooth, stony side of the riverbed lay a tunnel carved in the wet rock, large enough for a man to walk through. Centuries of water were still dribbling out of it when the group stepped inside the cave.

Addison's flashlight emitted a weak orange glow as the batteries ran down. Moving quickly, they followed the path deep into the mountain. As the flashlight began to sputter out completely, the group reached a steep chute, dimly lit by gray light. It was the only way out.

For a few minutes, no one could figure out how to climb the steep chute. The rock walls were too slippery, and the bottom of the vault was riddled with sharp stones that would filet any climber who chanced to fall.

"I know the answer!" Raj pointed to a crack leading directly up the rock face. "In mountain climbing, this is called a fist crack. You wedge your flat hand in the crack, like shaking hands. Once your hand is in the crack, you clench it into a fist. It anchors you to the rock and you climb straight up." Raj demonstrated the technique, spidering up and down the slick stone with ease.

Addison didn't love getting his hands dirty, but he didn't love being trapped in underground tunnels, either. When he slid his hand into the limestone fissure and flexed his fist, he found he could get a strong grip on the rock. Hand over hand, the team hauled themselves up the chute until at last they saw daylight. "Raj, I love it when your survival tricks actually work."

"Me too," said Raj, breathing fresh air. "Me too."

The group emerged in a secret valley, completely encircled by towering cliffs. Addison realized they had found the only passage into this hidden world. His pulse quickened when he gazed out at the field before him, covered in stone monuments. "A necropolis!"

"Wow," said Molly, taking in the view. "Wait, what's a necropolis?"

Addison tightened the strap on his messenger bag and scanned the barren ruins. "It means 'city of the dead.'"

Chapter Thirty-Nine
The City of the Dead

RAJ SCAMPERED UP THE bowl of the rocks and scouted the mountain below. A thousand feet down, he spotted tiny dots of people hiking up the mountain path. Their group was led by a woman dressed all in black. "Madame Feng. And the triads! They're coming."

The team joined Raj on the rocky ledge.

"How did they find us?" asked Eddie.

Addison frowned. "Maybe they forced Aunt D and Uncle N to cooperate."

Molly shook her head. "Maybe they heard Raj's avalanche and got curious."

Addison turned to Nobody. "Summon the Darkhad. This is Sir Frederick's 'city of the dead.' This must be where the triads are coming."

Nobody seemed thrilled to have the chance to use his two-way radio. He clicked it on, spoke excitedly in Mongolian, and gave Addison a nod.

"How long before the Darkhad arrive?"

"It is too steep for horseback. It could be hours."

"We need Dax for an extraction. See if your Mongol network can get him a message. They can reach him by phone at this tavern." He handed Nobody the business card for the Muddy Duck.

"Let's hope he's still in Mongolia," said Molly.

"He better be." Addison brushed dirt from his hands. "We're going after the golden whip." Addison watched Madame Feng's progress far below on the mountain. "How long before the triads catch up to us?"

"Not long," said I Don't Know.

••••••

The group climbed down off the lip of the crater and entered the city of the dead. Hundreds of white granite tombs filled the hidden hollow between the peaks of the sacred mountain. They crept under an archway built entirely of horse skeletons and down the center avenue, their feet crunching on gravel. They passed carved stone monuments to the great conquerors, Ögedei and Kublai Khan, their victories carved in relief on the base of the statues. They saw the tombs of Genghis's top men, Jebe and Subutai, two of the greatest generals in history. They wandered under the shadows of massive bone piles dedicated to the sky god and the steppe god.

"Why did the Mongols bury everyone aboveground?" Molly whispered.

"It's our tradition. We call it 'sky burial,'" said I Don't Know. "The older Mongols still practice it in the steppe."

The avenue led to a large stone door carved into the mountain. Addison had a pretty good feeling they needed to find a way inside. In front of the door sat a flat disk of rock, like the world's largest dinner plate, and in the middle of the plate was a pile of stones.

"A puzzle!" said Raj.

Eddie blanched. "Nobody touch it! It's probably booby-trapped!"

Addison studied the flat disk. "It's an *ovoo*. The Khan wouldn't want anyone visiting his tomb who wasn't a Mongol." He stepped close to the stone plate. "We have to walk around it three times clockwise."

Everyone circled the disk three times. It was decent exercise, but exactly nothing happened. Addison stood and frowned at the stone disk, but that didn't do anything, either. Then inspiration snuck up behind him and smacked him on the head. "We rotate the rock—not us!"

Addison grabbed an edge of the stone disk and pulled in a clockwise direction. He strained hard while everyone watched quizzically. Raj shrugged and joined in. Finally, with Eddie and Nobody's help, the heavy stone budged and began turning on an axle.

Everyone joined in, rotating the massive disk. They wound it three times clockwise and heard a loud, mechanical *click*, but nothing else seemed to happen.

"What are we forgetting?" asked Addison.

"You must place a stone on top of the rock pile," Nobody said.

Eddie spotted a conveniently located heap of rocks piled next to the *ovoo*. He fetched one and ran to drop it on the cairn of stones in the center of the plate.

"Wait!" Addison grabbed Eddie's wrist. "Remember the ceremony: it must be a white stone." They sorted through the gray and black heap of rocks and found only one white stone, the size of a baseball. Addison hefted it in his hand— it was heavier than the other rocks. He figured that was important.

Nobody had the longest arms—he placed the white stone on top of the cairn of rocks on the plate. It slid cleanly into place, pressing some ancient, hidden lever.

A loud grinding of stone sent Eddie racing for cover.

Addison's team looked up to see the large stone door creaking open in the sheer rock wall before them. The doorway was large enough for a man on horseback to gallop through. The group crossed inside the mountain.

They found themselves in a circular room with a high, vaulted ceiling. Enough light slanted through the doorway that Addison did not have to rely on his flashlight. In the center of the stone room sat a single white rock atop a pedestal. Doors were carved into the rock around the perimeter of the room, and beside each door stood an empty pedestal.

"Another puzzle." Raj glanced up at the stone carvings on the domed ceiling, searching for clues among the warriors and battles depicted in bas-relief.

Eddie wrung his hands. "We don't have time for all these puzzles. If we solve them, all we're doing is making Madame Feng's life easier when she arrives."

"We just need to work more quickly." Addison scanned the room, getting the lay of the land. "The entrance faces south. This room is a *ger*." He crossed to the center and spread out his arms like the pointers on a compass. "The west is the male side, the east is the female side, and the north is the shrine."

He moved to the rear wall and examined the shrine hollowed into the side of the mountain. It contained a few clay icons of horses, the paint faded and chipped. Designs carved into the wall were so worn by time, they were nearly indecipherable.

"What are we supposed to do at a shrine?" Molly asked I Don't Know.

"Pray, I guess."

The team knelt down before the shrine. This maneuver had done wonders in Kashgar and Karakoram, so Addison didn't think they were wasting their time. Still, they prayed for a minute and nothing much seemed to be happening.

"I Don't Know, you guys are always sprinkling your drinks in the air," said Molly. "Will that help?"

"Can't hurt." Addison unscrewed his canteen and spritzed water in the air by flicking his fingers. Everyone else did as well, except for Raj, who found it prudent to always conserve water when in the wilderness. They sprinkled water for a few more seconds, and again, nothing special seemed to happen.

"Wait a minute. Keep doing that!" Addison noticed a drop of water running down the cave wall, carrying away a few centuries of dust. Molly splashed water on the faded designs of the shrine. The dirt melted away, revealing a carving of a whip.

Addison rubbed water over the etching, reviving the faded paint. "A *golden* whip." He traced it with his finger. The tip of the whip pointed directly to a door on the eastern side of the wall. "I know what to do."

He crossed to the center of the room, plucked the white rock from its pedestal, and placed it on the pedestal by the eastern door. With a grinding of stone, the ancient portal swung open.

Addison's team coughed and waved away a few centuries of cobwebs and a billowing cloud of dust. When the air cleared, they saw a row of steps leading into the mountain.

Chapter Forty

The Tomb

ADDISON'S FLASHLIGHT WAS TAPPED, so Molly scrounged in her survival kit and found a magnesium flare. She struck it and held it aloft, showering red sparks in all directions. They crept into the tunnel under its crackling red glow.

Stairs carved into the rock eased their descent. The passage was wide enough to send echoes up and down the corridor. Carved stone demons leered from the walls of the cave. Skeletons of warriors flanked the tunnel, cloaked in dusty shrouds. Cobwebs had settled on the helms and dulled the blades of the axes. Addison saw the heaped bones of the butchered laborers who once carved this hidden tunnel.

The passage opened into a massive gaping cavern with a rough dirt floor. In the center was a large stone tomb. Addison removed his ivy cap and wiped the hair from his brow. "This is it. The tomb of the Khan."

"Death," said Raj. "The dark shroud that shields our mortal gaze from the light of destiny." Everyone turned to stare at him.

"Raj," said Addison, "someday you are going to be a big hit at dinner parties."

Nobody used Molly's flare to light the ancient torches anchored on the cavern walls.

The group crossed the chamber to stand reverently by the stone tomb.

Molly broke the silence. "So . . . where's the treasure? And where's the golden whip?"

Addison quoted Sir Frederick's clue. "'Know the Khan to open the tomb; know thyself to escape.' We have to try opening the tomb. The whip must be inside."

Nobody shook his head. "We cannot open the Khan's coffin. It's sacred."

Addison saw his point. He had a hard time picturing Sir Frederick rooting around inside a coffin as well. "His clue says we have to open the tomb. I don't see what our options are." He tried lifting the stone lid. Everyone pitched in to help. They strained until their faces boiled red. Nothing budged. The tomb appeared to be made of solid rock.

They scoured the stone sarcophagus for secret buttons or levers. Addison pushed and prodded like a Swedish masseuse.

"Are you sure this is the right coffin?" asked Molly at last. She was completely frustrated and completely covered in sweat. "Maybe we're on the wrong mountain."

"If you think this is a mistaken grave, you are gravely mistaken." Addison crossed his arms and pondered. The stone tomb was completely uninteresting in every possible way. There were no ornaments or impressive designs. It did not seem a proper resting place for one of the most power-ful people in history. "Okay, I'll admit, this doesn't seem like the tomb of a world conqueror. I've seen coffee tables that are nicer than this."

Nobody shrugged. "The Khan grew up poor. He was once a slave. Maybe he wanted something humble?"

Addison wasn't buying it. "What about the ten thousand horsemen who trampled his grave? What about diverting a river to cover it? What about murdering all the laborers? Why go through all that trouble and just have this boring lump of rock? This can't be the tomb—it's too easy."

Eddie was appalled. "You think this was easy? We crossed the entire Gobi Desert for this!"

Addison began pacing. Moving his feet helped jostle the neurons around in his brain, like shaking a snow globe. He left zigzagging tracks on the dirt floor. "The Khan's signature move on the battlefield was the false retreat. He was an expert at hiding his strength. This," Addison declared, pointing at the tomb, "is a decoy." He was now feeling quite sure of himself.

"All right, so where's the real tomb?" Molly gestured around the empty cavern.

Addison scratched his chin. He knew Madame Feng's team would arrive soon. He would hate to have come all this way just to see his hopes buried by a coffin. He kicked at the dirt. He kicked at the dirt a second time. He was about to kick at the dirt a third time when an idea struck him. "You know what's always bothered me? Why have ten thousand horses trample your grave and then divert a river over it? You don't need one if you have the other—it's overkill."

Molly frowned. "What's your point?"

"Mo, stick to me like a straitjacket. What if they're two separate things? We already diverted a river to reach the necropolis. What if this is where the horses trampled the earth to flatten it?"

"You're assuming they could even get horses up this mountain."

"They were the Mongol army—they could do anything."

Molly looked down at the cavern floor. "You're saying the Khan's tomb is underneath us?"

Addison nodded emphatically. "Why else is a cave

floor, inside a mountain, perfectly flat and covered in dirt?"

Molly raised her eyebrows. She studied the vast cave. "So the Mongols carted dirt inside this cavern, buried the Khan's tomb, and trampled the dirt flat to hide it."

"Precisely. Molly, you are easily in my top five favorite Cookes." Addison crossed to the stone sarcophagus. "*'Know the Khan to open the tomb; know thyself to escape.'*" He presented his case like a trial lawyer, making his summation before the jury. "Someone who truly knows the Khan would know this was not his coffin. And they would not dare defile a Khan by opening up his casket. We, my friends, are not supposed to open the sarcophagus at all."

"What are we supposed to do, then?"

Addison had a hunch he had a hunch. He hunched over. "We move the decoy." He pushed hard against the heavy stone. His team threw their shoulders in with him. It slid a few feet across the dirt, revealing a staircase burrowed into the earth.

••••••

Addison's group grabbed torches from the wall and descended the stone steps. Raj took the lead, scouring for booby traps. After fifty paces, the hallway opened into the largest cave Addison had ever seen or imagined. They held their torches high, peering into the gloom.

The cavernous chamber was piled with endless heaps of rubble, covered in a thick blanket of dust, as far as the eye could see. Addison could not mask his disappointment.

Eddie was outraged. "Sir Frederick left us all these clues just to lead us to a dust heap? Was he just playing a practical joke?"

Even Nobody and I Don't Know looked upset.

Addison couldn't decide his next move. He felt like giving up. Maybe, he thought, he should just wait for Madame Feng to arrive, and turn himself in.

Molly scanned the mountains of dust and surprised absolutely no one by breaking into a sneezing fit. The more she sneezed, the more dust she scattered in the air. It was a vicious cycle. When she regained control of herself, she did something that *was* surprising. She laughed.

Addison found this in poor taste. They had just been on a six-thousand-mile wild goose chase, and the last thing anyone needed was Molly to laugh about it.

Molly laughed harder. She moved to the nearby pile of rubble where her sneezing had scattered some dust. She took a deep breath and blew away more dust. She held her nose to keep from sneezing again. She plucked something out of the heap, blew on it, and polished it with her shirt-sleeve. She held it up for the group to see.

It was a gold coin.

Addison's eyes communicated this information to his

brain. His brain shook his head and ordered his eyes to double-check. He looked again. It was definitely a gold coin.

Addison's feet carried him to the nearest hill of gray rubble. He took a diver's breath and blew away a cloud of dust. The hill was a heap of gold. "Guys . . . I think we're in the right mountain."

The group fanned out across the giant cavern. Everywhere their footprints ran, they turned the gray dust to shining gold. Everywhere they breathed revealed more hilltops of glittering gold. Every object they touched turned gray dust to shimmering treasure.

Eddie's brain couldn't think of anything better to do, so it hung his mouth open and aired it out for a while. They were standing in an entire underground world of gold. Treasure from China filled the main atrium. The wealth of Persia was piled high in the next cavern. There were mountains of loot from Kazakhstan to Khwarezmia, from Kashgar to Kiev. The treasures of all the fallen empires sacked by the Mongol Horde.

Addison wandered in a daze. He admired the intricate silverwork of the Dariganga people. He hefted a scimitar gilded with the Sword Verse of the Qur'an, the sheath inlaid with rubies. He found a sultan's ivory chess set, the dark pieces carved with sapphires and the light pieces with emeralds.

In the center of the chamber was a high stone platform

that rose twenty feet in the air. It was decorated with jewels, weapons, and the bones of horses, slaves, and warriors.

Addison climbed the marbled steps to the Khan's tomb, sealed forever in a casket of ivory: the final resting place of the man who had conquered the world. Next to the tomb was a golden throne, and on the throne, a golden whip.

······

Nobody and I Don't Know dropped to their knees and bowed, pressing their foreheads to the ground.

Addison opened his messenger bag and found his father's copy of *The Secret History of the Mongols*. He read his father's signature on the inside cover and then rested the book on the golden throne of the Khan. "We did it, Dad."

His team mounted the steps and joined him at his side.

"You know," said Molly, "if you still want to be a stock-broker, all you need to get started is a few handfuls of this gold."

Addison realized what Molly had known all along: he could never give up archaeology. "This gold doesn't belong to us. It belongs to history."

Eddie stared at the mountains of treasure surrounding them. "Do you think the gold is booby-trapped if we try to take it? Like in the Incan treasure vault?"

"It might be. Sir Frederick didn't take any treasure, and he made it out. Maybe that's what the clue meant by *'know thyself to escape.'* We didn't come here for the treasure."

"Addison, what is the point of treasure hunting if we don't get any treasure?"

"The treasure is not the true reward, Eddie."

"Well, what is?"

"The adventure," said Raj.

"Knowledge," said Molly.

"This is," said Addison. He held up the golden whip.

Chapter Forty-One

The Golden Whip

ADDISON LIKED THE WEIGHT of the whip in his grip. The handle was braided with silver, and the eight feet of coiled, looping thong was constructed of interlocking golden links hinged together by a cunning design. He wondered what ingenious goldsmith had crafted it. Was it true the Khan had simply discovered the whip by a river as a boy and taken it as a sign he would one day rule the world? The truth was buried in the centuries.

Nobody watched him impatiently. "We're going to hide it in the forest, right?"

Addison's mind was racing like a gerbil on an exercise wheel. He thought about Sir Frederick's words: "know thyself." He could either save the whip or use it to save his aunt and uncle. Or maybe there was a way to do both.

"I have a plan. As soon as we get out of here, you alert the Darkhad. I trade the whip to Madame Feng for my aunt and uncle. Once they are safely free from her, the Darkhad ambush Madame Feng and retrieve the whip."

"It's too risky," Nobody said. "Madame Feng isn't going to go down without a fight. You blew up her palace, Addison."

"Technically, that was Raj, but I take your point."

"It was an honest mistake," said Raj. "It could have happened to anyone."

Addison stepped closer to the two Darkhad. "You said yesterday you'd choose protecting the Khan's relics over saving someone's life. But what would you do if it was *your* family?"

Nobody weighed it in his mind. He glanced at his sister.

I Don't Know nodded. "Addison's plan could work. The Darkhad outnumber the triads."

Nobody took a deep breath and looked at Addison solemnly. "You may take the golden whip. But touch nothing else."

Addison held the whip to his chest and nodded. Then he was on the move, descending the Khan's staircase. "We have to go quickly if this is going to work."

Eddie watched the team leaving. "Wait, just so I'm clear . . . no gold?"

······

The group raced out of the mountain tomb, crossed the hidden necropolis, and climbed down the slippery chute into the secret mountain passage. They emerged from the rocky hollow in the dry riverbed and dashed across the alpine meadow. Reaching the eagle cliff, they sprinted along the edge, searching for the spur that stretched across the gorge.

Molly scanned the line of the cliff wall and cried out.

The Darkhad chieftain was standing on the far side of the chasm, pointing angrily at the golden whip. "What have you done? Put it back!"

I Don't Know shouted back across the gorge. "It's all real, Uncle! Everything we've guarded for all these years!"

The chieftain drew his dagger and held it over his head. "I'll kill all of you!"

"If you kill us," said Addison, "who will know how to return the whip to Genghis's tomb?"

The chieftain hesitated. "What do you want?"

"I trade the whip for my aunt and uncle. Then you ambush the triads and retrieve the whip."

"I cannot gamble with the whip, and I cannot help you." He pointed to the river churning in the gorge a thousand feet below. "A Mongol may cross this river only to bury a Khan. And there has not been a Khan for five hundred years."

"You knew about the necropolis?" asked I Don't Know.

"I know many things. I know I will never break my vows. I know I will not help you play games with the triads. Return the whip to the tomb!"

Addison brandished the whip in both hands for the chieftain to see. "I'm handing the golden whip to Madame Feng. You can either help us or lose the whip forever."

The chieftain glowered at Addison. "I should have killed you when I had the chance."

"You may still get that chance. But first, help me. We can save my aunt and uncle and save the treasure!"

I Don't Know called to her uncle. "The triads are coming! Cross the river and help us!"

The chieftain brooded silently, then cocked his ear to the call of an ibex horn sounding an alarm. He stepped back among the pine trees and vanished from view.

"He'll help us, I know he will," said I Don't Know.

Nobody shook his head. "Stubborn man. He'd rather lose the whip than break the rules."

"We have to cross the river. Then your uncle can help us." Addison turned and raced toward the spur to make the leap back across the gorge. But by the time he reached the cliff's edge, the triads were already lining up on the opposite side, blocking his escape.

···

One after another, Madame Feng's crew leapt across the gorge. Even Aunt Delia and Uncle Nigel.

Addison counted nearly a dozen triads working their way up the side of the cliff. "I can't do this alone. We're outnumbered." He turned to Nobody. "Alert the Darkhad. Quickly!"

Nobody climbed up on a high rock and furiously blew a panic call on his ibex horn.

Molly surveyed the plateau for another route down the mountain. She saw they were surrounded by thousand-foot drops. "The triads are blocking our only escape. We're trapped up here."

Madame Feng inched along the cliff wall and stepped into view.

Addison turned to I Don't Know and gestured to the sword hilt strapped to her back. "How are you guys with those swords?"

"Not so great against guns."

Addison grimaced. He realized his best move now was to stall for time and hope the Darkhad would arrive. "Madame Feng, what a lovely surprise! We were just admiring the view. How did you find us?"

Madame Feng sidestepped her way along the cliff, edging closer to Addison. She called over the roar of the water that echoed in the vast ravine. "Your aunt and uncle finally became cooperative. I told them I still had you locked up and that if they didn't find the tomb, I would kill you."

"How clever!"

"It worked. Your uncle suddenly told me about the Great Taboo. He even seems to know clues to the treasure."

Addison shot a look at Uncle Nigel. There were fresh bruises on his stubbled jaw, and blood was crusted around his nose and lip. He looked wrung out like a sponge.

"Are the Feng casinos traded on the stock market?" asked Addison.

"Why, yes," said Madame Feng, confused.

"I hope your stock craters," said Addison. And he meant it to scorch.

Madame Feng shuffled closer along the cliff face, and Addison held up a warning hand to stop her.

"Remember what I offered you in your dungeon?" Addison held up the golden whip so that it cast dazzling sparkles in the afternoon sun. "If I get the whip, I get my aunt and uncle. You don't need them. This is what you came for."

Madame Feng gazed upon the Khan's whip, her eyes reflecting awe, wonder, and greed. She advanced along the rocky ledge.

Addison stretched his arm as if to toss the whip into the void. "I don't need the whip—I'll throw it away!"

Madame Feng froze. She was reading Addison and calculating.

He sensed her fear of losing the whip, and it gave him confidence. "Send my aunt and uncle over and I'll throw you the whip."

"You think I'm naïve? I can't trust the boy who burned down my palace!"

"I don't want to point fingers, but technically it was Raj who burned down your palace." Addison gestured to the top of the cliff, where the stony precipice met the plateau. "Let my aunt and uncle climb up to the summit. Then I will toss you the whip."

Madame Feng turned to her triads. "Let them climb!" she shouted.

Aunt Delia and Uncle Nigel found handholds and footholds and worked their way up to the crest of the cliff to where the sheer rocks rounded off to a plateau. The summit was crowned in a wide field of wildflowers. Hu trained his gun on the pair in case they tried to bolt before the exchange was made.

It was now time for Addison to toss the whip to Madame Feng.

She gestured impatiently. "What are you waiting for?"

Addison could stall no longer. He whispered to I Don't Know, crouched beside him on the ledge. "Where is your uncle? Where are the Darkhad?"

"He'll come," whispered I Don't Know.

Nobody scanned the opposite cliff and saw no sign of the warriors. "He won't break his vows by crossing the gorge. He's too stubborn."

Addison continued to hold the golden whip over the edge of the chasm. He ran his free hand through his hair, and his fingers came away wet with sweat. "I've stalled as long as I can. The Darkhad are too late."

Madame Feng yelled impatiently, her voice echoing back and forth across the abyss. "Toss the whip now or we shoot them!"

Out of options, Addison was winding up to toss the whip to Madame Feng when he heard the drone of an engine. He looked up to see a helicopter hurtling through the air. Addison, an eternal optimist, immediately assumed this was good news: perhaps Dax had acquired a helicopter pilot's license. When he saw the Russian flag on the large military chopper, he realized his situation was about to get much, much worse.

The golden eagles, agitated by the roaring blades, took flight from their nests, flapping in circles around the gorge.

Molly shouted to Nobody over the din of the chopper. "Where is your uncle? Blow the horn!"

Nobody desperately blew his ibex horn. He blew until his cheeks were red. He blew until the sound was swallowed up by the rumble of the helicopter. The chopper landed in the field, the wildflowers billowing under the gale of the blades. Still no Darkhad came.

Madame Feng and her triads trained their guns on the helicopter, watching nervously.

Addison gripped the whip in his hands. He watched Boris leap from the suicide doors of the chopper, followed by a platoon of *vori*. They seized Aunt Delia and Uncle Nigel, pinning their arms behind their backs.

Boris ignored the triads and their guns. He ignored Madame Feng. He confidently closed in on Addison, who backed to the edge of the cliff.

There was nothing behind Addison except a very long view of the valley and a very short trip down. "Hello, Boris. New pants, I see."

Boris looked down at his new leather duds and grunted.

"I know how the triads found us. But how did you?"

Boris stopped ten feet from Addison. Addison's whole group was cornered on the cliff's rocky brink. "We were eating lunch in the valley when the river suddenly dried up and reappeared a mile away. We got interested."

"Ah, yes. We started an avalanche. It's a long story." Addison looked over Boris's shoulder. The Russians outnumbered the triads and held the high ground, weapons raised. The triads clung to the rocks on the side of the cliff, aiming their weapons right back. Madame Feng's eyes darted back and forth from Boris to the golden whip.

Addison took a glance to his right at the one-thousand-foot chasm with the river churning far below. He saw no escape.

Boris stepped closer.

Addison held the whip over the precipice. The trick had worked once, so Addison had developed an affection for it.

Boris paused, calculating.

"Send over my aunt and uncle!"

The big Russian seemed to consider it.

Addison scanned the scene. His eyes roved to the chopper. A man in an elegant black suit stood by the suicide door, his face hidden in shadow. Addison felt fear, primal fear, in the pit of his stomach. The very sight of the man filled him with dread. Addison whispered a single word. "Malazar."

Boris read the fear in Addison's eyes. He took another step closer.

Addison stretched out his arm, threatening to hurl the whip into the void.

The *vor* only smiled. "You cannot destroy the whip."

Addison's arm quivered. He clenched his teeth.

The Russian took another step. "You are a Cooke. You spend your life saving these relics. It is in your blood, it is who you are. You'd sooner throw yourself off that cliff than destroy the whip."

Addison lowered his arm, defeated. He tossed the whip in the grass at Boris's feet. "Give me my aunt and uncle."

Boris turned to the *vori* who held Aunt Delia and Uncle Nigel pinned by their elbows. He gave a single nod of his chin.

The *vori* dragged Aunt Delia and Uncle Nigel to the side of the cliff.

Then they shoved them both over the edge.

Addison shouted.

Molly screamed.

Uncle Nigel clung to a rocky ledge, his other hand gripping Aunt Delia's wrist. Their feet dangled over infinity. Uncle Nigel's glasses slid from his face and tumbled hundreds of feet through the air. It was impossible to see where they fell; the canyon was clouded with mist kicked up by the river.

"Hang on!" Addison yelled.

Raj cupped his hands and shouted, "If you fall, aim for white water!"

Uncle Nigel's arm shook with the strain. His hand slid along the crumbling rock, losing its grip.

"Hang on!" Addison screamed again.

Uncle Nigel looked at Addison, his expression sad and vacant.

Addison realized that without his glasses, Uncle Nigel could not even see him.

Aunt Delia never screamed.

Uncle Nigel's hand slipped from the rock. He and Aunt Delia silently fell, vanishing into the mist.

Chapter Forty-Two

Malazar

ADDISON STOOD FROZEN ON the spot, unable to blink, unable to speak. Somewhere, he could hear Molly screaming. Eddie and Raj grabbed him by the shoulders, urging him to move. He stumbled over tufts of wild grass as though in a dream, barely aware of voices or the movement of his own feet.

Boris snatched the golden whip off the ground.

Madame Feng shouted. The triads opened fire.

The *vori* fired right back, pinning them down.

Boris trotted the whip back to the helicopter and handed it to Malazar. He pivoted and plodded back toward Addison, hollering over the roar of the chopper. "Now it is your turn. All Cookes must die."

Addison watched numbly as the big Russian swatted Eddie and Raj aside. Boris grabbed a handful of Addison's shirt to stand him up straight. Addison stared expressionlessly at the enormous fist swinging toward his gut.

The punch belted Addison back to his senses. His stomach seized up and he doubled over, unable to draw breath. He dropped to his knees, pain focusing his mind. He became aware of the battlefield. *Vori* were closing in on Molly, Nobody, and I Don't Know. Other *vori* were taking on the triads. There were still no Darkhad to be seen.

Boris wound up for a knockout punch to Addison's temple. Addison, unable to move or breathe, realized the blow might kill him. It was strange how the thought wafted into his mind, a simple objective fact: he was about to die. Addison was trying to think of something clever to say or do when he was greeted by the unusual sight of Tony Chin flying horizontally through the air.

Tony's foot connected with Boris in a devastating kick.

Addison's mind reeled, stunned to find himself still alive and breathing. It was a pleasant surprise. He stared, dazed, as Tony wrestled the bigger man to the ground. Tony did not stand much of a chance against the giant Russian. It seemed a pity; Addison rather liked Tony.

Tony rolled onto his back, frantically blocking Boris's punches with his elbows.

"Addison, your butterfly knife!"

Addison's stomach was slowly recovering from Boris's punch. He found himself able to take small sips of breath. Small sips were better than nothing. He drew his butterfly knife from his pocket and slashed at Boris.

The big *vor* rolled off of Tony and backed off a pace.

Tony grinned at Addison. "Remember, knife point down."

Addison nodded, flipping the knife in his hand with practiced ease.

Boris wheeled, seeking an easier target, and turned on Molly. His job was to eliminate Cookes, and it didn't matter which. "Come here, little girl." He swung an arm for her neck, hoping to clothesline her off her feet.

Molly's face was streaked with tears. She managed to duck the blow.

Boris overreached, his body overbalanced.

Molly saw her opening. She centered her weight and scooped her foot into the air, scoring a punishing roundhouse kick. She planted her foot right in Boris's kidney. Her balance, her breathing, her timing—she knew it was perfect.

The big *vor* stumbled backward a step, clutching his side, blinking his eyes in surprise.

Molly blew the strand of hair from her face. "I'm not a little girl."

Before Boris could respond, Tony Chin attacked him again.

Addison grabbed Molly by the arm. They slipped past Boris and Tony and sprinted across the field. Addison's mind was still in dull, ringing shock from the sight of his aunt and uncle falling into oblivion. He forced his feet to keep moving—he had a vague plan of reaching the river for safety. Eddie and Raj galloped alongside him.

Halfway to the river, Addison glanced over his shoulder to see Tony flat on the ground and Boris pounding toward them. Addison's team put on steam, but Boris's legs were longer, catching up quickly. The group's hundred-yard lead became ninety, and then eighty. Addison racked his brain for options. "Molly, your sling!"

Molly plucked the weapon from her survival pack and scooped up a stone on the run. She spun the sling over her head, wheeled on Boris, and loosed the shot.

The rock sailed three feet over his head. He was now only fifty yards away.

She snatched up a second rock on the fly and sent it sailing at Boris. It grazed his kneecap, but he kept right on coming. It was like flinging a pebble at a freight train.

Addison could see they weren't going to make it to the river—Boris was too fast. Addison had one last card to play. He drew his flare gun from his blazer, spun, and fired at Boris. He missed, sending a bolt of red fireworks sizzling across the plateau to explode over the valley. The daylight turned from yellow to red.

Addison had no more rounds for the flare gun. He could see no more stones for Molly among the wildflowers.

Raj stepped forward. "I've got this." He pulled a metal can from his pack and held it in front of his body like a talisman. He stood his ground, staring down Boris.

Boris saw they were no longer fleeing. He slowed to a stop and stared at Raj's can, amused. "What is that, a soda?"

Raj solemnly shook his head, no. "Bear spray."

Boris only had time to raise one eyebrow. Raj pulled the tab. A jet of pepper spray blasted Boris in the snout. He wailed like he'd bear-hugged a beehive.

Addison's team turned and bolted.

Boris, enraged, pulled out his gun for the first time. He jacked the slide and aimed through red and swollen eyes. His first two bullets fired wide.

Addison ran so fast, he thought his chest would burst. He wondered if anyone had ever died of a heart attack while trying to run from being shot by a gun.

"He's going to kill us!" Eddie shouted.

"Babatunde Okonjo!" Raj called.

"What about Babatunde Okonjo?" Molly hollered.

Raj sprinted faster and pointed ahead. "Run for the river! It only takes three feet of water to stop a bullet!"

"Are you sure?"

"All bullets up to fifty-caliber disintegrate in just under three feet of water!"

A third bullet whistled overhead.

Addison did not have the mental energy to question Raj. Besides, he didn't have a better plan to offer. He was glad they had diverted the river; it was closer now. The shock wave of a fourth bullet sizzled past his ear.

Molly's foot caught on a rock and sent her sprawling. Raj picked her up by the elbow. The group reached the riverbank.

"Dive!" shouted Raj.

They leapt headfirst into the river and swam, pulling hard, willing themselves deeper and deeper under the current.

Addison watched a bullet strike the surface of the water, flattening on impact. The slug slowed, tracing an arc through the water until it floated, harmlessly, past Addison's head. He reached out and cupped the bullet in his hand. It was warm to the touch.

More slugs carved paths through the water, streaking to a stop before they reached Addison's team in the depths. Together, they swam to the far side of the river, finally breaching the surface when their lungs were burning.

Molly clapped Raj hard on the back. "Raj, you saved me—you saved all of us!"

Raj blushed red and was unable to speak.

"Boris still has more bullets!" shouted Eddie, pointing across the river.

Boris's eyes were still streaming tears from the bear spray. He blinked hard and took careful aim at Addison.

Addison saw the moment Boris's gun barrel drew level with his right eye. That was when an arrow struck Boris in the thigh. He collapsed to one knee, firing his gun uselessly into the dirt.

The Darkhad climbed over the crest of the eagle cliff, loosing arrows and shouting their battle cries. Both triads and *vori* were driven before them.

Addison watched the triads form a protective circle around Madame Feng. Darkhad warriors charged the gang members, attacking with arrows, spears, and hand-to-hand fighting. Hu was tackled to the ground and lost in the melee.

Madame Feng called out to Tony Chin, begging for help, but could not remember his name. "You there! Do something! Help me!"

Addison saw Tony, battered and bruised, turn his back on Madame Feng. Tony waved goodbye to Addison and strolled away across the meadow, heading for a stand of trees. The Darkhad swept past him. He disappeared into the forest.

The Darkhad surrounded the Russians, who put up a stiff fight.

Nobody turned to Addison. "We have to join the Darkhad. They need us."

Addison nodded. "I'm sorry about the golden whip."

I Don't Know gripped Addison's hands in hers. "I'm sorry the Darkhad were late."

Addison shook his head. He was not ready to think about it. "Whatever happens, the Darkhad must divert this river back. There's still a chance the Russians will never find the entrance to the hidden valley."

Nobody urged his sister toward the battlefield. "C'mon, they need us."

I Don't Know turned back one more time and hugged Addison fiercely. She whispered in his ear. "I'm so sorry about your aunt and uncle." She turned and ran after her brother.

Addison watched the Russians retreat to their military helicopter, the Darkhad charging after them. To his surprise, the helicopter shut its doors to the *vori* and lifted off. He caught a glimpse of Malazar in the passenger seat, clutching the golden whip and abandoning his men.

Boris stood under the hurricane winds of the rotor blades and bellowed in rage.

The Darkhad fired arrows up at the fleeing chopper, the points bouncing harmlessly off the metal frame. The helicopter sped north, shrinking into the distance.

Addison wondered if his team could escape. He knew that soon the Darkhad would turn their fury on him.

Molly cried out, stabbing her finger at the sky. A plane

appeared along the ridge of the cliffs. It flew dangerously low over the rim of the gorge and stuck a short landing on the field of wildflowers.

"Dax!" Raj shouted.

Addison's group splashed into the river and swam across. Sopping wet, they hurtled over the hillocks of grass until they drew even with the plane.

Dax kicked open the door with his foot. He was already steering the plane due south for an exit.

Mr. Jacobsen barked when he saw the group. He tried to bound off the plane to greet everyone, but Dax held him by the collar.

Raj leapt aboard, calling over the roar of the engines, "I knew you'd come back for us!"

"Got a call at the Muddy Duck. Wouldn't have found you if you hadn't shot that flare."

"What airplane is this?"

"The Cessna Skyhawk," Dax said proudly.

Raj gave a thumbs-up. "She's beautiful."

Addison's team piled on board. Dax was already gunning the engine by the time Raj yanked the door shut and sealed it.

Darkhad warriors thundered toward the tiny plane, firing their weapons.

Dax aimed for the lip of the field. Just beyond it lay a thousand-foot drop. "One hundred yards of runway," he muttered. He kissed his finger and tapped a brand-new plastic frog on his dashboard.

Addison's team touched it for good luck.

Dax opened the engines up. The kick of speed flattened Addison's group against the back of their seats. The edge of the world rushed up to meet them.

The little plane plummeted right over the side of the cliff before catching wind. The engines revved higher, and the plane soared skyward.

Addison looked back through his window at the Black Darkhad screaming across the field, swords high over their heads, descending on the remaining Russians. He never saw what became of Boris. He didn't need to.

Dax packed on elevation, drawing the plane far out of the reach of Darkhad arrows.

Molly clutched Dax's arm. "We have to go back for Aunt Delia and Uncle Nigel. Maybe they survived the fall! Maybe they're down there!"

Dax surveyed the thousand-foot gorge. He grimaced and shook his head. "I can't get a plane in there—it's too dangerous. And the Darkhad will kill you if they find you."

Molly turned to Addison. "Nobody and I Don't Know—they trusted us. We have to retrieve the golden whip!"

"We will, Molly."

"How?"

Addison could only shake his head.

The mountains faded away into the distance.

They flew for a long time in silence. Raj, in the front seat, eventually explained to Dax everything that had happened.

Addison stared numbly out of his window, watching the earth roll away below. He did not speak for hundreds of miles.

They passed over the soot-stained skies of Ulaanbaatar and roared high above the blank canvas of the Gobi. Addison took off his uncle's medallion. He could not bear to wear it—he felt as if he did not deserve the honor. He shoved the chain into his blazer pocket.

Sunlight died in the west. Streaks of gold and orange light glimmered across the steppe. At last, Addison turned to Molly. "That was him," he said simply. "The man in the helicopter. That was Malazar."

Chapter Forty-Three

Goodbyes

DAX HAD NEVER HEARD Addison so silent. He put as many miles as he could between Addison and Mongolia, and finally glided the Cessna into Xilin Gol airport in the remote northern reaches of China.

Mr. Jacobsen loped alongside the group as they strode into the dusty terminal. Dax scanned the flights etched on a chalkboard. "If you catch the connection to Beijing, there's a direct flight to London. You should be okay from there."

Addison nodded. "What about you, Dax? Where are you heading?"

"Me?" Dax pulled the toothpick from his mouth and flicked it into the nearest trash bin. He checked the wind direction and squinted to the west. "I'm going to fuel up the Cessna and work my way back to Tanzania. See if I can work my way back into poacher poaching." He looked at Addison and squeezed his shoulder. "Take care, kid. And thanks."

"For what?"

"For reminding me that I don't always have to look forward. Sometimes you can find your way by looking back." Dax gave Molly's shoulder a squeeze as well.

She shook his hand. "Thanks, Dax. You saved our lives."

Raj, unable to help himself, hugged Dax around his waist. "Can I visit you in Africa sometime?"

Dax nodded and patted Raj on the back. "Anytime." He gave Eddie a thumbs-up, whistled to Mr. Jacobsen, and strode out of the terminal.

Addison pulled out Tony Chin's last credit card and turned it over in his hands. The lettering caught his eye. "You know, I never noticed it. But these are Feng Casino business credit cards. Madame Feng must pay Tony's account."

Eddie stared at Addison, mystified. "So?"

"So," said Addison, "business or first class?"

• • • • • •

With thunderstorm delays, Addison's team didn't land in London's Heathrow Airport until the following evening. Despite the first-class service, they were exhausted from travel and all the events of the previous weeks. They huddled together under the fluorescent airport lights, staring up at the departures with empty eyes.

"There's the 8:08 to New York," said Addison. "Gate forty-seven. You better hop, it's boarding soon."

"Aren't you coming?" asked Eddie.

"Molly and I aren't going back to New York."

Molly stared at Addison in surprise.

Addison had barely spoken in the past day. He'd been dreading this moment. "There's nothing for us in New York, Eddie. Not the museum, not the apartment. It's not safe for us."

As soon as Addison spoke, Molly saw the truth in his words. She still couldn't accept that Aunt Delia and Uncle Nigel were really gone. But without them, there would be no one to pay their apartment rent, no one to feed them, no one to protect them from whoever was after them.

"What will you do?" Raj asked quietly.

Addison took a deep breath. He felt hollow inside, but he didn't want his friends to know how helpless he felt at this moment. "We're going to find our other uncle. Uncle Jasper. He's here in England."

"But you barely know him!" said Eddie.

"We know him a little. We just haven't seen him in a few years."

"He's not crazy or anything?"

Addison answered diplomatically. "He's eccentric. But so are we. And Uncle Nigel told me Uncle Jasper will know how to keep us safe." Addison felt for the medallion in his pocket and added, "He'll have answers we need."

"You could stay with us on 86th Street," said Eddie.

Raj nodded. "You could stay with me if you don't mind sharing the apartment with my three sisters."

Addison shook his head. "I don't know what this prophecy is. I don't know who these people are or what they want. But I know I can't put you in danger."

Raj's brow creased with worry lines. "What about junior high? What about our adventures?"

Addison shook his head again. He didn't know. "Goodbye, Raj. Goodbye, Eddie." He meant to shake their hands. But he found he was hugging them.

Raj gripped him tightly. "That river. It was white water. Your aunt and uncle have a chance, Addison."

"Thanks, Raj."

Raj turned and hugged Molly as well. "If there's ever anything you need . . ."

"I'll call a Code Blue," said Molly.

Unable to speak more, Addison turned and left. Molly followed at his side. It took them an hour to pass through customs and get their passports stamped. When they finally stepped out of the arrivals terminal and onto the wet sidewalk, Addison found his uncle Jasper's address in his notebook. He turned up the collar of his blazer and hailed a cab in the London rain.

••••••

The black hackney cab left the hustle-bustle of the big city. Addison pulled out Uncle Nigel's medallion. Streetlights flickered on the metal and played on the ornate Latin inscriptions. He noticed a date engraved on the back and ran his thumb over it: 1307.

The tires hissed on wet pavement through the quiet suburbs. Soon they reached the countryside, dark and soundless but for the howling wind and tapping rain. They were far from the lights of civilization.

Molly peered out of her rain-streaked window. "Addison, where are we?"

"I have no idea."

At last the hackney turned off the main road, passed a wrought iron gate, and drove down a long driveway lined with towering pillars of Italian cypress. The driveway circled around a lake, through an orchard, and past a stable. It reached a sprawling lawn the size of a football field, the grass somewhat weedy and forlorn. An old gazebo, cracked and overgrown with vines, leaned beside a broken fountain.

The cab continued around a stand of apple trees, and a massive stone building loomed out of the darkness. It featured gothic spires and flying buttresses, and crenulations crowning the bastions of the towers.

"That is not a small house," said Molly, in wonder.

"That's no house," said Addison.

It was a castle.

Chapter Forty-Four

Runnymede

THE DRIVER BRAKED SMARTLY at the wide front steps of the manor and cocked an arm over the seat. "Two hundred quid."

Addison was aghast. "Two hundred British pounds? I can get a camel across the Gobi Desert for half that."

"Well, we ain't in the blooming Gobi Desert, are we, mate?"

"Seems a bit stiff."

The driver raised his voice over the rain pelting the roof of the hackney. "Drove forty-seven kilometers out of London for you, I did. Got to drive all the way back in this grotty, bleeding mess. I ought to charge you four hundred for this pleasure."

Addison realized he did not have any British money, or any money at all. Just as he was wondering what to do, his door was opened by a butler carrying an umbrella. Addison stared in amazement: an honest-to-God butler. Tuxedo tails and everything.

"I shall settle the charges, sir," said the butler with a voice as smooth as butter melting on a griddle.

"Two hundred quid." The cabbie sized up the butler's tuxedo and adjusted his price accordingly. "Plus a twenty-pound tip on account of driving in the blinkin' rain."

"You drive a hard bargain, sir." The butler produced the required banknotes and opened the door for Molly. "May I take your bag, madam?"

"I . . . I guess," said Molly uncertainly. She handed over her father's survival satchel, unsure if she should tip.

The butler helped Molly from the cab, closed her door, and shouldered her satchel, all while holding the giant umbrella perfectly still over Molly and Addison so that they did not get a drop of rain on them.

Addison admired this. "Addison Cooke," he said, smiling. "And my sister, Molly."

The butler studied their faces intently in the taillights of the hackney. Addison read a novel's worth of emotions passing behind the butler's eyes.

"As I live and breathe," said the butler at last. "It is a true pleasure to finally meet you. Jennings is my name." He shook both their hands. "Come inside, then. We'll warm up something for your dinner."

The cabbie, having counted his money, sped off in a hail of gravel.

Jennings guided them up the colonnaded front steps of the portico, through the wide double doors, and into the main entrance hall. Addison gaped up at the curved grand staircase, the marble pillars, and the magnificent crystal chandelier.

"You may set your bags there, Master and Lady Cooke. I shall take them upstairs for you." He shuffled out the umbrella. "You must be exhausted from your trip. I shall show you to your rooms in the east wing so you may change."

Molly was still wrapping her mind around the idea of having "rooms" in something called the "east wing." "We don't have anything to change into. We lost our clothes in a plane crash in Mongolia."

"My best suit," said Addison bitterly.

"I see," said Jennings. "In time I'm sure we will find a spare dinner jacket among your father's old things, Master Cooke. And perhaps something for Lady Cooke as well."

Addison pondered the idea of eating dinner in a formal dinner jacket and found it suited him right down to his wingtips. He realized his mouth was dangling open, so he shut it. It gave him something to do.

Jennings glided up the winding stairs. To Addison's

delight, the butler lifted a candelabrum from a wall sconce. "No electricity in this wing, I'm afraid."

"Why not?"

"Lord Cooke does not favor it."

"*Lord* Cooke," said Molly, perplexed. "You don't mean *Uncle* Jasper?"

"I mean your uncle, Lord Cooke. That was my reason for saying Lord Cooke."

"We're talking about Uncle Jasper, the man who can't drive a car and is banned from Monte Carlo for card counting?" Addison clarified.

"Yes. And we are also talking about Lord Jasper Cooke, the Seventeenth Earl of Runnymede."

Addison and Molly shared a look of confusion and bewilderment. They were quickly catching up to the fact that there were a few small details about their family that Uncle Nigel had failed to mention. "How old is this house?" asked Addison.

"The estate is one thousand years old, sir. This manor house was built atop the ruins of a Saxon castle." Jennings indicated a row of portraits along the upstairs hallway. The early portraits were Victorian, the later ones were Edwardian, and the last portrait displayed Uncle Jasper himself.

"Here we are. Your rooms."

Molly and Addison explored their adjoining rooms. If Addison's room had been any bigger, he could have hosted a soccer match. Molly was astonished to discover she had a four-poster bed. "You could sleep a Girl Scout troop on this thing!" she called. She and Addison had always shared a room and bunk bed, and she had never minded. Now she began to see there were other options in life.

"Are the accommodations to your satisfaction?" asked Jennings.

Addison settled into an armchair by his fireplace and called back across the room. "It will do, Mr. Jennings."

"Excellent. Lord Cooke will be most eager to meet you."

"Where is he?" asked Molly.

"In what room would you expect to find a Cooke?"

"The library," said Addison.

"Precisely," said Jennings. "It is in the western wing."

"Can you draw us a map?"

"I shall await you by the main staircase." Jennings turned and padded silently down the hall.

Addison and Molly did their best to spruce up their torn and dirt-streaked clothes.

•••••••

The siblings retraced their steps to the main staircase and called out Jennings's name. The butler appeared beside them as if summoned from a genie's lamp. He guided them across the vacant, drafty rooms of the castle until they reached the sumptuous library.

Addison took a few tentative steps across the plush Turkish carpet before he drifted to a stop, one hand on his chest. He felt he was having a religious experience, like a pilgrim entering a cathedral. The library was immense. Rolling ladders reached to the tops of the two-story bookcases. Spiraling staircases accessed hidden reading lofts tucked amid the rows. A grand staircase led to a balcony level, filled with still more shelves and cushioned window seats connected by zigzagging catwalks. The walls were hung with painted shields and decorated flags of coats of arms. Suits of armor with plumed helmets guarded the central aisle. A library globe, fully five feet in diameter, rested in its mobile cradle.

Jennings coughed discreetly, lifting Addison from his trance. As they padded across Anatolian rugs, passing taxidermy bears from the Hindu Kush mountains and stuffed Bengal tigers from the Indian subcontinent, Addison glimpsed shelves racked with herbs, potions, tribal masks, and ancient relics. Each aisle contained maps and corked specimens from dark and distant corners of the world: six-foot mahogany blow dart guns from Java, feathered spears from the Maasai warriors of Tanzania, bottled poisons from the ninja of the Iga Province in Japan, and strange herbal remedies from the Blackfoot American Indians of rural Montana.

Jennings arrived at a large rotunda, clasped his

white-gloved hands behind his tailcoat, and announced their presence. "Lord Cooke, may I present Addison and Molly Cooke, from the United States, by way of Mongolia."

In a button-tufted leather chair by the fire sat a man with twinkling blue eyes. He had the tanned and salted look of a man who'd lived many years on the sea. He sprang spryly to his feet and clasped Addison and Molly's hands, his face exuding warmth and sadness. "Has it finally happened, then? My brother Nigel and his dear wife, Delia. They've been taken! I am so sorry."

Addison admired his uncle's crisp and elegant British accent. "How did you know?"

"My sources in Asia. And I believe you've met Eustace at the Hong Kong museum. It's this bloody prophecy, you see. May I say 'bloody' around you? Forgive me, I'm not quite sure how to talk to young people. I'm not entirely sure how to talk to adults, for that matter. If it's all the same, I shall just speak to you as if you're adults. I have somewhat more practice with that."

"What is this prophecy?" asked Molly.

"Who is the Shadow?" asked Addison.

"Did he kill our parents?"

"And why were we never told about any of this?"

"Also, are we rich?" asked Molly.

"Rich?" asked Uncle Jasper. "In knowledge, perhaps. In history, certainly."

"Yes, but are we *rich*, rich?

"Heavens no," Uncle Jasper said, chuckling. "Not even a little bit."

"But this castle, the grounds . . ."

"Been in the family for ages. Costs a bally fortune to maintain. But we are academics, not bankers."

"But you have a butler!" said Molly.

"Jennings has a salary. He makes more than I do." Uncle Jasper gestured them to armchairs by the fireplace. He began filling a pipe. Addison was pleased to see it was the same sort of calabash pipe his uncle Nigel favored. "No, no. If you want to be rich, it's best not to become an archaeologist."

"You're an archaeologist like my father?" asked Addison.

"Your father was an archaeologist like *me*," Uncle Jasper corrected. He lit his pipe with a few meditative puffs. Molly rattled off three sneezes in quick succession. "Gesundheit, my dear. Forgive me, but it seems you both know almost nothing about our family. Your parents fled to New York to escape this blinking prophecy. Felt it was safer to keep you from me or from any ties to who you really are. But destiny has a way of unraveling the most well-intentioned plans, doesn't it?"

Addison and Molly began firing off questions like reporters at a press conference.

Uncle Jasper held up his hands. "All right, young Cookes.

You've been through more than anyone ever should. You require food and rest. Besides, there are some things that must be shown and not told. Tonight, you may ask me three questions and then Jennings will swoop you off to your dinner."

"Is someone trying to kill us?" asked Addison.

"Yes."

Addison gestured to the inch of bronze chain just visible under Uncle Jasper's collar. "Are you a member of some secret order, along with Uncle Nigel?"

"Yes."

"Are we safe here?" asked Molly.

Uncle Jasper looked deep into her eyes, considering. Addison marveled at how those eyes could contain so much humor and so much sorrow. "For now."

"Uncle Jasper, I put my trust in the Darkhad. I took the golden whip from the Khan's tomb and tried to trade it for Aunt Delia's and Uncle Nigel's lives. But I got them killed, and now the Shadow has the whip." Addison felt the edges of tears quivering in his eyes. He was ashamed, hoping nobody would see them in the dim light of the fire.

"Ah, the golden whip. No, no, Addison. You are looking at it all wrong." Uncle Jasper's face was lined with care. "You trusted your instincts. You knew to take the golden whip, and you were right."

"I was right?"

"It's not just a whip, Addison. Or a piece of archaeology. It has a purpose. That is why Malazar is willing to kill for it. It is very important."

"I don't understand."

"The *vori* were going to try to finish off your aunt and uncle no matter what you did. Handing over the whip didn't kill my brother, the Shadow did." Uncle Jasper drew on his pipe and squinted through the smoke. "But you were quite right to free the whip from the tomb, for now the prophecy can continue to unfold. You trusted your instincts—you believed in yourself."

"This prophecy again," said Molly, fighting a losing battle to snuff out a sneeze.

"All in good time."

"Why do they need this golden whip?"

"Technically, that's a fourth question, but I will let it slide. The Shadow needs many things, you see. The whip is part of a puzzle. And we need to be getting it back. And as for you," Uncle Jasper said, casually picking a piece of lint from his creased trousers, "you'll be wanting revenge, I suppose."

Addison raised his eyebrows. "How?"

"Are you learning to fight?"

"Barely." Addison admitted, thinking of his meager progress with his butterfly knife.

"A little," said Molly, remembering her roundhouse kick.

"Can you ride a horse? Wield a sword? Fire a bow and arrow? Can you climb? How far can you run? What languages do you speak?"

"We know a little ancient Greek and Latin."

"Not just dead languages. Living languages!"

"Well," Addison considered. "We're making good headway with English."

Uncle Jasper looked at him doubtfully.

"Can I ask you one more question?" said Addison.

"*May* you ask me," Uncle Jasper corrected.

"Why would we need to use swords and ride horses? Isn't that all old-fashioned?"

Uncle Jasper set his pipe down by an ashtray. "At any time in the past year, have you ever found yourselves in life-or-death situations where you wished you had these skills?"

Addison remembered Tony Chin easily besting him in a sword fight. He remembered nearly falling off his horse several times in the Naadam race. He remembered the terrifying rock climb entering the Khan's necropolis. He began to suspect that not everything he needed to learn could be found in a book. "As a matter of fact, yes."

"The world is full of ancient relics and people who will stop at nothing to steal them." Uncle Jasper loosened his tie, unbuttoned his collar, and drew out his medallion, glittering on its bronze chain. "Did your uncle manage to give you his medallion?"

Addison nodded.

"You may wear it for now, Addison. But eventually, the medallion must be earned."

"Can I earn one?" Molly blurted out.

"You *may* attempt to earn one," Uncle Jasper corrected. "If you choose." He rose to his feet. The butler had magically appeared behind them. "Jennings will prepare you a bite to eat. And then you must get a good night's sleep. Your training begins tomorrow."

······

That night, Addison stood by the window of his room. The rains had cleared, and a full moon lit up the gardens, the meadows, and the forests beyond. He knew he should feel tired, but his body was alert and his thoughts were racing like greyhounds on the backstretch. He needed to learn the secret history of his family. He needed to learn all he could about the Shadow. He needed to learn the prophecy.

The pain of losing his aunt and uncle came to him in waves. The image of their fall would not leave his thoughts. It was too close to the image of his mother's fall, printed forever in his mind's eye.

Addison drew the Templar medallion from his pocket. It gleamed in the moonlight. For the first time since losing his aunt and uncle, he hung it around his neck, the cool metal against his skin somehow electrifying.

There was a new feeling running in his veins. He was not a kid anymore, he sensed that. He had seen too much. He had seen the man responsible for the loss in his life: Malazar.

Addison stood with his bare feet on the wooden floor, watching the storm clouds swirling over the southern skies, and felt a new set to the features of his face, a new glint in his eye. A new mission in his life.

He needed to find out who his parents really were. He needed to retrieve the golden whip. And there was one more thing he needed most of all . . .

Revenge.

Author's Note

......

The Secret History of the Mongols was written shortly after Genghis Khan's death some eight hundred years ago. It is a long and challenging read because it was written in the days before there were Penguin editors. Thanks in large part to this biography, we know quite a lot about Genghis Khan's remarkable journey from kidnapped slave to world conqueror. It is a rewarding story if you can slog through it. *The Travels of Marco Polo*, also written nearly eight hundred years ago, provides similarly vivid detail about the empire of Genghis Khan and is a bit more readable.

In addition to Marco Polo, a number of European explorers traveled throughout the Mongol Empire. These include the Franciscan explorer Giovanni da Pian del Carpine in 1245 and the papal envoy William of Rubruck in 1253. Rubruck reached the Mongol capital of Karakoram and reported finding two churches and an active Christian community. The Knights Templar, a secretive European military order that reached the height of its powers during the time of Genghis Khan, also probably came into contact with the Mongols in some way. For instance, Rembald de Voczon, a Templar master, fought the Mongol Horde at the Battle of Mohi in 1241.

Much of the history of that time period has been lost. The old churches of Kashgar have either been destroyed or converted into mosques as the city's population has changed. The city of Karakorum was sacked by the Chinese in 1388 and is now buried under the earth. A small shantytown is all that remains. Some parts of the Erdene Zuu Monastery still stand, though the majority of the site was destroyed by a Communist purge in 1939. The Elsen-Tasarkhai dunes can be found near Karakoram. The Bezeklik Thousand Buddha Caves are to the south, in the Taklamakan Desert.

The Black Darkhad are an ethnic group in Northern Mongolia who trace their lineage to Bo'orchu and Muqali, Genghis Khan's generals who were tasked with guarding his shrine. The Darkhad maintain secret rituals and have kept a sacred flame burning in the shrine for eight hundred years. The shrine is said to contain some of the emperor's belongings, but not the body of Genghis Khan.

The Ikh Khorig, or Great Taboo, is a 240-square-kilometer area of the Khentii Mountains. In particular, the Burkhan Khaldun mountain is considered the most sacred place in Mongolia, partly because Genghis Khan himself ordered his descendants to worship it. No one besides the Darkhad are allowed to enter this land. Using satellite imagery, archaeologists have identified several possible sites for the Khan's final resting place inside the Great Taboo. The Mongolian government, out of respect for their history, has forbidden most excavations.

To this day, the location of Genghis Khan's tomb remains a mystery.

Acknowledgments

Thank you to Michael Green, Brian Geffen, Shanta Newlin, Katherine Quinn, Anna Jarzab, Kathryn Bhirud, Nicole White, and everyone in the Penguin family. Also thank you to Christopher Adler, Brianne Johnson, and my actual family.